THE CIDER MAKER'S SECRET

MATILDA LOCKWOOD

NIMBLE PIG PRESS

This is a work of historical fiction. While it is set in Herefordshire in 1763 and includes references to authentic places and historical events, the characters and their personal stories are products of the author's imagination. Any resemblance to actual persons, living or dead, is coincidental.

The Cider Maker's Secret
ISBN: 979-8-9933114-0-1
Cover design by Angelina Sakhatsa
Manuscript critiqued by Maria of Juicy Details Editing
Published by Nimble Pig Press, PO Box 489, Indianola, WA 98342

For information, visit:
https://www.matildalockwoodwrites.com/

Printed in the United States of America

First Edition

For the cider sellers, especially those at Washington state farmer's markets, who never once judged me for sampling my way through the stalls and calling it research.
Thanks for always sending me merrily on my way with sticky fingers and a full basket!

PREFACE

Historical Note

In 1763, Herefordshire was deep in cider country. Apple trees stretched across the hills, pressing houses worked from dawn until the light failed, and the rhythms of the year followed blossom, harvest, and fermentation. A good yield meant a good winter.

Then Parliament brought in the Cider Act. It placed a tax of four shillings on every hogshead of cider and gave excise officers the right to search private land to enforce it. Four shillings might sound small now, but at the time it could be between a quarter and nearly half the value of the cider. If a hogshead sold for 10 shillings, the tax meant a 40 percent increase. Even at 20 shillings, it was still a sharp 20 percent rise. In today's money, that's like adding somewhere between £50 and £120 per barrel.

The law fell hardest on regions like Herefordshire and Devon, where cider was a cornerstone of local trade. Protests were loud and long-lasting, prices rose, sales faltered, and some orchardists were forced to abandon their trade altogether. The tax was finally repealed in 1766, but by then the smallest makers had often sold off trees or land just to keep food on the table.

The Whitcombe orchard, Nathaniel's voyages, and the people you'll meet here are imagined. But the backdrop of steep hillsides, the early frosts, and the strain that a single Act of Parliament could bring to an entire county is entirely real.

This story unfolds in that moment of strain and change, when a good harvest might still save a season, and a single bad law could ruin it.

CONTENTS

CHAPTER ONE

THE PRESSING HOUR

HEREFORDSHIRE, ENGLAND, 1763

The scream tore across the orchard like a blade through wet bark.

Elizabeth Whitcombe didn't pause to think. She dropped the bundle of ledger papers she'd been reviewing on the table, tore open the front door and ran as she slammed it behind her, skirts clutched in one hand, boots slapping against the slick earth, shawl flying behind her like a pennant in retreat. The rain last night had left the ground sodden, and the air was thick with the scent of churned soil and bruised apple flesh. A breath ago, she'd been calculating yield per barrel. Now all she could think of was her young niece, Phoebe. Was she all right? And William, the orchard helper near her niece's age, who she knew had been working in the direction of the scream.

William had come to them at Michaelmas, thin as a willow wand after a rough year on parish aid. He slept above the press now and earned in coin and bread both, which suited them all fine so long as he kept within sight of John Thatcher, her cider master.

She passed the front hedge, heart pounding. The crows were already wheeling above the south field, black scraps of sky turned frantic. Beyond them, a shout rose: "Move! The beam's giving!" That was Thatcher.

Her feet flew faster.

As she crested the low rise above the press yard, the world slammed into clarity. The southwest corner of the cider barn—*her* barn, her father's legacy, the body of their labor—was collapsing in on itself. A ridgepole had split. One wall bowed outward like a kicked fence. Half the roof looked as if it had dropped in prayer.

"Phoebe?" she shouted.

A woman near the coop, shook her head. "She's with the hens, miss!"

Her lungs released, just barely...but the barn still groaned. A wheelbarrow was overturned. One of the Foxwhelp barrels had rolled straight into a support post and burst, froth and pulp spreading like blood across the stones. A chicken, feathers askew and wailing, danced in the wreckage.

"God's teeth," Elizabeth muttered.

Workers shouted, staggered. Ropes were hauled. Crates dragged clear. And then...

A voice rose from inside the barn. High, panicked. "Help! I'm stuck!"

Her heart seized. *William.* Only twelve years of age, a wiry little thing with more curiosity than caution; he was too eager to prove himself yet too young to know how, most times.

"William?" she called, sick with certainty, looking behind her at the shaken faces of the workers. "He's..."

"He's still in there!" One of the farmers gave an answering shout. "Went to clean the vat before the storm hit!"

Her legs moved before the words finished echoing. "John!" she bellowed. "Get a brace under that east beam! And find me rope...not twine, proper line!" She didn't wait for confirmation, nor warning. She dove into the ruin that was now the barn.

Inside, the air was thick as cider mash. Dust choked the light. The vat loomed to her right, the press to her left, both warped under pressure. Shattered slats littered the floor. The scent of fermentation was sharp and sour, burning her eyes."William!" she coughed, shielding her head.

"Here!" came the cry again, higher now, brittle with fear. "I...I can't move my foot!"

Elizabeth plunged deeper into the barn. Inside, the air was hot, sour, and stifling. Dust hung in streaks where daylight struggled through the gaping roof. The vat loomed to her right, the press to her left, both warped under strain. Broken slats, spilled pulp, and tangled rope covered the floor like battlefield debris.

"William!" she called, hand cupped around her mouth as grit rained from above. "Where are you?"

A muffled cry answered. "Here! Under the sacks! I can't get free!"

Turning in the direction of his voice, toward the mash trough, she spotted him behind it, one small foot pinned beneath a half-barrel. His cap was missing, his face pale and slick with cider pulp and fear, and the sight of him trapped there punched the breath from her chest.

"Don't move," she said, voice like iron drawn from the forge trying to convince not only him but herself. "You're not dying today; not on my land, and not under this bloody roof." She crouched beside him, bracing one shoulder against the old press and shoving with all her weight. The barrel shifted slowly, then rolled aside with a wet thud. William gave a ragged gasp and tried to scramble free, his boot sliding in pulp.

"Can you walk?" she asked, already reaching for him.

"I—I think so, Miss Whitcombe." His voice trembled. "My ankle's all queer."

"Lean on me." She hauled him upright with one arm and wrapped the other around his ribs. He clung to her, and his small frame reminded her of a sapling in wind.

Together, they limped toward the light. Every step sent a groan through the timbers above, the barn's bones unsettled and sullen. As they neared the doorway, Elizabeth caught a glimpse of what had failed: the beam above the press, blackened with rot, shot through with frass and fine webbing.

By the saints, she thought grimly. *How did no one see it?* She filed it away. Later, she'd dissect the damage like a wound. For now, there was a child in her arms, and the barn was groaning like it still meant to bury them.

Outside, the light hit her face like a slap.

Voices shouted. The bracing lines had been thrown. Someone—*thank God*—had brought real rope. John Thatcher barked orders from somewhere near the press yard. The barn creaked again, protesting the weight of rescue.

Elizabeth stumbled toward the haystack and eased William down into it. He clutched his foot and blinked hard, trying not to cry. "I'm sorry, miss," he whispered, shoulders hunched. "I only meant to clean it before breakfast...thought I had time—"

"Quiet, now," she said, not unkindly. She dropped to one knee and checked his ankle, fingers sure and swift. "It's swollen, not broken. You'll live. But next time, you shout before crawling into danger, not after."

He nodded, lips trembling.

Only then did she allow herself a breath. The worst of it was holding...for now. As she looked warily at it, the cider barn seemed to groan at her again, low and resentful, like a beast not yet finished with its tantrum.

Elizabeth rose from William's side, her skirts streaked with mash, one shoulder throbbing from the barrel heave. Around her, the yard stank of pulp and smoke, churned earth and panic. Ropes crisscrossed like crude stitches between the beams, anchoring the sagging bones of the barn to the old press frame.

John Thatcher, red-faced and muttering curses into his handkerchief, was just finishing the last of the bracing lines when Elizabeth stalked across the mud. "We need more rope!"

The south wall had all but folded. The press frame, God willing, might yet be saved. Two barrels lost. The roof gutter dangled like a drunkard's tooth. Her father's barn, built with war-worn hands and cedar, undone by rain and rot and time.

And she hadn't seen it coming. A familiar nausea began to take hold in her stomach, and a nasty voice whispered in her mind, not for the first time, that she'd never be able to do this alone. She was almost forty, unmarried, with several families of her workers depending on the Whitcombe Orchard turning a profit, and the new Cider Tax threatened to cripple her business. Not to mention, the unwelcome secrets she'd been discovering her late husband had left behind.

"Phoebe!" she suddenly called, her panic shifting. *If she had been hurt...*

"In here!" came her niece's familiar voice from the henhouse, muffled but indignant. "I'm not dead!"

Relief swept through Elizabeth so hard she almost laughed. "Good," she muttered. "But I might be. And it's not yet breakfast."

The henhouse door creaked open, and Phoebe emerged: hay in her hair, one stocking sagging, and a hen tucked under each arm. "I told them to stay put," she huffed, indignant. "But they panicked anyway. Chickens don't listen."

"Neither do apprentices," Elizabeth called back, too relieved to scold properly. "Mind you put them back and count the layers to make sure they're all accounted for in this mess."

Phoebe gave a dramatic salute, accompanied by a flapping wingtip, and disappeared again.

Elizabeth exhaled. Her hands were shaking. She clenched them into fists at her sides, and reminded herself that control was a habit, not a comfort. *One, two, three, four...*

Then, a new voice, deep and dry with amusement, drifted in from the west fence line. "Need a hand...or a miracle?"

She turned sharply.

A stranger leaned against the rail as though admiring the chaos. He was tall, sun-browned, and broad through the shoulders; his dark coat was mud-streaked, boots travel-worn. A coil of rope hung from one shoulder like a badge. To Elizabeth's discerning eye and the talks she had with American colonists, he looked like he belonged more to wind and timber than parlors or courtrooms.

"Are you offering one or the other, sir?" she asked, voice clipped. She had to admit, he cut a fine figure.

"Whichever's needed, my lady, provided you'll give me a moment of your time." He smiled, exposing a dimple in his left cheek that lent a boyish youth to his face she suddenly found irritating. How much of her time must she spent shepherding young men?

Her cider master John Thatcher left the post and joined them, eyes narrowing. "And who the devil might you be?"

The man vaulted the fence with a fluid ease, landing in the slush like he'd done it a hundred times. He straightened, brushing muck from his sleeves.

"Nathaniel Carter," he said. "I was meant to arrive with a handshake and a shipping proposal. But I gather your barn had other plans, and luckily I always carry extra rope when I'm on my horse."

"How fortunate for us." Elizabeth frowned. "What part of America are you from?"

"Virginia," he said, tipping his chin. "Left as much of the accent behind in port that I could."

"You brought rope," John grunted, not quite a welcome, but his expression indicated that he was finished hearing their banter.

"And a working knowledge of failing beams," Nathaniel replied. "My father was a carpenter. May I?"

Without waiting, he crossed to the damaged frame and studied it with a soldier's calm. In moments, he was threading a diagonal line across the structure, tensioning it with a makeshift pulley from the crate pile, tying off with crisp, competent knots.

Elizabeth watched him work. His hands were quick, efficient. But his eyes moved like a mapmaker's. Noticing, measuring, and learning the land without ever asking permission.

Heat skittered up her throat...part warning, part something irreverently alive. It had been years since a man's steadiness registered as anything but extra work for her. This one moved toward danger as if it owed him rent. Attractive, yes, in the way a rightly set beam is attractive: sound, clean, useful, and liable to crack your skull if you stand beneath it too long. She had no room for skull-cracking distractions. Not with ledgers to reconcile, mouths to feed, and a Crown assessor who would happily seize what the weather hadn't already taken.

"Do you do this sort of thing for fun?" she asked, arms folded.

"My grandfather taught usefulness before manners," he replied, tugging the line taut. "Barns don't wait for courtesy."

From the haystack, William piped up with a sniffle: "He's faster than John."

"I heard that," John snapped.

Elizabeth allowed herself the faintest exhale of amusement. She stepped forward, skirts heavy with cider and mud. "Mr. Carter. Why are you actually here?"

Nathaniel turned, rope over one shoulder, gaze direct. "I'm here for your apples."

Elizabeth's eyes narrowed. "You picked a dramatic method of inquiry."

"I wasn't aiming for drama," Nathaniel replied. "But I'll admit, your orchard has bite. I'd love a tour, if you'll indulge me."

She bit back a sharper reply, though her thoughts were already running ahead. *Who sent him? And why now...when the barn's broken-backed, the audit looming, and every barrel spoken for?* "Welcome to Whitcombe Orchard," she said dryly. "Wipe your boots before you cone in."

He bowed with a half-smile. "Gladly."

The yard had quieted. Workers moved with cautious energy, avoiding the worst of the mud. William had drifted away from the haystack, still favoring his foot, eyes wide with stunned admiration for the man who vaulted fences and knew knots.

Elizabeth folded her arms. "I'm afraid if you're here to buy cider, you're wasting time. The barrels are spoken for, and the Exchequer sees to it we've little left to spare."

"I'm not here for cider," Nathaniel said. "I'm here for your trees."

That stopped her. She stared at him. "*What?*"

"Specifically, your scions," he continued, as though it were nothing. "Whitcombe graftwood. I've tasted cider from your Redstreaks and Foxwhelps. They're bold, complex, unlike anything in the colonies. I want to establish orchards in New Hampshire, using your stock."

Her arms crossed tighter. "You want to ship my trees across the ocean." *The audacity of this man.*

"Not trees. Just clippings. Shoots. Graftwood. Nothing to harm the rootstock. I'll pay handsomely, of course."

"It's not about coin," she said, tone sharpening. "These trees are legacy. My father's hands were in every graft. My grandfather's in the original rootbeds. They're not for export."

Nathaniel nodded. "I understand. But legacy doesn't have to stay rooted to one soil. What your family grew here could flourish on both sides of the sea."

Elizabeth glanced toward the orchard rows: wet now from morning storm, but still proud in their posture. She saw the careful work in every stake, every shaping scar. Years layered in bark. "You speak as if you mean well," she said. "But men always do, until they've taken what they want." She took a deep breath. She hadn't intended to disallow so openly. She didn't like him, so why was she letting him affect her so?

"I'm not here to take," Nathaniel said. "I'm here to trade. Openly. Respectfully. On your terms."

She held his gaze a moment longer. There was something there...earnestness, or something well-performed. "I'll consider it," she said finally. It was a lie, to be sure...of course she wouldn't let this boastful snake walk away with her legacy. "No promises."

Nathaniel nodded, accepting this with grace, and she felt absurdly pleased as a result. "That's more than I hoped for."

A commotion stirred at the edge of the road: hoofbeats in churned mud. A rider approached at speed, his bottle-green coat vivid against the gray sky. He pulled up hard, dismounted, and strode forward with stiff posture and a scroll in hand.

Elizabeth's stomach sank. "Simms," she muttered.

The rider inclined his head. "Mistress Whitcombe." He held out the scroll, its red wax seal shining in the sun. "By order of His Majesty's Exchequer, a full audit of Whitcombe Orchard is scheduled for one week hence."

She took it with numb fingers, breaking the seal and scanning the parchment. Her jaw clenched. "This is our third audit this year."

Wainscott would come—the same inspector with the counting rod and the neat little book—set their barrel counts against the Excise register, and if the numbers failed to kiss, he could seize stock on the spot and fine her besides.

"Indeed," Simms replied. "Given reports of irregularities, the Crown deems it prudent."

"What reports?" she snapped, eyes flicking up.

He gave a thin smile. "The Crown receives information from a variety of sources."

Her mind raced. *The rot. The beam. Could someone have—?*

Nathaniel stepped forward. "Is this standard practice?" he asked, voice even.

Simms turned to him slowly. "And you are?"

"Nathaniel Carter. Prospective associate."

Simms offered no reply, only a dismissive glance, and turned back to Elizabeth. "Ensure your records are in order. The inspection will be thorough." Then he mounted and rode off, leaving rutted mud and tension in his wake.

Elizabeth stood in silence, the scroll curling in her hand. "Damn the Crown and its endless meddling."

Nathaniel shifted beside her. "If there's anything I can do to help—"

She turned on him. "You've done enough."

He stepped back, quiet.

Elizabeth could feel the day pressing in again...barrels lost, beams rotted, a stranger with questions, and now a week to prepare for inspection with half the ledgers water-spattered and the barn held together by rope and curses. She turned toward the orchard, toward the trees still standing, shoulders drawn. Her hair had come loose from its pins, her shawl hung sodden from one elbow, and the scroll in her hand flaked red wax like dried blood.

The sun was pushing through the cloud now, casting a thin gold sheen across the muddied yard. The orchard glistened in the distance, green and unbent, the only thing still standing proud.

Elizabeth stood at the edge of the wreckage with her shoulders daring to slump, scroll in hand, its red seal already flaking away like dried pulp.

Nathaniel Carter waited near the half-righted barrel cart, his coat slung over one shoulder, sleeves rolled above his forearms. He looked every inch the colonial tradesman: strong-backed, sea-burnished, and too observant by half.

Elizabeth didn't trust him. She didn't trust any man who arrived unannounced on the heels of ruin. But she'd seen his knots. His steadiness. The way he'd moved toward danger without waiting for permission.

That could be worth something, or it could be a liability.

"Mr. Carter," she called.

He turned, sunlight catching on his damp hair, a gleam of gold at his collarbone. "Mistress Whitcombe."

Her tone was clipped. "You arrived without letter, without reference, and on the morning my barrelhouse damn near crushed a child." She took a step closer. "Why? What could possibly make scions so important?"

Nathaniel didn't flinch. "Because the orchards in New York and Virginia are waning. Because the seedlines there are thin and inbred, and the men hawking cider in Williamsburg whisper about Whitcombe Redstreaks like legend."

"And yet," she said coolly, "they never whisper *my* name."

His smile faltered slightly. "That part, I gathered."

Elizabeth folded her arms. "I'm not interested in compliments. Or flattery dressed as commerce. If you've come to trade, you're late in the season for grafting and at least five generations early for buying me out."

"I'm not here to buy you out," he said firmly. "I'm here to earn your trust. And if I can, to build something worth the risk."

"With what collateral?" she asked. "A rope coil and a practiced smile?"

He laughed. "No. With ships. Colonial markets. And buyers who will pay triple for cider they can brag is English-born. What you grow here could root ten orchards in New England."

Elizabeth didn't answer right away. Her fingers curled tighter around the scroll. Her shawl was still heavy with wet mash, and her back ached from the barrel-lift. She was tired of always having to show off being clever, of having to stay meek enough so as not to raise eyebrows, of constantly outmaneuvering men who believed legacy was theirs by right. "I don't want to anchor anyone but myself," she said finally. "Do you know what it costs to keep this place running? What the Crown demands from a woman who dares to trade like a man?"

"I do," he said. "In Virginia, we call it robbery and serve it with molasses."

She smiled at that, a laugh threatening to escape as the corner of her mouth twitched. He saw it, and wisely said nothing.

"But you've been taxed more than coin," he added. "This land bears your name in every graft scar. And I mean to respect that."

Elizabeth followed his gaze to the orchard. "In case you didn't hear, the cider office is sending an audit. In seven days. I've no time to entertain maybes or silver tongues."

"Then let me help," he said. "Let me earn more than suspicion."

"If I entertain such a notion…" She eyed him, sharp and calculating. "You'll take orders from John. You'll not enter the stillroom, nor the graft vault. You'll keep your boots off the south slope. And you'll stay out of Phoebe's henhouse."

He raised an eyebrow. "Phoebe?"

"My niece. And she bites."

"I'll remember that."

From the haystack, William sneezed. The boy was still barefoot and fidgeting with the hem of his shirt. Phoebe's voice drifted from the henhouse a moment later: "You'd better not be bleeding on my feed sacks, Willie!"

Elizabeth didn't even turn. "One week, Mr. Carter," she said like an oath. "If your boots are still clean by then, if you catch my meaning, I might believe you mean to stay."

"And if they're not?"

She gave a thin smile. "You give me reason enough to toss you out and never bother with you again."

He grinned back. "Then I suppose I'd best start earning the dirt."

She watched him go, shoulders squared, gait sure, rope swinging from his hand like a flag of intent, and couldn't yet decide whether she'd just recruited a steward or invited a storm.

Either way, the reckoning had begun.

CHAPTER TWO

A FRUIT WORTH CROSSING FOR

The teacup rattled faintly as Nathaniel Carter set it down, willing his stomach to settle.

It was not the tea's fault. He had grown used to the bitter English brew, black leaf steeped too long, laced faintly with metal. He would never confess it to anyone in Virginia, but he no longer found it unpleasant. It was simply ill-suited to the sort of sickness that came from riding too fast on too little sleep after a sea voyage, with yesterday's apples and older regrets still roiling beneath his ribs.

The Red Hart at Ledbury had low beams, lumpy chairs, and a fire that smoked just enough to remind a man not to linger. But it also had a back corner that stayed mostly empty in the mornings, which was the reason Nathaniel had chosen it.

This morning, however, the corner had been claimed.

"You need a faster ship," said the man across from him, "or at least a slower conscience."

Miles Hardwick had the look, all too accurate, of someone who had been put out of three ports and welcomed in two. His cravat was hastily knotted, one boot still damp from last night's puddle, and a tobacco-stained paper rested between his fingers as if grown there. He leaned back with that particular confidence which made strangers forgive his trespasses, and friends overlook them altogether.

Nathaniel found himself smiling, though he kept his eyes on the tea. Miles's manner had that effect. He could turn a quarrel into a jest before the ale had reached the bottom of the cup. Yet now and again, the jest left someone else's pride in splinters, and Nathaniel was the one to sweep them up.

He had once seen Miles charm a ferry toll from a surly bargeman, only to hand the saved coins to a barefoot boy in the next village. Another time, Miles had insulted a ship's quartermaster so cleverly the man insisted on sharing his best tobacco in grudging admiration.

And there had been that evening in Portsmouth, when Miles relieved a drunken merchant of half his purse in a card game, then bought a round for the whole room, including the merchant. Nathaniel had laughed with the rest, but later, alone, he had wondered why the man's laugh had sounded hollow.

"I have a conscience quite suited to the work," Nathaniel said, setting the cup aside. "It simply does not clear customs as swiftly as you do."

"That is your trouble," Miles replied with a grin. "Trying to play fair in a crooked game." He leaned forward. "I know what you are after: old cultivars, deep rootstock, a lady orchardist with more grit than grace. The kind of legacy the London gentry would bottle and boast over."

"You have been listening in again," Nathaniel said.

Miles's grin widened. "I listen everywhere. A man learns more with his ears than with his boots."

He reached into his coat and slid a folded scrap of paper across the table. "There is a cutter anchored off Bristol. It leaves in eight days. You bring me a few grafts—clean and quiet—and I shall see them to Virginia. No tariffs, no questions."

"She has not given her consent," Nathaniel said, not touching the paper. "And that is smuggling."

"Barely. Call it gardening by discreet arrangement."

Nathaniel shook his head, though the corner of his mouth betrayed him.

Miles sighed, tucked the paper away, and rose. "Be noble, then. But when the Excise men start sniffing and the lady bolts the gate, remember that I offered a rope."

He clapped Nathaniel on the shoulder as he passed, leaving a faint smell of tobacco and rainwater in his wake.

When he was gone, the inn felt quieter, but not improved. Nathaniel reached into his satchel for his late mother's orchard journal, tracing the worn leather with his thumb. He had learned to work alongside Miles without tumbling into his schemes, but it was a harder thing than planting a tree to know when it was time to pull it up by the roots.

Inside, her careful script filled the pages: cultivar notes, bloom dates, graft pairings. The secret notes she'd kept from his father, who's always refused to listen. He flipped to one entry.

Foxwhelp – bittersharp. High tannin. Best blended. Ripens late. Watch for stem rot if damp persists.

A faded smear marked the margin. Blackberry jam, likely. She'd always read while eating breakfast.

He let his thumb rest on the page. If she were here, she'd have seen Whitcombe Orchard's worth in a heartbeat. She'd have known that trees grown on slope and storm bore the richest yield.

Nathaniel rubbed his jaw and rose. The orchard was waiting. So was Elizabeth.

From the ridge, Whitcombe Orchard looked orderly enough: a patchwork of gold and green stitched with footpaths and wind. But up close, it was no tidy quilt.

Windfalls lay bruised in the grass. Ladders leaned like abandoned spears. Branches creaked in the breeze above like sentries whispering warnings. The scent of ripening apples was rich...ferment and earth and something more wild than cultivated.

Nathaniel kept to the edges at first, noting the slope's drainage, the spacing of trees, the bark textures. Foxwhelps and Kingston Blacks flamed red and gold, streaked like fire against the green.

His mother had taught him to look for adversity. The best cider came from fruit that had endured. Without thinking about it, he pulled her cultivar book out again.

A sudden thunk interrupted his thoughts, followed by a child's voice: "Careful! That one's for vinegar!"

Nathaniel turned. A boy had just lobbed an apple into a wooden trug already half-full, and a girl no taller than his ribs stood nearby, hands on hips and scowl full of authority.

She walked with a marked limp, one foot turning inward with each third step, but her grip on the trug's handle was firm. A crooked walking stick jutted from her elbow like a banner, and her expression suggested she'd managed more chaos before breakfast than most men by noon.

"I said vinegar, William," she repeated, glaring toward the boy perched in the lower crook of a nearby apple tree. "If you bruise that one too, Aunt Lizzie will set you scrubbing the mash tub until your fingers prune."

The boy, maybe nine, with straw in his hair and boots far too big, scrambled down sheepishly and dropped the next apple gently into the trug. "Didn't mean to bruise it," he muttered.

Phoebe, clearly unimpressed, gave the apple a once-over and nodded with reluctant approval.

Nathaniel stepped closer, slow and deliberate. The girl's eyes flicked toward him.

"You're the American," she said, as if accusing him of something.

"I am. Nathaniel Carter."

She narrowed her gaze. "You don't walk like any Carter I know."

That drew a smile from him. "No?"

She shrugged. "There was a Carter in my grandfather's ledgers. He walked with a limp from a musket ball. You don't."

He chuckled, adjusting the orchard book under his arm. "I'll try not to disappoint. And you must be Miss Phoebe."

"Phoebe. Don't call me miss," she said quickly.

"Noted." He glanced at William, who was now crouching to stack apples by size. "You're both hard at work."

Phoebe tipped her chin toward the book. "Are you here to take notes, or take something from my aunt?" The step in her voice unnerved him.

"I'm here to offer something," he said. "Not take."

"Everyone says that." She turned back to the trug, as if he'd already had his chance.

Before Nathaniel could reply, a woman's voice called from the south slope. "Phoebe! Inside, now!"

Nathaniel turned. A gust caught the hem of her apron as Elizabeth Whitcombe crested the rise...dark hair coming loose in the wind, brow furrowed, sleeves rolled, boots stained with presswater. She looked carved from orchard soil itself.

For a moment, he couldn't move. *She's glorious.*

Phoebe groaned. "She saw me talking to you."

Nathaniel leaned down slightly. "I'll tell her I did all the talking, and you only practiced your withering glances."

Phoebe's lips twitched. "Deal." She limped toward the barn with William trailing behind, hauling the trug like a wagon through war.

Nathaniel stayed rooted until Elizabeth reached him. "Mister Carter," she said flatly. "You're early."

He nodded, anchoring a respectful look on his features. "You're busy."

She raised an eyebrow. "You noticed."

"I noticed many things," he said. "Your slope runs true. Your graft lines are older than the surrounding trees. And your niece gives orders like a magistrate."

A breath of a smile tugged at her mouth before she caught it. "Phoebe takes after her mother. Ruth could flay a man with half a phrase."

"And you?" he asked.

"Sometimes." Elizabeth's stare didn't soften. "I tend to prefer actions to flaying. Unless flaying is warranted."

"Actions, then," he said easily. "Show me something I'm not seeing."

She hesitated half a beat, no more, then tipped her head toward the lower row. "Come on. If you're going to pester me about scions, you can at least learn how not to ruin a mother tree with your questions."

The slope broke into shorter trees spaced closer together where wind worried at the branches. Here the rows were stitched with older stakes and newer twine, a palimpsest of seasons. Elizabeth stopped at a Redstreak with a stubborn cross-shoot and reached for the small pruning knife tucked into her apron band. She snapped the blade open with a practiced flick and steadied the shoot in her left hand.

"Most men," she said, "cut where it's obvious. They lop the thickest bit because it offends the eye. But the tree doesn't care for your sense of symmetry. She cares about where food flows." She touched a tiny swelling where the shoot met the spur. "You cut here, above a bud facing outward, and you leave a tongue for the graft to take when spring comes."

Nathaniel leaned in, but not so close as to crowd her. He didn't reach for the knife. He didn't advise. He watched the angle of her wrist, the way she set the blade and rolled it forward rather than hacking. He nodded once. "You're making a door, not a wound."

"Exactly." The slice was clean, one smooth pull. The little twig dropped, and already the cut looked purposeful, not violent. She glanced sideways and caught his eyes not on her face but on her grip. She saw the cataloguing there, the way his gaze noted how her thumb braced, how she kept the pad clear of the blade.

"You're the first man I've met who understands where to look," she said, assuming her usual dryness but unable to stop the warmth that rose in her chest. "They watch the knife. They don't watch the hand."

"Hands tell you what a person was taught," he said. "And what they had to teach themselves."

"Mm." She moved to the next limb and lifted it to show the callus line of an old graft. "My father put this in twenty-three years ago. He loved the neatness of cleft grafts. Said a tree ought to look like it meant to be a tree. I don't care what it looks like as long as it bears well and doesn't sulk."

"Whip-and-tongue?" he asked, gentle, testing.

"When I can. Tongue lets you lock it without strangling the cambium." She tucked the knife away. "You do listen."

"I was raised by a woman who could make a tree repent of bad habits," he said, smiling. "Listening was survival."

"Then listen to this. If you come at my trees like a raider—stripping viable wood, ignoring balance—I'll toss you off the south slope and call it charity." She set her palm against the trunk a moment, like a blessing, then dropped her hand. "If you come with care? We might talk."

"Care, then," he said. He didn't reach for her knife. "Show me where spring scion would come from, and I'll tell you how I'd package it to cross an ocean without rotting or sprouting."

"You'd tell me?" A brow lifted.

"Trading fair means showing your working." He crouched, checked the drip line, pinched a crumb of soil and rubbed it. "Drainage is clean. Your understory's thin. You mulch heavy at leaf-fall?"

"With pomace and straw. It keeps the roots temperate when the frost sulks overlong." She didn't bother to hide that she was pleased he'd read the ground correctly. "We'll talk spring. Right now, it's harvest. We mind what's in front of us, or else we feed vinegar."

From farther down the slope a crow scolded; the wind carried the barn's damp breath. Elizabeth slid the knife home. For a beat they stood close, both looking outward over the rows rather than at each other, the way two people stand when they are working the same problem from different angles.

"You hold the blade low to protect your thumb," Nathaniel said, almost absent, as if finishing a note to himself.

She felt the observation land. "I've grown fond of my thumbs," she said lightly. "And of doing things right the first time." Then, catching herself, she took a half step back. "Come on. Mr. Thatcher will be sharpening complaints like knives if I keep you out here."

"I'll try not to bleed on his floor," he said.

"That would be a first," she muttered, but the corner of her mouth tipped despite herself.

Before he could answer her, a voice called from below. "Lizzie! Press is acting up again. Barrel chute's slow."

The older man emerged from the open barn door, wiping his hands on a stained rag. His balding crown was ringed with cider-damp curls and his expression held equal parts irritation and affection.

Elizabeth didn't roll her eyes, but she came close. "Mr. Thatcher," she said. "You remember Mr. Carter."

John gave him a small grunt of acknowledgment. "From the colonies. I recall. Looking to bottle our secrets in a barrel, is he?"

Nathaniel offered a polite nod. "Not all Americans are pirates. I'm looking to partner or not at all."

Thatcher huffed. "Then come see what you're proposing to tie yourself to. She's beautiful, but temperamental."

"John!" Elizabeth warned.

Reddening, John held up his hands. "I meant the orchard, Miss Whitcombe."

"Hmm." Elizabeth gave Nathaniel one last, skeptical glance before falling into step beside the older man. Nathaniel followed, unsure if he'd just passed a test or walked into a fresh one.

As they approached the barn, Nathaniel spotted William again, now carrying a scoop and bucket, trailing behind Phoebe with the air of a loyal page. The boy paused to glance at Nathaniel, then quickly looked away and pretended to study a barrel. Nathaniel offered a subtle nod of greeting. William gave a shy half-wave.

The barn door creaked like a hinge on an old oath. Inside, the air shifted: cooler, darker, thick with the scent of fermenting apples, wet wood, copper, and iron.

Dust drifted in the shafts of morning light. The press squatted in the far corner like an altar, cords and levers coiled like entrails around its base. Barrels were racked high to the rafters. The low hum of effort and industry clung to every beam.

Nathaniel ducked beneath a timber brace and paused just inside. "It smells like ambition," he said.

"How romantic of you," Elizabeth replied without turning. "It smells like crushed apples, sweat, and three generations of bloody-mindedness."

He smiled. "Same thing?"

She moved to Thatcher's side without ceremony, skirt hitched, sleeves already smudged. He pointed to the jammed chute at the base of the mash tub. Elizabeth dropped to a crouch, hands already in motion.

Nathaniel stayed where he was, watching. She didn't gesture or ask anyone for help; knew what she was doing, and the barn moved around her accordingly. She wasn't decorative. She belonged here, and he felt his respect for her build.

There was dirt on her cheek. Her braid had loosened at the nape. She looked nothing like the merchant daughters of Virginia or the powdered ladies of Boston salons. She looked like someone who'd stood in storms and made them yield.

He suddenly, fiercely wanted to kiss her. Her wanted to tell her how beautiful she looked. Of course, he knew it would be unwise. "You don't oversee the work from a distance, then?" he said.

Elizabeth didn't glance up. "Not unless I want it done twice."

"I meant it as a compliment."

"Then phrase it more clearly next time."

"I'll try again." He bowed slightly. "You're extraordinary."

That earned him a flick of her eyes. "Now you're laying it on." She gave the chute a sharp tug. A slat popped loose with a wet thunk. A trickle of crushed pulp followed. "Clear," she called.

Thatcher pulled the lever. The press groaned once, then rumbled into motion, its ancient gears grinding with satisfaction.

He waited until the gears settled into their satisfied groan. "Since you prefer actions to flaying, let me put my purpose plain, so you don't have to read it in my boots."

She flicked a look at him that said go on or hang yourself, depending how he did it.

"I'm here to do three things," he said, voice low enough that only she and the nearest barrel could hear. "First, secure a reliable line for buyers in New England: men who will pay honest coin for cider they can prove is blended from Whitcombe cultivars. Second, rebuild my reputation by doing it aboveboard...no bribes, no backdoor levies, no games that risk the maker's name. Third, if we suit, arrange for spring scion wood under a written agreement that protects your stock, your brand, and your say-so at every turn."

"Brand," she repeated, skeptical, but interested despite herself.

"Your father's name is already a brand," he said simply. "People speak it when they don't know they're speaking it. I'm offering you markets you don't have time or inclination to court. I take the risk and the shipping; you take the margin and the control. If I fail you, I lose more than coin. I lose the one thing I came to mend."

"Which is?"

"My good name," he said, not softening it. "I worked too long under a man who taught me to cut corners and call it clever. I'm done with clever that rots the wood from the inside."

For a heartbeat the barn seemed to hold still. She studied him the way she assessed a barrel stave, testing for soundness no eye alone could see.

"Plain enough?" he asked.

"Plain," she said. "We'll see about true."

"That's fair."

Nathaniel stepped forward slowly. "You've got a late harvest? That would put anyone on the edge."

"Yes." Her voice strained.

"And enforcement on cider transport is tightening."

"I know that too."

He watched her rise and wipe her hands. "Then let me help mitigate the risk."

Elizabeth turned toward him, chin lifted. "And what exactly do you expect in return, Mr. Carter? What do you really want?"

The barn held still, as if listening.

"I want to bottle something honest," he said quietly. "Something worthy of its name. Without backdoors or bribes. Something to be proud of...there's no orchard I'd rather work with than yours." His father's face, making the shadiest deals at the risk of the Carter orchard, long since sold, flashed into his mind, and he pushed it away.

She studied him, unreadable. "Shame," she murmured at last. "Backdoors are where the real stories start."

Was she serious? He smiled. "I thought you preferred actions to flaying."

"I do," she said, walking toward the fermenting crocks. "But a well-aimed flensing has its place."

Nathaniel followed. "I'm not here to provoke."

"You're a man with polished boots, standing in my barn. That's provocation enough."

"You told me to keep my boots clean. Besides, I left the polish in Ledbury."

"Pity. It might've looked charming when you spill your first mash bucket."

At the long sorting table, apples gleamed in the half-light. Bitter-sharps, sweets, russets softening just at the edges. Nathaniel picked one up. "You sort by feel?"

"I sort by knowing what the hell I'm doing. And by not trusting hired men to tell a Kingston Black from a Redstreak blindfolded."

"Your niece could."

A faint smile, real and reluctant. "Phoebe could tell a graft from ten paces and name the mother tree besides. She was raised among apples."

He turned the russet in his palm. "You're building something that could last a hundred years."

"We'll see."

"You want to protect it." *How could he convince her?* "I understand that."

"No," she said. "You think you understand. But you don't."

Before he could ask what she meant, a crash sounded from outside, followed by Phoebe's shout and a startled yelp.

Elizabeth's jaw tensed. "And now comes Act Two." She strode toward the door.

Nathaniel lingered a beat longer in the scent and shadow of her barn. He'd been to countless orchards, walked countless rows. But none of them had pressed the air from his chest like this. None of them had her.

Outside, footsteps pounded the slope. Phoebe came into view first, dragging a half-filled trug behind her like a soldier returning from the front. Apples bumped against the sides, bruised but salvageable, and tucked beneath them was a worn book with a bent corner.

Nathaniel's breath caught, and even as he saw it in front of them, his blood felt cold as his hand reached into his vest to feel the pocket empty of its usual presence of his mother's cultivar book.

Phoebe plunked the trug down and held the book aloft with theatrical gravity. "You dropped this. Didn't peek."

Nathaniel stepped forward, greatly relieved and even more sheepish. How could he have been so careless? "Much obliged. You have no idea...I'd have been lost without this. Thank you."

Phoebe handed it over like a sacred relic. "Your handwriting leans to the left, you know. That's a good sign."

"I'll keep that in mind," he said, accepting the journal.

"You might be all right," she added, eyeing him. "For a Carter." Then she turned, stick tapping against her boot as she limped away. William trailed behind her again, still quiet, clutching a sack of rinds like it might explode. Phoebe rapidly instructions at him, and he obeyed with the long-suffering silence of a boy determined to stay on her good side.

Elizabeth appeared beside Nathaniel without a word. He sensed her before he saw her...an orchard presence, grounded and firm.

"She doesn't warm easily," she said, voice low.

"I take it as a compliment."

They stood in silence, watching the orchard stretch wide before them. The wind rustled through the branches, shaking loose a few late apples that thudded into the grass.

Nathaniel turned the book in his hand. "This belonged to my mother. She catalogued every cultivar we ever raised, every graft that failed and every one that took, even if my father never listened. She'd have loved this place."

"Did she..." Elizabeth raised her brows in sympathy.

"She died last fall," he whispered, and was horrified to feel tears come to his eyes. He blinked rapidly.

"I'm so sorry," she said, and he wished she hadn't. "My husband died last winter. What a gift that you were able to keep her book documenting your own family's legacy."

"We lost our orchard," he sighed.

"No!"

Nodding glumly, he continued, "Three Sisters Orchard in Virginia. The land was seized when I was a boy. My mother tried to fight it quietly, but we ended up moving to a Quaker settlement in Pennsylvania. My mother became a teacher there, but she never forgot Three Sisters."

Elizabeth didn't answer, but her gaze lingered on the cover. She seemed to recognize what it meant to hold years in ink and leather.

"Your orchard," he said, "has the same feel. That kind of memory."

"What failed her?"

Nathaniel sucked in his breath. "What do you mean?"

"She kept records. Tracked everything. So she didn't fail lightly. What took your orchard down?"

"Besides my father?" He swallowed, surprised at how much that question stung. "Sorry. Trees were good, debt was better at growing. My father defaulted on debts after one too many bad harvests. There was an exceedingly bad winter. And one mistake in trust too large to undo."

Elizabeth's jaw worked slightly.

Nathaniel adjusted the book under his arm. "I'm not here to take what's yours, Mistress Whitcombe. I'm here because I believe it's worth something...not just to bottle or buy. But to help carry forward."

From the slope below, Thatcher's voice rang out. "Hope he brought more than words, Lizzie. This land's buried enough of those."

Nathaniel sighed as Elizabeth's lips pressed into a line. "I'll come back tomorrow," he offered, "to lend a hand? No pretense. No promises."

She gave a small, unreadable nod. "Come early. We don't wait on slow hands."

He gave a half-bow, more instinct than performance, and felt a bit foolish. As he stepped back onto the lane, orchard book tucked safely beneath his arm, he resisted the urge to glance back.

The orchard would still be there tomorrow.

And, he hoped, so would she.

As he reached the lane's turn, he paused. From his satchel he drew a small, wrapped oilcloth bundle and unrolled it to check the contents: a narrow grafting knife, clean and keen, and a coil of linen tape. He didn't bring them out to boast; he only needed to be certain they were ready when spring came and this fragile possibility warranted steel.

Across the rows, a figure moved. Elizabeth, counting barrels with Thatcher, lips moving as she tallied. She adjusted a stack with her hip, then, without looking, reached to steady a ladder William shouldn't have climbed while she was turned. She wasn't watching the knife. She was watching the hands.

"Care," he murmured, rewrapping the bundle. "Start with care."

He slid the knife back into its case and kept walking, the orchard at his back and the shape of her grip clear in his mind. Tomorrow he'd bring work gloves and keep his tongue behind his teeth. He'd listen first. And if she allowed it, he'd earn the dirt.

Chapter Three

PRESSED HARD

S team curled from the kettle on the stillroom stove, releasing the scent of mint and sage as Elizabeth tipped dried leaves into the clay teapot with brisk efficiency. Behind her, John Thatcher sat hunched over the harvest records, rubbing his temple with fingers still scabbed from the barrelhouse collapse. The iron latch on the door clicked softly as the wind shifted, but the stillroom remained warm and quiet, an herbal refuge from the day's mounting weight. Elizabeth's hands were steady, but her mind churned.

A rustle came from just outside the shuttered window. Then voices. Boys' voices. Raised, laughing, mean.

"Oi—look who walks like a duck with a crutch!"

Elizabeth stilled, fingers curling around the teapot handle.

"She limp 'cause she stepped in her own shadow!"

A pause. Then came William's voice...younger than the rest, but clear and loud with purpose. "Leave her alone. She's braver than the lot of you. Least she's not scared of books."

But the other boys only jeered louder. One of them scoffed, "Books? That girl'd trip over a prayer book spine!"

"The nerve of those brats!" John hissed as he looked up from the table, already rising. "I'll send them running—"

"No." Elizabeth lifted a hand, eyes fixed on the window. "Let her handle it."

"Are you sure?" John frowned. "She's twelve."

"She's also sharp as a fresh graft and sick of being told she's breakable." Elizabeth moved to the door but didn't open it. "I won't teach her to hide."

Outside, the taunting had broken into scattered laughter, until something snapped sharply through the air. A rustling thwack. Then a yelp.

"She's got a weapon!"

"Run!"

More scrambling. Fleeing footsteps. A second of stunned silence.

Elizabeth opened the door in time to see Phoebe, standing near the orchard's east wall, gripping her walking stick in one hand and something else small, wooden, and unmistakably slingshot-shaped in the other. She adjusted the end of the stick, twisting the carved tip back into place with practiced ease. Her cheeks were flushed, jaw set. She didn't look toward the house.

John let out a low whistle. "Is that... new?"

"She's had it three weeks," Elizabeth muttered. "Built it with kitchen twine and a drawer handle."

"Remind me never to raise my voice in her direction."

Elizabeth stepped onto the stone stoop but didn't call to Phoebe. Instead, she waited as the girl turned, limping slightly, her gait stubborn as ever. William trailed her at a distance, shoulders hunched but eyes bright.

As they drew close, Elizabeth arched a brow. "Was that necessary?"

Phoebe lifted her chin. "I didn't aim for anyone's face."

"Small mercies."

William piped up, breathless. "I tried to stop them, but they just laughed at me too."

Elizabeth offered him a nod. "You've done fine, William. Go wash your hands before you touch anything with sugar in it."

He scampered inside.

Phoebe waited a beat longer. "I didn't want to make trouble."

"You didn't." Elizabeth opened the door. "You ended it. Good for you."

Phoebe's cheeks pinned and her mouth twitched. "Ruth would've told me to pray for their souls."

"I'm not Ruth."

"I noticed."

Elizabeth ushered her in, hand briefly squeezing her shoulder. Behind them, John shook his head with weary admiration and returned to the table. The stillroom's calm returned slowly, steeped in steam and ashwood warmth.

But something had shifted in Elizabeth's chest. Not pride, but a sharper feeling. The certainty that this orchard, this household, must not falter. Not when girls like Phoebe were learning to defend their place in it with wit, fire, and a slingshot carved from scrap.

A small shadow crossed the stillroom threshold and hovered there like a sparrow choosing a rafter. Phoebe didn't look at Elizabeth or Thatcher; she stared past them, toward the shelves where jars marched in orderly rows: rosemary, comfrey, pennyroyal, valerian. Her jaw had that rigid set Ruth used to get when she'd been wronged and would not make a sermon of it.

"Hand," Elizabeth said softly, already reaching for a clean cloth.

"Don't fuss," Phoebe muttered, but she didn't pull away. Her palm was scuffed and sticky with apple sap; a pink welt striped two knuckles where the slingshot band had snapped back.

"I will fuss exactly as much as a woman who owns vinegar and salt is allowed." Elizabeth dipped the cloth in warm water, wrung it out, and began to wipe. "And I will do it here, where boys who can't tell a graft from a gooseberry can't see you wince."

Thatcher cleared his throat. "I'll check the press," he said, already pushing back from the table. His eyes flicked to Phoebe in first pride, then a warning to be gentle at the corners, and he left them to it.

The door swung again, only half-shut, admitting a sliver of orchard light, and a taller shadow. Nathaniel Carter stood at the seam, hat in his hand, as if the hinge had surprised him into stillness.

"The north lane's clear," he said, keeping his voice low, as though announcing weather. "Lads have scattered."

"Did you run them off?" Phoebe asked, suspicious, chin tilting.

"No," Nathaniel said. "Just kept walking until they decided it was less interesting to make noise where I was going."

Phoebe considered this, then granted him the mercy of a small nod. Elizabeth noticed the way he stayed at the threshold, no farther, like a man who knew a room where women were working was a place to ask permission of.

"You may stand there," Elizabeth said dryly, "and refrain from opining."

"I am capable of both," he said, and, to his credit, proved it.

Elizabeth dabbed brine across Phoebe's knuckles. The girl hissed once through her teeth, then held steady, eyes on the ceiling beam where her grandfather had burnt the mark that named this room hers to tend. Elizabeth saw it land: pain, endured without performance.

"Tell me what you did," she said.

"What you told me, months ago." Phoebe lifted her chin toward the open window. "Count angles before you count enemies. I had the wall, my stick, and a straight shot between the chicken coop and the rain barrel. I didn't aim for heads. I reminded them I could aim."

"Good." Elizabeth wrapped a thin strip of linen. "And you?"

"I told William to get low," Phoebe said. "Then I told him not to cry where they could see."

Elizabeth's throat tightened. "Of course you did."

Nathaniel shifted, careful as a man in a chapel. "You built that slingshot," he said after a moment, not quite a question.

"Yes," Phoebe said. "Bend of hazel, drawer handle, twine from Aunt Lizzie's worst apron."

"It was not my worst apron," Elizabeth said, and Phoebe almost smiled.

Nathaniel let that sit, then added, "Your draw's clean. Knuckles will harden if you keep at it."

"I'm not keeping at it to prove anything," Phoebe said, wary again. "I did it to get them gone."

"Then you used exactly the right tool the shortest amount of time," he said. "That's better than proving things."

He didn't say brave. He didn't say inspiration. Elizabeth heard what he didn't do as distinctly as the words he chose. The boy's voices outside had been a nettle against her skin; his restraint cooled the itch without pretending it hadn't stung.

"You're bleeding," Elizabeth said, turning Phoebe's hand to check her palm.

"It's sap," Phoebe said, offended.

"And blood," Elizabeth returned, and tore a thinner ribbon of linen to bind the web between finger and thumb. "There. Move it."

Phoebe flexed. The wrap held. Her mouth wanted to quirk; she would not give it the satisfaction.

"You don't have to talk about it," Elizabeth added, gentler now.

"I won't," Phoebe said, equally gentle. "But I want to stay in the yard where people can see me not hiding."

"Then you will," Elizabeth said. "We'll sort apples where the sun can mind its own business."

Phoebe glanced past Elizabeth to Nathaniel, gauging him with the precise little head tilt she used on strange dogs and new men. "If you see them again..."

"I'll keep walking," he said. "And I'll carry a basket that needs carrying."

Phoebe seemed to accept the terms. She slid the slingshot from where it rode against her walking stick and set it on the table as if it were any other tool that had done its job. "William's in the yard," she said, abrupt now, purpose reclaimed. "He can't sort a Blenheim from a pippin when he's rattled."

"Go on," Elizabeth said. "I'll bring the vinegar apples and the 'mind your manners' voice."

Phoebe's eyes flashed with a small, fierce delight. She scooped up her stick, tucked the slingshot into the crook of her elbow, and limped out as if the floor had better learn to keep up.

The room breathed differently when she'd gone. Elizabeth rinsed the cloth and wrung it dry, then set both hands flat on the table to quiet the tremor that lurked when anger abated.

Nathaniel didn't move. He'd turned his shoulder slightly, giving her privacy without making a show of giving it. Through the open window came the orchard's ordinary sounds: bees, the soft clunk of fruit into a trug, William's voice trying on command the way his boots tried on size.

"You could have taken the stick from her," Elizabeth said finally, not looking at him. "Men like to call weapons 'too much' when a girl carries one."

"It wasn't too much today," Nathaniel said. "And it was hers."

Elizabeth looked up, surprised by the neat fit of that answer in the space where she expected a sermon. She found him watching the shelf labels instead of her...comfrey, yarrow, woundwort...as if he knew that sometimes being seen from the side was easier than square-on.

"I was not calm," she said, and it felt like confession.

"You were precise," he answered. "You made a room where she could come back to herself. I've seen boys who never get one."

She let that weigh them both. Her father had cut rooms out of chaos with lists and labor; Ruth with prayer and a keel of humor. Elizabeth had learned to do it with salt water, linen, the measured cadence of competent hands.

"I don't want her to learn that the only way she is left alone is if she's feared," Elizabeth said, voice low. "I want her to learn that you can be left alone because you belong."

"Then you'll show her belonging until the ground learns the trick," he said.

She almost laughed. "You make it sound like teaching a root to take."

"It is," he said. "Scar two tongues. Fit them close. Bind—not to choke, only to hold—then leave it alone long enough to choose itself." He gave a rueful tilt of the mouth. "I only ever learned that because a woman showed me how."

Elizabeth felt heat rise up her throat again, not anger this time. There was a steadiness in him that could have read as performance if he'd pushed it harder. He did not. He stayed near the door, boots quiet, hands empty, the opposite of a man who wanted credit for existing.

"You may carry a basket, Mr. Carter," she said at last, and heard the formality turn wry without her permission. "And you may remember that if you call her brave to her face, she'll think you've made her into a tale. She is not a tale. She is a person whose knuckles sting."

"Understood."

Elizabeth took down a small jar from the shelf, worked the cork free, and dabbed a smear of calendula in the linen where sap and blood had met. "Come on," she said. "Let us be seen not hiding."

He stepped back to let her pass, and when they crossed the yard together, she with the vinegar trug, he with an empty basket, both of them keeping a respectful pace behind the girl who had already sorted herself, Elizabeth felt the set of her shoulders change. Not lighter not safer, but steadier, as if a second hand had settled on the other side of the beam she carried and said, without asking to steer, I've got this edge.

***

It began with the pounding of hooves—fast and uneven—cutting through the orchard's hum of bees and soft wind. William's shout came next.

"Horse in the north row!"

Elizabeth turned from the barrelhouse door just as a bay gelding burst between two Blenheim trees, eyes rolling white, foam flecking its bit. Its reins dangled loose, one strap already looped around a low branch. The animal's flank heaved, tail lashing, each jerk threatening to splinter the grafted limb it had snagged.

"Mind the trees!" Thatcher bellowed from the far side, trying to wave it toward the open lane. But the more they shouted, the wilder the horse grew, sidestepping, backing into the next row, snapping twigs under its stamping hooves.

Nathaniel was already moving. He had vaulted the low fence without a thought, boots striking earth in a long stride. "Hold back!" he called, voice carrying like a whipcrack. "You'll drive him further in."

He slowed as he neared, his hands low and open, each step measured. The gelding's ears flicked toward him, then flattened again as the tangled rein pulled against its head.

"Easy, lad," Nathaniel murmured, his tone dropping to something near a drawl, the kind a man used on skittish stock back home. "You've only got yourself in a snarl. Let's see to it."

The horse tossed its head, forelegs lifting in a half-rear. Nathaniel sidestepped neatly, letting the hooves strike empty air before easing forward again, always at the edge of the animal's vision.

"William—quiet now—bring me the cut-knife from the fence-post."

The boy obeyed, creeping forward, wide-eyed. Nathaniel took the blade without looking, keeping his gaze steady on the gelding. His free hand reached toward the bit, slow as a leaf falling. At the last moment, the horse froze, snorting, breath hot against Nathaniel's palm.

"That's it," Nathaniel said softly. With one smooth motion, he slid the blade between the rein and branch, severing the leather. The gelding jerked once, then stilled, confused by the sudden freedom. Nathaniel stepped in close, catching the dangling strap before it could whip again, and laid his other hand along the sweat-dark neck. "You've run enough," he murmured. "Time to walk."

The bay's breathing slowed. Nathaniel led it toward the open gate, each step easy, unhurried, as if they'd always been companions.

Elizabeth exhaled only when the horse's hindquarters cleared the last row. Thatcher came trotting up to take the reins, muttering about careless neighbors, but William stayed rooted where he was, staring.

"That was... quick," the boy managed.

"Quicker than letting him take half the orchard down with him," Nathaniel said, passing the cut rein into Thatcher's hands.

Elizabeth's gaze found his, something unspoken in it...a mix of relief, gratitude, and perhaps the smallest thread of surprise. "My thanks, Mr. Carter."

Nathaniel tipped his hat, the barest smile playing at his mouth. "Would've been a shame to lose a tree like that."

As he walked back toward the barrelhouse, William fell into step beside him, still looking as if he'd just watched a conjuring trick. "You'll have to show me how you did that."

"Patience first," Nathaniel said, glancing down at the boy. "That's the real trick."

Behind them, the shaken tree shivered once in the wind, but held its apples.

***

Later that day, Elizabeth crouched near the edge of the raised bed, tugging the last of the summer's bloom from the roots, the stems brittle with age. She tied them in small bundles with twine, her fingers stained with the oil and earth. The scent clung to her sleeves, usually a comfort. But today, even lavender couldn't quiet the knot tightening in her chest.

Then, the sound of wheels on gravel.

The unmistakable scrape of iron-rimmed carriage wheels crushed fallen leaves in their path, cutting through the orchard's hush like a blade.

Her hand stilled. She didn't look up. Not yet. She knew that carriage.

It had not been enough to send Simms. Now, Sir William Rutledge himself had come to inspect the battlefield.

The wheels stopped just short of the cider house yard, the clatter replaced by the creak of polished leather boots descending from the step. She rose slowly, brushing the dirt from her apron, her pulse steady but high.

A black-lacquered carriage, the Rutledge crest emblazoned in gold, gleamed in the noon light. Behind Sir William stepped his steward, Henry Simms, expression as pinched as ever, and a magistrate's clerk in a drab coat with a large ledger in hand.

Not a surprise, but not welcome. Elizabeth didn't move from the garden. Let him come to me.

She turned another lavender bundle, her hands slow, deliberate. "Sir William," she said when he approached, her tone as calm as the cool air. "You're a long way from Ledbury. I trust it isn't my soothing herbs that drew you?"

His smile was carved marble. "I've always admired the herb garden you keep in addition to your orchard, Mistress Whitcombe. So much care for something so... delicate."

Elizabeth resisted the urge to fix her shawl. This was calculated. Public. Intentional.

"I understand you received official notice of the audit," Sir William said. "I thought it only proper to follow up."

"Your steward delivered it yesterday," she replied. "With great enthusiasm."

Simms, a stone-faced shadow behind his master, inclined his head as Sir William stepped closer. "Still. After I heard of your reaction, I wondered if such things are better discussed face-to-face. I'd hate to think of you... caught unaware in your near future. I'm not sure if you understand the severity of the situation. These audits can be so very thorough, and unforgiving."

Elizabeth smiled sharply. "Then it's fortunate I've nothing to hide."

"Oh, I wouldn't say that." His gaze lingered a moment too long. "Even good intentions make poor currency when the barrels are light."

"Thank you for your concern. It is unwarranted."

Behind him, the magistrate's clerk was pretending not to listen, but his ink-stained fingers twitched with anticipation.

Sir William lowered his voice, just enough that only she could hear. "Sell to me. Quietly. You avoid scandal, I absorb all debt, and your name remains respectable."

She didn't flinch. "No."

He leaned in slightly. "Or let the Crown pick your bones clean. And watch your workers scatter like dropped apples."

Elizabeth gripped the lavender bundle tighter. Her fingers were shaking, and she hated it. Hated the heat rising in her throat, the pressure behind her ribs, the way he made it sound like mercy. She drew a breath and tilted her chin. "Your suggestion is noted. But misplaced."

Sir William gave a slow, pitying nod. "I'm sure you'll do your best, Mistress Whitcombe. I've no doubt you'll be... remembered fondly." With that, he turned on his heel. The steward and clerk followed without a word, the scroll still unopened in the man's hand, more a weapon than a record.

The carriage door snapped shut. The whip cracked. And just like that, they were gone.

Elizabeth didn't move until the last of the dust settled behind the wheels. Then she slowly looked up and found half the yard watching her. No one spoke. She turned back to the garden, her hands white-knuckled around the crushed stems of lavender.

The scent had turned bitter.

The still room was cool and dim, its stone walls holding the chill even as the autumn sun warmed the orchard outside. It smelled of dried herbs and old wood, of rosemary, sage, and cider-soaked oak. Elizabeth shut the door behind her and leaned against it for a moment, letting the silence close around her like a cloak.

No eyes here. No whispers. Just breath and shadow and the soft creak of barrels aging in their racks.

She crossed to the worktable in the center of the room—scarred by years of labor, oil-darkened in places where her father's hands had once rested. She pressed her palms flat to the surface, willing it to hold her upright.

Sir William's words still rang in her ears. "*Watch your workers scatter like dropped apples.*"

She had stood her ground. She hadn't flinched. And yet, her knees felt unsteady now that no one was looking.

The barrel count wouldn't lie. Neither would the ledger. She could delay, deflect, pray for a strong late yield—but nothing could hide the fact that she was four barrels short and had no coin left to stretch.

She traced the edge of a small wooden spoon that lay beside the herb scale. Her father had carved it when she was ten. Said it was for "tasting what you've earned."

She had never used it.

Behind her, the door creaked open again. She didn't look. "I locked it for a reason," she murmured.

"Never stopped me before," came John Thatcher's gravelly voice.

She turned just enough to see him lean against the wall, arms crossed, his face drawn tight with what she suspected was concern disguised as irritation.

"I saw the carriage leave," he said. "Didn't look like a friendly chat."

Elizabeth let out a soft breath. "Rutledge wanted a performance. I gave him one."

"You gave him the sharp edge of your tongue."

"He deserved worse."

John didn't disagree. Instead, he walked slowly toward the table, glancing at the barrels stacked in the corner.

"Cider gods aren't smiling this season," he muttered. "Too much heat. Not enough rain."

"They smiled long enough to take my father," Elizabeth said, voice low.

John looked at her, longer this time. "He'd have cracked that lordling over the head with a cider stave, you know."

"I know."

"But you don't have the luxury of defiance anymore."

She turned sharply. "So I should sell?"

"No." John shook his head. "I think you should stop pretending you can fix this on your own."

The words hung in the air.

She didn't answer. Not right away. Her gaze dropped to the bundle of rosemary she'd been meaning to hang. She'd dried it in careful rows, clipped it just before bloom. The scent was strongest now: bright, medicinal, grounding.

"I've never had a partner who didn't make things worse," she said quietly.

"Then maybe it's time you found one who doesn't try to run the place over you."

She said nothing.

John stepped closer, lowered his voice. "You said no to Carter's offer? Or, you didn't say yes."

"Because he's here for the trees. Not the orchard. Not the people. Just the rootstock."

"Maybe," John said. "But he hasn't taken anything. And he braced that roof faster than I could blink."

She gave him a sidelong glance. "You blinked at least twice."

He snorted. "I'm serious, Lizzy. It's worth considering."

Her shoulders tensed at the nickname in his mouth. It softened something at the edge of her ribs, and she hated it. She had to stay strong, unyielding, or everything would fall apart.

She looked at the barrels again. Ran a hand across the sealed iron hoop of one near the door. Her cider. Her name. Her father's legacy. And the shadow of Rutledge creeping in faster than she'd expected.

"I'm not saying yes," she said finally. "I just... don't know if no is enough anymore."

John nodded, grim. "That's where it starts."

She exhaled slowly and reached for a clean cloth to wipe her hands. "I need to think."

"You need to decide."

They stood in silence, surrounded by the quiet pulse of cider breathing in its barrels and herbs drying to bone. Outside, the press groaned into motion again, its weight echoing through the walls.

Elizabeth closed her eyes, letting the rhythm of it steady her. Just for a moment. The still room was a sanctuary, but Elizabeth had learned the hard way that even sanctuaries had cracks.

She stood by the far wall now, fingers busy with what looked like work but was nothing of the sort. She was paring dried ginger root with a worn-handled knife, shaving it into fine curls for tincture. The scent was sharp and clean—something between lemon and heat—and she let it sting her fingertips to keep the rest of her steady.

When she couldn't fix a problem, she prepared herbs. It was how she survived her father's death. Her husband's debts. Every tax increase, every storm-lost harvest. Peel. Dry. Steep. Wait.

But ginger wouldn't fix four missing barrels. And it wouldn't fix the way her orchard now felt like it was listing beneath her.

She was just about to set the knife aside when she heard it: the creak of a boot on stone, softer than John's, slower than William's. She didn't turn.

"If you've come to offer unwanted advice," she said, "you're late to the line of men who've tried."

A chuckle behind her. American. Confident. Infuriating.

"I've enjoyed the fruits of my labors, and came to return your favor," Nathaniel Carter said. "You didn't quite slam the door in my face earlier, and I felt that showed restraint."

She still didn't look at him. "And now you've come to reward me with your presence?"

"I thought I'd try reason first. Then charm, if necessary."

Elizabeth turned, slowly, wiping her hands on her apron. "You'll find I'm immune to both."

Nathaniel stood in the doorway, coat off, sleeves rolled, hair still windblown from the orchard. He looked like someone who belonged everywhere and nowhere, a traveler with good boots and bad timing.

His gaze swept the room with mild curiosity. "I've been in cellars, cooperages, cider barns. But I've never seen one of these. Our family never had one."

"This is a still room," Elizabeth said crisply. "For drying, distilling, tincturing, bottling, and, on occasion, yelling."

"Useful place," he said.

"Not for lingering."

He took that hint exactly as well as she expected, which was not at all. "I'm not here to linger. I'm here to make an offer that doesn't insult your intelligence."

She crossed her arms. "You're already doing better than most."

He stepped forward and placed a folded sheet on the worktable beside the ginger curls. "One barrel. Your choosing. Uncut, unblended, your strongest label. I take it with me. Present it to the colonial guilds and shipping brokers. If it sells, we talk trees."

She didn't reach for the paper. "And if it doesn't?"

"Then you're out one barrel and a bit of pride."

She stared at him, weighing the risk. One barrel wasn't nothing. But it was something. And if it opened a market, if it bought her a season...

Nathaniel watched her, not smiling. Just steady. And she hated that it steadied her in return.

"You want the old bloodlines," she said. "The Kingston Blacks. The Foxwhelps. You want trees that drink hard and fruit late."

He nodded. "I want what you have. What no one else does. And I'm offering trade. Not theft."

"You're offering hope," she murmured. "Hope doesn't pay debts."

"No. But it buys time."

She looked at the paper again, then back at him. Her fingers twitched.

"I don't like needing help," she said.

"I don't like asking for it," he answered. "But I need this to work as badly as you do."

Her brow lifted. "What happens if you fail?"

His jaw tensed. He hesitated. "Then I go back empty-handed. And the business I was trying to build back home rots in the ground."

She blinked. She hadn't expected that. She expected deflection. A joke. A shrug. Not something that hit just close enough to sting.

He smiled faintly, and this time it wasn't self-satisfied. "You think you're the only one with ghosts in the trees, Mistress Whitcombe?"

She turned away before he could read too much in her face.

Behind her, she heard him shift. "I'll be in Ledbury until Friday. If you decide the gamble is worth the grain, send word."

CHAPTER FOUR

BARREL IN THE SHADOWS

W hen he left, she plucked a dried lavender stem from the bundle on the wall and broke it clean in two, the scent rising like smoke.

Taking a deep breath and seeking to distract herself with productivity, she crossed the room, pulled the basket of unopened letters toward her, and began slicing the seals open one by one.

Most were of little consequence, but last letter bore a familiar indigo wax seal of AL smeared by rain, as if the messenger had hesitated to deliver it at all. Elizabeth slid her finger beneath the flap and unfolded the page with a familiar heaviness.

From Anne Larton, Oakmere Vale

Lizzie—

You were right. The cider's turning. They say the Black-spotted Blenheims can't be salvaged this year. The rot's in the root, not just the fruit. The Excise sent a clerk last week—barely out of shortcoats—and he fined us three shillings for a "misrecorded cask." Peter says we'll pull through, but you know how he lies to spare me.

Tell me you've had better luck. And if not, at least tell me you've had better courage. You inspire me, you know.

Love, Anne

Elizabeth pressed the page flat against the table. The script shook at the edges. Oakmere was older than Whitcombe...older than most holdings in three counties. If they were failing, what hope had she?

She picked up another: black ink on coarse stock, from the Downes in Melverley. Three cider trees cut down by order of the sheriff for nonpayment. A stillhouse confiscated. A warning from the Cider Office that "all unregistered exports, including gifts, shall be construed as criminal acts against the Crown."

Her fingers tightened around the parchment. At the bottom of the stack sat a note from the Graces in Cheshire: short, blunt, unsigned.

They'll come for you next. Women like us make poor scapegoats, but excellent examples.

Elizabeth stared at the words for a long moment. She remembered the Graces' orchard: all sisters, no brothers, no sons. They'd trained dogs to guard the fermenting shed.

A kettle hissed, forgotten on the iron hook.

Across the room, Phoebe sat reading in the window nook, toes tucked up, her limp forgotten for a moment as she turned the pages of her novel with ink-smudged fingers. The breeze tousled her hair, and she muttered something under her breath...probably correcting the protagonist's poor choices.

Elizabeth looked down again at the letters. The ink. The warnings. The rot. The law. She swept them all into a neat pile and folded her hands atop them. "I won't lose this place," she whispered.

Phoebe glanced up. "Did you say something?"

Elizabeth forced a small smile. "Just thinking aloud."

The girl arched a brow. "Dangerous habit."

Elizabeth stood and walked to the open door. The orchard stretched beyond, lit now by the dappled sun of a breaking sky. The ridge tree stood firm at the far end, its graft scar half-hidden by leaf and shadow. She stepped out onto the path, wind lifting the edge of her apron.

Tomorrow would bring questions. Audits. And likely, more interference. But today...today the barrels were standing, the mash was sweet, and her niece had faced cruelty without crumpling.

The orchard still lived.

And she would make damn sure it stayed that way.

The light was turning, long and gold, slanting across the stone floor of the barrelhouse as Elizabeth stepped inside. The door creaked on its hinge, the scent of mash and musty timber thick in the air. A bird rustled in the eaves. One of Thatcher's new braces groaned faintly as the wind nudged the frame.

She moved through the rows, her fingers brushing the barrels like a priestess checking votives. Marked. Sealed. Legal. Safe.

All except one.

In the farthest shadowed corner, tucked behind an overturned apple crate and half a spool of rope, sat the cask she'd held back for her own cellar. Smaller than the rest. Sturdy and untapped. Foxwhelp and Kingston Black, with just a sliver of Sweet Coppin. The blend a little like Phoebe: unexpected, sharp, and hard to forget.

Elizabeth crouched beside it, her knees stiff, her skirts bunching at the hem. She ran a hand across the lid, traced the wood grain, and pressed her palm flat against the top as if she could hear the cider inside shifting with intent.

This was a gamble. A breach. A mark against her if discovered. But it was also hope in liquid form. If it impressed Carter's backers, if it made it past the harbormaster's nose and the Excise, then perhaps they had a chance at something more than just survival.

Elizabeth picked up the charcoal nub she'd hidden in her apron pocket. No elaborate mark. No crest or forgery. Just one letter, clean and dark:

W.

"For Whitcombe," she whispered, and suddenly grinned. "For women." *For the wildness that still ran in her late sister's blood and her niece's spine.* "For all of it." She reached for the linen square she'd brought and wrapped the stopper carefully, tying it off with twine like a gift she didn't dare name.

Behind her, the door creaked again.

"Ma'am?"

She turned...and stopped. William hovered in the jamb, and just beyond his shoulder Nathaniel Carter waited with his hat in his hands, boots clean, expression careful. He'd chosen not to cross the threshold until invited.

"Come in," Elizabeth said, because the barrel was already chosen and the clock was already ticking.

Nathaniel stepped inside, took in the single cask tucked behind rope and crates, and did not smile. "You picked your best."

"I picked what will speak," she said.

"Then we need the paperwork that keeps the Excise from deciding it's a confession." He set his hat on an upturned crate. "Tell me exactly what Wainscott counts."

"Barrels by tally mark and placement," Elizabeth said, already moving to the worktable. "Then he checks my ledger against the Excise register he carries. If a barrel appears on my page and not on his, or stands on my rack without a corresponding line, he calls it fraud, seizes stock, and fines me for the difference."

"So we give him a reason the numbers don't kiss," Nathaniel said. "And we put that reason on three sheets, each from a different angle, so if he tugs one, the others hold."

Elizabeth dipped her pen. "Name them."

He held up a finger. "One: Cooper's Docket says this cask left today for hoop repair after swelling and weeping at the chine. Cooper's dockets live in the gray between trade and tax; Wainscott can't count what's 'under repair.'"

A second finger. "Two: Assay Note marks it as a sample cask for assay, bound for the colonial brokers' guild. Samples not offered for retail are temporarily excise-exempt in transit. The note names the cask, weight, bung sealed with wax and gauze, expected return of empty."

A third. "Three: Gate Tally, our own carter's chit that records an outbound move by cart, signed with a hand Wainscott recognizes. Destination listed as farrier on the High Street, so no one reads 'inn' and thinks ale."

William's eyes were big as apples. "I can carry the farrier tale," he said.

"You'll carry the barrel and keep your mouth shut," Elizabeth said, but there was no bite in it. She slid parchment toward Nathaniel. "Write the cooper's docket. Thatcher's brother worked the hoops in Ledbury last winter; Wainscott has seen his marks."

Nathaniel nodded. "What's the cooper's surname?"

"Hollis."

"Hollis it is." He began in a neat, trade-plain hand: *Received of Whitcombe Orchard one cask (Foxwhelp/Kingston Black blend), chine seep, hoops to be heated and reset...*

Elizabeth pulled a second sheet and headed the top: *Assay—Not for Retail.* Beneath it she wrote, with ruthless clarity: *Sample for quality and proof; cask to return empty; duty not assessed while under seal.* She paused. "Exemption line?"

"Write 'Under Article for Samples and Assays' and name the steward who signed your last audit," Nathaniel said. "If Wainscott wants to sneer, he has to sneer up the chain."

"Simms," she said, and the nib scratched his name with satisfying malice.

William shifted his weight. "What about the empty spot on the rack when he comes to count?"

"There won't be one," Elizabeth said. "Thatcher keeps dummy barrels: sound hoops, stale must. We set one where this was, chalk it with the same tally stroke, and I mark my ledger with 'R' for Repair on the line so the missing volume is accounted for. If Wainscott demands a tap, I tell him it's newly racked and not yet proofed; he hates sticky floors more than he hates me."

Nathaniel added without looking up, "And the gate tally covers why no one saw it leave the lane: 'Moved by side path to avoid churned mud at the press yard.' Small lies smell like truth."

Elizabeth lifted the page to blot it, feeling the strange steadiness of a plan with three legs instead of one. "And if he asks why we sent a good barrel to the cooper and not a spoiled one?"

"Because it's a good barrel worth saving," Nathaniel said simply. "And because a cask that travels to assay ought to be worthy of its name."

She nodded once, satisfied against her will. "Sign the docket 'H. Hollis' with a scuffed hand," she said, sliding the first sheet back to him. "He writes like a man who fights his quill."

Nathaniel scuffed the signature believably and sanded it. Elizabeth filled the gate chit in her practical script and folded all three into a packet tied with twine.

She turned to William. "You'll take the barrel to the farrier's yard door, hand the packet to the man who says 'Blackthorn shoes don't hold,' and then you'll forget the words as soon as you've heard them."

William swallowed. "Blackthorn shoes don't hold," he repeated, reverent as a catechism.

Nathaniel crouched to the boy's eye level. "Mind your steps on the slope. Keep the cask low on your hip so it doesn't shout that it's full. And if anyone speaks to you—"

"I'm running vinegar to the farrier for rust," William said promptly.

"Good lad," Elizabeth said. She pressed the tied packet into his palm and then, after a beat, pressed her other hand over it. "Fast, and back by the ridge before the moon lifts."

He nodded, gathered the barrel as if it were heavier than it was, and slipped into the dusk.

As he vanished into the twilight, Elizabeth let her hands fall to her sides. She whispered, "Go fast, little barrel."

Because she'd done everything else she could. And now it would come down to fate, or skill, or the stubborn alchemy of apples pressed against the odds.

She turned back to the rows of barrels.

Tomorrow, she would wake early and check the mash. She would bandage John's arm. She would taste for sweetness and for trouble. And if the world stayed upright, she would teach Phoebe how to notch a graft on a younger tree.

But for tonight, she would walk the orchard once more. And let herself believe, just for an hour, that the W she'd written stood for something that might survive.

The kettle had cooled, but the air still held the warmth of steeped sage and crushed mint. Elizabeth sat at the worktable, ledger open, pen idle. Outside, the wind combed softly through the trees, brushing the shutters with a hush like breath held.

Phoebe entered quietly, walking stick tucked close, book still clutched in one hand like a shield. She hesitated at the threshold.

Elizabeth looked up. "Done tallying?"

"More or less." Phoebe crossed the room in a lopsided rhythm. "William took it?"

"He's already past the ridge."

Phoebe sat, curling her legs beneath her, resting her bad foot with a small, nearly inaudible sigh. "He's brave."

"He's careful," Elizabeth corrected. "Which is braver."

They sat in silence a moment. The candle between them crackled faintly.

Phoebe ran her finger along the grain of the table. "Do you think it'll matter? The barrel?"

Elizabeth didn't answer at once. Her gaze flicked to the window, where the moon was just beginning to rise beyond the orchard slope. "If it doesn't," she said finally, "then we try something else." Watching her niece and noticing the hollows under her eyes, she asked, "Are you sleeping at night?"

Phoebe nodded, but her eyes stayed on the table. "I had another nightmare about the fever."

Elizabeth's breath caught.

"I remember Mama crying. Not just at night. She prayed with her hands shaking. And I remember thinking, 'If I live, she'll stop.' But when I woke up... she cried harder."

Her aunt pressed her lips together.

"I thought I was being punished," Phoebe said quietly. "That I'd done something to deserve being twisted."

"You hadn't." Elizabeth's voice was sharper than she meant. She softened. "You haven't."

"She said the gods would choose. But I think the fever did."

Elizabeth looked down at her hands. There was always something under her nails now: earth, pulp, bruised skin. "Your mother wanted to believe. In order. In cause and consequence. That suffering meant something."

"She was wrong."

"Yes." Elizabeth didn't flinch.

Phoebe stared at the candle. "I don't want to believe in punishment. Or fate. I want to believe in grafting. In roots. In things you can fix with your hands."

Elizabeth smiled, a small one, and reached across the table. Phoebe didn't hesitate. Their fingers met and held.

"You know the tree near the west slope?" Elizabeth said. "The one with the twisted graft?"

Phoebe nodded. "The bark bulges on one side."

"It shouldn't have taken. Not cleanly. But it held. And now it gives the best early crop we have."

Phoebe looked up at her. "Even when it's not perfect?"

Elizabeth's eyes warmed. "Especially then. A burly tree that stands the test of adversity is the best kind."

"The audit..." Phoebe blinked fast, once. "You're going to fight them, aren't you?"

"Yes," Elizabeth said.

"I know you don't have an heir. You could just sell to Sir Rutledge and it would be so much easier for you..."

"You're my heir, and I don't steer into easy. Don't be ridiculous." She rolled her eyes. "Of course I'll fight. For the orchard. For you. For everything they think I shouldn't be able to do without a man to sign for it."

Phoebe leaned forward, resting her cheek on the back of Elizabeth's hand. "Then I'll fight too."

The candle flickered between them. Outside, somewhere in the dark, an owl hooted once. *A good omen*, Ruth would have said. Elizabeth chose to believe it still might be.

The house settled into its evening creaks. Thatcher's footfalls faded. Phoebe's door clicked. Elizabeth gathered the three scrapings of sand she'd used to blot the assay note and tipped them back into the dish.

"You write like a woman who expects to be argued with," Nathaniel said from the doorway.

She didn't start. She'd known he hadn't gone far; the stillroom breathed differently when it was only hers. "I write so that when the arguing starts, the paper does some of it for me."

He stepped in, slow, palms empty. The packet copies lay between them on the table, one for the cooper's box, one for her ledger, one to flash like a shield if Wainscott pressed too close. Elizabeth reached for the ledger; he reached at the same moment to steady the ink well as the table wobbled.

Their hands met not palm to palm but along the cuff, the edge of his sleeve taking a crescent of her wet ink. She should have snatched back. Instead they both held still, two competent people correcting for a wobble, breath caught in the same small hinge of time.

"You've blotted yourself," she said at last, but the dryness in her voice came a half-second late.

"Cost of doing business," he said, softer than before. He didn't let the inkwell tip; he didn't try to cover her hand with his. He simply stayed where the table needed him and watched her write R in the ledger margin beside the absent cask's line: Repair Hollis.

"There," she said, and underlined once. "If Wainscott reads left to right like a Christian, he'll see the story the way we tell it."

Nathaniel's mouth tipped. "And if he reads like a miser?"

"Then he'll follow the numbers to the gate tally and trip over his own suspicion." She took the packet copy meant for her shelf and reached past him to set it high. The brush of her sleeve against his forearm was nothing at all and entirely too much. He didn't move. Neither did she.

"You hold the pen low to protect your thumb," he said, same steady notice as in the rows.

"I like my thumbs," she said. "And clean cuts." She slid the ledger shut and only then withdrew her hand from the space his steadied.

"Thank you," she added, and surprised herself with how little it cost to say it.

"For the ink?" he asked, glancing at the mark he'd carry out of her house.

"For not trying to carry what isn't yours," she said. "For holding the edge of the board when I needed the other hand."

He nodded once, as if accepting terms, not triumph. "I'll walk the lane and look for William's return," he said. "If anyone's watching, they can count my boots instead of your barrels."

"Mind the mud," she said.

"I'll earn it," he answered, and stepped back through the door. The air he left behind felt warmer than the stove deserved.

Elizabeth reopened the ledger, touched the drying R, and let herself breathe. The story would hold enough for a first look. The rest would be work, and work she knew how to do.

She flexed her ink-stained fingers, the ghost of his sleeve still a crescent on her cuff, and blew out the candle.

By the time the house had gone quiet, Elizabeth had relit her lantern and stepped out beneath the orchard's stars.

She didn't need light to walk these rows; her boots knew the way, even in darkness. But still she brought the flame, a small flickering defiance against what might come next. The barrel was gone, the risk already taken. William had carried it straight to the Red Hart under cover of dusk, saddlebag sealed, no questions asked.

She'd thanked him with an apple from her own hand. He'd grinned and taken off like a fox on a dare. *Good lad.*

Now the orchard held its breath.

Elizabeth trailed her fingers along the rough bark of a Blenheim tree, then paused beside a younger grafted limb, still bound in muslin. The scent of ferment and crushed skins hung on the wind. Somewhere, a fox barked.

She crossed toward the ridge slope, lantern swinging low. The moon glinted off the leaves, silvering the shadows. Here stood the old one...the tree with no name. Her father's notes had called it "Root 9A," but that never suited. It was just hers, though the graft had twisted wrong at the start. The bark puckered along the join. But it held.

She touched it gently. "Still growing," she murmured.

Behind her, the house was only a dim silhouette now. Phoebe would be asleep or pretending to be. The girl never liked goodbyes, even to days.

Elizabeth let her hand drop.

Once, this orchard had meant routine. Now it was resistance. Not just to Rutledge, or the Exchequer, or men with polished boots and patronizing smiles, but to the rot that said she couldn't survive without a name beside hers on the deed.

She looked up at the stars, sharp and clear above the trees. Somewhere across the sea, Nathaniel Carter and his men would open the barrel. She didn't trust him. Not yet. But the cider was real. And that was a beginning.

Her breath misted in the air.

This land already held her sister. Had almost held Phoebe. Had swallowed her husband's body like a seed too bitter to sprout. But still she walked it. Still she planted. Still she named. Beneath the ridge tree, she knelt and pressed her palm to the earth. "Let this be enough," she whispered.

The graft held. The night held. She rose and walked back toward the house. And from a second-floor window, faint and flickering, a candle still burned.

CHAPTER FIVE

A BARREL AND A BLUFF

BRISTOL PORTS

The fog over the Avon was thick enough to taste. Nathaniel Carter stood on the damp planks of the quay, collar turned up against the chill, and watched a pair of dockhands maneuver a crate of saplings into the yawning belly of the Mary Belle. He'd already paid the captain—three guineas for space enough to wedge the bundle between two casks of tobacco—and was silently calculating how much of the bark would still be green when they reached Virginia.

These scions were from Haverford Green orchard, a modest holding east of Ledbury whose bittersweets sold well enough in the taverns of Bristol. It was not the prize he sought at Whitcombe, but the deal kept his hands in the trade and his name in the mouths of the merchants who mattered.

Behind him, Miles Hardwick's voice cut through the gulls' cries. "Tell me you didn't waste prime cargo space on twigs."

Nathaniel didn't bother turning. "Rootstock. Blenheim, Egremont Russet. You'd sell your own mother for half the price these fetch."

"Aye, but I can sell your share of French brandy in half the time," Miles said cheerfully, sidling up with a ledger under one arm. "You've a berth going back empty...fill it, and you can afford all the lady orchardists you like."

Nathaniel took the folded bill of lading from the captain, tucking it into his coat. "I'm not looking for 'all' of them. Just the ones with the right trees. And if I can get the best..."

"Whitcombe." Miles grinned. "You've been sighing in that direction for weeks."

Nathaniel turned, finally, meeting his friend's gaze with a dry look. "I've been working in that direction. There's a difference."

They walked together down the slick quay, past barrels of salted fish and stacks of wool bales. A boy darted between them, carrying a coil of rope, and Nathaniel stepped aside automatically, his hand still half on the packet of saplings as if it were a living thing that might bolt.

"You keep chasing these honest ventures," Miles said, "you'll die with clean hands and empty pockets."

"Maybe," Nathaniel said, scanning the tide for the next incoming ship, "but the pockets will be mine."

Miles snorted, peeling away toward a tavern where half his business was struck. Nathaniel stayed at the water's edge a moment longer, eyes on the anchored ships. Somewhere out there was the cutter that would carry Whitcombe's grafts—if Elizabeth agreed. If she didn't...

He glanced back toward the warehouse, where the captain's men were still stowing his saplings with a care he'd paid dearly for. If she didn't, he'd be stuck with another season of patchwork deals: a barrel here, a crate there, never enough to stake his claim.

The tide shifted. Lines groaned against the bollards. Nathaniel straightened his coat, squared his shoulders, and went to check the rest of his cargo.

The trees were only twigs now, but in Virginia soil, they could grow into something worth crossing oceans for.

***

Nathaniel Carter adjusted the collar of his coat as he stepped into the muddy square, boots skidding slightly on the slick cobbles. A low mist clung to the eaves of the rooftops, softening the crooked outlines of Tudor timbers, but the market was already bustling. Smoke curled from cookpots. A cart laden with split firewood creaked past, and somewhere nearby, a woman hawked crabapples in a voice roughened by cider and weather.

He tucked his hands deeper into his coat pockets and made a slow circuit of the square, trying not to look like a man stalling.

Brass candlesticks winked from one stall. A baker's boy with ash on his sleeves waved a tray of scalding oatcakes overhead. Beside the posthouse, a broadside was being nailed to the wall, its title writ in gothic black: ROYAL DUTIES ON FERMENTED GOODS. A cluster of townsfolk stood gathered around it, muttering.

"Another tax?" said a potbellied man in a stained apron. "They'll be taxing the froth off the ale next."

"Already are," came the reply. "And cider, same as brandy now. As if we were selling poison instead of breakfast."

The tension was woven into every corner of the market...every wary glance, every muttered curse. The Cider Act had gone through like a blade. He'd seen it in Devon, in Bristol, now here. Growers folding their presses. Merchants hedging their bets.

But he wasn't just hedging. He was gambling.

He made his way to the cooper's yard on the edge of the green. The place smelled of wet pine and pitch, and the man inside—balding, brawny, flecked with sawdust—barely looked up as Nathaniel approached.

"Yours'll be ready for loading come sundown," the cooper said. "That is, if the lady sends it."

"She will." Nathaniel made the words sound easy.

The cooper gave him a look that said he wasn't fooled. "Hope you've better luck than the last fellow tried to buy from her. She sent him home with a sprained wrist and nothing else."

Nathaniel offered a faint smile and a half-lie. "I've been told I'm more charming."

He turned before the man could press further and walked back toward the square, boots slipping slightly in a patch of churned mud. Above him, a skein of crows passed low, wheeling east toward the hedgerows. He should have felt the anticipation of success.

Instead, all he felt was time ticking.

If she didn't send the barrel... if she'd changed her mind, or lost her nerve, or simply decided he wasn't worth the risk...

Everything fell apart.

His backers would cut him off. His own name, already frayed by failure, would mean nothing. He'd have to slink back to Virginia and tell what was left of the orchard he'd tried.

He passed the King's Arms and paused beneath the overhang. A drayman was unloading barrels from a branded cart, heavy casks sealed with thick red wax, marked BRISTOL DISTILLERY. Apple brandy. Government registered. Properly taxed.

The drayman tapped each barrel with a practiced knuckle, nodding at the sound.

Nathaniel stared, breath souring in his throat.

He'd had a shipment like that once. Stamped and ready for the schooner. But the hold had flooded during loading. Two cracked. A third split from the swell. By the time the ship left port, the rest had gone to vinegar. The captain had dumped them in the Chesapeake. His backer had dumped him not long after.

He hadn't shipped anything since, until now.

If Elizabeth came through. If the barrel bore up to the voyage. If the cider tasted as good as it had in that stillroom, under her wary gaze and firelight glinting off copper pots...

God help him, he'd gambled his second chance on a single barrel from a woman who might never say yes.

Nathaniel turned away from the cart and exhaled through his teeth, dragging a hand through his wind-tossed hair. The fog was lifting, and with it came the scent of roasting chestnuts and woodsmoke from the nearby green. A dog barked once and was silenced by a curt voice. He checked the sky. Noon approaching. If there was no word by now...

No. Not yet. He wasn't finished. And she hadn't said no. Not yet. He adjusted his coat, squared his shoulders, and walked toward the alley behind the posthouse, where the light narrowed and the shadows stretched long.

The alley behind the posthouse was little more than a cleft between buildings, damp and sharp with the smell of ink, mold, and spent tallow. A sagging beam leaned low overhead, and moss crept up the stones like slow fire. Nathaniel ducked beneath the lintel and stepped into the narrow shade, one hand deep in his coat, the other wrapped around a folded parcel of papers.

He knelt beside an overturned crate and spread his tools across it...parchment creased from travel, a flask of ink, and a battered satchel containing a wax seal and two quills, one whittled down from an older goose feather. He laid down a silk handkerchief first: London make, old but clean, to keep the ink from soaking up the alley's damp.

The documents weren't falsified...more like reinterpreted.

A colonial goods license. A shipping manifest listing "agricultural tinctures and samples." A merchant's charter signed in Williamsburg, whose ink had long since browned with age.

He uncorked the ink and dipped the finer quill.

From: Whitcombe Orchard, Herefordshire.

To: R. H. & Co., Philadelphia, Province of Pennsylvania.

Contents: One cask, fermented juice of malus domestica, known cultivar: Kingston Black. For sampling and classification purposes only. Not for retail.

He paused. The lie was nestled between the lines...not in what he claimed, but in what he avoided.

The Cider Act made it plain: no alcoholic cider, especially not fermented at home and sent without Crown review, could be exported without a formal Excise license. No woman could ship it herself, widow or no. And certainly not to a partner overseas without naming an official distributor.

But one barrel, just one, might pass unnoticed, buried in a larger shipment or declared as a tincture. If she had marked it. If she had meant it.

Nathaniel's breath fogged in the close air. He dipped the seal into the wax and pressed it to the page, smudging the edge. It wasn't perfect. But it looked plausible.

He folded the parchment into a waxed packet already labeled with the rough stamps of a Bristol trade company. It wouldn't fool an inspector for long, but for an honest porter, or a dockmaster skimming ledgers at dusk, it would pass.

"Apology or proof," he murmured aloud, binding the string tight. "That's what one barrel can be."

If it failed, he'd take the blame. He had enough credentials to shield Elizabeth. Enough guilt, too.

But if it succeeded...if R. H. in Philadelphia deemed it worthy...then the next packet would carry saplings. Grafts. The thought was thrilling.

He slipped the packet back into his satchel and straightened, wiping moisture from his knee. A breeze stirred the alley's shadows, and from the square beyond came the faint call of a boy advertising chestnuts. He hesitated, glancing toward the high street.

Still no cart. No word.

But he trusted her more than he wanted to admit. She had not said no. And that, in itself, was something, coming from a woman with her convictions.

He adjusted his coat, squared his shoulders, and stepped back into the mist-thinned light...his gamble sealed, his name on the line.

By late afternoon, Ledbury's market was thinning. Rain had threatened all morning, but now it hung low and sulky in the sky, weaving mist through the blackened chimney stacks. Merchants were packing up carts with chapped hands, calling to one another through the damp.

Nathaniel stood by the cooper's shed, boots planted in gravel, collar turned high. He told himself he wasn't watching the road.

And then he heard it: a cart wheel squealing, a wooden rattle against uneven stone, and looked up.

John Thatcher was coming down the lane at a steady pace, his broad frame unmistakable, one hand guiding a two-wheeled cart drawn by a small piebald horse.

Jogging beside him, cheeks pink with effort, was a boy no more than fourteen, scarf askew, one glove missing, the other clutching something wrapped in muslin.

William.

Nathaniel stepped forward just as the boy caught sight of him.

"Mr. Carter!" William called, breath puffing in clouds. "It's here, it's really here!"

Thatcher gave Nathaniel a small nod as he halted the cart. "She sent the lad, but I told her I'd see it handed over myself. Figured you'd prefer that to trusting a boy with a barrel and half a promise."

The lad puffed his chest a little but didn't argue.

Nathaniel's gaze had already locked on the cask, oak-banded, sealed with fresh wax, and marked in bold charcoal strokes with a single, deliberate letter: W.

It took a second to breathe.

"Miss Whitcombe said to give you this too," William added, thrusting the muslin bundle up with two hands. "She said it wasn't for eating."

Nathaniel took it carefully. The muslin was warm from the boy's hand. Inside, sprigs of lavender and rosemary, slightly crushed. Still fragrant despite the chill.

And tucked between them was a note, folded once. He opened it.

One barrel. The rest is your gamble. —E.

He read it again. And again. A hopeful smile spread over his face.

Thatcher had unhitched the cart and was checking the wax seal with practiced eyes. "Well made," he said quietly. "Fresh off the rack. She packed it herself."

William leaned in. "She said if you drop it in the river, she's not making you another. Ever."

A quiet laugh broke from Nathaniel's throat before he could help it. He reached out and ran one gloved hand across the cask's curve. The wood was smooth. The seal solid. The mark hers. He wouldn't let her down. "You came a long way," he murmured, voice low. "Let's see how far you'll go."

Thatcher turned toward him, steady. "She said this is your test. Not hers."

The cart was hitched again, this time for the short journey to the river staging yard. Nathaniel watched them lead it away, the barrel rocking gently between the wheels, the faint scent from her note still on his hands.

The river yard ran on habit and suspicion. Men in blue coats chalked tallies on crates; a clerk with a purpled nose wrote in a neat, pinched hand that looked like it had never touched tar. When Thatcher rolled the cart beneath the hoist, a yard foreman with a salt-tangled beard rapped the cask with his knuckles and cocked his head.

"What's this, then?" he asked without looking up.

"Repair docket," Thatcher said, producing the folded slip with the ink barely dry. "Hoops heated and reset by Hollis if needed, else straight to sample."

"Sample?" The foreman finally looked. "There's duty on cider, and double if it's called brandy by the wrong man."

Nathaniel set his palm on the rim, steady as if he meant to hold back the river with a hand. "Assay: Not for Retail," he said, and slid the second paper across the plank: *Sample for quality and proof; cask to return empty; duty not assessed while under seal. Under Article for Samples and Assays, signed, Steward Simms.*

The foreman's eyes flicked at the name like a fish at a fly. Not love; recognition. He sniffed, then jerked his chin at the yard clerk. "Read it."

The clerk obliged, the words small and tidy in his mouth. "Gate tally?"

"Here." Nathaniel laid the third chit down. Moved by side path to avoid churned mud at press yard. The line sat there, small and plausible as a scuff. "You can count the cart marks on the lane if you like."

Thatcher folded his arms. "Or you can help a working man keep a good barrel from swelling to vinegar while we argue."

The foreman grunted, re-rapped the wood, and glanced at the wax. "Seal's sound."

Behind Nathaniel, a familiar voice arrived smelling of tobacco and opportunity. "Or we grease the rope and call it afternoon," Miles Hardwick drawled, already fishing in his coat for a coin he shouldn't have had so ready.

Nathaniel didn't turn. He kept his hand where it was, the calm of it louder than a shout. "No grease," he said. "We're aboveboard, or we don't sail."

The clerk's quill paused, just a tremor, but the foreman's mouth twitched, not quite a smile. He took the Assay note, folded it, and tapped the wax with a thumbnail. "You'll get me the empty back," he said.

"You'll get it," Nathaniel replied. "I'll sign for the return myself."

The foreman slapped the plank twice, quick as a drumbeat. Two hands appeared to hoist. The sling took the weight, the barrel rose, and for a breath Nathaniel's chest rose with it, held by the same rope. He didn't release his breath until the cask settled into its berth between tobacco and wool, chocked with care. The W on its head faced inward now, protected by ordinary things.

"Manifest?" the clerk asked, already impatient.

Nathaniel slid a folded sheet across: *Agricultural tinctures and samples, sealed. Destination: Philadelphia*. The clerk stamped it. The foreman scratched a chalk mark on the sling post. The river moved, indifferent and approving.

Miles exhaled a laugh through his nose. "You do love to make a sermon of paperwork."

"Paper holds," Nathaniel said. "Bribes don't."

The foreman had already turned away. Thatcher gave Nathaniel one short nod, the kind of acknowledgement that men trade when work had to be done exactly right, and whistled to William, who stood a little taller than when he'd arrived.

"Back to Ledbury," Thatcher said, taking up the cart's shafts. "Tell your aunt the river took what it was owed, and not a drop more."

William flashed a grin at Nathaniel as if they'd jointly stolen a march on the Crown. Then he ran, scarf flapping, boots slapping puddles in a rhythm that sounded like we did it, we did it all the way up the lane.

It was a dare. A wager. A beginning. And he was not about to let it fail.

Evening settled over Ledbury like ink spilled across vellum...slow and steady, seeping into corners and crevices. The King's Arms was quiet now. The hearth snapped and sighed, casting flickering shadows against the oak-paneled walls. Two travelers played cards at the far table, their voices low, the scrape of coin softer than the fire's hiss.

Nathaniel sat alone near the back, waistcoat unbuttoned, shirt sleeves pushed to his forearms. His coat hung behind him, damp at the shoulders. The scent of rosemary clung faintly to him.

Before him, a ledger lay open, its header neatly inked:

Whitcombe, Single Barrel Projection.

Beside it sat a second book: worn, leather-bound, its pages foxed and dog-eared. His mother's orchard cultivar book. The same one she had carried through frost seasons and harvest days, her notes penned in a tidy but sharp hand. He flipped to the page he'd marked with a ribbon.

Foxwhelp x Redstreak — hybrid trial.

And beneath it, scrawled in a margin faded by time and thumbprints:

Good yield in cold years. Better after grief.

He stared at that line for a long moment, not breathing.

His quill hovered, ink pooled on the nib. In his mind, he saw her again, grey wrap tight around her shoulders, sleeves rolled to the elbow, a grafting knife held like a duelist's blade. He could still hear her voice. "Too shallow and you'll stunt the limb. Too deep, and you'll kill it."

She'd made him feel the bark beneath his fingers. Made him wait. Made him watch how the sap bled before the knife was allowed to cut again.

"I don't know if I can," he'd said once. Twelve years old. Mud on his knees.

"Then you're learning," she'd replied. "Only fools are certain."

He blinked the memory away and dipped the quill. A line, then another. Projections. Trade routes. Names of merchants who might take a second shipment if the first succeeded.

He glanced again at the muslin bundle now resting near the inkwell. Lavender and rosemary. Not for preservation, not really. For belief. For memory. A woman's message, unsigned except for the one letter painted in charcoal on the cask.

W.

Whitcombe.

He set the quill down and pressed his fingers against the ledger's edge. He wanted to be worthy of the risk she'd taken. Worthy of her

name on that barrel. And God help him, he wanted her to believe he
was.

He turned the lavender sprig between thumb and forefinger until
the oil rose. Then he pulled a clean half-sheet toward him and wrote
carefully, not courting poetry, only clarity.

Mistress Whitcombe,

*The cask marked W is aboard under assay. Papers held—, cooper's
docket, assay note (Simms named), and gate tally accepted. I signed to
return the empty and will send proof by the same hand.*

*If it passes in Philadelphia, I'll bring you figures you can test with
your own numbers. If it fails, the loss is mine, not yours.*

Your word was enough; I will work to be worthy of it. —N. Carter

He sanded the ink, folded it once, and sealed it with plain wax, no
crest, no flourish, and slipped the note into a smaller muslin wrap with
the rosemary she'd sent him, as if to answer herb for herb. A boy from
the taproom agreed to carry it toward Whitcombe at first light for a
copper and a heel of bread.

When the door shut behind the boy, the room felt steadier, like a
beam with a second hand on it. Nathaniel closed his mother's book
and, before he could think better of it, added one more line to the
ledger under Projection:

*If accepted: next voyage, contract terms for spring scion wood (written,
protective of stock and name); buyers' line: R.H. & Co., Philadelphia;
contingency if W is refused: cut losses, deliver empty, send apology.*

He read the words again. He read apology like it was a kind of prayer
and protective like a promise. Then he blotted the page, blew out the
candle, and let the scent of rosemary and ink lay its weight on the
room. The ship would take the tide at dawn. He would take whatever
came with it.

CHAPTER SIX

A THORNY OFFER

M iles was waiting at the Red Hart's back table, hat tipped low and a bottle already open between them. The tavern's smoke-laden air curled in the lamplight, turning the space into a den of shadow and whispered deals.

Nathaniel slid into the bench opposite, shaking the rain from his coat. "You sent word like it was urgent."

"It is." Miles poured him a measure without asking. "The Whitcombe woman's got the stock we need. She's stalling. We stop her other deals, she comes to us."

Nathaniel took the glass but didn't drink. "You mean cut her off from her buyers."

"Not cut off. Persuade. Apply a little pressure in the right places. A delayed payment here, a sudden tax inquiry there...next thing you know, she's looking for a safe harbour, and there we are with the berth already cleared." Miles leaned in, grinning like a man explaining the rules of a game. "It's clean, no one gets hurt, and it works."

Nathaniel turned the glass in his hand, watching the amber swirl. Outside, the wind battered the shutters. "No."

"No?" Miles's brow lifted. "We've been talking about this for months. We just tip the scales..."

"She's not cargo, Miles." Nathaniel set the glass down. "You don't shove a deal through her door and expect her to take it. She's got her land, her people..,"

"She's got a ledger that says she'll need our money by harvest." Miles's tone sharpened. "I thought you wanted these trees. I thought you wanted a foothold in Virginia again."

"I do," Nathaniel said evenly. But his fingers tightened on the edge of the table. Miles was right about one thing: Whitcombe was vulnerable. If they didn't act, someone else—someone less scrupulous—would see the same weakness and strike first. It was the kind of opening Nathaniel had made his living on. Back in Virginia, he wouldn't have hesitated.

But Whitcombe wasn't just any orchard.

He thought of the ridge tree at dusk, the smell of crushed apple skin on his hands, the way Elizabeth's gaze steadied like an anchor when she looked at her land. He'd seen her face in the candlelight after the audit notice came, tight with resolve, not fear, and he'd felt the strange weight of wanting her to win, even if it cost him.

"I'm not burning her orchard to plant mine."

Miles sat back, studying him. "You've gone soft on her."

Nathaniel didn't answer. Soft, maybe. Or maybe it was something else...something he couldn't quite name that felt like loyalty.

"If she sells me those scions," he said at last, "it'll be because she chose to. Not because I took away every other choice."

Miles gave a low laugh. "Soft, stubborn, and broke. A fine combination."

"Maybe," Nathaniel said, rising from the bench. "But the orchard's still hers. And I mean for it to stay that way until she decides otherwise."

Miles swirled his own drink, eyes narrowing. "Careful, Nate. You keep playing gentleman, and someone else will take what you were too polite to reach for."

Nathaniel pulled on his coat and stepped out into the rain without answering. The wind off the Avon was sharp, and the thought of Miles's warning clung like wet cloth. But the image of Elizabeth Whitcombe kept him walking, mile after mile, until the dark broke into the soft outline of its trees.

***

The morning mist had burned off by the time Elizabeth heard his voice again: low, confident, and far too familiar.

"Beautiful day for stubbornness," Nathaniel Carter called from the orchard gate, leaning against the post like he'd been born to it.

Elizabeth didn't look up from her ledger. She sat on the cider house bench, tallying the week's yield in chalk beside a row of empty jugs. "I don't recall requesting commentary from the hedgerow."

"Just returning the favor. I brought better boots and worse judgment."

"Charming," she said without looking at him,

"I'm honored to have your barrel," he replied easily, stepping through the gate like he belonged there. "And I came to talk about what grows beside it."

Her chalk paused mid-stroke.

"I said yes to one barrel," she said, finally lifting her eyes. "Don't press for cuttings too."

"I'm not pressing," he said. "I'm asking, politely."

From the far side of the barn, Phoebe's voice floated over—clear, cheeky, and just breathless enough to betray a recent sprint. "He's terrible at polite," she muttered loud enough to be heard.

Elizabeth smothered a smile. "She's not wrong."

Nathaniel grinned toward her. "Sharp tongue."

"Yes," Elizabeth said. "And more than enough reason not to wager anything untested."

Phoebe appeared in the barn's open doorway, a hen tucked under one arm and a half-eaten apple in the other. Her braid was coming loose, apron lopsided and streaked with straw. "You going to argue all day?" she asked. "Because the chicken's getting bored."

"And where's William?" Elizabeth asked, narrowing her eyes at the apple. "I told him to check the coop gate."

"He's chasing the red one again," Phoebe replied. "Said she looked at him funny." Nodding in Nathaniel's direction, she added, "He's still here, so I'm guessing he hasn't stepped on any grafts."

"Yet," Elizabeth muttered.

Nathaniel raised his hands. "Still offering reverence."

Phoebe arched a brow. "Is that what you call it?"

"Phoebe," Elizabeth warned.

The girl grinned and disappeared back around the barn, the hen squawking softly and her boots thumping a youthful rhythm on the packed earth.

Elizabeth turned back to Nathaniel, her expression guarded. "I'm not going to be your supplier, Mr. Carter. I'm not risking my orchard to line someone else's purse."

"I'm not asking for a supplier," he said. "I'm offering a stake."

"I already gave you a barrel."

"You did. And I'm grateful. But you said yourself: as the land's always been under threat. You said they'd come for it, stamp by stamp." His voice lowered. "I want to help keep it yours."

She glanced toward the barn where Phoebe had vanished, and her voice went softer. "This place isn't just mine. It hasn't been for a while. I've got mouths to feed, and I can't trust that everyone I meet has their best interests at heart, let alone mine."

When she looked back at Nathaniel, her eyes were steady. "You'll get your barrel. You'll get your verdict. And if the verdict's good, then we'll talk. Not before."

He nodded. "Fair enough."

She crossed her arms. "And if you so much as look at a cutting before then—"

"I'll return to the colonies in disgrace," Nathaniel finished, watching her face for a smile. He was rewarded by one in her eyes.

They walked in silence.

The orchard had dried just enough to keep her boots from sucking at the earth, though Elizabeth still picked her steps carefully. She didn't glance at Nathaniel, who followed a pace behind, but she could hear him: his stride steady, his breath quiet.

It unnerved her, the way he let silence stretch like a canvas, waiting to see what she'd paint on it.

They passed under a row of Redstreaks, fruit clustered high, thick-skinned and late to soften. She paused near one tree, tracing her fingertips along a branch's lower swell. "These were my father's last planting," she said. "He spaced them for air. Told me that cider's sweetness starts with what doesn't rot."

Nathaniel nodded without smart remarks, hands clasped behind his back like a man in a chapel.

She hated that he was learning. It meant he might stay.

"You'll find the soil thin in this quadrant," she added. "Good for the tannins. Harsh on the knees."

"So you planted what could fight for its flavor," he said, reading it like a code. "Not what looked pretty in bloom."

Elizabeth slowed but didn't reply. That was the trouble with a man like him: he listened too well. He heard meaning in bark, in silence, in the way she held her knife before she pruned.

They reached a Foxwhelp row next, with older, knotted trees bearing graft scars so deep they looked like open mouths. Her father had once joked that if the orchard ever spoke, it would speak in Foxwhelp first.

Elizabeth reached for one branch, touching the thick seam where two bloodlines had met and healed. "Phoebe asked last week if she was more like her mother or me," she said, surprising herself with the admission.

Nathaniel turned his head slightly. "And what did you tell her?"

"That she was a graft," Elizabeth replied. "Took rough, but she's holding." She didn't add that Phoebe had gone quiet for a long moment afterward, then whispered, 'Then maybe I'll bear both fruits.' It had nearly undone her.

They walked a few paces more in quiet.

"She doesn't limp much," he offered gently. "A strong sapling you've raised there. Is the father still alive?"

"She doesn't like pity," Elizabeth said. "Neither did Ruth. But Ruth didn't believe in doctors. Or variolation. Said if God wanted the pox to pass over her house, He would. Ruth kept her own name for Phoebe," Elizabeth added, voice even. "As for her father...Ruth never spoke him, and there was no license to bind it."

"She didn't survive the pox."

"No. I'll never know why I was left to raise my sister's child."
Elizabeth's voice was flat. "But it changed everything."

A breeze rustled the leaves above them. The orchard whispered. She
kept her arms folded tightly.

"She walks with a twist now. Twists her stories too—reads them
behind hay bales, keeps them under flour sacks like she's smuggling
saints." Elizabeth gave a dry laugh. "Her mother would've burned
every page of those."

"But you let her read."

"I let her decide what stories matter," she said.

Nathaniel nodded, his voice quiet. "That's more than most girls
get."

They rounded the slope to a lower field, where the Hagloe Crabs
hunched like gossiping old women, dense and half-feral. The branches
clawed the air, fruit bitter and sharp. Elizabeth ducked beneath one
and stopped beside a tree with a splintered limb mended in wax and
pitch.

"This one split last year," she murmured. "Phoebe helped bind it.
Her hands are clever when she forgets to hide them."

Nathaniel crouched to inspect the binding. "Did she learn from
you?"

"She learns from everything," Elizabeth said. "Even from things
that fail."

There was a pause.

"Like that barrel?" he asked softly.

She met his eyes, and for a moment, there was no orchard...just her,
the weight of her name, and the man who kept asking for a piece of it.

"I'll take the risk," she said. "But not for you."

He nodded. "For her, then."

Behind them, a crow lifted from a branch with a rattle of wings. The trees were still now, heavy with waiting.

Nathaniel stepped back respectfully. "Show me the tree you're proudest of?"

Elizabeth hesitated. Then she turned down a path edged with moss and shade and didn't look to see if he followed. Of course he did. As they walked, she glanced sideways just once and said lightly, "If you've told that shipmate of yours, Hardwick, about the cuttings, I'll see you both skinned with your own bramble wire."

Nathaniel raised his brows. "I haven't. And he'd only smuggle them in pickle jars if I did."

She gave a tight-lipped smile, more a warning than a joke. "Don't test me, Carter."

They turned down toward the hollow, where the orchard's oldest trees stood close and bent-backed. The light shifted here, dimmer, green-gold and hushed. Elizabeth's boots squelched slightly in the damp loam as she moved toward the gnarled tree that had once marked the edge of her father's boundary row and stopped.

The bark was tufted. Not with moss or lichen, but with something unnatural...soft white clusters like wool caught on thorns, except they moved. Squirmed.

She swore under her breath and stepped closer, squinting in horror. *Woolly aphids.*

One of the branches oozed slightly where the bark had been pierced. Another showed signs of rot near the base—thin rings of mildew creeping up from the roots like a slow poison.

"Hell," she said, crouching. "Not again."

Nathaniel moved beside her, expression shifting from curiosity to concern. "Root rot?"

"And invaders." She scraped a bit of the bark back with her nail. The flesh beneath was spotted, brown-veined. "Damn it all."

"Bad cluster?"

"Could be worse. But if it spreads—"

"Has it reached the Foxwhelps?"

"Not yet," she said tightly. "But the ground's too damp down here. Should've cleared the run-off. I knew it. I've known it for weeks."

Nathaniel crouched beside her, squinting at the infestation. "It's early enough to treat. You've got soap and lime?"

"Yes," she said. "And vinegar steeped in tobacco. My father's recipe. But it won't hold if we don't regrade the slope."

Nathaniel tilted his head, thoughtful. "What about spiking the roots with ash and boiling down horsetail? We used to do that for fire blight; my mother swore by it."

Elizabeth looked at him, surprised.

"I listen sometimes," he said. "Even to women."

She barked a short laugh despite herself.

Then her expression turned grim again. "Phoebe walks past here every morning. I should've noticed. I should've seen it before her."

Nathaniel didn't answer right away. He ran a gloved hand along a healthy branch above the rot. "You're walking the whole orchard on your own," he said finally. "You can't blame yourself for every pest with wings."

"I can, and do." She stood, brushing her skirt clean. "When I'm gone, it needs to hold."

Nathaniel stood with her and surveyed the hollow. The air smelled faintly of sap and decay, overlaid with the sharper tang of cider in late season, what the old growers called blister-sweet. "I can help dig," he offered. "If you'll trust me with a spade."

"You want to earn your barrel now?"

"No," he said. "I want to understand what I'm risking it for."

A breeze stirred the trees overhead, and a few yellowed leaves fell in slow spirals. Elizabeth crossed her arms. "Come tomorrow at dawn. Bring gloves."

"I always do," he said.

They stood a moment longer in the shadow of the blighted tree. She glanced toward the slope where the hill rose gently back toward the house. Somewhere up there, Phoebe would be reading again, wrapped in one of the old wool shawls, eyes narrowed at a page, unaware of the creeping rot just down the hill.

Not everything needed to reach her.

Elizabeth turned. "Let's go."

Nathaniel followed her out of the hollow, steps light, hands empty. But he didn't look like a man who'd come away with nothing.

By the time they reached the stillroom, the light was going gold at the edges. The long table near the window was scattered with drying herbs and half-filled jugs, the air thick with the scent of vinegar and bruised mint.

Phoebe sat on a low stool near the hearth, scratching at the wax tablet she'd claimed as her ledger. A small apron hung from her shoulders, streaked with apple pulp and soot. Her left foot was propped on a wrapped brick still warm from the fire.

When she saw Elizabeth, she straightened, too quickly.

"I didn't touch the iron press," she said.

Elizabeth arched a brow. "Then what's dripping onto your skirt?"

Phoebe looked down. A thin ribbon of cider foam clung to the hem. She grinned. "William tried turning the crank himself. Said he was 'practicing manly arts.' Nearly pinned his own fingers."

From the back room came a muffled clatter and a boyish yelp.

Elizabeth sighed, but her tone was fond. "Tell him the next time he wants to impress a girl, he might try not bleeding on the tools."

"I'll embroider it on his cap," Phoebe said cheerfully, and bent back to her work.

"Since you're both under my feet," Elizabeth said, tapping the long table, "we'll make use of it. Lesson time. If you can carry a stick and count to ten, you can keep an orchard alive."

Phoebe brightened, already pushing the drying herbs aside to clear a space. William tumbled in from the back with a wet sleeve and a grin, then froze at Elizabeth's look and wiped his hands on the rag by the door.

Elizabeth set four things on the table: a whole apple, a bowl of pomace from the press, a short green twig with two buds, and a young whip-thin sapling with trimmed roots wrapped in damp cloth.

"Names," she said. "Out loud. We use our mouths so our hands don't forget."

She touched the bowl. "This is pomace: what's left after we crush the apples. It's skins, pulp, seeds, and stem pieces. It looks like waste." She scooped a small, gritty handful and let it fall back. "It isn't. We feed the orchard with it. We spread it under trees after pressing so the ground holds water and the soil gets richer. If we toss it in a heap and forget it, it rots and draws flies. If we lay it right, it becomes food for next year."

"So... yesterday's press becomes next year's sweetness," Phoebe said, studying the bowl.

"Exactly." Elizabeth nudged the twig with her knuckle. "This is a scion. Say it: sigh-on. It's a cutting, a one-year wood from a tree we like. We take scions when trees are asleep."

"Winter," William chimed in.

"Winter," Elizabeth repeated. "When the sap is low, buds tight. A sleeping branch travels well and keeps its instructions inside." She tapped the little sapling. "This is rootstock. The roots and lower trunk of a young tree. Rootstock is chosen for what the ground needs: strong roots, good disease resistance, the right size so we're not picking with ladders to Heaven."

Nathaniel stayed quiet, only leaning in enough to see which buds she pointed to, the way he'd watched her knife hand: eyes on the method, not the mouth.

"Put them together," Elizabeth said, "and you have grafting: two pieces growing as one. We do that in spring when the sap wakes up and wants to knit. Not in summer. Not in harvest. And certainly not in the rain, unless you're fond of mold." She looked at William. "Are you fond of mold?"

"No, ma'am," he said fervently.

Elizabeth pulled a small pruning knife from the shelf and set it on the table. She picked up the scion and held it so both children could see the buds. "These are buds. They point the way the new shoot wants to grow. When we graft, we mind the direction. We want the first push to go outward, not crossing back into the tree like tangled thread."

"And we mind our thumbs," Phoebe said, deadpan.

"We do." Elizabeth smiled despite herself. "Now. There are many ways to join wood." She glanced at Nathaniel. "My father loved the showiness of a cleft graft: split the rootstock and wedge the scion in like a book in a shelf. It works. But I prefer whip-and-tongue. It's tidy. The cuts fit close, the bark lines up, and it holds without choking."

She made two brisk, small practice cuts on a scrap stick, one diagonal "whip," then a short inner slice, the "tongue." "See?" She slid the two pieces together. The seam nearly vanished. "The trick is lining up the cambium, that thin green layer under the bark where the tree actually grows. Bark to bark is nothing. Cambium to cambium is everything. Line that up, tie it with soft tape, then leave it be. No picking. No peeking. Growth needs quiet."

Elizabeth set the scrap stick into Nathaniel's palm to show the angle. His hand dwarfed the knife, and when her thumb corrected his grip, his breath hitched. "Close," she murmured. "Closer." He wasn't watching the blade anymore.

William's brows knit. "How do you know you lined the green right if you can't see it?"

"Practice," she said. "And paying attention. We don't rush. We don't hack. We look, we set, we tie, we walk away." She nodded toward the window, where rows sloped down the hill. "The orchard forgives many things. It doesn't forgive careless."

Nathaniel's mouth tipped; he didn't add a word.

"Now the year," Elizabeth went on, drawing a quick circle with chalk on Phoebe's slate and marking the four corners. She wrote plainly as she spoke, her script big enough for William to copy.

"Winter," she said, tapping the top. "Pruning and planning. We cut out dead or crossing wood when the trees are asleep. We collect scions near the end of winter, keep them cool and wrapped so they don't wake too soon."

"Spring," she marked the right side. "Grafting time, bud-swell to first leaves. We set scion to rootstock, we tie, we seal. We also watch for blossom; that's late spring. Bees work then. We don't spray harsh things when bees are busy unless we want empty branches come autumn."

"Summer," she marked the bottom. "We thin fruit so branches don't break. We fight pests and drought. We water slow and deep if we must. We mend stakes. We keep grass down so mice don't nest at the base and chew bark."

"Late summer to autumn," she marked the left side. "Harvest and pressing. We pick what's ready: bittersharps later, sweets often first. We press, we rack to settle, and what's left is pomace, which goes back under the trees when the pressing's done." She looked at Phoebe. "Say it through."

Phoebe recited, eyes on the chalk wheel. "Winter prune, spring graft, late spring blossom, summer thin and tend, late summer to autumn harvest and press, then feed with pomace."

"Good." Elizabeth wiped a corner of the slate and added a narrow band across "spring" and "autumn." "We do small tasks all year: sharpen tools, check ties, walk rows. But we don't pretend everything happens at once. Anyone who tells you the trees will blossom on the same day you prune them is selling you a story, not an orchard."

William grinned. "And you don't buy stories."

"I buy work," she said. "Now, two quick fixes you'll see again tomorrow." She pointed to the pomace. "When we finish pressing, we spread this under the drip line, the ring on the ground where rain falls from the branches. Not right up against the trunk; leave a little bare earth so the bark can dry."

She lifted the scion again. "And when we store scions for spring, we keep them in a cool, damp bundle, wrapped in damp cloth or packed in clean sand in the cellar, so they don't sprout early. Label them. Always label them. A scion without a name is a stranger who will disappoint you."

Phoebe raised a hand like a pupil in a rare good school. "What about root rot in the lower hollow? Where does that fit?"

"Summer and autumn," Elizabeth said. "Drainage is wrong there; we'll fix the slope so water moves. We'll spike around the roots with ash, dose the soil with mild soap and tobacco vinegar, then a tea of horsetail and lime to dry the surface and harden the new skin. That buys time. The real cure is air and angle; the water has to leave."

Nathaniel glanced toward the door, then back at the slate. "You'll want open channels cut before freeze," he said, tone careful.

"We will," Elizabeth said. "Tomorrow at dawn we start the trench. Phoebe marks the line. William digs first spit. Mr. Carter hauls and minds his thumbs."

William puffed up with importance. Phoebe tried to hide a smile and failed.

Elizabeth set the knife aside and pushed the bowl of pomace toward the children. "Feel," she said. "Tell me what it says."

Phoebe plunged her fingers in without hesitation. "It's damp but not sloppy. Feels like spongey bread. Still warm from the press."

"Good," Elizabeth said. "Spread when it's like that. Not when it's wet as soup. If you can wring juice from it, you're inviting mold. If it's dust, the wind steals it."

William pinched a seed free and held it up. "Can we plant these and skip the graft?"

"We can," Elizabeth said. "But seeds are lottery children. You plant ten, you get ten strangers. If you want another Foxwhelp, you graft from Foxwhelp. If you want another Whitcombe Redstreak that tastes like ours, you graft from our tree. That's how we keep a name honest."

Nathaniel's gaze warmed at that, but he still didn't interrupt.

"Questions?" Elizabeth asked.

"What if the tongue split goes crooked?" William said.

"Then you stop, you cut again, cleaner and shallower. Never force a bad fit. A bad fit fails in wind." She met his eyes. "There's no shame in a second cut. There's shame in pretending the first was good when it wasn't."

Phoebe straightened, serious now. "What if someone calls my walk a flaw and says I won't hold?"

Elizabeth's answer was immediate. "Then you show them you've already held." She tapped the grafted seam she'd made in the practice wood, the two pieces now tight as one. "A strong join isn't lack of scar. It's life through the scar."

The stillroom went quiet but for the faint pop of the hearth. Elizabeth let the lesson rest a breath, then clapped once, businesslike. "Right. Put it to use. William, take this pomace to the Redstreak row and lay a ring a hand's breadth from the trunk, thin as a shawl, not thick as a quilt. Phoebe, fetch the label sticks from the cupboard; we'll mark the scion bundle by mother tree and date. If I find one stick without a name, I'll make you both copy it ten times."

"Yes, Aunt," Phoebe said, already limping briskly toward the cupboard.

William hefted the bowl and staggered cheerfully for the door. "Thin as a shawl! Not thick as a quilt!"

When they were gone, Nathaniel brushed a fingertip across the chalk wheel Phoebe had drawn. "You make it sound simple."

"It is," Elizabeth said. "Simple isn't easy. The season forgives poor poetry. It does not forgive poor timing."

He huffed a laugh. "I'll try to mind both."

"Do," she said, but there was a note of fondness she hadn't meant to give.

Phoebe reappeared with a fistful of label sticks and a coil of twine. "If we mark the scions this winter, can I help tie them? I won't peek."

"You may," Elizabeth said. "And you'll write the names big enough that John Thatcher can read them at arm's length without squinting."

"He always squints," Phoebe said.

"Then bigger," Elizabeth returned, deadpan. She gathered the twig and the young rootstock, set them side by side on the table, and rested her hand lightly across both. "Look," she said, softer now. "Different strengths. One has the roots. One has the fruit we want. Neither is enough alone."

Phoebe's expression went fierce and proud at once. Nathaniel's stayed steady, but something in his shoulders eased, as if a weight he'd been carrying found a second set of hands.

Elizabeth lifted her palm. "Back to it," she said briskly. "Tomorrow we trench the hollow, and next week we thin the Hagloes. Pruning is for winter. Grafting is for spring. Blossom is late spring. Harvest is late summer to autumn. Anyone who says otherwise can come explain it to the bees."

Nathaniel watched her with quiet interest, his hands still tucked in his coat pockets. "You keep her close to the grafts," he murmured. "That's rare."

Elizabeth began rinsing her hands in the basin by the window. "She asks better questions than most grown men."

"Then I hope I've earned the right to ask one more."

She dried her hands slowly, not turning. "Ask."

Nathaniel hesitated. Then: "If the test barrel passes, and the investors come, what happens to this? To her? To you?"

Elizabeth faced him fully. "That depends on who's asking."

"I'm asking as someone who might want to stay," he said. "Not to own. Just to build."

She held his gaze, cool but not cold.

Behind them, Phoebe cleared her throat, loudly, and said without looking up, "If he does stay, he'll need better shoes."

Elizabeth didn't smile, but she did reach for a fresh jar of vinegar and a bundle of thyme. "You'll both need better shoes," she said. "If we're culling trees tomorrow."

Nathaniel stepped closer to the table. "Should I bring my own pruning knife?"

"Borrow one of mine," Elizabeth said. "But mind the edge. It knows what it's doing."

He touched the stem of the apple still in his coat pocket and nodded. "So do you."

Elizabeth looked out the stillroom window, past the barn and the garden and toward the orchard's sloping rows.

"We'll see."

CHAPTER SEVEN

THE APOTHECARY

L edbury carried the scent of yesterday's rain, hearthsmoke curling from chimney pots, wet timber and sod clinging to the undersides of carts. Nathaniel Carter kept one hand in his coat pocket and the other lightly on the satchel slung at his side, boots slipping once on the glistening cobbles as he turned onto Church Lane.

The apothecary's shop leaned against its neighbor like a woman whispering secrets. Black timber, sagging beams, a sign that read *M. Morgan, Herbalist & Remedy-Maker* in peeling red paint. A faded sprig of tansy hung from the lintel, warding off flies or spirits, depending who you asked.

He pushed the door open.

Inside, the air was thick with rosemary and vinegar. Dried herbs hung like sleeping bats from the low rafters: bay, pennyroyal, catmint. Shelves were stacked with glass bottles labeled in slanted copperplate: Willow bark, dock powder, wormwood elixir. A cast-iron scale rested beside a chipped mortar bowl so worn, it looked as if it had ground down time itself.

A voice called from the back, firm and unimpressed: "If it's teeth you want pulled, try the stableboy with the pliers. If it's bleeding you're after, fall on your own blade."

Nathaniel smiled politely. "Just remedies, Mistress Morgan. Not martyrdom."

A curtain twitched. M. Morgan emerged, a wiry woman in her sixties, silver braids coiled like rope atop her head, apron stained with tincture. Her gaze was sharp as sour cider. She gave him a look like a man she'd already seen too many of. "Ah. Colonial," she said. "You reek of apples and trouble."

"Just the apples," he said. "Mostly."

She looked him up and down. "You here for something foolish, or something desperate?"

"Both, probably." He pulled a folded list from his pocket. "Wormwood, tobacco leaf, lime powder if you've got it. I've seen them work on woolly rot. Long shot, but..."

"Colonial cures," she muttered, but not unkindly. "Mud-blood remedies for land that's turned soft."

He said nothing, letting her move among the shelves like a storm in controlled descent.

"And what's the other parcel for?" she asked after a moment, pointing at the second line on his paper.

Nathaniel hesitated. Then: "Chamomile. And sweet flag root, if it's mild."

She raised a brow. "Not for rot, then."

"No." He cleared his throat. "There's a girl on the orchard. Bright. Brave. Bit fierce, really. Her gait's crooked, and the others sometimes forget she can still outrun them in wit."

Morgan hummed, measuring chamomile into a muslin pouch. "Clubfoot?"

He nodded. "Scarring from smallpox, too. Her mother was the sort who thought prayer worked better than variolation."

"Typical." She tied the pouch neatly and set it on the counter. "What's she reading?"

Nathaniel blinked. "Excuse me?"

"You said she was bright. Brave. I assume she reads."

"She was reading a strange novel the other night. Something with highwaymen and secret wills."

Morgan gave a rare smile. "Then I'll add lavender. Courage isn't worth much without imagination." She tucked a sprig into the pouch and slid it across to him. "Tell her it's for calm. And cleverness."

Nathaniel accepted it with more care than he meant to show. "Thank you."

"She sounds worth grafting to," Morgan said quietly. Then, with briskness: "That'll be two shillings even. You're paying orchard tax by way of conscience."

He paid, tucked both parcels into his coat, and stepped back into the light. The bell above the door gave a tired jangle as he closed it behind him.

By the time Nathaniel reached the stillroom, the door was propped with a wedge of applewood and the table looked like a small post office. Elizabeth had made a neat "Mail" shelf from an old crate: three pigeonholes chalked Cooper, Solicitors, Crown.

"You've built a government," he said, setting the herb parcels down.

"I've built reminders," she corrected, sliding a twine-tied packet into Cooper. "Hollis: cooper's copy of the repair docket and our promise to return the empty. Why it matters: if Wainscott questions the missing cask, Hollis's ledger will agree with mine. Same story, two mouths."

She tapped the middle slot. "Solicitors Bennett & Frye. My first letter asked about inheritance and trading rights as a widow; their reply"—she lifted a fresh sheet—"finally states I may contract in my own name so long as I can show clear books. Why it matters: it shuts Sir William's favorite argument and gives me legal footing to sign export agreements if I choose."

The last slot held a folded notice with a dull seal. "Crown/Excise. Receipt of my earlier petition and a circular on 'Samples and Assays.' Why it matters: it's dull, which is perfect; the rule that keeps our assay note ordinary rather than suspicious." She slid the circular across. "Keep a copy with your manifest. If a dock clerk frowns, you show him the Crown taught you the rule."

Nathaniel skimmed, nodding. "Three legs to the stool."

"Exactly," she said, then flicked a glance at the smaller pouch. "And that?"

"Chamomile, sweet flag, for calm and cleverness, the apothecary swears." He paused. "And lime and tobacco for the woolly rot."

"Good." The corner of her mouth tipped. "Put 'cleverness' under Phoebe and the rot under Tomorrow."

Elizabeth unstoppered a jug and set a row of bottles for tincture between them. "If you're here, you're useful. Wax these," she said, pushing him a brush and a dish of warm wax. "Thin coat. Think 'shawl,' not 'quilt.'"

He obeyed, serious as if waxing held back the Crown. The vinegar rose sharp; he half-sneezed and caught himself.

"Careful," she said, deadpan. "We lose more men to salads than to swords."

He choked on a laugh. "I'll add it to the ledger: 'Felled by vinaigr
ette.'"

"Spell it right," she said. "Wainscott counts vowels."

She labeled while he waxed, swift, tidy script: tobacco vinegar,
wormwood wash, horsetail tea. When the table wobbled, both reached
to steady the same bottle; his sleeve took a crescent of her wet ink.

"You collect these on purpose," she said, eyes flicking to the mark.

"Souvenirs," he said lightly. "Proof I helped without breaking anything."

"Low bar," she murmured, but her mouth softened. She handed
him a sprig of lavender. "For the apothecary debt."

Phoebe limped through, caught the lavender behind his ear, and
paused. "Fashion," she pronounced. "Keep it. It improves your
boots."

"We're saving for better shoes," Elizabeth said, straight-faced.

"For him?" Phoebe asked.

"For both of you," Elizabeth said, and Phoebe left satisfied, the
room lighter by a measure neither of them named.

They worked in easy silence a minute more: wax, label, set. The
ordinary rhythm did what ordinary rhythms do—it made space for
breath. When the last bottle cooled, Elizabeth touched the Mail shelf
with a knuckle. "Three stories aligned," she said. "Paper doesn't win
the harvest, but it keeps the floor from vanishing."

"And the floor is what I stand on," he said, softer than he meant.

"Try not to track mud over it," she returned, equally soft.

He set the brush down, gave a small nod that looked a lot like a
promise, and reached for his satchel. "I'll take a look from the ridge,
then back to town to keep the letters moving."

"Mind the slick stones," she said, eyes on her labels.

"I'll earn the dirt," he answered, and stepped into the afternoon smelling faintly of vinegar and ink.

The ridge above Whitcombe Orchard sloped soft and green beneath Nathaniel's boots, the soil still damp from the previous night's rain. Wind caught at his coat, lifting the edges like a sail, and brought with it the layered scent of the valley: wet grass, pressed skins, faint woodsmoke, and something sweeter he couldn't name.

He reached the ridge's crest and paused.

Below him, the orchard opened like a hymn. The trees curved in long rows toward the house, their leaves just beginning to yellow at the edges, thick with fruit. From this distance, the bruised bark and curling leaves of the afflicted row weren't visible, only the order, the shape, the ache of something tended for generations.

He squinted, spotting movement near the south edge of the cider house.

Elizabeth stood there, chalk in one hand, a barrel stave in the other. Her sleeves were rolled, apron knotted at the back, and a smear of cider stain darkened one hip. She was speaking William, who nodded earnestly as she pointed to a stack of half-labeled casks. His feet were too big for him, but his grin was steady. He trailed after her with a piece of charcoal in one hand and something suspiciously sticky in the other.

Nathaniel watched as she leaned in to correct the tilt of a marking line. Her hair was tied back in a loose scarf, wisps curling at her temples. She laughed at something the boy said, quick and open, and the sound of it reached him on the wind.

He loved the way she let herself laugh like someone who hadn't forgotten how.

His fingers found the satchel strap slung at his hip. Inside, the herbal parcel rustled against his mother's cultivar book.

Beneath it was the tin of lozenges he'd picked up on instinct. For Phoebe. He hadn't meant to remember her this often. She wasn't central to the trade, nor part of the negotiations. But her presence was there: quick, bright, edged with something he couldn't quite name. He remembered how she'd watched him on that first day with sharp-eyed suspicion. The way she'd stood with one hip cocked, chin high, as if daring the world to underestimate her one more time.

Don't call me brave. That voice again, small and fierce. That's what people say when they mean pitiful.

He'd liked that. And the way Elizabeth had answered without missing a beat: You're not pitiful. You're impossible.

The lozenges were softer than most. Beet sugar, not treacle—easier to chew. He'd picked them because they'd suit someone who spent more time reading than speaking. Someone who might not like sweets but could use a small, tangible grace.

His gaze returned to Elizabeth.

She was directing two of her workers now, pointing toward the western rows, her movements calm and exact. William trailed her again, this time carrying a slat of slate board almost as tall as he was.

Nathaniel exhaled and set a hand on the trunk of the ridge's lone tree. The bark was moss-soft, cool beneath his fingers.

This was no longer about proving himself to men in Philadelphia or answering Miles's impatient notes about buyers and shortcuts. It was about this. This orchard. These people. That girl. This woman.

He closed his eyes and murmured one of his mother's old lines, something she'd said over every graft she ever made:

"Graft with intention. Bind with hope."

Then he opened them, took one last long look at the cider house below, and turned toward town, the orchard shrinking behind him, but not fading.

The hearth at the King's Arms crackled low, the fire settling into a steady orange pulse. Nathaniel sat alone at his usual table, coat slung over the bench beside him, a tankard of ale gone warm at his elbow. The inn was quiet save for a dog snoring in the corner and the scrape of a broom from the kitchen door.

In front of him lay his leather-bound book of cultivars, pages yellowed and softened with time. A pressed leaf curled at the edge, and beneath it, a folded letter: thick parchment sealed in red wax.

He'd known what it would say. Still, his fingers hesitated before breaking it.

Crack. Red flakes of wax dusted the table.

Mr. Carter,

It is now mid-October. We have received no confirmation of shipment. The merchant ship from Bristol departs in nine days. If your orchard contact cannot produce what was promised, we will consider the offer void.

You are not the only bidder.

Sentimentality is not a currency we trade in.

—R.H.

Nathaniel stared at the page, pulse steady. He let the letter settle like a weight. He did not sigh. He didn't curse. He simply leaned back and looked toward the low-beamed ceiling, as though answers might be scored there among the smoke-dark timber.

Nine days.

Nine days to prove a woman's gamble hadn't been a mistake. To prove that what they'd bottled, marked, and shipped was worth more than coin. That legacy had value, even if Miles would scoff at the thought.

He looked down at his ink-stained, scarred hands. They'd once buried his mother beneath a pear tree. They'd grafted scions into old wood, pulled Elizabeth's boy from under a splintered beam, and carried more than his share of barrels.

But they hadn't built anything here. Not yet.

He reached into his satchel and turned the tin of sugar lozenges for Phoebe in his palm, remembering her crooked posture, the sharpness in her voice. She was just a young girl. But there was something in her eyes that was bursting with hope: a fierceness, like bark over new growth.

Girls like her didn't get legacies written for them. They made their own.

His mother would have said: *Tend those girls gently. They're grafted tighter than you think.*

Setting the tin down, he opened his mother's book and found her handwriting in the margin of a pruning diagram.

You plant for someone else's shade. That's the whole of it.

Nathaniel breathed in. Then dipped his pen in the inkpot.

To R.H. in Philadelphia,

The barrel has shipped. One cask, hand-marked.

Sharp, clean, old bloodlines. If it survives the crossing, we move to saplings.

I vouch for its line.

—N. Carter

He let the ink dry slowly as the fire whispered low. Then he sealed the letter with his mother's bone-handled signet—the one shaped like a blooming apple.

And before folding the paper, he added a final line:

Whitcombe. First of the old line.

Not Carter. Not failure. Not compromise.

Whitcombe.

He closed it with care, as though sealing something sacred.

If the cider passed muster, if the orchard held, if Elizabeth let him stay long enough to be of use—he could build something worth grafting into.

The taproom had emptied by the time Nathaniel stirred the hearth one final time, coaxing the coals into a slow, smoldering glow. The barkeep had long since banked the lamps, and only the faint hiss of the dying fire and the creak of ancient wood remained.

He sat at his corner table, coat folded over the bench, the sugar lozenge tin resting beside the cultivar book. His hand lay open across the spine and he traced the edges of a leaf pressed between the back pages. A Spitzenburg, flattened long ago. Once bright crimson, like spilled wine...now pale, papery gold. Fragile, but not gone.

He remembered sitting beside his mother's worktable as a boy, watching her sort scion wood by moonlight. She'd spoken to each branch like a prayer: this one will bear, that one won't. He'd asked once how she could tell.

"You don't," she'd said. "But you bind it anyway. You give it time. You wait."

The wax-sealed letter sat on the edge of the table, stamped and ready. Across from it, Elizabeth's unsigned note, the one she'd tucked into the barrel parcel with no greeting, just the challenge: *One barrel. The rest is your gamble.*

He opened the cultivar book and slipped her note between the pages, just beneath a diagram of bark-cleft joins.

And then, carefully, he turned the tin of lozenges over in his palm.

It had been a small errand. An afterthought, at first. But something about Phoebe: her sharpness, her limp, her pride. The way she'd glared at him for calling her brave. The way Elizabeth had let her speak freely, even defiantly.

He hadn't come here planning to care about a disabled girl with a book of nonsense, or to let his heart begin to ache for a stubborn orchard mistress with cider on her apron and grief in her voice. He certainly hadn't come to feel responsible.

Yet here he was, writing letters to Philadelphia and buying lozenges for a girl who might never thank him, but might remember.

And that, somehow, mattered.

He pressed his palm to the cover of the book, letting the weight of it settle.

The fire cast long shadows on the walls, soft and shifting, like branches in wind. He stood there a moment, letting the hush wrap around him.

Then, out loud, and almost without meaning to, he said:

"She didn't ask me to graft anything. But God help me...I already have."

CHAPTER EIGHT

THE FIRST OF THE LINE

The orchard was quiet that morning, the kind of quiet that felt intentional, like the trees had drawn breath and were holding it. Elizabeth moved along the southern rows with her ledger under one arm and her pruning knife sheathed at her side. The earth still bore a slick sheen from last night's mist, and her boots sank just enough to remind her that rot never waited for permission.

Behind her, faintly, came the sound of Phoebe's voice, half-recited lines from *The Female Quixote*, the words lilting through the air in uneven cadence as she paced the hen-yard path with a stick tapping the stones. Elizabeth smiled faintly, then sighed. Ruth never would've approved of that book. "Brain fluff," she'd called it. "All corsets and nonsense." But Ruth was gone. And stubborn, clever little Phoebe, was still here, with her pocked skin, her twisted gait, and her fierce insistence on walking every row herself come spring.

The Kingston Black ahead leaned westward: too heavy in the crown, like an old man nodding off mid-sentence. Elizabeth crouched at the base of its trunk, fingers brushing bark grown rough with time. The graft seam was thickened, familiar, but something caught her eye. A second line. Smoother. Shallower. Tucked beneath lichen and old wax.

Her thumb found the edge and stilled. The breath caught in her throat.

No.

This wasn't hers. The angle was wrong. The cut too high, the join too fragile. She brushed further and found another on a Hagloe Crab twenty yards up. And again, near the hollow elm. Three trees, all scarred by a hand that hadn't known patience. Or hadn't cared to.

Thomas.

The orchard didn't speak, but her pulse did. Tight and fast.

She knelt in the grass, one palm pressed to the trunk, one to her thigh. "He didn't trust my judgment," she murmured. "Only the fruit." *And wasn't that the oldest rot of all? Love that claimed to trust but never let go of the knife.*

Phoebe's laugh rang faintly from the kitchen stoop, bright, clipped. Elizabeth straightened slowly. There was no reason to worry the girl. Not over ghosts and graft seams. Not yet.

She turned and began back toward the cider house, steps firmer now, ledger shut tight under her arm. Inside, she slid it onto the shelf beside the harvest charts and reached instead for the blank folio she'd started days ago, the one without a family crest, without a husband's signature. She opened it and wrote:

South row. Three trees. Unauthorized grafts. Root inspection pending.

This book, at least, would tell the truth. Even if the others never had.

And across the yard, Phoebe's voice rose again: halting, determined, reciting something about storm-wrecked castles and steadfast sisters. Elizabeth swallowed a strange lump in her throat. There were many things she could not undo. But she could hold fast to what still grew. And to the girl who, for all her crooked steps and quiet questions, never stopped walking forward.

A flicker of movement beyond the stoop caught her attention: William, running back toward the stable with a sack of barley nearly dragging behind him. Too small for the load, but determined not to drop it. Phoebe had told him to leave her to the apples, and he had obeyed, though not without a sulky scuff to the stoop with his heel.

Elizabeth watched him go, lips thinning. He'd need tending, too. In time. But one root at a time.

And as she turned to gather her tools, her eyes fell on the old ledger again: the one Thomas had signed in heavy, prideful strokes. She thought of the letter still unwritten on her desk. If rumors were stirring in town already, rumors of saplings wrapped in oilcloth, of barrels hiding cuttings...it would not take long for the talk to reach the wrong ears. Miles Hardwick had grinned last week at the very idea, like it was a game.

The law had favored signatures, not sweat. And women's names came last, if at all.

She set her pruning knife down with care. The orchard's secrets were older than any of them. But the reckoning would be hers to write.

Elizabeth crossed the barrelhouse yard with a folded rag in one hand, wiping apple residue from her palm. The sun had burned the mist off the high ridge, but here, in the press-yard's crook, the light slanted cautiously, leaving every warped board and rusted nail looking more like a warning than an accident.

She heard the sound before she saw it, chalk against wood, brisk and deliberate. She turned the corner.

John Thatcher was crouched at the far end, a stub of lime chalk in his hand. He was marking an X beside the rim of a cask that sat two rows too far down.

"John," she called, voice even.

He didn't look up. "Yes, mistress?"

She walked closer, slow but direct. "That one's not part of the final press. It's mash from the late cider run. Still fermenting."

He wiped his hand on his breeches and rose, slow and stiff. "I'm marking estimates. It'll hold near thirty."

"I adjusted the count this morning," Elizabeth said. "That barrel's not ready for seal. Not until the froth's drawn off and tested."

His mouth thinned. "That's not what Thomas would have said." *There it was.* The splinter, beneath the veneer.

A breath snagged in her throat, not surprise, not pain exactly, but a kind of familiar ache. "No," she said. "It's not. Because I am not just my late husband, and that's a bloody good thing, co sundering how he left the place."

The yard went quiet. Even the clucking from the henhouse seemed to still.

Phoebe was seated just beyond the barrelhouse doors, peeling apples into a chipped basin, her shawl pinned tight around her shoulders. At the sound of Elizabeth's voice, her hands paused, just for a moment. Then the paring knife resumed, steady and small.

Beside her, William sat cross-legged with a buttered crust in hand, watching with wide eyes. He didn't understand the full tension, but he knew enough to hush.

John didn't speak, but she saw the shift in his stance. The way he straightened, as if reminded who'd kept this place standing. Or who was still trying to.

Elizabeth didn't wait for apology. She turned and walked back toward the stillhouse, boots ringing slightly on the edge of the stone threshold.

Inside, she let the door close with more force than necessary and pressed her forehead against the cool plastered wall.

She hadn't meant to snap. Not fully. But it was the second time that day a man had tried to measure her by her husband's shadow. And she was tired...tired of trying to lead without bruising egos, tired of polite resistance being mistaken for weakness.

Behind her, she heard the creak of the cider house stool and the scrape of a knife in a basin. Phoebe had followed her inside, quiet as a shadow, and taken up the task again without asking. That was the girl's way. She didn't need to be told what mattered, only trusted to help bear the weight of it.

William peered in through the open door, then, sensing no shouting, disappeared again.

Elizabeth didn't speak. But she did not ask Phoebe to leave, either. The two of them worked in silence for a long moment, one bruised, one patient, both watchful.

Some orchards were passed down with deeds and signatures. Others, like this, were inherited one root at a time.

And this one, Elizabeth vowed again, would not be lost. Not to rot. Not to ghosts. Not to men who looked past her to find the name they wanted written above hers on the barrel.

That afternoon, the wind shifted.

Elizabeth straightened, the bruise of anger cooling into something more useful. "Enough sulking," she said, voice even. "We're doing a live count."

Phoebe set the paring knife down at once, eyes bright. "Which row?"

"South racks, bays two through four," Elizabeth said. "The ones Wainscott will start with because the light hits clean there and he likes to feel clever."

John Thatcher wiped his palms and muttered something under his breath about men who liked to feel clever, but he fetched the chalk and the hoop-tester mallet. Elizabeth lifted her ledger from the shelf, the new folio, not Thomas's old book, and tucked a stub of graphite at the spine.

They stepped into the barrelhouse. Cool air, apple-dark. Elizabeth's candle threw steady light; dust motes turned lazy in the beam.

Nathaniel's shadow filled the doorway a heartbeat later. He'd come in quietly, as if the house itself had called him. "Trouble?"

"Verification," Elizabeth said. "You can hold the chalkboard or the peace."

"I'll try both," he said, taking the slate Phoebe thrust at him.

"Count and call," Elizabeth ordered. "John, rap and listen. Carter, read head marks and cooper brands aloud. Phoebe, tally strokes. I'll reconcile to the ledger and the gate chit."

They moved.

Bay two: John rapped the first head, solid, tight. "One," Phoebe said, chalk tapping the slate. Nathaniel read the scuffed brand on the croze. "Hollis—H.H.—stroke three." Elizabeth found Hollis 3 on the ledger line and marked a neat tick. Next cask: "Farm-coopered, barley twist hoop, stroke one." Tick. Third: "Hollis, stroke five. Bung wax fresh." Tick.

The rhythm steadied everyone's breath. Rap, read, write. Wood told its small truths.

Bay three, half-shadowed beneath a brace: John rapped; the note came back blunter. He squinted. "New rack, not settled." Elizabeth wrote NR in the margin and kept going.

Bay four: Nathaniel bent to the second cask, thumb wiping dust from the head mark. "Hollis... H4—stroke two."

"H-H," John snapped, quick as a lash. "Not 'H4'. You colonials and your tidy numbers, those are letters. That's Hollis twice. Family mark."

Nathaniel blinked, then nodded once, short and clean. "You're right. H.H. stroke two." He didn't defend. He corrected, voice steady. "Good catch."

Elizabeth's pen paused a fraction. She'd expected a flinch, maybe a boast to cover it. He gave neither. She marked the line and moved them on.

Three more heads, clean. Then—

John rapped another and frowned. The sound came back hollower than its neighbors. "That one's light," he said.

Nathaniel read the head mark. "Hollis, stroke four, chalk tally 'I'."

Elizabeth ran her finger down the ledger column. "Hollis, stroke four should sit in bay three, not four. Volume noted 'thirty-one and some.'" She looked up. "We're missing a cask...or one wandered."

Phoebe leaned closer, eyes quick. "The chalk tally slash is tilted wrong," she said. "Yours angle left, Aunt. That one angles right."

"Which means someone copied the mark and got sloppy," Elizabeth said. She set her palm to the head and pushed. The cask shifted too easily, weight off the bung. "Dummy on a real line," she murmured. "Who moved it?"

Silence. Then William's small voice floated from the doorway, guilty as a cat with feathers on its whiskers. "I did."

He edged in, cap in hand. "I was sweeping the aisle. Mr. Thatcher said keep the lanes clear and I—there wasn't space, so I slid this one here and put that other one there. I thought the slash was just a slash."

John's mouth opened, but Elizabeth lifted a hand. "No shouting. We're glad you told us." She nodded at the next bay. "Show me where you slid the other one."

William led them two rows down. There, half-hidden by a coil of rope, sat a cask with the correct weight under John's mallet and the proper tilt to its chalk stroke. Nathaniel read the head: "H.H., stroke four." Elizabeth's ledger line smiled back at her.

"So we'd have looked light in bay four and heavy in bay three," Phoebe said, satisfied. "Wainscott would have loved that."

"He'd have called it deception and seized two to make a lesson," Elizabeth said. She drew a square bracket in the margin joining the two entries and wrote in bold, legible, strokes: *Variance A: Lane sweep moved cask H.H./4 from B3→B4; dummy left in B4. Corrected—E.W.* She handed Phoebe the graphite. "Write the same on the slate. Big."

John grunted. "We'll re-rack now."

"Not yet," Nathaniel said, crouching to eye the dummy. He tapped its stave gently. "If a clerk insists on a tap test, this one won't stand it. Better we swap it for a tighter dummy from the north wall, the one with the sound hoops and stale must." He looked to John. "Or you can tell me I'm wrong and I'll fetch what you say."

John studied him a beat, then gave a short nod. "You're not wrong. Get the north dummy, then." To William: "And you, mind your marks. Tilt left. Always left."

"Yes, sir," William said, color high, relief higher.

Nathaniel moved quick and sure, rolled the better dummy in, and they made the exchange with quiet competence. Elizabeth adjusted the ledger: B3 restored; B4 dummy replaced (sound), then drew a neat R beside the repaired line to remind herself of the earlier story. When she looked up, Nathaniel was already offering her the bung cloth to keep her hands clean.

"Thank you," she said, and meant it.

They finished the run. Tally: twenty-one present; twenty-one accounted; one variance corrected; one dummy replaced; one notation added.

At the end, Elizabeth shut the ledger and rested both palms on the cover. "That's what Wainscott will try to do," she said. "Find the moment the story wobbles and stick a finger in the crack."

"Then we close the crack," Nathaniel said.

John slid the chalk behind his ear and looked at Nathaniel, not unkind. "You read our letters wrong and didn't flinch when told. That'll do."

"I've earned worse corrections," Nathaniel said, dry. "Better to be scolded by a cooper's mark than by a magistrate."

Elizabeth let herself note privately that he'd taken the set like good joinery: pressure applied, no splinter. "Phoebe," she said, "copy the Variance A note into the new folio. Big script. If I'm struck by lightning tomorrow, I want you to be able to find it fast."

"Yes, Aunt." Phoebe's grin flashed, bright as a coin. "Tilt left. Always left."

William hugged the broom with new reverence. "I'll sweep after we count next time."

"You'll ask first," Elizabeth corrected. "Then sweep." She lifted the ledger again, weight familiar and, for once, a little lighter. "Back to work."

They dispersed, the air in the barrelhouse easier by a hair. Outside, wind worried the eaves, but inside, the numbers held.

It swept through the orchard in low, deliberate gusts, rattling the shutters and curling stray leaves along the kitchen steps. Elizabeth was peeling back parchment from a new stack of cider seals when the gate latch clicked, and a familiar voice sailed over the hedge like a fox pretending to be a songbird.

"Brought eggs! And a warning...but the eggs are fresher."

Elizabeth sighed and stood. "You'd make a poor town crier, Hester."

Phoebe, seated cross-legged by the hearth with her leg braced out awkwardly, looked up from her lap. She had been threading twine through a patch of calico scraps, an invention of her own for holding together the broken basket handle. "I'd say a middling one," she offered dryly. "Depends on the news."

The old woman herself appeared around the corner of the kitchen stoop like a wandering storm: patched skirts, striped shawl, and her usual gleam of mischief. "That girl's sharp," she said, jerking her chin toward Phoebe. "Takes after her aunt, poor thing."

"God help her," Elizabeth muttered.

"Too late for that," Hester said cheerfully, placing the egg basket on the stone step. "Seven total. Two with speckles, one with a hairline crack. I brought the cracked one on purpose; some truths are better broken than swallowed whole."

Phoebe snorted but kept her eyes down.

William sat on the floor nearby with a basket of withered apples and a wooden spoon, contentedly smacking the fruit and pretending it was science. At the sound of Hester's voice, he looked up and grinned.

"I told him to go run pest patrol," Phoebe said, jerking her chin toward William. "He said he's experimenting on whether apples bounce."

"They don't," William offered solemnly, holding up a dented one as proof.

"Good lad," Hester said. "Learn early, the laws of fruit and fate."

Elizabeth lifted one egg to the light, rotated it, then returned it to the nest of straw. "You didn't walk the ridge for gossip."

"Course not. I brought speculation." Hester leaned against the doorframe like it belonged to her. "Word is cider's fetching double in Bristol. Especially when bottled by a widow with good cheekbones and an American loitering in her barrelhouse."

Elizabeth didn't look up. "Is this matchmaking or tax advice?"

"Same thing these days," Hester said. "And don't bother denying it. I saw him. Blue coat, bold boots, and a grin like a fox in the grain bin."

Phoebe looked up, eyes narrowing. "Is this the same fox who trampled the mint bed last week?"

Hester let out a bark of laughter. "Oh, she's clever. Keep her close."

"I do," Elizabeth said quietly.

There was a pause then, just long enough for the wind to rattle the windowpane again.

"And what are they saying in town?" Elizabeth asked, tone sharper now. "Truly."

Hester's mirth ebbed, replaced by a sharper gleam beneath her silver curls. "Some say Americans are smuggling saplings. Hollowing out barrels. Wrapping cuttings in oilcloth and sealing them with false names. Clever devils. Always wanting what our roots know."

Elizabeth's hand stilled on the egg. "Is that so."

"Wouldn't know anything about that, would you, love?"

"I wouldn't," she said, flatly.

Phoebe shifted by the hearth, the patched twine loop slipping off her fingers. Elizabeth caught the motion in her periphery, the way her niece's jaw tightened, the way children always heard more than they were meant to.

William began quietly humming to himself. He was young enough not to understand, but old enough to feel the room change.

Hester saw it too. But her smile softened, just a touch.

"Well. If you need more eggs, send the girl," she said, nodding toward Phoebe. "Her eyes are honest. And her tongue, I reckon, sharp enough to make the foxes behave."

Phoebe's chin lifted. "I'm learning to swear in Latin."

"Saints preserve us," Hester said, already turning. "You'll be running the whole orchard next."

Elizabeth watched the older woman pass through the gate. She reached into the basket, plucked the cracked egg, and tossed it firmly into the refuse bin. Then she looked back at Phoebe, who had returned to her patchwork twine like nothing at all had changed.

But Elizabeth knew better. Phoebe was listening, learning, carrying every tension the way young trees carried frost damage: silent, but permanent.

That evening, a thick, locally made beeswax candle sputtered once before settling. Elizabeth dipped the nib anyway.

She sat at her small writing desk in the corner of her bedroom, sleeves rolled to the elbow, fingertips stained faintly with cork dust. The sky beyond the casement was gunmetal grey, and the orchard below had gone still...too still, like it knew what she was about to do.

She hesitated over the greeting, then scratched:

To the office of Mr. W. Harding, Solicitor, Chancery Lane, London

It felt strange, writing it out. Stranger still doing it without telling John, or even Phoebe. But if the Crown's steward arrived before harvest, and the audit came down hard, she couldn't be left defending the orchard on hearsay and vinegar-stung hope. She needed precedent. Paper. A foothold in a world that had always tried to price her out of her own soil.

She began to write.

Regarding estate inheritance, cider rights, and landholder protections for widow proprietors under current excise laws...

Each word scraped. She hated this kind of writing—cold, bone-dry. But it was what men recognized. What courts understood. What Ruth, were she alive, would've called "prudent," even as she rolled her eyes.

A faint knock sounded on the doorframe.

Phoebe stood there, wrapped in a knitted shawl and clutching a candle stub of her own. Her twisted foot made her lean slightly to one side, but she held her weight steady. "You're still up," she said.

"So are you."

"I had a dream about the storm," Phoebe admitted. "The one two winters ago. When the apple shed roof tore off."

Elizabeth softened, but only just. "It held, didn't it?"

"You stitched it with harness straps," Phoebe said, stepping closer. "You said it was 'good enough for snow and judgment.'"

Elizabeth huffed faintly. "I was tired."

Phoebe hovered a moment, then asked, "What are you writing?"

"Something I hope I never have to send."

Phoebe's gaze flicked to the sealed page, the knife beside it. She didn't ask more. Just said, "If something happened... what would happen to me?"

Elizabeth stilled.

Phoebe had never asked. Not like this. Not directly. And now that she had, it was like the orchard itself had leaned in to listen.

"You would stay," Elizabeth said at last. "Here. On this land. With the trees and the house and the still room." She met the girl's eyes. "And if anyone tried to take that from you, I'd raise hell."

Phoebe nodded slowly. Then: "Even if the law said otherwise?"

"I've outlived a husband, a tax shift, and the frost of '59," Elizabeth said. "The law doesn't scare me half as much as losing what's mine."

Phoebe tilted her head. "Even if what's yours wasn't always supposed to be?"

Elizabeth looked down. "Everything worth keeping requires a choice. And I chose you, Phoebe. I'll choose you again."

They stood in silence. Then Phoebe said softly, "I heard Hester, earlier."

Elizabeth looked up.

"She said I'd be running the orchard next."

A pause. "Would you want to?"

Phoebe lifted one shoulder. "Maybe. If the orchard wants me."

Elizabeth crossed the room and brushed a thumb gently against her niece's cheek. "It does. And so do I."

Phoebe blinked hard, then turned without another word and slipped back down the hall.

Elizabeth stood a moment longer, watching the place where she'd gone. Then, very quietly, she folded the letter and slid it beneath the old grafting knife in the drawer. Lantern in hand, she stepped out into the orchard.

The flame guttered once, then steadied. The rows breathed around her in their hush: no owl, no fox, just the sound of her own footsteps through damp leaves.

She followed the ridge path past the Foxwhelps and the twisted Hagloes, her thoughts snagging on root seams and bruised memories.

The Bloody Turk stood just ahead, hunched as ever. She raised the lantern.

There it was. The scar. Too shallow, wrong-angled, not hers. Thomas had touched this tree without telling her. Bent it to his will. And the bark had healed over it anyway...misshapen but surviving.

She crouched, pressed her hand to the seam. "You didn't trust me," she said aloud, softly. "Only what I could grow." She straightened, but the hurt didn't lift. She looked to the ridge above the eastern rows, where sometimes Nathaniel walked with his hands in his pockets and too much weight behind his gaze. He wasn't there tonight.

But maybe one day he would be. She hated so much she yearned for the thought. She barely knew the younger man, but she'd enjoyed his company far more than she'd expected,

Elizabeth turned back toward the house, the lantern swinging low. Her boots left no clear trail, but Phoebe's small candle still glowed faintly from the upstairs window.

The orchard would survive.

But what it became next, that would be Elizabeth's choice. And Phoebe's.

CHAPTER NINE

A QUESTION
OF ROOTS

T he sun was low enough to bake the barrel hoops but not enough
to dry the mud beneath them.

Nathaniel Carter crouched beside the cracked barrel like it had
insulted him personally, one palm braced against the swollen wood,
the other wiping pitch from his breeches. The ground sucked slightly
beneath his boots, thirsty and resentful.

"Hoop's gone slack again," John Thatcher muttered beside him,
arms crossed, a chunk of pitch in one hand. "Either the wood's warped
or someone forgot cider expands in heat."

Nathaniel didn't rise to the bait. "I've met coopers who'd blame the
moon before blaming their craftsmanship."

John grunted. "Moon's more consistent than most men."

They were alone behind the cider barn, out of earshot but not out
of scent, and Nathaniel closed his eyes briefly to savor the aroma of hot
oak, bruised apple skin, and faint acid tang of ferment. A half-dozen
barrels lined the shaded wall, some already sealed and chalked with

Elizabeth's unmistakable script. The one before them—mid-sized, iron-banded, leaking slow at the seam—was salvageable, if barely.

Nathaniel held the hoop in place as John tapped a new stave into the belly with a mallet carved from ash.

"You do this often?" John asked, eyeing his grip with suspicion.

"More than I wished I had to," Nathaniel said. "Pear cider's worse for warping. And Virginia summers'll swell a cask like a pregnant goat."

That earned the smallest twitch at the corner of John's mouth. Not quite a smile. A reluctant, male acceptance of humor involving livestock.

"Still," Nathaniel added, squinting against the sun, "I'd rather patch a dozen barrels than read one Exchequer notice."

"Then you're mad or new." John passed him the steaming pitch ladle with the caution of a man handing over a pistol. "Mind your hand. Pitch's gone dear since that naval fire off Portsmouth. No room for waste."

Nathaniel dipped the brush, let the tar run, and sealed the seam with the precision of someone who'd done worse jobs for less thanks.

"You keep at this," John said after a pause, "you'll ruin your merchant hands."

Nathaniel glanced up. "They've survived storms, blisters, and a Boston tax clerk named Orville with halitosis and a grudge. I'll risk a blister."

That drew a grunt of amusement. Nathaniel pressed the moment.

"Tell me, John…how long do I need to sweat in your yard before you stop thinking I've come to sweet-talk your mistress out of her orchard?"

John didn't answer right away, and he watched the pitch settle into its seam like a wound sealing over. "That depends," he said finally. "Are you trying to sweet-talk her?"

Nathaniel took his time aligning the hoop. "Not at the moment."

"She'll know if you are."

"I'm beginning to suspect she'll know even if I'm not."

They worked in silence for a beat, the only sound the soft hiss of tar against damp wood and the distant call of a child's voice, high and breathless.

"Is that William?" Nathaniel asked, glancing toward the orchard's edge.

John nodded. "Trying to outsmart the hen again. Nearly cracked an egg in his pocket earlier. I told him to stay where it's shaded."

Nathaniel smiled faintly. "He reminds me of my cousin at that age. All elbows and questions."

"Boy's got heart," John said. "But he'll lose a thumb if he keeps reaching for tools too big for him."

"He tried to help with the barrel earlier."

"And wore out halfway through. Elizabeth sent him off with a damp cloth and a warning. He listens better to Phoebe anyhow."

Nathaniel nodded, then frowned slightly. "He shouldn't be doing the heavy lifting."

"He isn't. Not alone." John looked at him more squarely. "She sees to that. You might've worked with men who use boys wrong. We don't."

Nathaniel met his gaze. "I know."

He didn't mention his would-be partner Miles. Some men offered speed and shortcuts, and some let boys do a man's work for the sake of profit. And some, like Elizabeth, ran their world differently.

They finished the sealing quietly, the seam trued and hardened beneath the pitch. When Nathaniel rose, his back ached, but the sense of earned satisfaction grounded him.

"Next barrel?" he asked. "Or do I get promoted to apple peeler?"

"You're too full of words for peeling," John muttered. But his voice had softened.

Elizabeth didn't slow when Nathaniel approached, but she looked up. "Good afternoon."

"And to you. That barrel held," he said conversationally, falling into step beside her.

She glanced sideways. "Held now, or held long enough to claim credit?"

"I only claim what I patch with my own hands," he said. "Which makes me, in this case, moderately useful."

"Hm." A noncommittal noise. She brushed a hanging branch aside. "Useful men tend to want thanks. Or favors."

"I'm already in possession of your favor," he said. "You sent me a barrel."

"That was business," she replied. "A gamble."

She stopped at the edge of the Bloody Turk row, where the oldest grafts knuckled low against the soil. The trees here were scarred and sloped.

"My husband grafted this stretch," she said, voice lower now. "He rushed it. Didn't ask. Didn't wait." She knelt by one trunk and peeled back a layer of bark near the base. "Didn't seal this one properly. It healed wrong."

Nathaniel crouched beside her, squinting at the seam. "Still bore fruit?"

"Some. Not what it might've."

Their shoulders nearly touched. The tree above them creaked softly.

"I know what you're about to say," she said.

"Do you?"

"That I should cut it and start again."

"I wasn't going to say that," he murmured.

"No?"

"I was going to say it's not too late. If the sap's still moving, the
graft's still trying."

She blinked, startled by the gentleness in it. "You sound like a
romantic."

"I'm a cider man," he said. "We drink rot and call it gold."

That pulled a quick, startled laugh from her.

Nathaniel leaned back, grinning. "There it is again. That sound.
I've missed it."

"Oh, you uncouth man." She stood and dusted off her skirts. "I
don't have time to laugh."

"I've seen you with Phoebe," he said, more softly now. "She makes
you laugh. Or maybe you make her braver, and the laughter follows."

Elizabeth stilled.

"She's clever," he added. "And sharp. Like someone else I'm getting
to know."

Elizabeth didn't meet his gaze. Instead, she looked up at the trees,
letting her breath settle. "She walks the rows in spring, even when her
foot's bad. Says it helps her learn the orchard's pulse."

"She's learning from the best."

The praise settled like warmth between them. Elizabeth looked at
him again, her expression unreadable. "You walk through my orchard
like it's scripture."

He tilted his head. "Isn't it?"

Elizabeth led him to a small clearing where the trees opened just enough to let in the angled light. At its center stood one solitary tree, low and wide-limbed, hunched like a woman braced against wind. Her branches were thick with scars, her bark riddled with seams, but the leaves glowed gold in the afternoon hush, and the fruit she bore clustered bold and blood-red.

Nathaniel slowed. "She looks like she's survived three wars and a famine."

"She has," Elizabeth said. "That's Old Widow."

He moved closer, letting his fingers hover just above the bark. "Your father tried to cut her?"

"Twice. I begged him not to. Said I'd manage the graft myself. I was fifteen, and too stubborn to know better." She pointed toward the lowest limb, where a thick old seam swelled around the branch like a scar wrapped in prayer.

"You did that?" he asked softly.

"It was messy," she said. "Ugly. But it took. Eventually." Her hand brushed a curl of moss from the seam. "She didn't bloom again for years. Then one spring—right after my mother died—she burst into fruit like a miracle."

Nathaniel looked at her, not the tree. "Sometimes grief waters things. Even when we don't want it to."

She didn't answer right away. She just kept her hand pressed to the bark. "It's not a pretty tree. And she never bears much. But the cider she gives..." her voice dipped reverently, "It's sharp at first. Then soft. Like she's warning you not to get too comfortable."

Nathaniel chuckled once. "She sounds familiar."

Elizabeth raised an eyebrow.

"I meant Phoebe," he said, grinning. "But now that I've said it aloud, I realize it might be both of you."

She almost smiled, the looked away toward the tree line. "Phoebe calls this her favorite. She says the bark's shaped like a crown if you squint sideways."

Nathaniel knelt and looked, tilting his head. "I see it."

"She doesn't kneel," Elizabeth added, softly. "Not if she can help it. Not even to pick windfall. Says she'd rather stoop crooked than look like she's bowing."

"I can understand that," Nathaniel murmured.

A sudden thump and clatter echoed from farther down the hill, followed by a high, sheepish voice calling out, "I didn't mean to!"

Elizabeth sighed. "That'll be William. Phoebe's likely got him moving ladders he's not tall enough to lift."

"She seems to manage him."

"She manages most things," Elizabeth said, without affection but with fierce respect. "Even when the grown men don't."

Nathaniel smiled faintly, watching her face soften just slightly as she said it.

They stood together a while, not speaking. The orchard moved faintly around them...wind in the higher branches, the rustle of a pigeon, the hush that came before a storm or something else changing.

Elizabeth turned toward him then, close enough he could smell the cider tang of her sleeve, the faint trace of mint on her breath. "If you're waiting for permission," she said, voice low, "I don't give it easily."

Nathaniel didn't move. "I don't take it lightly."

Their eyes held.

His hand lifted slightly, just enough to brush the edge of her fingers where they rested on the trunk. "I'd ask to kiss you," he whispered hoarsely, desire in his voice, "but...."

Elizabeth didn't pull away, but she did speak. "Not here," she said, voice steady. "Not under her branches." A pause. And then, so quietly he nearly missed it… "She'd see."

Nathaniel smiled, but it was the quiet kind, almost solemn. "Then let her stand guard." And he stepped back.

The orchard let the moment pass between them like a breath. When William's voice rang out again—a startled yelp, the scrape of a boot, a loud whisper of "Sorry, Phoebe!"—Elizabeth didn't flinch. She turned, finally, and walked toward the sound, her steps sure again.

And this time, Nathaniel didn't follow. He rested his hand where hers had been. The bark was warm.

They reached the crest of the north slope just as the light began to thin. The orchard stretched below them, rows etched in russet and deepening green, smoke curling from the kitchen chimney, a few scattered voices rising from the barrelhouse yard.

Elizabeth stood still. Nathaniel did too, only just behind her.

"This was my mother's favorite view," she said at last. "She said it made the orchard look obedient."

Nathaniel smiled softly. "It's the only time it looks small."

"She liked things small," Elizabeth said. "Contained. Predictable."

"And you?"

She hesitated. "I like what endures."

A gust of wind stirred the grass at their feet. From somewhere beyond the trees came the sound of a child's laugh, quick and bright, carried far by the breeze.

Nathaniel turned slightly. "Phoebe?"

Elizabeth nodded. "She plays a game where she names the trees after people in her books. She's been trying to decide if the Redstreaks are more like slippery villains or misunderstood aunts."

He chuckled. "She's a good reader."

"She's better than I was. And she won't kneel, even when the other girls tease her for walking slow."

"She shouldn't," he said, quiet but certain.

Elizabeth glanced at him.

"I meant it," he said. "You're raising something in her that might outlast all of this."

Silence again, but not empty. Nathaniel's gaze drifted to Elizabeth's hands, still dirt-stained from pruning, one faintly nicked at the knuckle. "You never stop."

"There's too much at stake." Elizabeth took a deep breath. "I don't know why I'm telling you this, but a half-dozen of my workers have just been hired away from me. All of them said it was because they were offered more money. I did some asking around, and they've all gone to those who have offered to buy from me." Her breathing was coming to her more rapidly. "There are so many things to juggle, and if I stop, it'll all come crashing down."

"You carry this alone." His voice held no pity, for which she was grateful.

"I have no choice," she sighed. "I won't sell my Richard until it's turn from my fingers, and I won't marry and be livestock to a smirking lord old enough to be my father. Not that there would be any suitors at all, if not for my orchard." She stopped, out of breath.

When the air was still again, Nathaniel said, very quietly: "Let me help more, Miss Whitcombe."

Elizabeth turned to him fully now, her face unreadable in the last light. "Why? What's in it for you?"

"For a graft that might take," he said. "For a chance to make something that holds."

She looked out over the orchard. "If I give you that chance," she murmured, "and you lie to me..."

"I won't."

She looked back at him. "I've patched every wound this place could bleed. I've named every tree, buried the blighted roots, raised a girl who limps through rain and still finds ways to run. You don't get to ruin that."

He held her gaze. "I don't want to ruin it."

"Then don't make promises you can't keep."

"I'm not." A pause. "But I'll make one now."

She waited.

Nathaniel stepped beside her, close but not touching. "Whatever takes root here, I'll guard it. Even if it isn't mine."

Elizabeth didn't know what to say.

The sound reached them first, an ugly choke from the barn followed by Phoebe's clarion: "Press is slipping!"

Elizabeth was already moving. "If that cheese breaks we lose the lot," she said, skirts gathered, boots biting the slope. "Warm night like this, and the mash will sour before dawn."

Nathaniel kept pace. "You've got room to rack it off if we get the run going?"

"Barely," she shot back. "And Wainscott's due to nose the counts tomorrow at first light. If the racks read light, he'll say theft and call it a lesson."

The barn swallowed them into cider dusk: cool air, iron, wet wood. The big screw press hunched like an altar; the cheeses—m, cloth-wrapped layers of pomace, were stacked crooked under the platen. A wedge had slipped; juice bled down a seam and puddled underfoot.

John Thatcher braced the capstan bar with his shoulder and grunted without greeting. "Wedge came loose; the plank's bowing. William, fetch the spare slat—no, not that one, the true one—"

"I've got the slat," Nathaniel said, sliding in at the base. He shoved the bowed plank out, elbow to wood, and shouldered the true in its place. "Hold the weight."

"I'm holding," John growled. "Lizzie—"

"On it." Elizabeth was already at the brake, hand on the iron pawl, eyes narrowed. "Phoebe, fold the cloth tighter on cheese three. No fingers near the edge. William, you stand by with the pails; if the overflow starts, you run it to the settling tubs."

The press groaned like an animal settling into its harness.

"Capstan," Elizabeth said.

Nathaniel and John took opposite ends of the long bar; Elizabeth stepped between them to set the pawl. "On my call. Quarter turn. Breathe with it, not against it."

They pushed.

The screw creaked; the platen descended a hair. Juice bright as coin began to thread down the grooves, clear at first, then clouding as the pressure found pulp.

Elizabeth watched the stack like a hawk. "Again. Easy. Keep it even."

They heaved another quarter turn, bodies close in the cramped bay, heat waking in shoulders and palms. Nathaniel matched John's rhythm, eyes on Elizabeth's face for the moment she would lift two fingers—hold—or flatten her palm—give.

Phoebe, steady as any journeyman, slid a hand-spike beneath the sagging edge of cheese three and levered it true. "Now?" she asked.

"Now," Elizabeth said. "Lock."

The pawl clicked. The stack held.

Nathaniel swallowed back a laugh. This was work you felt in the teeth. He shifted grip; the capstan bar brought his shoulder almost into Elizabeth's. He could smell vinegar and mint and the faint smoke that lived in the timber.

John jerked his chin. "Again."

They leaned. Quarter turn. Another. Juice ran stronger, the rills joining into a small river threading toward the chute.

"Keep it breathing," Elizabeth murmured. "Don't crush it to bitterness."

Nathaniel glanced down; her palm, nicked at the knuckle, guided the brake like a musician's hand. He followed the tempo. He'd hauled sails with worse partners.

The platen sank another thumb-width. The cloths held. Phoebe's mouth was tight with concentration; William's eyes were huge above his pails.

"Overflow," William yelped.

"Angle the trough," Nathaniel said, already sliding a shim under the lip. "There—"

"Good," Elizabeth said, quick and cool. "Phoebe, take a wrap off cheese one and pull it snug. That's it. Carter, with me."

She grabbed the second capstan bar. He took the third. They moved together, two points on a clock face, bodies crossing and recrossing in the cramped half-circle. Forearms brushed; her sleeve left a comet of juice on his cuff.

"Your bar," she said, breath quick now, "is uphill. Give me the weight on two now."

He gave it. The screw bit; the whole stack settled with a satisfying sigh. Juice coursed bright into the waiting vat.

"Hold," she said, palm lifted. The brake caught. The barn exhaled with them.

John listened at the stack the way a cooper listens at a cask. "She's singing," he pronounced. "Slow turns to finish."

Elizabeth nodded. "Quarter. Then eighths. We'll not wring tannin for pride."

They worked the arc in smaller bites, the press's complaint lowering into a contented hum. The orchard sounded here more than it looked: chuff of breath, clip of pawl, the soft patter of cider threading to vat and bucket, William's careful shuffle to the settling tubs.

Nathaniel's palm burned. The capstan chewed through old callus and made a new one. He didn't loosen his grip.

Elizabeth saw it. "Last lift," she said, voice gentler than orders. "Then rack."

"Last lift," he echoed.

Together, they eased the final eighth. Juice streamed briefly then slowed to a thin, steady line. Elizabeth tapped the pawl home. "Done."

A small cheer burst, unbidden, from William; even John allowed himself a grunt that almost counted as approval.

Elizabeth stepped to the flow and dipped two fingers in the stream, tasting like a priest at communion. "Foxwhelp in front," she said, pleased. "Redstreak behind. Clean. No crush." She tipped her hand toward Nathaniel. "Here."

He touched his fingertip to hers, then to his tongue. Tart, bold, promising. His eyes met hers over the taste. "Old bloodlines," he said softly. "First of the line."

A flush rose in Elizabeth's cheeks. She turned to business. "Rack it off before the vat turns sulky," she said briskly, but the corner of her mouth tugged up. "Phoebe, mark the first run. William, mind your slop; if you baptize your breeches I'm not mending them."

They moved into the racking: ladles, funnels, a length of clean hose. Nathaniel steadied the vat; Elizabeth set the head of the hose and drew the first siphon, quick and practiced. The amber line slid into the waiting barrel with a sound like rain in a cistern.

"Bung cloth," she said.

Nathaniel passed it. His hands were shaking now, not from strain, but from the skin split opening at the heel of his palm. She noticed the bead of red through cider stain.

"You'll salt that if you touch the wormwood jar," she said. "Give me your hand."

He offered it without a quip. She took it, workmanlike at first, then softer as the sting registered in his jaw. She fetched a strip of clean linen from a peg, dipped it in apple vinegar, squeezed it once, and wrapped his palm with a surgeon's efficiency. Vinegar bit; he didn't flinch.

"You tie like someone who's mended a season's worth of fools," he said, attempting lightness.

"I tie like someone who expects people to return the next day and finish what they start," she replied, a half-smile finally visible. She smoothed the knot with a thumb, and her hand rested a breath longer than necessary on his wrist. A charge crossed, the kind that lived in good work done shoulder-to-shoulder.

John pretended not to see any of it. "Bung's at two-thirds," he announced. "She'll take another ladle."

Elizabeth and Nathaniel moved again, bodies finding the same lane around each other without collision. When the barrel finally thudded full, Elizabeth set the bung, sealed the wax, and chalked the head in her tight hand: W, First Run, Clean.

They stood in the hush that follows crisis. Outside, evening swelled; inside, the barn seemed wider.

Phoebe wiped her hands on her apron and surveyed the stack with an unabashed pride that would shame a magistrate. "We saved it," she declared.

"We did," Elizabeth said. She looked at Nathaniel. "Together."

He nodded once, the word fitting somewhere deep he didn't show. "Together."

She reached for the last strip of linen, glanced at the nick on her own knuckle, and hesitated. He saw it, caught her wrist lightly, and turned her hand palm-up. "My turn," he said.

His touch was careful, not claiming. He wrapped the small cut with the same crisp knot she'd used on him, then pressed the loose end flat with a thumb. Their hands paused, his over hers, hers steady under his, each feeling the pulse in the other's fingers before letting go.

John clapped dust from his hands like a man ending prayer. "That's enough romance for a barrelhouse," he said dryly. "Phoebe, mark the book. William, sweep after the drip stops. Carter, if you're staying to be useful, put those shoulders on the capstan again; we've another stack to breathe down."

"Aye," Nathaniel said, grinning despite himself.

Elizabeth lifted the slate and added one neat line beneath the day's tally: Press run saved: Wainscott cannot claim light. She set the chalk down and caught Nathaniel's eye.

"Go wash," she said, softer than before. "You smell like victory and salad."

He laughed, the sound low, new. "I'll add it to the ledger. Value: enough."

She didn't stop him when he reached for the capstan again. She stepped in at the brake. And when the bar swung past his bandaged hand, the back of his wrist brushed hers in that small, ordinary way that holds more meaning than a speech.

They turned the screw. The barn breathed. The night came on, and the cider ran.

CHAPTER TEN

CIDER AND SMOKE

T he first breath of morning bit clean against Elizabeth's cheeks as she stepped into the orchard yard, boots crunching through crisp hay and yesterday's leaves. Steam curled from the barn roof, and she inhaled the cider-sweet scent of crushed fruit already beginning to ferment in the early press buckets.

The press itself stood squat and proud near the barrelhouse, a stack of grooved oak and iron bolts: old, but well-cared-for. John Thatcher and two younger lads were adjusting the frame when she arrived, but it wasn't John's bark she heard next.

"That pulley's leaning harder than a Bristol banker. Left shim's out of line."

She didn't need to look. "And what exactly would you know about cider presses, Mr. Carter?"

Nathaniel straightened from where he'd been crouched, sleeves already damp with mash and his coat discarded neatly over a fence post.

"Only that the right wedge prevents heartbreak." He offered a crooked smile. "And bruised toes."

Before Elizabeth could reply, a small voice added: "I said it first."

She turned.

Phoebe stood just outside the barn door, broom handle tucked under one arm and hair braided too loosely for propriety. Her right boot was scuffed from the uneven yard, and the laces tugged askew around her twisted foot, but her eyes were sharp, watching the frame with narrowed focus.

Nathaniel offered a slight bow. "She did. By a full minute, I'd wager."

Elizabeth crossed the yard to inspect the press, fingers trailing along the beam. "That pulley's been fussy since midsummer."

"I heard it shift," Phoebe said quietly, tapping the broom against her boot. "It scraped wrong."

John gave a grunt of grudging approval. "Good ear."

At that moment, a boy came skidding around the corner of the shed, barely eleven, red-cheeked and breathless, hauling a splintered rake far too tall for him.

"She hears everything," William piped, puffing from exertion. "Like a fox in church."

Phoebe flushed but didn't look away.

Elizabeth looked at her. She was standing straighter now, despite the crooked set of her foot, and her knuckles were red from the chill. The sight pierced her sharper than she'd expected. She forced a nod toward the kitchen stoop. "Fetch the drying cloths, please. They'll be needed soon."

Phoebe darted off, limping but swift. William trailed behind her, dragging the rake with exaggerated importance.

Elizabeth turned back to the press. She sniffed the air near the vat and caught the first sharpness of the season's pulp. Redstreaks, mostly. Small, early, high in acid.

"We're not pressing to drink," she said. "Just to test the ferment and color. A poor start predicts a poor season."

"I've heard that," Nathaniel said. "Old wives' tale in Virginia says the first batch of cider can sour a courtship if you taste it before noon."

She gave him a dry look. "Is that your excuse?"

"Always."

A bark of laughter from John made her start. He rarely found Nathaniel amusing. But perhaps, just today, the promise of cider had softened more than apples.

They loaded the mash together, shoulder to shoulder at the press. Elizabeth worked swiftly, arms practiced and sure. Nathaniel kept pace, sleeves rolled and eyes on her hands. The rhythm settled: mash, press, crank, strain. The screw groaned low as the first juice dribbled into the collecting bucket.

"You've a streak on your sleeve," he said, nodding toward her bodice.

She looked down, sticky pulp staining the edge of her chemise. "I know."

"I could..."

"I don't need rescuing from apple juice," she said, reaching for the crank.

"But it's plotting against you," he joked. "Sticky rebellion."

She smiled, despite herself. "It'll have to try harder."

Phoebe returned with the cloths just as the cider gave its first sharp lurch, and juice spilled over the lip of the bucket with a sound like a toast being poured. William trailed behind, carrying a bundle of rags tied with twine and looking immensely pleased with himself.

John peered in. "Color's fair. A touch green at the rim."

Elizabeth bent to inspect. The juice gleamed gold-amber in the light, with a halo of fizz already beginning to rise.

"Let it breathe an hour," she murmured. "Then we'll see if it sings."

Nathaniel stepped back, boots soaked, arms streaked with foam. "If it sings, do I get to say I helped?"

Phoebe, standing just behind him again, replied, "Only if you didn't spill any."

He turned, mock-affronted. "Unforgiving. Like her aunt."

Elizabeth's brow arched. "Then you're learning."

He grinned. "Close enough."

She turned away before he could say more, not trusting the warmth rising in her chest, nor the way he'd begun to look less like an intruder, and more like a man who knew how to hold his place in a storm.

The hour didn't pass politely.

A cough rattled up from the press, a stiff, wooden protest, followed by a sour little hiccup in the drain. The flow narrowed to a sulky trickle.

John muttered, "Told you the spindle thread would balk," and bent to the screw's iron collar. "There's play in the nut. If the thread chews itself, we'll spend a week nursing splinters and pride."

Elizabeth slid in under the beam, palms flat to the frame. "Not on my watch." She glanced at Nathaniel. "You know a hungry thread when you hear one?"

"Sounds like a fisherman lying about the size of his catch," he said, crouching at her side. "Gnaws at the story."

"Mm." She tipped her head at the capstan. "We ease back a quarter, wedge the bed true, and coax, not bully, the screw into a clean lane."

"Quarter back," John echoed, moving to the pawl.

Phoebe appeared with William in tow, both carrying wedges like ceremonial offerings. "We brought the good ones," she announced, chin up.

Elizabeth took the shorter wedge, tested its grain with a thumbnail, then pressed it into Nathaniel's palm. "You're on the low side. Heel the frame with this when I say. If you jam it early, we crack a plank and all this goes to vinegar and stories."

"Copy your lead," he said.

She tossed him a look that might have been approval. "On my call. Breathe with me. Ready...now."

John slipped the pawl; Nathaniel and Elizabeth eased the capstan a hair counterclockwise. The press sighed; the cheeses settled, cloths creaking softly.

"Hold," she said. "Wedge."

Nathaniel slid the wedge under the bed, feeling for the honest bite. "It's not catching."

"It will." Elizabeth shifted her shoulder against the frame and nudged with the heel of her hand. "Now."

The wedge seated with a clean, satisfying note. Nathaniel grinned despite himself. "Music."

"Keep listening," she said. "Wind on. Eighth turns only."

They brought the screw forward by breaths, not boasts. The groan smoothed. The sulky trickle fattened again to a steady line.

William exhaled like a bellows. "It's working."

"Because we didn't panic," Phoebe said primly, eyes bright. "And because Aunt Lizzie likes the good wedges."

"Because the good wedge had a steady hand," Elizabeth corrected, letting the pawl catch. She looked at Nathaniel then, a measuring glance. "Men rush a problem and call it bravery. The orchard calls it waste."

"Then let's not waste," he said gently.

She nodded once. "Hand me the lamp."

He passed it in. She raised the light and squinted along the spindle's threads, counting silently. "There's wear near the collar," she murmured. "We'll pack the nut with tallow and linen tomorrow. It'll buy us through the week."

"Or I can turn a new linen wrap tonight," Nathaniel offered. "We used to do it in Virginia when the mill screw chattered."

John's grunt was grudgingly warm. "You at least sound like a man who's ruined a good screw before."

"Twice," Nathaniel admitted. "Third time I learned to listen to women who knew better."

Elizabeth huffed, the closest she got to a laugh with her head under a beam. "Flattery's cheap. Put your shoulder on the capstan."

They wound again. The rhythm returned, push, breathe, lock; push, breathe, lock, tight as a hymn.

The drain cleared its throat and drank properly. Juice ran bright, lively as gossip.

"Color's back," John said, peering. "She's come round."

Phoebe leaned in to watch the stream, solemn as a midwife. "It sings."

"Because it was heard," Elizabeth said, stepping out from under the frame and shoving damp hair off her brow with the back of her wrist.

Nathaniel straightened with her. Close in the cramped bay, they nearly bumped shoulders; he checked himself an inch shy and she didn't move away. He saw pulp on her sleeve, a nick along her knuckle, a fleck of iron dust caught at her temple.

"You've got a smear," he said, reaching without thinking, then stopping with his hand suspended. "May I?"

Elizabeth stilled, amused. "From apple or iron?"

"Iron," he said.

"Then yes," she allowed. "Apple stains are trophies; iron tells tales out of turn."

He brushed the gray fleck away with the pad of a finger. His touch was careful; her pulse jumped once under the skin at her temple and settled.

Phoebe, who missed nothing, handed up a rag like a priest distributing a sacrament. "For competence," she declared.

Elizabeth took it, eyes still on Nathaniel, and wiped the iron from her skin. "For steadiness," she said pointedly. "That's what I value in a partner, any partner. Someone who can hear a wrong note and set it right without making a parade of his own helpfulness. Someone who keeps his footing when the floor goes slick and doesn't tear the thread trying to prove he's stronger than wood."

Nathaniel's smile was small and real. "Understood."

"Good," she said, the word landing like a seal on a barrel head. "John, bring the tallow when that bucket's clear. Phoebe, mark a red dot on the spindle collar. William, you'll fetch the linen strips from the stillroom, folded, not in a knot, or I'll set you scrubbing."

William was already darting toward the door. "Folded! I heard it!"

"Doubtful," Phoebe muttered, but her grin betrayed her.

Nathaniel shifted to the far side of the press, shoulder to the capstan again. "Quarter on your call," he said.

"Your ear's improving," Elizabeth replied.

"So's my luck," he said, then made a face at the press. "Don't tell the thread I said that."

"Superstitious?" she asked, deadpan.

"Pragmatic. I've learned not to taunt timber."

"Good," she said again, and signaled. They turned the eighth together.

When the pawl clicked into place and the flow held happy, Elizabeth reached for the little brush and dipped it in tallow, dabbing the exposed thread lightly. "This keeps the song sweet," she said.

"Then I'll bring more tallow," Nathaniel answered. "And fewer opinions."

She cut him a look sideways. "Keep the opinions if they come with the right wedge."

"Noted," he said.

Work resumed: that companionable quiet where bodies know what the next motion is before anyone speaks. Phoebe set out the clean cloths in two neat stacks: tight weave, loose weave; William returned with a proper roll of linen for the spindle packing and only stepped in one puddle.

When the mash settled obedient again and the vat drank without complaint, Elizabeth finally stepped back. The knot between her brows loosened.

"Crisis over," John decreed. "For this half hour."

Elizabeth turned to Nathaniel, mouth quirking. "You can stay."

"I didn't realize I'd been reapplying for the job," he said.

"You always are," she said. "Everyone is. The orchard doesn't hire for charm."

"Unfortunate," he murmured. "It's one of my cheaper tools."

"Retire it for the afternoon," she said, already reaching for the next straining cloth. "Bring me your shoulders and your ear."

He shouldered in beside her without another word. As they lifted the damp cloth together, his bandaged palm grazed her wrist; she steadied the cloth, and briefly, deliberately let her thumb press his pulse once, a silent acknowledgment.

"Steady," she said.

"Steady," he echoed.

The press breathed. The song held. And for a scant, generous moment, so did they.

By midday, the pressing yard was thick with apple pulp and clamor. The sun burned off the early chill, and every surface—skin, cloth, wood—gleamed with cider sheen.

Phoebe sat cross-legged near the press, polishing a row of clean bottles with the corner of her apron. Her small hands moved with care, but her eyes never stopped scanning the workyard, her gaze flicking from barrel to boy to beam.

William passed her, arms loaded with pails, one handle dragging in the dirt.

"You'll spill that," she warned.

"I won't," he said, then sloshed half the contents on his breeches. He swore softly.

Phoebe smirked. "Told you."

"I'll clean it!" he hissed, glancing toward Elizabeth's direction.

"She saw already."

He groaned and thumped toward the trough, trailing apple skins and pride.

Nathaniel passed behind them with a straining cloth in hand, holding it high above the collecting vat as juice dripped in a steady stream. "William!" he called. "Tell Thatcher the second mash is ready for turn."

William dropped his bucket with a squelch and tore across the yard in a gangly blur.

Phoebe rose slowly, favoring her right foot. She dusted her skirts and limped after him.

"Do you always walk behind him like a keeper?" Nathaniel asked gently, falling into step beside her.

"I walk where I like," Phoebe replied, glancing up. "He just ends up ahead."

Nathaniel grinned. "Fair answer."

He handed her a clean cloth without ceremony, and she took it as if it had been her idea.

"Why do you stay?" she asked suddenly, wiping the lip of a bottle. "You've seen the orchard. You've gotten your barrel."

Nathaniel slowed. The press creaked behind them; the smell of mash was thick in the air. "I'm still learning," he said.

Phoebe gave him a sideways look. "About apples?"

"About your aunt."

She didn't respond. Just polished with greater precision.

Nathaniel tried again. "My friend Miles might come by soon. You met him yesterday? I heard he came by to pay a visit." It had actually been William who'd mentioned that Miles had done so without telling him, and while Nathaniel had been occupied. It had irked him.

Phoebe made a face. "He smells like vinegar and swears worse than William."

"Accurate," Nathaniel said with a chuckle. "But sometimes useful."

"He cheats at cards."

"You caught him?"

"I caught him letting William win."

That surprised a laugh from him. "Sharp eyes."

"I listen."

Nathaniel looked down at her, small but straight-backed, her foot braced slightly outward for balance, her mouth set like a girl twice her age. "You always listen?"

"When I shouldn't," she said, and then quickly, "but I don't always tell."

Nathaniel sobered a little. "That's a rare skill." Phoebe shrugged, and Nathaniel let the quiet stretch.

Back at the press, Elizabeth called something indistinct, her voice commanding but calm. John responded with a grunt, and the crank turned once more.

"She says if I learn all the tree names," Phoebe said quietly, "she'll teach me grafting."

"She will," Nathaniel said. "She wants someone to carry it forward."

"I already do." Phoebe turned back to her bottles, but her next breath came easier.

By midafternoon, the golden sheen of the first press had deepened, darker now, denser, filled with the promise of longer ferment. Elizabeth stood beside the testing vat with her sleeves rolled to the elbow, watching the bubbles rise. John had gone to fetch a second straining sack, and William was somewhere in pursuit of a chicken with escape artistry beyond its size.

Nathaniel had not made himself scarce. He stayed after the testing, rinsing buckets, stacking barrels, handling the crank with the quiet competency of someone who'd labored before and wasn't afraid to sweat again.

But as the light slanted westward, Elizabeth noticed the shift. The way he stood still too long. The way his gaze kept flicking toward the road. "Expecting someone?" she asked, not looking up from the vat.

He didn't answer right away. Then, "I don't know." That wasn't like him. Not the Carter who'd swaggered through her orchard with charm tucked behind his teeth.

Elizabeth turned slightly. "What is it?"

Phoebe had been nearby—folding drying cloths and sorting them by weave, the way Elizabeth had taught her—but now she paused too, one hand still on the table, head tilted just enough to suggest she was listening.

Nathaniel reached into the satchel he'd left near the shed. From it, he withdrew a folded letter sealed in cracked red wax.

Elizabeth's breath stilled. She recognized the seal immediately: *Wetherstone.* Her late husband's solicitor.

Nathaniel offered the letter carefully. "Arrived with the merchant's post. The innkeeper thought it odd...a solicitor sending duplicate notices by hand. But I've a feeling yours isn't the only orchard with ghosts in its books."

Elizabeth took it without thanks. She slit it open with the edge of her nail.

Phoebe didn't move, but Elizabeth felt her eyes like a weight balanced on her shoulder.

The letter was brief.

Mistress Whitcombe,

In reviewing the 1762 filings for the Trewyn-Orchard trust, it has come to our attention that one cask—numbered 14-KB—was exported without a final customs seal affixed to its ledger copy. The cask is referenced in the midseason yield reports but does not appear in the excise collector's stamped receipts.

While this may have been a clerical oversight, please be advised: the omission constitutes a potential violation under Section VI of the Revised Excise Code.

A formal inquiry may accompany the Crown audit should this matter remain unresolved.

— H. Wetherstone, Solicitor on Retainer to the Late Mr. Whitcombe

The lines blurred slightly.

Elizabeth blinked and realized her hand had clenched, crumpling the page.

Nathaniel reached out and gently steadied the edge to keep it from tearing. His fingers brushed hers, warm and solid.

She looked at him. "14-KB was pressed last August. He handled the export himself."

"I thought he was already unwell?" Nathaniel asked.

"He was." Her throat tightened. "But not so far gone he couldn't forge a ledger line."

Phoebe made no sound, but she had stopped folding. Elizabeth could see the stillness in her posture. Sharp as flint, that girl.

"And now it's yours to answer for," he said grimly.

Elizabeth stepped away, folding the letter tight again with practiced, almost savage precision. The breeze shifted, carrying chimney smoke and the faint sweetness of overripe apples gone too soft in the sun.

"I could help," Nathaniel offered. "With the solicitor. With the audit. Whatever you need."

She didn't turn. "Why?"

"You know why."

"I want to hear it," she said.

He exhaled slowly, voice lower now. "Because I've stood in that place. Where someone else's foolishness lands in your lap, wrapped in polite ink and threats. Because I know what it is to feel the weight of a name you didn't soil."

Phoebe looked up.

Elizabeth felt her watching like a mirror held from a small hand, angled just enough to show what she didn't want to see. She stared at the press, cider hissing softly in the vat. "I can't afford to lean on anyone else," she said.

"I'm not asking you to lean," Nathaniel said gently. "Only to know I'm nearby."

Elizabeth turned then, not toward him, but toward Phoebe. The girl was folding again, slowly, one cloth after another, hands careful and neat. "I'll be inside shortly," Elizabeth said to her. "Tell Mrs. Merritt to keep the fire low. It'll spoil the pulp otherwise." Phoebe gathered the basket of cloths and walked away.

Later that evening, the press had stilled. The vat cooled. And inside the kitchen, the scent of apples had yielded to something sharper: cider vinegar and burnt starch, a sign that someone had forgotten the pot too long over flame. Elizabeth stirred the mash anyway, slow and steady, anchoring herself in motion. Beside her on the hearth, Phoebe sat cross-legged, pretending to sketch but mostly watching Elizabeth's every movement with hawk-like precision. The child was too quiet. Which meant she'd understood more than she let on.

"You're not writing," Elizabeth said without turning.

Phoebe dipped her quill and began a line—uneven but bold. "Just thinking what to call the barrel."

"Which one?"

"The one that caused all the trouble."

Elizabeth paused. "You name the barrels?"

Phoebe looked up with a faint shrug. "Only the ones that misbehave."

Elizabeth let the smile come, faint but real. "And?"

"I was thinking Sir Falsebottom," Phoebe offered. "Or Lord Wastrel. Something properly titled."

Elizabeth snorted once. "Very proper."

A knock at the frame made both their heads turn.

Nathaniel stood just beyond the threshold, hat in hand. Behind him, William jogged up the path clutching a bundle of linen that was clearly too large for him, nearly tripping over the step. His cheeks were flushed, curls damp with the effort of keeping pace.

"I told him not to run," Nathaniel said as William wheezed into the kitchen. "But he's convinced speed can solve linen collapse."

"I'm practicing," William said through a breath, depositing the bundle beside the door. "For when we send cider to London."

Elizabeth raised an eyebrow. "Planning to carry it yourself?"

"I might," he said defiantly, before catching Phoebe's eye and grinning. "Unless you name it Lady Sourpint."

Phoebe didn't look up, but her smile was unmistakable.

"Go wash," Elizabeth said gently. "Both of you."

The children scattered, William to the pump, Phoebe out to the bucket behind the stillroom.

When they were gone, Nathaniel stepped inside, quieter now. He reached into his coat and withdrew a sheet of paper, creased but unsealed. "This came with the merchant's packet," he said. "It's from Rutledge."

Elizabeth's breath cooled. "What does he want?"

Nathaniel held it out. "To 'offer guidance,' which I suspect means influence. Or ownership. Or worse."

She didn't take the paper. "You read it."

"I did."

"And?"

"He's watched you from a distance," Nathaniel said carefully. "Enough to know your cider is better than what's sold in Bristol, and your orchard's better managed than most men's."

"He'd never say that aloud."

"He doesn't have to," Nathaniel said. "He uses the word potential eight times."

Elizabeth finally took the letter. Her jaw tensed as she read the first few lines.

"He thinks I'm vulnerable."

"He thinks you're exceptional. Which is worse, if he wants something."

She folded the paper tight. "If I tell him to go to hell?"

Nathaniel shrugged once. "He'll smile, wait, and write again."

The fire popped.

Elizabeth stared into it. "I won't sell. Not now. Not while she's still mine to tend."

"She's not just yours," Nathaniel said quietly. "You've made her theirs too."

Elizabeth glanced toward the pump, where Phoebe and William were arguing about who got the dry towel.

"They don't know that yet," she said.

"They will," he replied. "They already act like it."

Elizabeth sighed, and for just a moment, closed her eyes, and let herself feel the full weight of the year.

The blight. The barrel. The dead man's signature haunting her ledgers like a stain.

She opened her eyes. "You'd better check the vats," she told Nathaniel. "If the Foxwhelp's turned, we'll need to pull early."

And without waiting for an answer, she crossed the yard, toward the darkening cider, the hard-won grafts, and the storm she was bracing to meet.

***

The rain hadn't stopped since dawn. By midday the orchard's narrow river was running high and fast, shoving at its banks like it meant to break them. Nathaniel stood on the slick plank that led to the landing stage, shoulder braced against a cider barrel bound for the Red Hart. The rope under his boot was tight as a drawn bowstring.

"Easy there," William called from the far side, his cap dripping, pride in his voice at being trusted with the work.

"I've got it," Nathaniel said, then the barrel lurched, the rope snapped tight, and his feet vanished out from under him.

The river swallowed him in one violent gulp. The cold was a fist in his chest; he couldn't breathe, couldn't see. Current slammed him sideways, spinning him until the sluice gate flashed in his vision: black, jagged teeth. A heartbeat to think: if it catches me there, I'm gone.

"Rope!" William's voice cracked like a boy's, high with fear.

A coil arced through the air. Nathaniel lunged, missed, lunged again. The hemp slapped his palms, burned, but he clung to it like breath itself. The current wrenched hard...

...and Elizabeth was already on the bank, skirts sodden, both hands locked on the rope, digging in without hesitation. Behind her, Phoebe planted her walking stick in the mud and shoved her weight into her aunt's back, bracing them both. No pause, no question, just immediate movement.

Nathaniel's shoulder screamed as the rope went taut, but they held. William was scrambling down the bank now, water up to his knees, grabbing Nathaniel's coat. Together, the three of them hauled him inch by inch out of the current's grip.

His boots hit shallows. Mud. Then he was on his knees, coughing river water into the grass.

Elizabeth still had the rope in both fists, breath sharp, eyes fixed on him like she wasn't going to let go until she was certain. "You're mad," she said, voice low now, but steady.

"Not mad," Nathaniel panted. "Just...careless. I'm so sorry. You saved my life...I can never thank you enough."

She caught his scraped knuckles, turning them to the light. River silt rimmed each cut; she wiped it away with her kerchief, the cloth darkening as if it swallowed his foolishness whole. He meant to apologize again. Instead, when her thumb circled his pulse, the word stuck to his tongue. They stood too near; she was first to step back.

Phoebe pressed a handkerchief into his hand, useless against the water streaming off him. William grinned in relief, babbling how close it had been.

Nathaniel shuddered. All he could feel was the pull of that rope in his palms, and the knowledge that when the river tried to take him, they hadn't even thought about the risk...they'd just held on.

CHAPTER ELEVEN

STOWAWAYS

The scent of oak and ferment hung in the air, thick as breath in a sealed room. Morning light sliced through the high barn slats, striping the packed earth floor in gold and shadow. Somewhere above, pigeons shuffled across the roof beam, and William, all elbows and dusty boots, hummed a crooked tune as he rolled a hoop of iron toward a row of sealed casks. He made a show of steering it like a ship's wheel, then dropped it with a clank that made the pigeons flap.

Nathaniel stood with the barn ledger propped on a crate, the chalk-powdered barrel lists arrayed before him. He balanced a black-lead stick in one hand and squinted at the looping figures in Elizabeth's distinctive hand.

Barrel 5A – Redstreak Blend

Barrel 5B – Same

Barrel 6 – Foxwhelp (Unfiltered)

Barrel 7 – Blotched skin, cider service only – do not sell

He scanned down the column. Then back up. Then across to the barrel wall, where mismatched numerals gleamed in chalk-white curves.

Something was off.

Barrel 8 was missing from the ledger entirely. So was 11. Yet he could see them from here, lined up neatly beneath the west wall, wax-stamped and sealed in a way that looked rushed, too neat. He tapped the page lightly and frowned. "William?"

The boy looked up from his crouch near a vat of coopering tools, his cheeks pink from exertion. "Yes, sir?"

"You help mark these?"

"Nah. Just carried 'em over. Miss Whitcombe writes the numbers. John checks twice, like always."

A soft voice piped up from behind a stack of sacks. "Sometimes I check them, too."

Nathaniel turned. Phoebe sat cross-legged on a low stool in the corner, a half-used chalk slate balanced on her knee and her boots not quite reaching the floor. Ink smudged the side of her wrist. She had copied the ledger entries into her own careful script, each numeral exaggerated, slanted in mimicry of Elizabeth's hand. "She lets me copy when I finish my fractions," she added, not looking up. "It's good practice. For when the orchard's mine."

William made a face, half a smirk, but didn't contradict her. He glanced at her chalkwork, then looked away quickly, as if aware she'd surpassed him in this arena.

Nathaniel smiled despite himself. "Well then, she'll need to get you your own barrel chalk."

Phoebe shrugged, eyes still on her slate. "I'd rather have my own orchard."

Across the barn, the wax seals on the unlisted barrels gleamed faintly red in the rising light. Nathaniel turned back to the ledger and made a note in the margin, leaving space...something was off in the numbers, and not just an oversight.

He thought briefly of Miles. The man had warned him about this: how local estates sometimes hid surplus in plain sight. "If it looks too tidy, it usually is," he'd said over a pint at the dockside inn. "Barrels don't align themselves unless someone's hiding the gaps."

The numbers stayed in Nathaniel's head, sharp and stubborn.

Nathaniel kept scanning, ledger, wall, ledger, until the silence turned solid.

He tapped the margin with the blacklead. "All right. I'm going to speak this out so we hear it before Wainscott does." He angled the ledger so both children could see. "If an inspector walks in and finds two sealed barrels that aren't listed here, he won't assume 'honest mistake.' He'll say three things, in plain terms."

William stopped fiddling with the hoop. Phoebe's chalk stilled.

"One," Nathaniel said, holding up a finger, "that we've got unregistered casks: juice pressed and stored without a matching line in the excise book. That's 'light barrels' in their language. They treat that like you've hidden coin under the floorboards."

William swallowed. "Even if it's just because someone forgot to write it?"

"He won't care why," Nathaniel said. "He'll say the Crown was cheated a stamp."

He raised a second finger. "Two: he'll call these dummies...decoys to cover a shortfall. If the count in the tax book says thirty and the barn shows thirty-two, he'll claim someone padded one side or shaved the other. Either way, it reads like falsifying."

Phoebe's eyes narrowed. "But Aunt Lizzie always checks."

"I know," he said softly. "But Wainscott doesn't know her. He knows ledgers. And ledgers with gaps make men like him feel clever."

A third finger. "Three: if he connects a missing barrel number to a shipment, say, one that went out when no seal was stamped...he'll call it diversion. That's a neat word for 'you sent cider off-book.' He will use bigger words: 'contravention of Section this and sub-article that' but what he'll mean is smuggling."

William's mouth fell open. "We didn't smuggle anything."

Phoebe didn't flinch. "What do we do?"

"First," Nathaniel said, voice even, "we label the problem ourselves, not let him label it for us." He set the ledger on a crate and chalked three calm, tidy lines:

• *8 — pressed, awaiting seal (froth test pending)*
• *11 — recount vs. stock (moved during bracing)*

He looked up. "If these truly are part-ready or mis-shelved, we say so before he 'discovers' it. That turns a crime into a process."

Phoebe nodded once, like a clerk hearing minutes. "And if they're not?"

"Then we fix the truth," he said. "John and I will lift the bungs and take a whispering taste. If they're young, they wait. If they're mis-set, we move them under eyes, not behind crates. Either way, the ledger gets the exact note that matches the floor."

He crossed to the two suspect casks, crouched, and ran a knuckle along the wax. "Seal's sound but too clean," he murmured. "Likely new." He pointed to the chalk on Barrel 11. "And that hand isn't Elizabeth's, see the loop?" He glanced back at Phoebe. "Yours?"

She flushed. "I... copied a 1 as a 7 once. Aunt Lizzie made me rewrite the whole page to feel how a number sits. But I didn't mark those."

"Then someone rushed," Nathaniel said. "Rushed work looks dishonest even when it isn't."

He straightened, met both of their gazes. "Listen to me, and carry this to anyone who asks you questions with a friendly smile: Every barrel in this barn has a twin line in this book. If we're not sure, we say, 'Mistress Whitcombe is correcting today's count; you can watch her do it.' We never say 'I don't know' to an excise man. We say 'I'll show you.'"

William nodded vigorously, desperate to be useful.

Phoebe, chin high: "What will Wainscott say next?"

"That we forged a paper to ship one barrel as a 'sample,'" Nathaniel said, not blinking. "He'll say the form is a fig leaf."

"Is it?" William blurted.

"No," Nathaniel answered, very calmly. "It's a petition to be heard by men who wouldn't otherwise let a woman speak in trade. That's different." He softened his voice. "And it's my name on that risk, not your aunt's."

Phoebe studied him a heartbeat too long. "He'll still try to pin it on her."

"He'll try," Nathaniel agreed. "So we make him work for it, with clean counts, clean marks, clean mouths."

Elizabeth's step sounded in the yard. She appeared in the barn doorway, hair caught back, sleeves rolled. Her eyes swept the scene, registering the chalk in Phoebe's hand, the worry on William's face, the way Nathaniel stood between the ledger and the barrels like a hinge.

"What have you found?" she asked.

"Two tidy lies waiting to be told about us," Nathaniel said, steady but not alarmed. He tapped the ledger. "I've written the plain-speech version so we can own the corrections before Wainscott does. Barrels Eight and Eleven: one likely unsealed, one mis-shelved and mis-marked. We'll open, taste, date, and match, then you annotate in your hand while I move them into light."

Elizabeth's gaze held his for a long breath. She read the margin notes, the restraint in his tone, the absence of panic.

"All right," she said. "We show our work." She reached for the bung-pull. "Phoebe: fresh page. Title it 'Inspection Pre-Count' and write today's date big enough a magistrate can see it from the road. William: water and cloths. Mr. Carter, you'll pour."

"And answer," he said quietly.

"And answer," she agreed, sharper. Then, to Phoebe, almost off-hand: "If Wainscott says the word 'smuggling' in this barn, you will not react. You will keep writing. That's how we win."

Phoebe's mouth set. "Yes, Aunt."

"Good," Elizabeth said. "Let's leave the man nothing easy."

They set to it:,methodical, unhurried, the barn echoing with the small, decisive sounds of work that knew exactly what it was correcting.

The sun had begun to tip westward, catching the orchard in gold-edged shadow. Nathaniel waited beneath the hazel tree near the edge of the grove, sleeves rolled, satchel slung over one shoulder. He'd lit the small barrel fire ten minutes before, and now steam drifted lazily from the shallow water within, a trick he hadn't used since he'd been brought out to be consulted on an orchard in Annapolis. The scent of boiled bark and smoke curled through the air, edged faintly with wormwood and wet oak.

He crouched by the barrel, holding the limb Elizabeth had cut yesterday, inspecting its angle, cambium, scars. Miles's voice rose in memory: "You can steam a lie into anything, if you boil it long enough." Nathaniel shook the thought away. This wasn't that kind of heat.

A rustle at the edge of the clearing made him glance up...not Elizabeth, but Phoebe. She stood at the path's bend, her small form framed by the slope, one hand gripping her walking stick, the other holding something wrapped in damp cloth. "She said you'd need this," Phoebe announced, approaching with her careful, deliberate gait. "The limb. She was trimming the old Gold Parmain."

Nathaniel took the offering with care, unwrapping the branch. "Thank you. Is she...?"

"Right behind me," Phoebe said, already turning to go. Then she paused, head tilted slightly. "Are you really going to steam it?"

"I am," he said. "Old method from Maryland. Makes the cambium bend better. Less likely to split when it's bound."

"Will it hurt the tree?" she asked, not with fear, but with the scientific interest of someone already imagining her own experiments.

"No," he said. "Sometimes heat makes things more willing."

Phoebe frowned thoughtfully. "So does time. But not everyone waits." Before he could respond, she added, "I'll leave you to it. My aunt says I'm not supposed to be near open flame." She vanished back into the trees, her voice trailing behind her like a wisp of cider-scented wind.

Elizabeth arrived a moment later, boots brushing fallen husks, pruning shears still tucked into the belt of her work apron. "Was that Phoebe?"

"She brought the limb. And left me with a proverb," Nathaniel said, holding up the branch.

Elizabeth's expression softened at that, and she crouched beside him at the steaming barrel without a word. He passed her the coil of linen and took up the pruning blade, its hilt worn smooth with use. Steam rose between them as bark softened, cambium revealed. They worked in a rhythm that required no discussion. Only memory. Only care.

The bark gave way cleanly under the heat. Elizabeth held the limb as he made the first cut, then bound the graft with a smooth wrap, her hands deft and steady.

Somewhere beyond the trees, Phoebe hovered at the edge of the path, watching, unseen, taking mental note of every motion, every tool, every silence that stitched a wounded branch back into belonging.

The last of the sun had sunk behind the ridge, leaving only a fringe of silver light bleeding across the orchard. Nathaniel and Elizabeth walked in silence, the steam from the grafting pit still rising faintly behind them, like breath from some great creature left sleeping among the trees.

She walked just ahead, boots sure over the uneven grass. He followed without hurry, satchel slung low, hands still smelling of wax and bark.

"Do you always work alone like that?" he asked quietly.

Elizabeth didn't turn. "Most men who offer help do so with strings attached."

"Not all of us come with string."

"No," she said, dryly. "Some come with linen tape and resin."

He huffed a low laugh. "Fair."

They reached a row of younger Dabinett trees: late fruiters, dense with green shadow even in fading light. The scent of cider mash drifted faintly on the breeze from the barn below. Elizabeth slowed her steps.

"I saw Phoebe at the edge of the grove," Nathaniel said, almost offhand. "She brought the limb. Then vanished like a scout on assignment."

Elizabeth let out a breath that was almost a sigh. "She likes to observe before she decides who's worth her time."

"She's a sharp eye. Strong sense of timing."

"She has to," Elizabeth replied. "She doesn't get the luxury of stumbling."

He nodded, accepting the truth in that. "My mother had rows of pears," he offered. "Early-ripening. Soft skin, weak hearts. She talked to them like they were daughters. Said they bruised from too much wind or not enough praise."

Elizabeth's brows lifted.

He shrugged. "I thought it was foolish, growing up. But now..." He hesitated. "Now I talk to bark and roots like they might remember me." A pause. Then, quieter: "The year it was seized, we lost the whole lower slope. Late frost, root rot, deer damage. I tried to graft. Too late. Too clumsy. I didn't know what I was saving."

Elizabeth's voice came low. "But you tried."

"I failed."

She didn't answer, but she didn't walk faster either.

They reached the orchard gate. Elizabeth paused there, one hand on the worn wooden post. Behind her, in the distance, a small shape moved across the upper path: Phoebe, walking slowly toward the house, head down in thought. William followed at a distance, rolling a dented tin hoop with a stick, half-lost in his own game.

Nathaniel followed Elizabeth's gaze. "They remind me of all the reasons it matters."

"She sees more than she says," Elizabeth murmured. "And someday, if I've done anything right, she'll grow what I didn't know how to."

He nodded. "Then you've done something right already."

Elizabeth looked at him, and her hand lingered on the gatepost a moment longer.

"That graft," he said. "It'll hold."

She met his eyes. "We'll see if it bears." Then she turned, slipped through the gate, and vanished into the dusk.

Nathaniel stayed behind, watching the steam fade behind the trees. The heat had gone. But not from his chest.

By dawn, the orchard steamed faintly in the valley's hollows, last night's mist lifting slow off the grass. Inside the press barn, the scent of apple pulp clung to everything: boards, boots, skin. The vat had cooled overnight, and John Thatcher was already wrenching the screw tighter by the time Elizabeth arrived.

Phoebe was there too, perched on an overturned crate near the edge of the platform, ledger open across her lap, stub of chalk in hand. She wasn't supposed to be helping. But neither Elizabeth nor John had told her to leave. And that was nearly the same as permission.

William, yawning and tousled, stood beside John with a cloth bundle of fresh rags under one arm and cider flecks already on his sleeves. He was clearly proud to be included, though still half a head shorter than the press table. His job, unofficial but sacred, was to carry emptied baskets to the wash trough and refill them with clean straw liners, work he performed with solemn care.

Nathaniel was already at the crank, sleeves rolled, hair damp at the temples. He looked up when Elizabeth entered but didn't speak, just nodded once, eyes steady.

She returned the nod and moved to inspect the bucket below the press. "Ferment's clearer today," she said, crouching. "Foam's breaking faster."

"I noticed," Nathaniel said. "Color's richer too."

Phoebe piped up from her perch. "You can tell by the rim, can't you? Like a tea ring."

Elizabeth blinked. "Where did you hear that?"

"You said it last year. When William spilled the August batch."

William turned bright red. "That was an accident!"

Phoebe looked smug.

Elizabeth fought a smile. "You were listening?"

"I always listen," Phoebe said solemnly.

Nathaniel passed her the chalk. "Then why don't you mark the rim line for the first pour, little steward."

Phoebe did precisely, with her tongue sticking out slightly at the corner. William leaned in, watching her work with undisguised admiration.

They pressed in earnest then. The crank groaned, the juice flowed, and sunlight spread slowly across the barn floor like an unrolling carpet of gold. The air filled with the scent of crushed fruit and warm wood.

Elizabeth worked opposite Nathaniel, the rhythm wordless. Their hands brushed once across the mash tub. Neither pulled back. Phoebe saw, of course, but said nothing. She only turned a page in the ledger and drew a small tree in the margin, its roots curling beneath the numbers.

When they paused to rest, Elizabeth leaned back against the beam and took the ladle William had left to scoop a taste of the morning's press.

She held it out.

"Go on," she said to Nathaniel.

He raised an eyebrow. "Is this a peace offering?"

"It's a test," Phoebe corrected. "If he flinches, the batch isn't ready."

Nathaniel grinned, took the ladle, and sipped.

He didn't flinch.

"Redstreak and Dabinetts," he said, nodding. "But the acid's higher than yesterday."

Elizabeth folded her arms. "Because I cut the mix."

"Cut it?" Phoebe echoed, intrigued.

"Mixed the bins differently," Elizabeth explained. "Sometimes balance isn't what you plan. It's what you adjust for."

Phoebe nodded slowly, committing that to memory.

Nathaniel handed back the ladle. His fingers lingered on Elizabeth's just slightly.

"You adjusted well," he said.

She didn't reply. But she didn't step back either.

Phoebe watched them for a moment, then looked down at her chalk drawing again. She added two tiny figures standing beneath the tree she'd drawn: one with curls, one with rolled sleeves.

Then she closed the ledger without a word.

Outside, the sun kept rising. Inside, the mash kept pressing.

The stillroom was warmer than the kitchen, heat banked low, air sweet with apple and sharp with vinegar. Rain ticked at the shutters, a softer echo of the river's earlier roar. On the table lay a coil of rope, dark with wet, the last few feet stretched out and straight so it could dry without kinking.

Nathaniel sat on the bench, hair still damp, shirt changed, knuckles scraped raw under a clean strip of linen. Elizabeth stood across from him with a small bowl of calendula salve and a roll of narrow bandage. She didn't speak at first. She unwound the wet rope to check the splice, laid it flat again, then dipped two fingers in the salve.

"Palms," she said.

He offered them. The left shook, just once, a memory of the river still lodged in muscle. She pretended not to feel it as she smoothed the salve over the burned grooves the rope had cut.

"You know better than to brace a barrel at flood," she said, not unkindly.

"I do," he answered. "And I knew it before my boots left the plank." He watched her hands. "You were very fast."

"I've pulled lambs in a spring torrent," she said. "Rope doesn't frighten me."

"Losing people does," he said, quiet.

Her eyes flicked up. "Yes."

They let the word sit. Rain ticked. Somewhere above, a settling beam gave a small, tired sigh.

She wrapped the bandage and tied it off with a square knot he recognized from the bracing lines. "There," she said. "You'll feel it in the morning."

"I feel it now," he said. "Mostly the part where Phoebe planted herself like a dolmen behind you and shoved."

"She cheats physics," Elizabeth said, and the corner of her mouth lifted. "Don't praise her for it. She'll start lifting the house to see if it can be done."

"She already has," he said, and they both smiled.

Elizabeth set the bandage roll aside and rinsed her fingers. "We need a rule," she said without turning. "Two, in fact. First: no one crosses to the landing alone in a rain that fattens the ditch. Not you. Not William. Not me."

"Agreed," he said at once.

"Second: if the river looks like teeth, we wait. Pride doesn't lift a barrel."

"Pride nearly took my head off," he said. "I'll sign your rules in blood if you like."

"Ink will do," she said dryly, reaching for the ledger she kept for house safety. She wrote without hurry, carefully, the way she wrote numbers that could be held up in a court—and then turned the book for him to sign below her name. He did, bandaged hand careful.

She blotted the page. "There. The river has to argue with both of us now."

He watched her close the ledger and slide it into its place under the shelf where she kept tinctures. "Thank you," he said.

"For what?"

"For not scolding me in front of the boy," he said. "And for... not letting go."

Her jaw touched a softer line. "I wouldn't."

"I know that now," he said. "I felt it in the rope."

Silence again, but it wasn't empty. It felt like standing in a press yard after the screw settles, pressure easing, purpose remaining.

Elizabeth reached for another length of clean cord, then hesitated and set it down. "I don't say this for comfort," she began, eyes on the knot she'd tied, "but so we can work. If the river had taken you..." She swallowed once, plain and unadorned. "It would have made the audit easier. Fewer risks. Fewer men to defend. And yet I didn't think about the audit for even a breath."

He didn't move. "What did you think about?"

"Keeping you," she said simply. "Choosing you. Over barrels and ledgers and what men will say later."

Nathaniel's breath went a little ragged. He looked down at his bandaged palms, then up again. "Then let me choose you back."

Her eyebrow lifted.

He nodded toward the rope. "When the river runs high, I'm at the gate, no more lone errands to spare my pride. When Wainscott walks in, I take the first questions, no more leaving you to carry someone else's sins because you're the one with a roof. When Miles turns up with his shortcuts, I say no out loud where your people can hear me." He paused. "And if there's risk to be put on paper, we write my name on it first."

She held him in a long, measuring look. "You're fond of promises."

"I'm fond of keeping them," he said. "You like steadiness; I can give that."

"I like competence paired with steadiness," she corrected. "Men are steady as stones when they're wrong."

He laughed, breath easing. "Then watch me be right twice before breakfast."

"We'll see," she said, but there was warmth in it.

He flexed his fingers, testing the ties she'd made. The bandage held, snug but not strangling. "Good knot."

"Square," she said. "Holds true if both ends pull."

His breath hitched. "Is that your warning?"

"It's my preferred design," she said, and finally allowed herself to lean an inch closer, as if to check the knot, though they both knew it was permission to be near. From this close he could see the tiny freckle at her temple, the stray wisp of hair that had escaped her scarf, the faint iron trace still at the edge of her nail from earlier.

"Thank you," he said again, voice low now. "For choosing."

"Don't make me regret it," she said, equally low.

He didn't reach for her hand; he lifted his bandaged palm instead, and she set her fingertips against the linen just for a beat, feeling the pulse beneath. Not a kiss. Not a vow spoken twice. But something planted.

Phoebe's stick tapped once in the hall. She appeared in the doorway, took in the scene: rope laid out, ink drying, hands bandaged, and nodded like a tiny magistrate.

"Good," she said. "Rules."

"Rules," Elizabeth agreed. "Tell William."

"I already did," Phoebe said, and vanished, stick tapping a measured beat. "I told him the river has teeth."

When she was gone, Elizabeth drew the wet rope toward the hearth and looped it wide to dry. Nathaniel rose, slower than usual, as if standing too quickly might wake whatever had just settled in the room.

"Back to the barn?" he asked.

"In a minute," she said. "Let the river hear us not rushing."

He stood beside her in the stillness, watching the rope steam just a little, and felt, for the first time in a long while, like he belonged to something he hadn't built alone.

***

The Red Hart's back room was warm with firelight and thick with the smell of smoke and spilt ale. Nathaniel sat with his boots stretched toward the hearth, coat loosened at the throat. It had been a long day hauling stock down to the quay, and he'd been looking forward to nothing more than a glass and the quiet.

The latch lifted.

A woman stepped in, skirts brushing the jamb, hood shadowing her face. Lamplight caught the pale line of her cheek, the dark sweep of hair, and for a stunned instant Nathaniel's chest jolted...Elizabeth!

She came toward him slowly, unfastening the hood. The scent of some floral water drifted ahead of her. "You're Nathaniel Carter?" Her voice was pitched soft, coaxing.

He half rose without thinking. "Aye, I..,"

The hood fell back, and the illusion shattered. The mouth was painted too red, the smile too polished. Not Elizabeth. Not even close.

Behind her, Miles leaned on the doorframe, grinning like a man who'd won a bet. "Thought you could use some company. Consider it an investment in morale."

Nathaniel frowned. "You shouldn't have."

"I should. You've been walking around like a parson on fast-day. Loosen your collar, Carter." Miles tipped an imaginary hat to the woman and sauntered out, the door swinging shut behind him.

Nathaniel stood there for a long beat, the fire snapping in the grate. She had nice eyes. A warm shape in the lamplight. A red-blooded man could take what was offered and no one would fault him for it...God knew he'd been too long without a woman's touch.

But the thought curdled almost at once. If he touched her, he'd be pretending she was someone else. Pretending she was Elizabeth. And that wasn't fair, to either of them. "You've come for coin," he said finally. "My heart belongs to another, but I'd like to help."

"Much obliged." Her smile wavered. "And supper. I'd like to eat tomorrow."

He reached for his purse. "You've other work?"

"Not steady. I mend linen for the boarding houses when they'll have me. Mostly they don't."

Nathaniel poured her a measure of brandy, set a coin beside it. "Then tell me about the mending. Show me how to stitch a tear so it doesn't pull again. You can take the rest of the bottle for the trouble."

She blinked at him, unsure whether to laugh, then settled into the chair opposite. Her fingers were deft even in the dim light, and as she worked, the edge in her voice eased.

By the time the cloth was mended and the fire burned low, Miles had not returned, no doubt disappointed his game had come to nothing. Nathaniel walked her to the door, pressing the coin into her palm. "You'll not want for supper," he said.

She studied him a moment. "And you'll not want for decency. That's rarer than you think."

When she was gone, Nathaniel sat back down, watching the last ember crackle to ash. The heat in his chest earlier hadn't been hunger, it had been hope. And he wasn't about to waste that on a shadow of the real thing.

The door creaked again. Miles stepped inside, eyebrows raised. "Well? She worth the silver?"

"Not in the trade you intended." Nathaniel didn't look up.

Miles leaned against the wall, smirking. "Don't tell me you turned her away. God above, Carter, what's happened to you?"

Nathaniel took his time answering, turning his empty glass in his hands. "I've a taste for other things."

Miles barked a laugh. "Other things, or a certain orchard keeper?"

Nathaniel met his gaze, steady and unflinching. "Doesn't matter. Leave it alone."

Miles's smile thinned, as if he'd seen more than Nathaniel meant him to. But he only shrugged, pushing off the wall. "Suit yourself. Just don't expect the world to wait for you."

"I don't." Nathaniel poured himself another measure, the firelight catching in the amber. "But I'll wait for what matters."

CHAPTER TWELVE

THE WIDOW'S LEDGER

The stillroom was colder than usual, though the window was shut and the early sun shone through its warped panes, making colors on the wall that looked like warm molasses. Elizabeth Whitcombe sat at the small desk in the corner, coat draped over her shoulders, ink drying too slowly in the chill. Her fingers smudged the edge of the parchment as she turned another page in the orchard ledger too quickly, too roughly, and cursed under her breath.

She'd copied these entries herself only last harvest, with her late husband coughing in the next room and tax rumors thick as woodsmoke in every conversation. But even so, something didn't add up.

Three barrels. Stamped, tallied, taxed.

And five that had gone missing from the list entirely.

Her eyes traced the space between numbers...barrel #116 straight to #120, as if the others had never existed. But she remembered them. Remembered the days they'd rolled hot from the press, steaming faintly in the frost air, and how Whitcombe had sent them "off to Bristol" without a receipt, without a word.

She'd been in mourning by then...for her father, not her husband. She hadn't yet known she'd have to mourn twice in the same winter. And certainly not for the things he'd done in her name.

Elizabeth leaned back and pressed the ball of her thumb to her temple. Her braid scraped against the back of the chair as she breathed through her teeth.

If she amended the ledger now, it would look like forgery.

If she didn't, the gap alone could ruin her when the inspector came.

1763 law was cruelly clear: any discrepancy in barrel count, any number that didn't match the excise register, was presumed intent to defraud. The orchard could be fined, her barrels seized, her right to produce stripped like a title she'd never fully been allowed to wear.

Plainly put: if the numbers in her book didn't match the Crown's book, the Crown would call it cheating. "Light barrels" meant you hid cider to dodge a stamp. A missing ledger line read as you lied on purpose. And if a barrel had moved without the right mark, they didn't say "oversight" they said smuggling. One mismatch, and the Exchequer would treat her as if she'd stolen from the King.

Her eyes drifted to the pen beside her hand.

It had belonged to her father. The nib was worn, the handle ink-stained where her thumb always pressed hardest. She picked it up now, dipped it in the bottle, and brought the tip to the margin beneath barrel 115.

She hovered.

There was room to fit the names. To forge them. Five quick strokes, just enough to fill the gap and make it all look intentional. A tidy lie. An invisible lie.

But her hand didn't move.

She could almost hear Miles Hardwick's voice from the week prior as he leaned on her orchard gate and offered to "smooth the paperwork" like he had for a ciderworks near Colwall. Called it just a matter of ink and good sense. She'd sent him off with a look sharp enough to peel bark.

Let him chase shortcuts elsewhere.

Across the room, the hearth ticked. A wind stirred through the stillroom flue and rattled the glass. Her eyes flicked briefly toward the small shelf in the corner, where Phoebe's chalk slate still rested from the day before, half a cider tree drawn with uneven roots and crooked limbs. A scrap of apple bark was tucked beside it like a gift. Elizabeth didn't look at it long.

She exhaled and set the pen down with precision. She reached instead for a fresh booklet, still unmarked, and cracked it open at the first page. Its binding creaked softly. The paper was smoother than her usual ledgers, meant for seed records, not cider weights.

She took up the pen again and wrote on the top line:

PRIVATE ACCOUNT – Autumn 1763 – E. T. Whitcombe

No initials but her own. No shared names. No ghost pressing the nib at her hand.

She turned the old ledger facedown to the ink blot itself on the wood, and began, slowly, carefully, to write what no one else would see.

By midday, the sun was too warm for October. The air clung damp in the barrelhouse yard, thick with the sweet rot of windfalls. Elizabeth strode across the packed earth toward the cooper's chalk table, skirts lifted slightly above her boots. She was still thinking about the blank pages she'd begun that morning. The act of it, starting her own ledger, felt both rebellious and insufficient.

Phoebe was nearby, seated on a low bench by the far wall, sorting fallen apples into bruise-heavy and salvageable piles. Her back was straight, her right foot angled slightly outward...the twisted one never quite settling comfortably in its boot. A sun-faded bonnet shaded her face, but Elizabeth could feel the child's attention even when her hands were still.

Not far off, William was dragging a half-empty basket toward the wash trough, his small boots skidding slightly in the mud. He'd been unusually quiet since the coopers' assistant made a careless joke about "cripples and widow-work" under his breath that morning. Phoebe hadn't said a word in response, but her sorting had grown remarkably fast and ruthless after that.

Elizabeth found John Thatcher bent over the barrel rack, marking rings with a stub of chalk. His shirt clung to his back with sweat. A strip of apple pulp was caught in his collar. He didn't notice her until she cleared her throat.

"You marked those wrong," she said flatly.

John didn't look up. "Didn't touch the numbers."

"You didn't touch mine," she clarified. "I adjusted the count this morning. Those five aren't cleared for press."

He set the chalk down slowly. "That's not how Whitcombe marked them." He always spoke about her late husband as Whitcombe, and her as Lizzie. Suddenly she hated it.

"I'm Whitcombe now." Elizabeth folded her arms. "You want the rest of *your* name, John, you'd best remember mine."

Behind her, Phoebe's small hand paused mid-reach, an apple half-turned in her palm.

The silence that followed was sharp as pruning wire. John wiped his hands on his trousers and turned.

"I meant no offense."

"You marked them for pressing." Her voice was tight. "They were already suspect when the ink dried last season. You want to see this orchard fined before the audit even begins?"

"I want to see the orchard stand." John's voice didn't rise, but it had a weight in it. "You've been changing things...barrel counts, field schedules, quiet talk with the boy and the American. We've worked these fields longer than he's known how to spell 'Redstreak.'"

Her pulse ticked once in her throat. "So your quarrel is with Nathaniel."

"My quarrel," he said, "is with not knowing whose books we're following."

Elizabeth stepped forward. The heel of her boot crushed a fallen apple to pulp.

"Then I'll be plain," she said. "These barrels don't move unless I say so. My late husband left enough ghosts. I'll not let his mistakes damn this harvest."

John looked at her for a long moment. Then, without a word, he picked up the chalk and wiped the numbers clean.

"I'll make the count match yours," he said. "But you should tell the others. Before the steward comes asking. Before someone like that shipping man, Hardwick, starts whispering about new leadership again."

Elizabeth's jaw tightened. She hadn't realized Miles had spoken with John, too. She hadn't realized how quickly Miles sowed doubt.

She didn't answer. Her heart was pounding, not just with anger but with something colder. A creeping awareness that even the people who'd stood beside her in wind and rain still looked sideways when it came to power. A woman's title might be inked into a will, but not into the bones of a place.

Elizabeth stopped three paces on and didn't keep walking. She turned back.

"Not whispers," she said. "We do this in the yard where everyone can see."

Within the half hour, the barrelhouse doors were thrown wide and a plank table dragged into the light. The cooper's chalk lay beside a clean sheet of foolscap. Elizabeth set out three things with the kind of precision that made men take note: her house ledger, the cooper's rack list, and a blank page titled in a firm, dark hand:

WHITCOMBE ORCHARD — PRE-COUNT ADDENDUM, MICHAELMAS 1763

(To be read beside the house ledger and the Crown register.)

Workers drifted in at the edges curiously. Hester arrived with her egg basket and a look that dared anyone to call this improper. M. Morgan, the apothecary, had come for thyme and stayed on the stoop, arms folded, sharp eyes missing nothing. Phoebe took the stool nearest the table, slate ready. William stood square as a fencepost with a stack of fresh cloths he'd insisted were "for official business."

Nathaniel didn't take the table. He took the work: bungs, cloths, a bucket, keeping the movement smooth while Elizabeth kept the center.

"John," she said evenly, "call the barrels in order."

He cleared his throat. "One hundred thirteen: Kingston Black. Stamped and sealed."

"Read," Elizabeth said. Phoebe murmured the matching line from the ledger. Elizabeth noted it on the addendum with a steady scratch of her pen.

"Fourteen," John went on. "Redstreak blend."

"Read." Match. Note.

They moved briskly; open, glance, taste if there was any doubt, reseal, write. When they reached the suspect corner, Elizabeth didn't slow.

"Barrel One Hundred Sixteen, unlisted in the house ledger," John said, voice carefully neutral.

Elizabeth looked at the gathered faces before she looked at the cask. No flinch. "Open."

Nathaniel worked the bung. The smell was sound—young, not green. He tipped the thinnest taste to the rim, held it to the light. "Redstreak heavy, pressed late. It belongs to last harvest, but it's not gone."

Elizabeth nodded once. She wrote, clean and large:

116: PRESENT ON FLOOR; UNLISTED. TASTED SOUND. MARKED TODAY FOR SEAL.

"Read," she said.

Phoebe read it back, steady as a bellman.

"Next," Elizabeth said.

"Barrel One Hundred Seventeen, missing," John called, checking the rack gaps.

"Note it," Elizabeth said, and her pen didn't falter:

117 — NOT PRESENT; SEE CROWN REGISTER FOR STAMP.

She looked up so they'd hear the plain speech beneath the ink. "If it's stamped there and absent here, the gap is location, not honesty. If it's absent there and present here, we show why." Her voice didn't rise. It didn't need to.

When they reached One Hundred Twenty, the wax looked too clean. Nathaniel crouched, ran a thumb across the stamp. "New seal," he said. "Set in the last week."

Elizabeth didn't blink. "Whose hand?"

John hesitated. "Mine."

There was a stir. Elizabeth didn't look away from John. "Why?"

"Thought to tidy," he said. "Gap made me itch."

She let the honesty land, then nodded. "We don't tidy over truth. We tidy toward it." To Phoebe: "Write:"

120: SEALED LAST WEEK BY J. THATCHER; ENTERED TODAY.

She set down the pen and looked up at the yard, letting the words carry beyond the table. "This is what Wainscott will try: to make a gap into guilt. We meet him with a book anyone can read."

Hester snorted approval. "Make him do sums where all the children can see."

Morgan's mouth twitched. "Decent medicine."

When the addendum page was full, Elizabeth sanded the ink, tipped the sheet to dry, then laid it flat again. "Signatures," she said. "Witnesses to the count."

She didn't push the pen to Nathaniel; she placed it in John's hand first. He signed, jaw set. Hester signed next, "H. Merritt, eggs and sense" earning a ripple of laughter that eased the tight shoulders around the yard. Morgan followed with a brisk "M. Morgan, apothecary." Nathaniel signed last, neat and small, not reaching for the center.

Elizabeth added her name across the foot, E. T. Whitcombe, and the page, suddenly, looked like ballast.

She folded it once and slid it into the ledger. "This sits with the house book," she said. "When the inspector arrives, this is the first page he sees, and the last he leaves with."

"And the missing stamp?" Morgan asked, practical to the bone.

Elizabeth's mouth thinned. "Carrick & Plympton can hunt their ghost in their own closets. We won't forge a dead man's mark."

"That's steadier than most," Hester said, satisfied. "And harder to argue with than a prayer."

Nathaniel exhaled a breath he hadn't noticed he'd been holding. Not relief; confidence. She had given everyone a script that was not a lie.

As people dispersed, Phoebe lingered, running a fingertip along her aunt's signature as if memorizing the shape of it. "Will he still say smuggling?"

"He might," Elizabeth said. "You will keep writing."

Phoebe nodded, grave. "And I will spell it correctly."

"Do," Elizabeth said, and the ghost of a smile flickered. "It'll save us ink in the appeal."

Nathaniel fell into step beside Elizabeth as she gathered the sand shaker and the seal. He didn't offer praise; she didn't need it. He only said, as if naming a weather:

"You just made the orchard speak."

"And you poured when I said pour," she replied. "That's what I value."

"Not charm?" he teased, very quietly.

"Competence," she said, even quieter. "Steady competence."

He took that like a charge, not a flirtation. "Then I'll be steady."

She turned the sand shaker once in her palm, considering him. "So far," she said. But the glance she gave him held more promise than warning.

The knock came just as the kitchen clock struck three. Elizabeth paused, one hand buried in flour, the other resting against the rim of a cracked bowl. She hadn't been expecting anyone, not today, and certainly not someone arriving by the front path instead of the orchard gate.

From the hearth rug, Phoebe looked up from a stack of weath-er-creased story pages she'd been copying. Her lips were stained with blackberry juice, though she'd insisted she wasn't eating them.

"Stay there," Elizabeth said, gently but firmly.

Phoebe nodded and tucked her legs beneath her, though the crutch she'd leaned beside her slipped sideways with a clatter. She righted it, then stared fixedly at the door as if willing it to reveal its secrets.

When Elizabeth opened it, she found young messenger Thomas, cheeks flushed and coat too large, one muddy boot half-untied. He thrust a bundle wrapped in oilskin into her hands before she could speak.

"From the solicitor's office in Ledbury, miss," he mumbled, eyes on his boots. "Said it was urgent."

"Did they give you a name?" she asked, already inspecting the seal.

Thomas shrugged. "Just said it came by special rider. Clerk looked like he'd swallowed a wasp, ma'am."

That sounded like Plympton.

Elizabeth reached into her apron and handed him a copper half-penny. "Tell your uncle thank you. And mind the ditch when you pass the south lane, it's washed out again."

"Yes, miss." He darted off, boots thudding, the coin clutched tight-ly in his hand.

The bundle was still warm from his chest, but the wax seal remained crisp: red, dry, and stamped with the insignia of Carrick & Plympton, her late husband's estate solicitors. She shut the door with her hip and set the package down on the wide oak table, brushing aside a bowl of chopped quince and the torn corner of a market list she'd never finished.

Phoebe was watching. Her pockmarked cheeks were unreadable, but her hands were tight around the handle of her crutch again. "Is it bad news?" she asked softly. Her gaze didn't leave the bundle as Elizabeth loosened the knot.

The letter's wax cracked with an audible snap. "Go on, then," Elizabeth said without turning. "Wash those fingers before you smear blackberry on my accounts."

Phoebe hesitated, then limped obediently toward the side basin, one hand trailing the bench for balance. Her steps were careful, but her ears were tuned like a wire.

Elizabeth waited until the girl was out of direct line of sight before she unfolded the letter and read.

Madam,

Per the Excise Office circular of Michaelmas Term, the assessor Wainscott is scheduled to attend your premises five days from the date of this notice to reconcile orchard ledgers and bonded receipts.

You are advised to have on hand the following: the house ledger; the cooper's daily tallies; any private account books reflecting stock movements since last harvest; and the stamped manifests corresponding to barrels numbered 116–120.

In light of the recent communication from the Excise Office and in anticipation of the forthcoming inspection, we are compelled to inform you that discrepancies have emerged in the submitted records from the harvest of the previous year.

Specifically: five barrels were listed as transported under the Whitcombe name to a bonded warehouse near Hereford.

Only three stamps were ever processed by Crown assessors...

The words blurred. But not because her eyes failed her.

Because the truth was simple.

He'd done it. James. Or someone under his name, which made little difference now. Five barrels, moved or sold or gifted or gods-knew-what, two unstamped. Two ghosts in her ledger.

The solicitor's note didn't threaten outright. Not yet. But the message was clear: produce the stamps, or prepare for seizure.

Elizabeth folded the parchment once, twice, neatly, slowly. Then crossed to the hearth, where the ash box lay beside a small pile of unburnt pinecones and yesterday's coals. She opened the iron lid, scooped out the warmest ash with the edge of the hearth brush, and laid the wrapped bundle gently beneath it. The gray flakes coated the parchment like snow.

Phoebe had returned and was watching her again, silent as breath.

Elizabeth reached for the small cast-iron apple press weight that had sat on the hearth since her father's day: circular, worn, and heavy as a regret you couldn't bury.

She placed it atop the ash, atop the bundle, without a word, where it would stay where no steward would think to look.

Phoebe edged a step closer. "You're not burning it?"

"No." Elizabeth wiped her hands on her apron, then met the girl's eyes. "Some things need remembering. Even if they never get spoken."

Phoebe's brow furrowed, but she nodded. "If they come asking, I didn't see anything."

Elizabeth exhaled...not quite a laugh, not quite a sob. "You saw everything, my girl. But thank you all the same."

The child turned back to her seat, dragging her crutch beside her with an uneven thump. Elizabeth stood alone by the hearth a moment longer.

The press resumed before sunrise.

The first clang of copper startled the crows from the south hedgerow, their black wings slicing the pale sky as Elizabeth stepped into the barrelhouse yard. Her boots stepped over bark mulch, damp with dew, and the air smelled of pulp and steam: sharp, ripe, almost holy.

Inside, John Thatcher had already cranked the beam into place. William, still blinking sleep from his eyes, was arranging the cloths for the pomace as best he could. He carried them carefully, like folded flags. The boy didn't speak much during the morning pressings, but his hands moved quickly when John barked instructions.

By the time the second press was lowered, Nathaniel appeared in the open frame of the east door, sleeves rolled, hair damp as if he'd washed in the basin just to feel clean before seeing her.

He crossed the yard in silence, lifting a half-drained vat with ease, and took his place beside her.

For a while, they worked without speaking. The cloths were heavy, the mash uneven. She showed him how to shift the weight with his heel to balance the run. He adjusted the pressure. Steam rose. The cider darkened with the second press...thick and gold and full of memory.

A sound from behind, the scrape of John's boots, broke the moment. William's small voice followed, asking for fresh cloths. Elizabeth straightened, blinking as if pulled from a dream.

"Would you check the eastern bins for me?" she said to Nathaniel, her voice low. "Some of the Tom Putt apples may be too soft to keep."

He caught her meaning in an instant. They stepped out together, past the barrelhouse door, into the strip of orchard where the low sun painted the leaves in brass and green. Here, the hum of the press was muted, and the air smelled of apples still clinging to the branch...sharp and sweet, tinged with the faint musk of damp bark.

A lone bee droned lazily between windfalls. Somewhere above, a thrush shifted in the branches, sending down a flutter of loosened leaves. An apple fell with a soft thud onto the grass, rolling until it rested against her boot.

Between the rows, they stopped.

He caught her watching his mouth. She caught him watching her hands. A moment passed with no words, just the slow drift of a leaf settling in the path.

Then he stepped closer.

She whispered, "Nathaniel..."

And then he kissed her.

It was not gentle.

It was not hasty.

It was slow, steady, certain...like pressing weight into pulp and knowing the sweetness would rise. His hands found her waist as if they had always belonged there. Her fingers curled into his collar, anchoring herself to something that felt dangerously like truth.

When they broke apart, breathless, he said only:

"I'm not here to steal what's yours. I'm here to help you keep it." His voice lowered. "Though damn it, I didn't intend to fall for you."

She closed her eyes for a moment. Far off, the press hissed in the catch tray. A bee dipped between fallen apples. "I know," she whispered. And still, she didn't step away.

Two days passed like apples rolling downhill: small jolts, constant motion. On the third morning, the Ledbury bell tolled noon, and Phoebe, who counted everything, announced from the yard gate without ceremony, "Three days."

Elizabeth didn't correct her. The addendum lay dry in the ledger. The barrels sat where anyone could see them. If Wainscott wanted shadows, he'd have to bring his own.

CHAPTER THIRTEEN

THE LINE IN INK

T he woman at the table was dressed in dove-grey silk and carried the air of someone who thought she was doing Elizabeth a favor simply by sitting in her kitchen. She introduced herself as Mrs. Armitage, and she'd brought her daughter, a pale, sharp-faced girl of about twelve, who drifted through the doorway with a simper and too much perfume.

While Elizabeth poured tea, Mrs. Armitage launched into a smooth recitation about "relieving you of the burden of such an expansive property" and "allowing you to retire in comfort."

Phoebe, tasked with bringing in a fresh loaf from the pantry, found her way blocked by the girl.

"You limp," the girl said in the same tone one might use to point out a stain. "Does it hurt?"

Phoebe kept her voice even. "Not as much as your manners must."

The girl's eyes narrowed. "Mama says people like you shouldn't be in charge of anything important. You drop things. You fall over. You..."

"I can graft a tree better than you can spell your own name," Phoebe said, and pushed past.

The girl's cheeks flushed. She stepped sideways just as Phoebe passed, catching the handle of the heavy flour bin with a quick, deliberate jerk. The lid banged open, flour dust billowed, and Phoebe stumbled into the corner post, catching herself on her bad leg. Pain spiked, but she stayed upright.

"What was that noise?" Elizabeth's voice carried from the kitchen.

"Nothing," Phoebe called back, forcing her face smooth. "I just stumbled."

Elizabeth appeared in the doorway, eyes flicking from Phoebe to the mess of flour. Her expression tightened...not quite anger, but disappointment. "Perhaps we'll have you stick to the ledger work for now. Leave the heavy carrying to William."

Phoebe's jaw clenched, but she only nodded. "Yes, Aunt."

Mrs. Armitage and her daughter left half an hour later, the offer for the orchard politely but firmly refused.

It was two days before Elizabeth heard the truth: William, working beside her in the barrelhouse, muttered something about "that spiteful little hen knocking Phoebe into the post." When Elizabeth pressed him, he told her everything.

Elizabeth said nothing then, but that evening she found Phoebe in the grafting shed, quietly trimming a Blenheim scion.

"You've been wasted on ledgers," Elizabeth said, leaning against the doorframe. "You're back to grafting and barrel-marking. And the next time someone knocks you about, you tell me. No matter who they are."

Phoebe looked up sharply. "How did you...?"

"William can't keep his mouth shut," Elizabeth said, smiling faintly. "And I'm glad of it this once."

Phoebe's shoulders eased, and she bent back over the scion, the quick, deft cuts of her knife speaking more than thanks could.

Elizabeth watched her a moment longer, then said, "A straight graft grows strong. But a crooked one that holds? That's the one worth keeping."

***

The orchard yard was quiet in the early haze, its trees trembling in the faint breeze as if unsure whether to hold on to summer or let autumn begin its work. Dew clung to the lower leaves and slicked the wood of the cider press, where Nathaniel paused, gloved hands at his sides.

Elizabeth Whitcombe was already there.

She stood just beyond the Redstreak rows, her hair twisted up beneath a kerchief, bodice laced snug over her linen shift. Her sleeves were rolled to the elbow. She moved with practiced efficiency, checking the small scabs forming on the bark where yesterday's pruning had opened tiny wounds.

Phoebe was a few yards behind her, basket in one arm, her gait uneven as she followed the rows with deliberate steps. One foot dragged slightly in the damp grass, but she kept pace, stopping now and then to pick up dropped twine or note a withered leaf. She didn't speak, but she watched sharp-eyed and unblinking, as if the orchard's secrets were hers to audit too.

And trailing a few paces behind was William, sleeves too long, the ends of his breeches damp with dew. He tugged a small cart with visible effort, frowning in concentration as he tried to wheel it over a rut.

When it stuck, he gave it a frustrated kick—but Elizabeth's gentle call corrected him before the second.

Nathaniel had half hoped Elizabeth wouldn't be there yet. He'd half hoped she would.

He hadn't slept. He'd walked the orchard's perimeter three times before dawn. The kiss still sat in his chest like a match struck and left burning. He'd meant it...not as pretense, not as flirtation. As something...earned. Or at least offered in the hope it could be.

But this morning Elizabeth didn't look flustered or changed in the slightest.

She glanced his way only once, brief as a blink, then returned to showing William how to brace a limb with cord. Her voice was low and clear. Not cold, but cool.

Nathaniel moved to the barrels at the edge of the cider barn, keeping his posture relaxed, though his stomach had knotted itself into something tight and hollow. He busied himself checking a row of staves for warping. A few needed new bands. One had gone soft at the base.

He could feel her near, hear her voice over the rustle of leaves and soft scrape of twine. She was laughing quietly at something John had said about a wayward hen roosting in the wrong rafters.

She didn't laugh like that with him.

And it shouldn't have stung, not with the brief tone they'd known each other. But it did. He gripped the barrel edge tighter than necessary.

A cluster of birds lifted from the distant hedgerow, wheeling over the orchard as the light sharpened. Nathaniel watched them a moment, then turned back to his work, jaw set.

Last night, her mouth had been soft and certain beneath his. Her breath had caught. Her fingers had lingered at his coat lapel. And something in him had answered, something that hadn't stirred for years.

And now, the morning was just that: morning.

Phoebe crouched in the grass now, inspecting the edge of a root flare the way he'd seen Elizabeth do a dozen times. She whispered something under her breath. A verse, maybe. Or a quote. She liked stories: castle romances, he remembered. "It's bowed on the west side," she murmured, tapping the flare with a stick. "It'll take water wrong."

John Thatcher, passing nearby, glanced over and muttered, "She's not wrong."

Nathaniel scraped a palm across his jaw, resisting the urge to look at Elizabeth again. Not because he didn't want to, but because he wanted to too much. He bent to test the barrel again and muttered, "Right. Then we start fresh."

Behind him, a twig snapped softly. Phoebe was moving toward the house now, basket in one hand, trailing a line of twine behind her like breadcrumbs. She walked as though daring the path to betray her. And beside the apple rows, Elizabeth Whitcombe moved like the wind had never touched her.

Like last night had never happened.

And like Nathaniel Carter hadn't once dared to hope it had meant more than the cider he still hadn't drunk.

The midday sun slipped in through the warped shutters of the King's Arms taproom, throwing dusty shafts of light across Nathaniel's table and the untouched mug of ale beside his papers.

He hadn't drunk from it.

The taste of the orchard—of her—still lingered in his mouth, and he didn't want to wash it away. Not yet.

The letter had come folded tight and clean, sealed with the mark
he recognized at once: R.H., stamped in crisp wax the color of blood.
He'd opened it with steady fingers, but they hadn't stayed steady long.

He reread the lines now, ink sharp on the page:

Carter—

*The barrel arrived intact. Unblemished, and in better form than
your last attempts.*

The contents? Exceptional. Tannin holds. Clarity is pure.

Our taster called it "ambition aged in oak."

*I want saplings. You told me the orchard had line worth preserving.
If the cider bears it, the trees must.*

Secure rights. Secure wood. I want roots by spring.

Nathaniel stared at the words. Saplings. Roots. As if she were just
a vendor. As if her orchard were a catalog entry. As if Phoebe didn't
walk those rows with stubborn steps, treating bark like scripture. As
if William's small hands hadn't been clumsy on the cords this morning, and Elizabeth hadn't corrected him with that patient calm that
belonged more to guardians than landowners.

He folded the letter once, then again, sharper than needed. The wax
cracked faintly. He slipped it beneath his mother's old cultivar ledger
and let out a slow breath.

This was the plan. This had always been the plan. The barrel had
been a test, yes, but now it had passed. And the next step was clear:
negotiate for saplings. Secure rights. Persuade, pressure, close.

But now, the thought made his skin crawl.

He couldn't strong-arm her. He wouldn't. Not after watching her
show Phoebe how to split deadwood from a limb like it was an act
of survival. Not after seeing William nearly drop a brace and hearing
Elizabeth gently call, "Again, lad, this time, think it through," with no
bite in it.

Not after feeling the quiet conviction in her kiss...like she knew exactly what she could lose, and kissed him anyway.

He reached for a fresh sheet of parchment and dipped his pen.

Whitcombe Orchard Inventory Request

To Mistress Elizabeth Whitcombe,

If agreeable, I'd like to begin documenting your grafting methods.

Not for sale. Not for trade. For record. For preservation.

Your orchard carries more than yield—it carries story.

I'd like to see it honored in ink.

He paused.

Then added:

And I'd ask your permission first. Always.

When he finished, he set the pen down and pressed his signet into the sealing wax. The old apple-blossom imprint held, clear and firm.

No demands. No stakes. Just a request.

It was all he dared ask...for now.

He sat back in the dim gold of the tavern light, hands folded over the sealed note, and wondered if she'd open it with the same stillness with which she'd met his eyes this morning.

Still, composed, as if nothing had changed.

And yet everything had.

The stillroom felt like a chapel at matins. Elizabeth set the sand shaker, the seal, and her cleanest sheet of foolscap in a neat row before she sat. The window threw a thin blade of late light across the table. She breathed in once, steadying her wrist.

At the top she wrote, plain and large:

To the Office of the Excise, Hereford District

For the attention of Assessor Wainscott

Her pen hesitated only long enough to gather ink.

Whitcombe Orchard—Petition for Reconciliation on Inspection
Day and Relief from Summary Seizure

Sir,

I write as widow-proprietor of Whitcombe Orchard, Whitcombe
Lane, parish of Ledbury. In preparation for your attendance five days
from receipt of circular (Michaelmas Term), I petition:

1) That our enclosed Pre-Count Addendum (executed this day
with signatures of yard witnesses and cooper) be accepted for reconciliation beside the house ledger and your bonded register;

2) That barrels numbered 116 and 120—present on the floor, one
sealed last week by my foreman to prevent spoilage—be heard for nunc
pro tunc stamping on payment of duty and fee if you find the contents
sound and of last year's press;

3) That any penalty on "light barrels" be tolled where the deficit
arose during the illness and subsequent death of my husband, who
kept the ledgers that season;

4) That, pending your decision, stock be secured under my seal and
bond, not seized.

Grounds: Section VI of the Revised Excise Code punishes intent
to defraud; it does not forbid reconciliation where the fault is proved
clerical, or where stock is present, sound, and openly declared before
inspection. The Michaelmas circular invites "all books, tallies, and
private accounts reflecting stock movement." I enclose such; the orchard stands open.

As widow-proprietor, I claim the same standing as any master of
manufactory under the 1758 amendment respecting a wife continu-
ing a trade. I alone bear the risk and the duty. I meet you in the open
with the truth and the tax ready in my hand.

Plainly: the numbers in my book and the Crown's book do not
match because a dying man handled them badly. The barrels are here.

They are counted. I ask leave to pay what is owed and mend the record in your sight.

Respectfully,

Elizabeth T. Whitcombe

Whitcombe Orchard, Ledbury

She sanded the ink and read it once through, lips barely moving. It was not pretty. It was a plank laid over water.

A cough sounded in the jamb. John Thatcher leaned in, cap in hand. He had the look of a man who'd come to protest and decided against it halfway across the yard.

"You'll send that tonight?" he asked.

"Yes."

He nodded at line two. "You're asking him to stamp in arrears."

"I'm giving him a lawful way to say yes," she said. "And a difficult way to say no."

John's mouth twitched. "That's craft."

She set the petition aside and drew a second, smaller sheet.

Schedule and Witness Notice

Wainscott: On inspection, barrels to be produced in this order...

Witnesses present: J. Thatcher (cooper), H. Merritt (egg-seller), M. Morgan (apothecary). Yard open, gate unbarred.

"Names carry weight," Elizabeth said. "Women's, too, if they're the ones men ask for eggs and medicine."

John made a quiet sound of agreement. "You want me to walk it to the post?"

"I will."

"You'd better not," said a new voice.

Nathaniel stood just inside the door, hat in hand, hair damp from the lane. His coat was unbuttoned at the throat, and his eyes went first to the petition, not to her.

"You shouldn't carry the Crown's temper by yourself in the dark," he said lightly, but there was nothing light under it. "Let me take a copy and send a rider from Bristol besides."

"I don't need an American shield," she replied, too quickly.

"I wasn't offering a shield," he said. "Only a duplicate."

He stepped closer and set a small parcel on the table. "Better iron-gall. The inn's pot runs thin." He opened the stopper and tipped a dark, clean line into her inkwell. "Yours is honest. This will make it legible."

Elizabeth did not thank him. She dipped the nib and began a fair copy in a hand even steadier than the first. He stood out of the way, out of the light, and tore a strip of clean wove for her blot when she needed it without waiting to be asked.

At the signature he said, very soft, "Do you want it witnessed now?"

"By whom?" she asked.

"By the people it affects," he said. "Not me."

She hesitated. Then she called, without raising her voice, "Phoebe."

The girl appeared as if she'd been waiting on the other side of the wall, ledger hugged to her chest, chalk dust on her sleeve.

"Read it," Elizabeth said.

Phoebe read from "I petition" to "mend the record in your sight" carefully. When she finished, she did not look at Nathaniel. She looked at her aunt. "It says the truth the way a clerk can't wiggle out of," she judged.

"Then sign as witness," Elizabeth said.

Phoebe lifted her chin and wrote P. Whitcombe in the corner, small but uncompromising. John added his name beneath. Hester would add hers in the morning; Elizabeth could already hear the eggs in that signature.

Nathaniel reached for wax. "You'll want a clean seal," he said, warming the stick over the coals and letting it pool just so. He didn't touch her hand; he set the bone-handled signet within reach and stepped back. She pressed it home herself, apple blossom sharp, un-questionable.

"Two packets," he said. "One to Hereford by the night post. One to Bristol with a rider who owes me a favor. If Hereford delays, Bristol will have put your request in the clerk's mouth by breakfast."

"And my words?" she asked.

"Unchanged," he said. "Copied neat, not softened."

She studied him a heartbeat longer than necessary. "That's what I value," she said. "Clean work. No embroidery."

His smile was quick and gone. "Then I'll keep to thread and leave lace to other men."

He wrapped the duplicate petition against pasteboard, tied it off with thin twine, and wrote the Excise address in a hand made for ledgers and manifests. Not elegant. Legible.

"I'll walk with you as far as the gate," he said. "Then John can scowl me back to the road like a proper watchdog."

"John doesn't need help scowling," Elizabeth said, but she rose. The stillroom felt warmer when she stood.

At the door, Nathaniel paused. "One practical thing more," he said. "When Wainscott comes, seat him where the light falls on your page, not his. Then ask him to initial every line he refuses. Clerks hate signing their own hard hearts."

Elizabeth's mouth curved despite herself. "You've spent time with clerks."

"I have debts to them in ink," he said. "And some grudges."

She tucked the sealed packet beneath her cloak and reached for the latch. He opened the door for her and did not follow through it. His palm hovered a hair's breadth from the jamb, the way a man guards a candle in wind. Not touching her. Guarding the draft.

"Come back," she said, "when the rider's on the road. I'll want to know which horse to pray over."

"I'll bring the name," he said. "And more ink."

She went into the lane with John at her flank, the packet firm beneath her arm, the petition solid as a stave under her hand. Behind her, in the low room smelling of vinegar and mint, Nathaniel Carter blew out the lamp, then relit it with a spill so the room wouldn't go dark between one light and the next.

***

They returned just before the clock struck nine. Phoebe was waiting at the table with the sand shaker set like a sentinel and a slice of bread wrapped in cloth that she pretended not to have saved.

"Rider took it?" she asked.

"He did," Elizabeth said. "Both."

Phoebe nodded once, as if she'd expected nothing less. Then, shyly fierce: "You wrote like a master."

Elizabeth rested her palm on the petition's twin, her copy, and felt the steadying weight of it. "We'll see," she said. But her voice held iron.

Nathaniel reappeared at the threshold, rain on his shoulders and the name in his mouth. "Merritt's bay," he reported. "Takes the Ledbury road as if it owes it money."

Elizabeth exhaled a laugh she hadn't meant to let out. He didn't pocket it. He only nodded, as if the sound itself belonged with the day's work. Then he set a fresh, stoppered vial beside the inkwell and left his hand there just long enough for his knuckles to brush the wood near hers.

Not a touch. A measure of distance. Chosen, and understood.

"Good ink," he said.

"Good copy," she answered.

"Good luck," he offered.

"We make our own," she said, and closed the ledger on the line she'd drawn that afternoon, the one in ink that a clerk would have to cross out in front of witnesses if he meant to move her.

The orchard was quieter in the evening. The wind had gone soft, brushing the leaves with the hush of a hand smoothing a child's hair. Nathaniel found her beneath the slope of the eastern hill, where the Dabinett trees grew gnarled and dusk-burnished.

Elizabeth was bent at the waist, inspecting a graft line by lantern light. Her skirts were dusted with bark shavings. A curl of hair had escaped its pin and clung to her cheek, but she didn't brush it away.

She didn't look up as he approached. "I'm not hiding barrels," she said, her voice low and calm, "if that's why you're here."

"I didn't think you were," he replied.

That earned him a brief, cool, beautiful glance.

He held out the sealed letter. "I wrote this today. You can read it later. Or not. But I thought it right to ask."

She took the note slowly, deliberately, but didn't break the seal. "What is it?"

"A request," he said. "To document the grafts. The methods. Not for trade. Not for investors. For the record."

She raised a brow. "You want to make a book of my trees."

"I want to make sure they're remembered. Even if the land changes hands. Even if the laws shift again. The way you've kept them alive—your spacing, your rootstocks, your timing—it's worth putting down."

A pause. Not long. But not short, either. Then she dared him, "And if I said no?"

"I'd respect that."

Another pause. Longer this time.

Behind her, the lantern flame wavered in a soft gust, its light catching on the scars at the base of the nearest tree. The graft seam glowed gold for half a second, then darkened again.

She looked away, toward the slope. "You'll begin with the Redstreaks. The early rows. You wait for me to walk them. No guesses."

"I wouldn't dream of it," he said, and meant it.

She tucked the letter into her bodice, as neatly as one might pocket a pruning knife. "And Phoebe, if she gets in the way..."

"She won't," he assured her. "She's a smart girl, and I'd be a smart man to work patiently around her, as it should be."

Elizabeth exhaled. A sound like bark splitting. "She's what makes me risk all this," she said. "Not profit. Not reputation. Her. This orchard...if I lose it, I lose what I promised her I'd protect."

He took a slow step closer, until the scent of ciderwood and drying leaves filled the space between them. "I won't be what undoes that."

***

By dawn, the cider yard thrummed again with motion. The sun rose honey-pale through the orchard mist, and already the air smelled of pulp and woodsmoke, of effort and yield.

Elizabeth rolled up her sleeves and tied her apron tighter. The press's old lever had been coaxed back into place, the troughs scrubbed. John was already checking the racks. William moved crates with both arms and a stubborn little grunt, his curls damp with early exertion. The boy's legs were still too short for the barrel step, but that hadn't stopped him from trying.

The mash cloths were still damp from rinsing, and the flywheel creaked like a weary saint.

He worked beside her now, sleeves rolled, coat shed, hair damp at the temples. Not too close. Not too far. His movements mirrored hers...efficient, wordless, precise.

She slid a wedge beneath the barrel spout. He passed her the brace without asking. It was a companionable, working silence.

Phoebe stood off to one side on her stool, chin lifted as she watched the rhythm of the press: her eyes tracking lever, pulp, cloth. One of her hands was smudged with chalk from marking barrel heads yesterday. She didn't interrupt, but simply observed, as if studying the language of cider by ear.

When the juice began to run thick and gold, Elizabeth let herself watch it for a moment. The first yield. Steady and strong...a little late, but sound.

Nathaniel handed her the ledger without a word. She took it. He said, lightly, "You're not going to let me ink a single line, are you?"

"Not yet," she said.

He nodded, as if that was fair.

They moved as one for the better part of an hour, shifting pressings, checking pulp weight, balancing mesh layers. When her braid began to slip, he offered her a kerchief without speaking. She took it, bound her hair again, and just barely caught the respectful look he gave her. Her knees felt weak, and she shook her head free of the clouds that threatened to muddle it.

Phoebe coughed gently behind them, the soft sound of a throat cleared by someone who would never interrupt but wished the mash flow to stay even. Elizabeth smothered a smile.

Later, as the sun cleared the trees and John called for the midday break, she walked with Nathaniel to the edge of the orchard, where the last of the windfalls were gathered in baskets. William was curled beside one, nibbling bread crust and swatting at a bee with his hat. He grinned up at her, gap-toothed and triumphant, as if this were battle won.

A lone sparrow darted from the grass and startled a laugh from her...quick, sudden, unguarded.

"You haven't laughed in three days," Nathaniel said.

"I've been busy."

"I noticed."

They stood beneath the Widow tree then, its limbs heavy but still holding. She touched the scarred branch near the base, where a graft from Thomas had failed long ago and one of hers had taken root in its place.

She said, "I used to think legacy was about permanence."

"And now?"

She looked up at him. "Now I think it's about what you leave breathing behind you."

"I'd like to help it breathe longer."

Elizabeth reached into her apron and pulled out the folded letter he'd given her last night, still unopened.

Slowly, she broke the seal.

He stood very still.

She read in silence. Then closed it and returned it to her pocket. "I'll walk the northern rows with you," she said.

"I'll bring good ink."

A pause.

"And apples," he added, a little sheepish.

She smirked. "You'd better."

CHAPTER FOURTEEN

THE VISITOR

The morning had broken mild, but Phoebe insisted on wearing her red shawl anyway. She looped it like a sash and limped beside Elizabeth through the yard, her sketchbook pressed to her chest.

"Say it again?" she asked.

Elizabeth barely glanced up from the barrel tally. "Pomace."

"Pom-iss?"

"Pom-ace," Elizabeth corrected, drawing out the soft final syllable. "It's what's left after pressing."

Phoebe wrinkled her nose. "It sounds like a villain's name in a castle novel."

"Then write it down," Elizabeth said, softening. "You'll remember it that way."

Phoebe stopped to jot it in her notebook, printing each letter with careful gravity. Her fingers were ink-stained and calloused from clutching pencils too long. When she caught Elizabeth watching, she straightened and asked, "Do the Excise men ever care about pomace?"

Elizabeth's steps slowed. "Not unless someone tries to ferment it."

Phoebe nodded, considering this with the solemnity of a steward's apprentice. "So if we left a pomace barrel out and called it stew, they couldn't tax it?"

"Not unless it started to bubble," Elizabeth said dryly. "Then they'd call it criminal."

Phoebe grinned, then faltered. "Will they be angry, Aunt?"

Elizabeth tucked a loose strand of hair behind Phoebe's ear and looked out across the yard, where the press shed stood like a dare. "We're not doing anything wrong," she said. "But that doesn't mean they won't want something."

Phoebe chewed her lip. "Because we don't have a man to speak for us?"

"Because they think we shouldn't be able to speak for ourselves."

Phoebe's gaze flicked to the barn. "Will you lie to them?"

Elizabeth met her eyes. "I'll protect what's ours."

That seemed enough for now. Phoebe turned her attention back to her notebook. "Then I'll protect it too," she said. "With my words."

Elizabeth's throat tightened. She reached for Phoebe's hand. "Go find William. He should be in the loft helping John. See if he needs help moving the skins, but walk, not run. I mean it."

Phoebe turned dutifully and limped across the yard, chin high, notebook clutched like a banner.

Elizabeth watched her go, then turned toward the press house. The barrel manifest was tight this time...she'd made sure of it...but she still felt the weight of every mark, every seal. The sky above was too clear. The kind of clear that made you nervous for what might break it.

She checked the folded packet beneath the tally slate, a copy of the petition she'd sent to the county solicitors. A quiet insurance: signatures from the cooper, the parish clerk, even the Crown's own gauger, all testifying that Whitcombe cider had paid its due.

If the inspector arrived spoiling for quarrel, this paper, her mother's careful plan, would be her shield. Not ironclad, but enough to make him think twice.

When she heard hooves on the lane gravel, she already knew.

The low thud of hooves turned every head in the yard.

Elizabeth straightened by the press house, heart already quickening. The rider came into view through the split gate—dark coat, stiff posture, reins held in a hand too careful to be neighborly. A silver crown glinted beneath his lapel.

Phoebe reappeared from the stillroom path, brows drawn. She stopped short of Elizabeth and clutched her notebook to her chest. "Is that one of the tax men?" she whispered.

Elizabeth gave the faintest nod. "Inside. Now."

"But—"

"No argument, Phoebe. Go."

Phoebe obeyed, darting behind the nearest door—but not before pressing her book into Elizabeth's hand. Her thumb marked a page where she'd drawn an apple tree sagging under too much fruit. A quiet offering.

The Excise man dismounted and looped the reins over a fence post, like he meant to stay through supper.

"Mrs. Whitcombe," he called. "Lovely morning."

Elizabeth stepped forward, shawl pinned neat, voice firm. "Inspector." Her expression told him she did not approve of the unannounced company.

"We're meant to catch you as you are," he explained to her accusatory face, smile thin. "Not as you'd prefer to be."

She didn't return it. "Then I hope you're fond of damp cuffs and stubborn barrels."

They traded formalities like stones skipped over water. He mentioned the Stamp Act's creeping arm. She ignored the word audit. But her thoughts leapt sideways, to the unsealed barrel tucked in the loft's shadow.

A blur of movement caught her eye: William. The boy tore in from the orchard path, hair wild, boots too big. She gave the barest tilt of her chin. He swerved at once toward the cider barn without a word, small and fast as a sparrow. Good lad.

The inspector flipped open his ledger. "We'll begin with your press records. I'll expect the count, sealed yields, and varietals since Midsummer."

"You'll have it," Elizabeth said. "Though I'd have preferred notice."

"Where's the fun in that?" he replied, stepping toward the barrels.

Phoebe's face appeared at the loft window, eyes huge. Just a sliver of her shadow showed, enough to tell Elizabeth she'd disobeyed. But wisely.

The inspector stopped before the first rack and tapped a seal. "What's your wax compound?"

"Elderberry ink with ash wax. It holds in cold and doesn't flake in transit."

He sniffed the disc. "Thin. Borderline unclear."

Before she could respond, another voice broke in.

"Apologies...am I interrupting?"

Nathaniel emerged from behind the stack, coat rumpled just enough to suggest haste. A scroll of parchment was tucked under one arm, and his smile radiated colonial ease.

Elizabeth didn't blink. "Not at all, Mr. Carter. The inspector was admiring our sealant technique."

Phoebe pressed her fingers to the glass.

Nathaniel bowed. "Nathaniel Carter, formerly of Virginia. Temporary guest of the orchard. I have a particular interest in sealing methods...mild obsession, really."

The inspector grunted at the name of the state, but turned back to his ledger.

They continued the inspection. Nathaniel asked idle questions at all the right times, stepping into the inspector's path just enough to slow him. Elizabeth realized he was running interference; not carelessly, but with just enough flash to be remembered and enough ignorance to seem harmless. She wondered just for a moment if he'd learned it from Miles Hardwick.

He shot Elizabeth a sidelong look that carried a flicker of mischief, the same glint she'd seen when they'd argued over stillroom measures two nights before...his jest about her weighing spices by stubbornness, hers about his colonial talent for reckless guesses.

The memory steadied her; even now, danger smelled faintly of rosemary and laughter.

The inspector moved toward the shed's lean-to.

Elizabeth's breath caught.

Nathaniel was faster.

Ink spilled. Parchment unrolled like a conjurer's trick. A crock of boiled syrup, placed with uncanny luck, cracked open across the stones.

Phoebe gasped audibly.

The inspector swore and jumped back, boots catching the slick. "God's teeth, what..."

"Begging pardon," Nathaniel said, crouching to collect the wreckage. "Didn't see the crate. Slippery things, these Gloucestershire mornings."

John appeared just then with a marked barrel, switched earlier by William, if all had gone well. He slid it into place beside the others like it had always been there.

The inspector dabbed syrup from his coat with a kerchief and grumbled through the rest of the count. When he finished scribbling his provisional report, he didn't linger.

Elizabeth kept her expression even as he swung into the saddle, but inside she ticked off each paper now in play:

Solicitors' petition: proof of dues paid.

Cooper's bill of lading: every barrel accounted for.

Crown gauger's note: date-stamped and signed.

A trifecta of signatures, each a small hedge against the next official who fancied himself wolf among her trees.

Elizabeth watched him mount and ride off, dignity dampened. She turned back toward the press house. William peeked around the corner, cheeks red. Phoebe's eyes were still in the window, wide and clear. Elizabeth didn't wave her down.

She just nodded once, slow and deliberate. Phoebe didn't look away.

The silence after the inspector's departure was the kind that didn't quite settle. It hovered like vapor after a frost, or the kind of stillness that came before questions.

Nathaniel brushed syrup from his sleeves, jaw working in thought. Elizabeth crouched by the flagstones where the ink had spilled. The parchment, now mostly ruined, lay coiled nearby, edges soaked through.

John stepped up with the decoy barrel, pausing only long enough to murmur, "That one's sealed proper. No one'll ask again."

Behind him, William emerged from the barn's shadow, face flushed from exertion. He didn't speak, just gave Elizabeth a quick nod and darted off again toward the press house, as if afraid lingering too long might undo their luck.

Elizabeth stood, rubbing her fingers clean on her apron. The syrup had left a dark line along the hem of her sleeve.

Phoebe's face was still visible in the upper window. She hadn't turned away.

"You did well," Elizabeth called up softly, knowing she'd hear.

Phoebe lifted her hand slowly in response, then ducked back out of sight.

John grunted. "Girl's got eyes like a falcon. Lad too," he added, glancing toward where William had gone.

Nathaniel stepped beside Elizabeth and lowered his voice. "That was close."

"You timed it perfectly," she said, not looking at him.

"I learned from a man who thrives on last-minute theatrics," Nathaniel muttered. "Miles would've thrown the whole barrel down the slope and claimed it was possessed."

Elizabeth gave the ghost of a smile.

Nathaniel tilted his head. "Not the worst idea, honestly."

"She's watching," Elizabeth murmured, her gaze returning to the window.

He followed her eyes. "Then I'll behave."

John snorted. "God help us."

They stood like that a moment, three adults who had just pulled off a crime that wasn't really a crime, but could be punished like one all the same. The air smelled of apples, ash, and vinegar. The kind of scent that stayed in your clothes even after scrubbing.

Phoebe's silhouette vanished from the window.

Nathaniel shifted. "She'll ask questions."

"She always does."

"Will you answer them?"

Elizabeth looked down at the syrup-dark smear along the stone.

"I'll tell her we made a choice," she said. "And that I made it for her."

Nathaniel nodded solemnly. "Then let her know I stood behind it."

Elizabeth didn't answer, but her expression softened by a fraction. Then she turned and walked toward the press.

Nathaniel fell in beside her, brushing a smear of syrup from his sleeve. "Next time," he murmured, "let me spill the ink earlier and save your heart the gallop."

"Next time," she replied, a wry tilt to her mouth, "bring less syrup." His low laugh followed her.

The house had long since gone still, save the whisper of wind through loose thatching and the faint creak of old rafters. Elizabeth sat at the corner desk with the shutters cracked just enough to catch the scent of cold cider air. A taper flickered beside her, throwing faint shadows across the ledger. Ink-stained fingers hovered above the page.

Behind her, Phoebe lay curled on the settle, the red shawl gathered around her like a banner fallen in sleep. Her sketchbook was tucked beneath her chin, as if she feared someone might steal the words she'd written.

Her foot stuck out from under the quilt, twisted outward at the angle it always fell. A streak of ash still marked her cheek from when she'd helped by the hearth.

Elizabeth glanced once at the clock face—nearly midnight—and then again toward the darkened stairwell.

"William's sleeping," Phoebe mumbled suddenly, voice muffled. "He asked if the inspector was a soldier."

Elizabeth looked back. Phoebe hadn't opened her eyes, but her body had stiffened with half-wakefulness.

"I told him no," the girl continued, "but it felt like maybe."

Elizabeth's pen hovered, then dropped.

"I told him he was safe now," Phoebe added softly. "Was I right?"

Elizabeth crossed the room and knelt beside her.

"You were right to say it," she murmured, brushing a curl from the girl's forehead. "That's what matters."

Phoebe's brow furrowed in sleep. "Is lying always protection?"

Elizabeth hesitated.

"Not always," she said quietly. "But sometimes silence does more harm."

She waited for more, but Phoebe had already slipped back into sleep. Elizabeth stood, returned to the desk, and stared at the open ledger. For a long time she wrote nothing.

Then, deliberately, she flipped to the back pages, not the formal section for Excise entries, but the blank ones kept for thoughts too heavy for daytime.

She dipped the quill.

We lied. And it worked. But the lie left a residue...something I can't scrub off.

She saw everything. I think she always will.

And still she gave me the sketch. Bent tree. Too much weight. A warning? Or forgiveness?

Her hand trembled slightly. She paused, re-read, then crossed out the last line. The ink smeared.

Nathaniel's words came back unbidden.

You're not the only one who lost something worth grafting.

She thought of Ruth's voice from that last winter, shaking with fever and fury: "If you plant for yield, you'll get fruit. If you plant for roots, you might get legacy."

The wax seal sat in its dish, cold.

Elizabeth turned to the next page. She picked up the pen again, not for the inspector, but for herself.

If she remembers the lie, I hope she also remembers this:

We chose to protect what grew here, even if the roots run crooked.

Even if the fruit takes a strange shape.

She sealed it shut with wax and let it cool.

Then, after one last look at Phoebe, who had now fully buried her face in the quilt, Elizabeth blew out the taper.

The darkness settled, soft and cool.

***

The first light came amber-gold, bleeding through orchard limbs still heavy with dew. Elizabeth stood at the edge of the press shed, sleeves rolled, jaw set. Her hands already bore a smear of pulp, and her breath rose in the crisp morning chill like something half-caught between exertion and resolve.

The press wheel groaned once, then settled.

John adjusted the feed lever, his face pinched with fatigue. "Not bad for a haunted orchard," he muttered.

Elizabeth didn't smile. "Don't tempt the saints. We're not out of it yet."

Behind her, Phoebe crouched beside the barrel stack, notebook open on one knee. She'd appointed herself cider tally-keeper that morning, though Elizabeth hadn't asked her to. Her grip on the charcoal stub was sure, if smudged, and her brows furrowed with each clunk of apple mass hitting the press.

"You'll spoil that skirt," Elizabeth called over, not unkindly.

Phoebe didn't glance up. "Already did. But I'm making symbols so I know how many turns it takes for each press. John says the grind's thicker when apples are underripe."

John raised an eyebrow. "I did?"

She nodded solemnly. "You muttered it while stirring."

Elizabeth blinked. Then, softly: "That's exactly right."

Nathaniel entered a moment later, sleeves rolled, coat forgotten. He glanced toward the child, then toward Elizabeth, as though checking which battlefield he was walking into.

"Press need another hand?" he asked.

John grunted. "Unless you want me to drop from the wheel, yes."

Nathaniel stepped in wordlessly, grabbing the bucket and aligning it beneath the press spout. The cider poured thick, cloudy and rust-hued, with foam that caught the light like old gold.

Phoebe looked up briefly, then back to her notes. "This one's got the smell of rutabaga," she announced.

Nathaniel paused. "Is that... bad?"

She shrugged. "Might just mean it's strong."

Elizabeth caught his eye and let herself laugh.

The morning wore on in quiet rhythm: crush, turn, pour, seal. Phoebe stayed close, occasionally handing cloths or brushing pulp toward the bin with a broom nearly her height. Her foot dragged slightly with each step, but she didn't stop.

William emerged once from the house, hair tousled and dragging a crate too large for him. Elizabeth intercepted him gently and sent him back inside with a cup of warm cider and strict instructions not to carry anything until his head stopped spinning. He obeyed without protest...rare for him.

John broke open a crate of wax discs for sealing, and Nathaniel leaned closer to Elizabeth, voice pitched low. "We should talk."

She didn't look at him. "We're working."

"Exactly," he said. "Which means we've earned a little truth between turns."

She set a lid on the next barrel, firm. "You first."

He hesitated. Then: "I won't ship another cask without your say-so. No signatures forged. No barrels smuggled. If you want to tell me to pack off home and rot beside a Black Twig tree, I'll go."

Elizabeth said nothing.

Phoebe glanced up from the corner and said, unprompted, "If he lies again, you should throw cider at him."

John muttered, "Waste of good cider."

Elizabeth half-smiled. "It's her orchard too, in a way."

Nathaniel looked over at the child, who pretended she hadn't heard.

"I wouldn't lie to her," he said quietly. "Or to you."

Elizabeth sealed the next barrel. Her hands were steady, but her voice was softer now.

"Then stay," she said. "And work."

Chapter Fifteen

A CONTRACT OF THORNS

Nathaniel Carter sat hunched over the small writing table in his room at the King's Arms, sleeves rolled, collar unfastened, hands stained with ink and cider both. He hadn't lit the hearth. A fire felt dishonest. The room was damp with late-autumn chill and the scent of smoke-damp wool.

The sealed letter from R.H. lay off to the side, its wax firm, its edge folded neatly. He hadn't read it again. He didn't need to.

The cider was extraordinary. Send saplings next.

He'd won the bet. He'd played the merchant's game. And it left him feeling like a man who'd stolen the prize from a child's hand.

Nathaniel leaned back, letting the chair creak beneath him. His mother's cultivar book lay open to a page marked with a faded ribbon. Her slanted notes curled in the margins: "storm-leaned graft," "watch tannin bite in drought," "roots hold where pride fails." Each phrase struck harder now, as if written to him across time.

He had risked her name to stake a claim on another's.

No...on Elizabeth's. And not only hers. Phoebe's too.

He glanced again at the invoice tucked beneath his elbow, stamped with a Philadelphia trade mark he and Miles had doctored together in the taproom after too many pints and too much boldness.

Miles had grinned when he'd handed back the paper. "One barrel, one fib. Could be worse. Could be war."

Nathaniel hadn't laughed then, and he didn't laugh now.

He reached for a clean scrap of parchment and scrawled a line in his sharpest hand:

You gave me something honest. I risked it like a thief.

He folded the note, but didn't seal it.

From below, a burst of laughter drifted up from the inn's taproom...men trading barbs and bitter tales over ale. He thought of Miles again, how easily his friend wore risk like a second coat. How he never looked back.

But Nathaniel did. And that was the difference.

He tucked the note into his coat pocket alongside the ledger Miles had once suggested might fetch more than cider in the right company.

"Burn it or bury it," Miles had said. "But if you show it to her, do it clean."

Nathaniel stood, looped his mother's book with its leather tie, and cinched his coat. He looked to the pale windowpane. A chill hung in the air, thick with the scent of apples gone soft in cellars.

Outside, the bell at St. Anne's tolled midday. It was time.

He stepped out, the unsealed letter in his pocket, and headed toward the one person who had every right to send him packing.

But if she didn't...

If she let him stay...

He would earn it. Graft by graft. Even if it drew blood.

Hours later, Elizabeth was kneeling beneath the Old Widow tree with a blade in her palm and thorn-twine tucked in her apron when she heard the crunch of boots behind her.

She didn't look up. "Wrong day for pleasantries, Mr. Carter," she said, the words flat as the blade she held.

"I'm not here for pleasantries," Nathaniel replied.

Elizabeth stood slowly, brushing damp soil from her skirts, her gaze fixed on the scarred bark of the tree rather than him.

"Then what? Another offer for me to chew on? Or another smile meant to soften my temper?"

"No offers. No smiles," he said. "Just the truth."

She crossed her arms. "Dangerous habit for a merchant."

"Dangerous habit for a liar."

That earned him a glance.

He stepped into the broken shade beneath the tree, coat unbuttoned, collar askew. Rain clung to the brim of his hat, but he didn't remove it. He looked like a man who had worn pride too long and now stood without it.

"I forged the shipping papers," he said. "To get the barrel out."

The orchard seemed to hold its breath as her mouth dropped open.

"I didn't forge the cider," he went on. "That was yours. Yours in method, in mastery, in name. But I slipped it through customs as a colonial sample, agricultural goods not for sale. It might pass. Or it might come back on me."

Her mouth was a hard line. She said nothing.

"I used my contact in Ledbury, Miles Hardwick. He's dealt with these things before."

"I'm not interested in your accomplice."

"He wasn't an accomplice," Nathaniel said. "Just... a man with quicker hands than mine and less to lose."

"And yet it's my orchard in the barrel," she said. "My soil. My risk."

"I know," he said.

He reached into his coat and held out the folded paper.

She took it, hesitated only a moment, and opened it.

You gave me something honest. I risked it like a thief. I'm sorry.

A gust stirred the branches above them. The rain began again, light but steady.

She looked up at him. "I don't forgive this."

"I don't expect you to."

"But I don't throw you out either," she said.

That startled something in him, and he didn't hide it.

"You said you'd take the punishment," she added. "That includes my silence. My scrutiny. And my choice of when—if—I trust you again."

"I'll take it," he said quickly.

Her voice softened. "This orchard holds more than barrels and trees. You saw that, didn't you?"

He nodded. "I did."

She glanced toward the stillroom slope, where the roof peaked above the rise. "Phoebe's been tracing graft lines in the ledger. She knows them better than John."

Nathaniel blinked. "I believe it."

"She watches everything," Elizabeth said. "And she remembers."

"I know," he said quietly. "She asked me if trees could remember, too."

Elizabeth looked back to the Old Widow. "They do. They remember what they survive."

The wind pulled at her apron strings. Her face was unreadable. "She deserves better than a man in our lives who gambles what isn't his."

"Then I'll earn the right to stay. Even if it means starting at the root."

"You tangled yourself into the branches, Mr. Carter. And you did it with thorns."

"I'll bleed for it."

By the time Nathaniel reached the barrelhouse, the sky had gone pewter-gray, and thunder grumbled like a pensioner with sore knees.

He ducked under the lintel just as the first cold drops began to fall. Inside, the air was thick with tannin and wood, as if the beams themselves had soaked in a century's worth of cider talk.

Barrels lined the walls in tidy stacks, chalk marks glinting faintly like ghost script. A small figure in the shadows was tugging at a crate...William, sleeves too long, face smudged with orchard dust.

"Mind your back, lad," John Thatcher called without turning. "Don't wrench yourself over half a dozen bottles."

William huffed. "I wasn't..."

"You were," John said, setting down his mallet. "Go help George with the strainers. And tell him not to boil the cloths this time; we need 'em thick."

William's boots thumped as he scampered off.

John finally turned, wiping his hands on his apron. "You're a day late to start fixing things, Carter."

Nathaniel hung his coat on the hook by the door, rainwater dripping to the stone floor. "Better late than silent."

John gave him a look. "She told me about your conversation."

"Everything?"

"The papers. The barrel. Your name on the ledger. All of it." John studied him in the dim light. "Well. Either you're honest now or stupid."

"Both," Nathaniel said.

John moved to the nearest barrel, thumbed the chalk line, then took up the hammer. "Men like your friend in Ledbury...what's his name? Miles?"

Nathaniel stilled. "Yes."

John spat in the dirt. "I've met his kind. Slippery as pressed pulp. Always two pints ahead of regret."

"I didn't follow his lead," Nathaniel said. "I asked his help. That's different."

"Not different enough, if it puts her orchard on the line."

"I didn't name her. I didn't name the estate."

"You named yourself," John said. "That's enough to tie the knot if the wrong man tugs the rope."

Nathaniel leaned against the barrel rim, the chill of it seeping through his shirt. "I'm not here to justify it. I'm here to stay. If I'm allowed."

John lifted the mallet and drove it into the bung. "Then act like it."

"I'm trying."

"Try harder," John said, wiping froth from the rim with his thumb.

Nathaniel glanced at the shelves of applewood staves, at the chipped tally board Phoebe had scrawled on last week with careful letters, her face set with the kind of intent no child should have to wear.

"She asked me once if trees could remember," Nathaniel said. "Phoebe, I mean."

John looked up.

"I didn't know how to answer," Nathaniel added. "But I'd like to learn."

John raised a brow. "Learn what, exactly?"

"How to scent a yield," Nathaniel said. "How to read tannin before it's writ. How not to waste what's been weathered."

John gave a grunt that might've been either approval or gas. "Come earlier. Before first light," he said. "No scent on your skin. No chatter in your head."

"No perfume," Nathaniel said dryly. "Got it."

"You're not forgiven," John added. "You're tolerated. There's a difference."

"I'll take it."

John rapped the barrel shut, then turned toward the darker corner, where more casks stood like sentinels in the gloom. "She's inked herself into this orchard," he muttered. "Don't think you'll blot her out."

"I don't want to," Nathaniel said. "I just want to be in the margin."

John said nothing more.

Rain drummed harder overhead, and the men stood quiet beneath the beams, among apples pressed into ghosts and promises not yet broken.

***

Elizabeth stood where the path narrowed between two old Foxwhelps, the soaked hem of her skirt heavy with orchard mud. Rain dripped steadily from the lower branches, darkening the earth into clay, but she didn't move. She hadn't moved since she heard his footsteps on the slope minutes ago.

Nathaniel slowed as he reached her, careful not to crowd.

"I wasn't sure you'd come," she said, not looking at him.

"You knew I would."

She didn't deny it.

The orchard breathed around them...wet bark, crushed moss, the faint yeasty ghost of ferment from the nearby press. Thunder muttered from across the valley, and far off, the church bell tolled its slow quarter chime.

Elizabeth's fingers closed around the pruning knife at her sash, feeling the worn grain of its handle. "I read your ledger," she said at last. "The one with the shipping projections. Every line looked like a row you meant to plant."

Nathaniel's gaze didn't waver. "I was trying to grow something that might bear fruit... somewhere I hadn't already blighted the soil."

"And you thought this orchard was your second chance?" When he didn't respond, she added, "You still do."

He sighed. "If you want me to walk away right now, I can. But I still think I can help both of us."

She turned toward him now, eyes unreadable in the fading light. "And if it costs me everything?"

His throat tightened. "Then I was never worthy of it. Or of you."

"You lied," she accused. "You didn't ask. You used me."

"I did," he admitted. "I took what wasn't offered. And I'll spend the rest of my life trying to give it back."

She studied him: wind-rough hair, jaw shadowed with rain, collar slightly askew from his run uphill. "I don't forgive men who use my trees without asking," she said.

He nodded once, solemn. "I know."

A gust of wind shook droplets from the high boughs above, pattering like coins into the grass.

Then softly, almost unwillingly, she said, "But I admit, you didn't use the trees."

He held his breath. Could it be she wasn't going to throw him out?

"You asked about every graft. You listened. You knelt to check for root rot when John wouldn't stoop. You remembered the name of my father's oldest tree." Her voice was thin and strange. "You used me, Nathaniel. Not the orchard."

He stepped closer, slow, careful. "And that's worse."

"Perhaps," she said. "Because I gave you nothing. And you still made it matter."

A beat passed. Then another.

"I still want to map the graft lines," he said. "Not for your investor. For history. For your legacy." He gestured around them.

She said nothing, but her glance shifted briefly down the path toward the stillroom, where lamplight flickered faintly behind the shutters. "Phoebe asked you if trees remember? I asked her, last winter, if she knew what she'd inherit. She didn't answer then. But I think she knows now."

Nathaniel swallowed. "She deserves something worth keeping."

"I won't forget what you did. But I might, with time, remember what you're still willing to do." Elizabeth hesitated. Then finally, quietly, she reached for his hand.

His fingers curled into hers like they'd always known how.

Elizabeth's hand tightened almost imperceptibly, as though she meant to pull away and changed her mind at the last instant.

"There's something I've never told anyone," she said at last, voice scarcely louder than the wind through the Foxwhelps.

Nathaniel waited, the rain pattering like a thousand slow clocks around them.

"When the fever took my sister," she began, eyes fixed on the dripping grass, "I kept hearing her voice after. Not in dreams—awake. I would turn, certain she was behind me, certain I'd left her somewhere. Even now, some nights, I'm afraid that if I stop working, if I let the house fall quiet, I'll hear her calling again and realise I've lost her twice."

The confession hung in the wet air, raw and shivering.

Nathaniel squeezed her hand, careful as if holding a fresh graft. "You haven't lost her. Memory isn't absence."

"Memory isn't enough," Elizabeth whispered. "Not when you're the one left."

He drew a slow breath. "Then let me help you keep the living safe. Phoebe, William, John, and you. I'll guard what breathes, not to own it, but because I know what it is to lose and be left looking over your shoulder."

Her gaze flicked to him, the stormlight silvering her lashes. "You'd do that?"

"Until the orchard forgets my name," he said, and the words carried no claim, only quiet promise.

For a heartbeat the only sound was the soft rush of rain through the branches, as if the trees themselves approved the vow.

They stood that way beneath the rain-dark leaves of the Foxwhelps, the world dimming by inches, wind in the trees, mud on their boots, her hand in his.

***

By the time Nathaniel reached the stillroom door, his boots were soaked through, and the edge of his coat dripped cider-mud onto the flagstones. A low lantern flickered inside. He paused before knocking.

Through the ripple of wet glass, he saw Phoebe.

She was seated on a small stool beside the drying shelf, a half-folded page balanced on her knee. Her walking stick rested against the counter. A single beeswax taper lit her from one side, turning her sharp little profile into shadow and glint.

She didn't look up. Nathaniel opened the door softly.

"You're late," she said, not turning.

"I've had a day of it."

"You look it." She sniffed. "You smell like you fell in a barrel."

He smiled faintly. "Wouldn't be the first time."

Phoebe lifted the page from her lap and held it out without rising. "You left this under the Foxwhelp ledger."

Nathaniel took it. His own notes: sketches of the western slope, graft lines traced in charcoal, scrawled alongside guesses about soil depth and tree age. "Thank you."

"She knew you were drawing maps. She let you keep doing it anyway."

He nodded. "I know."

"She's not the forgiving sort," Phoebe added.

"I know that too."

Phoebe finally looked at him, steady, unwavering, clever beyond her years. Her smallpox scars were soft in the candlelight. "She doesn't tell me everything," she said. "But I see more than she thinks."

"I suspect you do."

Phoebe tapped her finger once on the parchment in his hand. "Just make sure if you're writing our orchard down, you get the names right. The ones that matter."

Nathaniel blinked. "Which names?"

She pointed to a margin where he'd written "*Old Widow?*" beside an unlabeled rootstock sketch.

"That's *not* the Old Widow," she said. "That one's mine. She grafted it the spring I arrived. It didn't take for a year. But it's holding now."

He stared at her, something in his chest hitching. "You've got your own tree?"

She shrugged. "Not many girls do."

"I think that should be in the map," he said.

Phoebe offered a tight nod and returned her attention to a drying rack of pressed blossoms.

Nathaniel stepped back into the night. The door clicked shut behind him.

Across the slope, the orchard whispered with wind and rain. The candle still burned in the stillroom, casting Phoebe's shadow in long lines across the wall: slim, crooked, and unmoving.

He thought of Elizabeth's voice beneath the Foxwhelps, of the grief she had carried like a hidden root, and felt the weight of his own promise settle deeper than any ledger line.

This, he realised, was the work worth guarding: not barrels or grafts, but the fragile chorus of those who remained.

She was part of the orchard now. And he would not risk her again.

Miles's voice rose unbidden in his memory: casual, charming, dangerous: *One barrel, Carter. One name. You want your legacy back? Play the Crown like they play us.*

He had. And now he would spend the rest of the season untangling it.

Nathaniel looked out across the orchard one last time before turning for the dark path back to the inn.

No more lies. No more sleights.

Only the memory of her confession, and the vow he'd made in answer, would keep him steady when the next storm came.

From now on, only truth. And graft by graft, he would earn the right to stay.

Even if it drew blood.

CHAPTER SIXTEEN

THE SAPLING

E lizabeth crouched beneath the sweeping shadow of the Old Widow tree, fingers tucked into the folds of her apron to find the small bone-handled knife she always used for spring clefts. The grass was still damp from dawn, the air heavy with the scent of lichen and old bark. She could feel the way the earth held moisture..soft, willing, good for taking root.

Behind her, Nathaniel stood silent, boots planted respectfully beyond the dripline. He held the wax bundle and linen strips as she'd asked, one in each hand like ceremonial offerings. The way he stood, quiet and hatless, made it feel less like orchard work and more like a rite.

She didn't look at him as she cleared the rootstock, brushing away a tuft of moss with her thumb. "Didn't expect you to be on time."

"I didn't want to miss it," he said softly. "You don't graft with just anyone."

Elizabeth gave a faint, amused snort. "No, I suppose I don't."

She reached for the scion branch. It was slender but straight, trimmed the evening before from a variety she'd been nursing along the east wall: a stubborn Kingston crossbreed with tight buds and rich promise. She held it up, weighing the cut, then met Nathaniel's eye.

"You think it's ready?"

He stepped closer, eyes on the wood, not her. "It's strong through the cambium. Clean taper. If it were mine, I'd risk it."

"It's not yours."

"Not yet." That earned him a stern glance.

Elizabeth turned back to the tree. "Hold the wax packet ready. You'll see it blister once the sap starts to rise. That's the moment."

"I know that one." His voice was gentle, without challenge. "You taught me."

The bark of the Old Widow creaked faintly as she braced her hand against the trunk. She remembered the first time she'd been allowed to cleft-graft alone, age sixteen, sweating through a homespun shift, her father watching with arms crossed, withholding praise until the buds took. This tree had survived frost, locusts, and canker. It had no business still bearing. And yet...

She sliced the rootstock with care. The sound was sharp, a wet peel, the wood parting just enough to invite the scion in. Nathaniel didn't speak as she worked. He offered the tools only when she reached, his hands steady and warm beside hers.

As she slid the graft into place and tied the linen band tight around the join, her fingers brushed his.

Neither of them moved.

A robin chirped overhead, absurdly loud.

Elizabeth stepped back first, wiping her palms on her skirts. "The cut's true."

Nathaniel looked down at the little grafted stem, now swaddled like a wounded limb. "And the season's forgiving."

She hesitated, then reached for his hand. She found herself absurdly calmed by the rough brush of her fingers over his, threading them together like twine through the cleft.

Nathaniel didn't let go of her hand, not even when she let out a breath and turned slightly, as if half-ashamed to be the one who'd reached first.

"Phoebe'll want to see this tomorrow," Elizabeth murmured, glancing back at the graft. "She's been tracing graft lines into her copybook like they're spells."

He smiled. "Then I'll make sure it holds."

A flicker of thought crossed his mind, unspoken but sharp. Miles would call this foolish...too slow, too sentimental. He'd say you don't linger on roots when the ship's already leaking. But Nathaniel wasn't interested in the kind of legacy Miles admired anymore.

The graft was done. The wax sealed. The linen wrap tucked smooth. And still they stayed.

The orchard stretched quiet around them, hushed in that sun-warmed way of late morning when everything seemed to hold its breath. A breeze rattled through the high branches. The air smelled of sap and new leaves and something else he couldn't name.

"I remember," Nathaniel said after a moment, "my mother's first pear tree."

Elizabeth didn't speak, but her eyes flicked up to his.

He smiled—not the cocky smile, not the one he used for tavern lies and customs agents—but the one that came without defense. "She grafted it against my father's advice. He said the wood was too wet, the season too short. But she swore the tree had stubbornness in it. Said it reminded her of a mule she once owned. Or married."

Elizabeth huffed, amused despite herself.

"It took," Nathaniel continued, his thumb brushing gently across hers. "But crooked. The graft grew sideways. Bloomed late. Bore maybe three pears the first year, all lopsided and thick-skinned."

"Did she cut it down?" Elizabeth asked, voice quieter now.

"No. She baked them. Claimed ugly fruit held better against fire."

Elizabeth smiled.

"She said," Nathaniel added, mimicking his mother's drawl, "'Pretty things lie about what they're made of. But anything ugly that still grows...that's got truth in it.'"

Elizabeth turned fully toward him, her shawl slipping slightly off one shoulder. He reached up and fixed it slowly, as if any sudden movement might break the spell. Her breath caught when his knuckles grazed her collarbone. She didn't step back, and neither did he.

"And are you ugly fruit, Mr. Carter?" She tilted her chin. "I fear you are too comely for such a label."

"I think I'm still fire-toughening," he murmured with a blush.

She gave a soft laugh, and then his mouth was on hers.

This kiss wasn't like the one beneath the Bloody Turk. That one had been surprise and ache. This one burned slow, deep, rooted in her heart. His hands settled low on her waist; hers curled into the collar of his coat. He angled his head and deepened it, and she answered with a sound from the back of her throat that nearly undid him.

They kissed like the orchard didn't matter, like the graft hadn't been sealed, like the season would never end.

And when she finally broke the kiss, her lips still brushing his, she didn't move far. "Don't think this means I trust you," she whispered.

"I wouldn't dream of it."

"But you can stay."

His eyes darkened. "How long?"

She lifted one hand, trailed a finger down the lapel of his coat. "As long as you know when to stop."

"Then I'll stay very carefully." He bent his forehead to hers.

Elizabeth didn't answer, but her hand remained against his chest. The trees shifted overhead. And beneath the old boughs of the Widow tree, where sap ran new through healing wood, neither of them moved for a long time.

***

Later, Elizabeth leaned back on her palms, tilting her face toward the light. The graft behind them glistened faintly with fresh wax, a blackened seal snug at the join like a secret. The bees had returned to their low murmuring in the nettles. A bird scolded them from a nearby branch.

Nathaniel broke the silence first. "I've never planted anything with someone else before." He plucked a blade of grass, twisted it once, then let it fall. "Always seemed too... personal."

Elizabeth raised an eyebrow without turning. "Then don't botch it."

A beat, and he laughed, a low, warm sound that settled deep in her ribs and tickled her undercarriage. "Noted."

They sat that way for a moment longer, the hum of summer crawling slow around them. Elizabeth glanced sideways at his profile—creased at the brow, shadowed by sun. Not so careful now. Not so guarded.

He said, quieter, "Did you ever think of having children?"

It wasn't a question she'd expected, but she didn't flinch. "Once," she said. "Twice, maybe. But I thought of those thoughts like harvests. Some years give. Some don't." She plucked a stem of sorrel, rolled it between her fingers. "The land didn't take kindly to hope in those days. And neither did the man I married."

Nathaniel was silent. Then, "He didn't want them?"

"Oh, he wanted heirs. Something to hand his name to." She shrugged, bitter-edged. "But he didn't want softness. And children are softness, for a long while."

Nathaniel looked down at his boots, then up again. "My mother lost two. Never named them. Just planted rosemary." He paused. "Said that way, the grief made something grow."

Elizabeth turned her head. His eyes met hers. "Do you want them?" she asked bluntly.

"I don't know," he said, after a long moment. "I think... if the place was right. If I could offer something more than a name."

Elizabeth studied his face. "It's not the land that decides. Or the name. It's the care."

He nodded.

Then she leaned in, and kissed him first this time.

It was slow, deliberate, a curve of her mouth over his that took her breath with it. She cupped his jaw. He pulled her closer...one arm slipping around her waist, the other anchoring him in the grass.

Her hand curled into the back of his shirt. His mouth opened against hers, answering the call she hadn't spoken aloud. They kissed again, and again, hungrier now, lips brushing, then claiming, teeth catching briefly on lower lips. The sun pressed warmth into her back. The world narrowed.

His palm skimmed the side of her ribs, thumb finding the curve of her stays. She gasped softly into his mouth, then broke the kiss just long enough to whisper, "Not here."

He stilled.

Then, forehead pressed to hers, breath ragged, he said, "Alright."

His hand moved back to her waist. "Not here," he repeated, softer, like a promise.

They stayed that way, entwined in grass and light and grafted hopes. Her hand remained against his chest, just over his heartbeat.

A ladybird landed on Nathaniel's shoulder.

Elizabeth spotted it mid-sentence and smiled despite herself. "Don't move."

He froze, hand half-raised. "Is it something venomous? English spiders? Colonial spies?"

She leaned in and gently brushed the ladybird onto her fingertip. "No. Better. A sign of a good graft."

"Superstition?" he asked, eyebrows raised.

"Science," she replied primly. "Or so my grandmother claimed. Ladybirds only settle on trees that promise sweetness."

Nathaniel leaned closer, voice low. "Is that why you finally let me near this one? Sweetness?"

Elizabeth gave a dry laugh. "I was hoping for obedience."

He grinned. "Then you've clearly chosen the wrong man."

She rolled her eyes and let the ladybird climb a twig before flicking it gently skyward. It spun a lazy arc, wings flaring red against the deepening sky.

"I'll take the omen, though," she added more softly. "Phoebe would say it's the orchard blessing us. She's writing orchard omens into her copybook now...claims the last time she saw a ladybird, it crawled onto her inkpot and left a blot shaped like a heart."

Nathaniel smiled. "Then I suppose we ought to behave."

Elizabeth arched a brow. "That's not what she wrote in the margins."

A rustle behind them made her straighten.

William's voice rang out from somewhere near the north row: "Mistress Whitcombe? Someone nicked the barrel chalk again!"

Nathaniel startled and nearly tipped sideways into the sapling. Elizabeth swatted his shoulder, whispering, "Up! Up, you fool!"

They scrambled apart just in time for William to round the tree. He was a tangle of elbows and curiosity, face freckled, a smear of apple pulp across one cuff. He squinted at the scene before him: Elizabeth flushed, Nathaniel trying to look casual, the graft glistening between them.

William raised an eyebrow. "Everything alright?"

Elizabeth, too quickly: "Yes. Grafting."

Nathaniel, too cheerfully: "Just sealing the join."

William narrowed his eyes. "Well... don't seal yourselves into anything you'll regret." Then, with a shrug, he turned. "Barrel chalk, though. Gone again. Probably Miles's doing, he was nosing about earlier."

That stopped Nathaniel cold. "He was here?"

William nodded. "Just after breakfast. Said he was checking a delivery list. Pocketed an apple, too."

Nathaniel muttered something under his breath.

Elizabeth gave him a sharp look. "Should I worry?"

"Not unless he starts asking about saplings." Nathaniel's jaw was tight. "Miles is useful, when he wants to be. And careless, when he thinks no one's watching."

Elizabeth's gaze flicked toward the house. "Then I'll keep my watch sharp."

William had already vanished around the bend, humming tunelessly to himself.

Nathaniel sank back into the grass with a theatrical sigh.

"You nearly got us caught," Elizabeth said, swatting his arm again.

"I was seduced by sap and superstition."

She smirked. "That old American excuse."

Nathaniel grinned. "Speaking of American things, did I ever tell you there's a superstition back home that cider makes a man more agreeable in marriage?"

Elizabeth arched a brow. "Is that a proposal or a confession?"

"Depends," he said, reaching for her hand. "Have I been agreeable?"

She didn't answer with words. Just rested her palm in his.

They stood slowly, brushing off leaves, lint, and bits of orchard from their clothes. At the base of the Old Widow, the waxed graft caught the light.

Elizabeth pressed her fingers to it gently. "Let's see what you become," she murmured. "You seem to have volunteered to be a caretaker of my orchard, and I may regret it, but I can't help but appreciate what you've brought us."

"A caretaker," Nathaniel repeated. "I'm honored to be called such by you, and it's a title I bear with joy."

She smiled. Then, quietly, they walked back toward the house together. Two figures between rows, trailed by the scent of grafting wax, crushed sorrel, and something softer still. Something like beginning.

Up ahead, light spilled from the kitchen window. Through the wavering glass, the faint silhouette of Phoebe's bent head moved behind the curtain, half-shadow, half-sun. She was hunched over the table, quill in hand, the tip of her tongue poking out as she worked. Beside her sat an open page of graft diagrams, neat lines, careful inkblots, and what looked suspiciously like a tiny ladybird sketched in the margin.

Nathaniel paused by the door. Elizabeth reached first for the latch, then hesitated. "She's asking questions now...about bloodlines and inheritance. About what happens to an orchard when the last Whitcombe dies."

Nathaniel's voice was steady. "What did you tell her?"

"That rootstock isn't the same as fruit." She gave him a wry smile. "And that some things grow stronger when grafted across the old divisions."

Inside, Phoebe looked up from her copybook. Her eyes, so like Ruth's, and yet entirely her own, were bright with something she wasn't yet naming. She reached for her ink again and began shading in a new diagram, this time with two branches joining clean at a seam.

A sharp rap at the door cut across the quiet. Phoebe startled, her quill blotting the paper; William nearly dropped a jar.

Elizabeth crossed to the threshold and took the folded envelope from the post rider, her name etched in a clerk's neat hand. She broke the seal and scanned the single page. Her mouth tightened.

"From the solicitors?" Nathaniel asked.

"Yes." She read aloud, voice clipped. " 'Pending review of the late Whitcombe will, our office cannot yet determine lineal succession. We await confirmation of the colonial property register, presently delayed by the Crown Excise dispute. We will advise when records are released.' "

Phoebe frowned. "So... no answer?"

"No answer," Elizabeth said, folding the letter with deliberate care. "Only another delay."

William muttered, "They've had months."

Elizabeth set the page on the table, palm flat. "If the Crown ledger is the knot, I'll pull at another thread. My father's tithe accounts are still in the vestry. If the vicar kept the old orchard deeds, they'll prove what's ours without waiting for London to remember we exist." Her voice carried a quiet resolve that stilled the room.

Nathaniel watched her, saw the steel beneath the weariness, and felt the tug of it in his chest.

He drew a breath. "Elizabeth...when I first came, I thought the orchard was a way back to Philadelphia. Buyers, barrels, a tidy profit to make me respectable again."

Her eyes met his.

"But it isn't that any longer," he said. "The buyers can wait. What matters now is this place, and the people who keep it breathing. Phoebe. William. You."

A flush rose in her cheek, but she didn't look away.

"I want to guard what you've built," Nathaniel went on, softer. "Not to own it, not to hang my name on it, only to see it stand when the Crown ledger finally notices. That's the work worth doing."

For a moment the only sound was the small scratch of Phoebe's quill as she resumed shading the joined branches, as if to seal his vow in ink.

William passed behind her, carrying a stack of emptied jars in his arms and muttering about how no one ever returned the chalk with the lid on.

Nathaniel leaned closer to Elizabeth. "He'll make a fine orchard man, that one."

Elizabeth arched a brow. "If he lives long enough."

"Or if Miles doesn't lure him off to be a courier smuggler first."

She gave a tired, fond laugh. "Let's not borrow mischief. There's enough to tend already."

A quiet settled again.

At the door he paused, his brow to hers, heat gathering where they almost touched. "Let me carry the heavy things," he said, reaching for the latch. "Not the truths," she answered...and opened the latch herself.

CHAPTER SEVENTEEN

THE INK AND THE WOUND

The light through the window was watery and gray, the kind that made dust look like fog and thoughts sit heavy. Nathaniel stood by the hearth with one boot unlaced, the other forgotten halfway on, staring at the red wax seal he'd broken with a shaking thumb.

The courier had arrived at dawn, paid to ride straight from Bristol, mud-splashed and stone-faced, with no time for tea. The letter had no sender's name, just a sigil in the wax he recognized: an old Bristol contact who owed him honesty, if not hope.

He read the lines once. Then twice.

Four seized by dawn. Smugglers in irons. Two orchards burned under seizure protocols. Cider marked with non-native stamps now suspect. Colonial-linked shipments flagged. Widow-run holdings seen as prime vulnerabilities. The new orders from London read like a noose.

Nathaniel closed his eyes and swallowed hard.

He had gambled on a single barrel. One hand-lettered "W" looping across wax and wood. He had called it proof, not knowing the price.

"She sent one barrel," he muttered. "And I sent the Crown an invitation."

The floor creaked beneath his weight as he shifted, knees locked. Outside, the market square murmured to life, vendors barking early prices, the clatter of carts hitting cobblestones. Somewhere out in the yard, a boy's voice hollered about a chicken loose near the woodpile: William, likely, loud enough to stir the roosters. But here, in the hush of the room, only the crackle of the fire answered.

He dropped the letter onto the chair beside him. It curled at the edges like scorched bark.

On the table sat his mother's old cultivar book. Elizabeth's folded note rested inside the front flap, creased now from rereading, soft at the corners where his thumb had lingered.

He thought of the orchard. Of the graft beneath the Old Widow tree, still tender. Of Elizabeth's hands, stained with wax and ash. Of her lips, parted against his just two nights before, fierce with want and edged with restraint.

And behind her, the girl who traced grafts in pencil, speaking little and seeing too much. He remembered how she'd tucked a scrap of paper into the ledger the day before: a sketch of the Old Widow, the new scion labeled with looping letters: Hope, maybe.

There was more than cider at stake. More than land. He looked again at the line in the letter, widow-run holdings, underlined twice in the margin. "She's not a liability," he said aloud, quietly. "She's the reason it's worth anything at all."

And it wasn't just her. There was a girl in that house with ink-stained hands and questions about whether trees could remember. The Crown wouldn't see her, but he did.

The Crown wanted barrels and names. And Elizabeth had given him both.

The fire popped behind him, low and bitter.

He ran a hand through his hair and sat hard on the edge of the bed. No time for panic. Just movement and action.

And risk.

A second slip of paper had come folded inside the Bristol letter: blue clerk's stock, thin as onionskin. He hadn't noticed it until it slid free and landed by his boot. The seal was plain; the hand was not.

Wainscott.

Nathaniel unfolded it and read the single sentence twice.

In light of London's recent seizures, the Excise Office advances its Herefordshire inspection to three days from receipt.

Three. Not five. Not a gentleman's courtesy. A blade.

He exhaled through his teeth, slow and controlled. They'd have a steward counting staves and sniffing wax before week's end, with questions sharpened by panic and orders sharpened by fear. If there was any mercy, it would not be in ink.

"Three days," he said to the empty room. "Then they walk her rows."

He folded the notice and tucked it with the Bristol report. The math in his head shifted with a click: routes closed, barrels still cooling, grafts still tender, a widow expected to answer for a dead man's ledger.

***

The air inside the stillroom was thick with the scent of damp wood and long-dried apples, the kind of warmth that settled in the grain of the beams and creaked when no one was moving. Nathaniel sat at the long bench beneath the north window, sleeves rolled, ledger open, and a contract draft resting beside it, unsigned.

He stared at the page like it might reprimand him.

Everything was ready. Ink, wax, the legal wording. The transport risk had been weighed, mapped out to the coin. He'd even copied the botanical notes from Elizabeth's ledger into neat, investor-worthy language. The letter from R.H. had practically gleamed with anticipation: *Exceptional. Untamed. Plantable legacy. Confirm sapling shipment.*

He reached for the quill, then stopped.

Instead of signing, he drew a clean sheet of foolscap from beneath the ledger. The paper crackled...too fine for lies. He dipped the quill and began slowly, deliberately.

Conditions have changed. Saplings postponed.

His grip tightened.

The Whitcombe line is not to be touched without her consent.

No flattery. No plea. No mention of the forged barrel tag or how close the Excise man had come to lifting it. And nothing—not yet—about the other letter in his coat pocket demanding debt repayment. That truth still weighed too close to bone.

He paused.

Miles would've laughed at this..,called it cowardice, or worse. *"You've got the wood, the tools, the shipping name. Just cut clean and run it. If she won't sell you the graft, take the branch."*

Nathaniel set his jaw.

Miles could say such things...Miles, who once bartered an entire shipment's safety for a favor from a port customs man's mistress and hadn't blinked when the barrels arrived soaked and shrunken from heat. Charm didn't root legacy. It burned it.

This orchard wasn't a bargain to be won. It was hers. And lately, it felt like it belonged to more than her alone.

He looked toward the stillroom's far wall, where Phoebe's makeshift study corner had been set up: half a bench, a sloped writing board, and a scattering of copied graft diagrams. Her inkwell still held flecks of dried violet. A sheet of paper rested open, forgotten. On it, he could just make out a young apple tree, roots drawn like a heart.

He signed the letter without further pause.

—*N. Carter*

Caretaker.

The word had settled into him. Not agent. Not claimant. Not thief. Caretaker.

He hesitated, then turned the page and added a second line, deliberate as a signature carved in sapwood:

Henceforth your dealings are with me alone. Any levy, seizure, or prosecution arising from prior consignments is to be laid under my name, not Mistress Whitcombe's.

There. It cost him nothing but ink and possibly everything else. Fines. Irons. A transport ban. But if the Crown wanted a neck to fit its collar, it would not be hers.

He sanded the line and watched the grains drink the wet shine away.

Nathaniel folded the page, sealed it with wax, and pressed the apple-blossom imprint from his mother's old ring into the warm red circle. Then he picked up the original contract, grand projections, tidy margins, calculated freight costs, and slid it into the ash bucket beneath the bench.

He didn't burn it, but he buried it all the same.

He crossed the yard at a trot and found her on the stillroom step, sleeves rolled, hair pinned high, a curl gone free against her temple. She looked up, catching the set of his jaw before he spoke.

"What now?" she asked, already braced.

He held out the blue slip. "Wainscott. They've advanced the inspection. Three days."

Her gaze flicked over the line; her mouth didn't move. "Of course they have."

He kept his voice even. "I've written Philadelphia. No saplings. No contracts. The next letters say this plainly: they deal with me, not with you. If the Crown or any buyer wants a name to hang trouble on, it will be mine."

"That's not how the law reads," she said. "They'll hang trouble where it sticks."

"Let them try," he answered. "I'll step in front first."

Wind lifted the edge of her apron. Behind her, Phoebe's quill scratched faintly, a steady little heartbeat in ink.

"Why?" Elizabeth asked. Not sharp. Not soft.

"Because I came for buyers," he said, "and I found something worth more than coin. I'll take the fines. I'll take the risk of irons if it comes to that. I'll stand between the steward and your door. Not for profit. For you. For her." He tipped his head toward the window where the girl's shadow moved. "For this orchard that keeps choosing to live."

A long breath moved through her. "Three days," she said.

"Three," he echoed.

"Then we use all of them," she said. "Clean ledgers. Honest counts. No gaps to give them rope."

"Aye."

She nodded once. "Go, then. Tell John. And bring me the old wax...if the steward doubts our seals, he can watch me pour them myself."

He almost reached for her hand. Instead he bowed the smallest fraction and turned back into the yard at a run.

***

The ridge was quiet at dusk, save for the crunch of his boots over half-frozen turf. Nathaniel stood where the orchard dropped off into a shallow vale, letter in hand, its edges curled from the ride and the pocket's heat.

He hadn't meant to read it here. But when the boy from Worcester handed it over, silent but for the rustle of mail and the twitch of his outstretched hand, Nathaniel had walked until the house was a silhouette behind trees.

Now, wind hissed through stripped branches as he unfolded the page.

Sir, the debt long-held under the Carter name has been purchased by Fenwick & Grimley of Threadneedle Street. Terms unchanged. Payment required within thirty days or land will be seized and auctioned under default clause. No extensions, no indulgence. This is final.

He read it again.

The paper weighed less than an apple blossom, and carried more threat than any storm.

Threadneedle Street. That wasn't colonial. That was Crown-tied and street-savvy and utterly without mercy. Fenwick & Grimley didn't extend terms. They carved legacies cleanly and sold the bones.

Their orchard in Virginia...the ridge where his mother had planted her last tree before the fever took her, the same soil she'd named as dowry in a faded church book, which he'd bought back as soon as he'd been able to...was no longer his in principle. Only in days.

He slid the letter into the inside pocket of his coat, feeling its edge like a blade.

The sun had dropped low. Across the orchard, shadows stretched long between bare rows. The young graft beneath the Old Widow tree lay somewhere in that silence, wax still fresh, its join still uncertain.

He should have told Elizabeth. About the debt. About the Philadelphia sponsor. About how close he'd come to turning her orchard into a ghost ledger for smuggled saplings.

But what would that make him? Another man who came with promises and left her with consequences?

Miles would say: Tell her later. Or don't. Just get what you came for. Miles, who once offered to "smooth" a customs delay by threatening a clerk's mistress with exposure—and had smiled when the bribe worked faster than truth.

But Nathaniel wasn't that man, not anymore.

Not since Phoebe had stared him down over a cider barrel and said, "You here to take notes or take something?"

Not since Elizabeth had placed her hand in his and said nothing at all...and it had meant everything.

He drew his coat tighter. *Let Miles take the shortcuts. Let Grimley tally his debts.*

He was here. He'd made his choice. And he wasn't leaving without planting something better than what he came for.

The cider barn creaked around him, ribs of oak groaning as the wind pressed in from the north. Nathaniel lit only one lantern, setting it on the low workbench. Its glow reached no farther than the straw-laden floor and the rows of dormant barrels hunched like sentinels in the dark.

Nathaniel crossed to the potted Old Widow sapling near the rear wall. Beside it, the new graft. Wax-tight. Linen-bound. No darkening at the cleft.

Still, he crouched and touched the edge with a fingertip: cool, firm, unsplit.

But he'd seen grafts like this before: ones that held beautifully through one season, then cracked open at the first hard freeze. It wasn't the knife that undid them. It was the silence afterward. The forgetting. "Some wounds seal fast," he murmured, "but not clean."

The lantern crackled behind him. The air smelled of straw, burnt sugar, and pressed bark.

He stood and moved to the workbench, brushing aside curlings of applewood. His satchel lay open beside the ledger. He took out a square of parchment, dipped the quill, and began a new letter.

Bowman—

Bowman— Crown pressure's tightening and the inspection has been advanced to three days. Saplings must wait. Seizures hit Worcester. Barrel routes unsafe. Hold back publication. Spring, if I survive it, will yield better stock.

His hand hesitated, ink beading.

He thought of Miles again: leaning against a post in the Ledbury inn weeks earlier, grinning like the devil had loaned him teeth.

"You could run this quiet," Miles had said. "Ship under your own name. Blame the orchard when it's seized: say the widow was ignorant. Nobody questions a man with a writ and a white cravat."

Nathaniel hadn't answered then. He did now.

He wrote:

If the line survives, it will be by care, not cunning.

Then added:

I'll owe you freight come April. But don't count me dead yet.

He signed it:

—N. Carter

Caretaker.

A pause.

Then, as if summoned by some deeper need, he removed the sealing knife from its sleeve. Its blade, dull from orchard work, still caught the light along one worn edge.

He meant to tap the wax candle stub. Instead, he caught his thumb.

Just a brief, shallow nick. But the blood welled up fast and round. One bead fell before he could stop it, dark red on cream paper, soaking into the word line.

Quickly, he folded the letter with the stain intact, pressed the warm wax seal into place with his mother's apple-blossom ring, and let the blood dry as ink beneath.

Then he sat, exhaling slowly. The barn was quiet. The trees outside stirred but did not answer.

He looked toward the corner shelf where Phoebe's small cloth parcel still sat, wrapped around a leather-bound copybook. She had forgotten it yesterday while sketching barrel fastenings. Her diagrams were careful. Precise. One leaf showed graft joints, another the curl of a fruiting spur, and one, near the back, bore the pale smudge of her thumbprint in ash. He remembered her saying, "If a tree remembers where it was cut, maybe it also remembers who helped it grow back."

Legacy didn't come cheap. It didn't come fast. And it didn't come from men like Miles. Nathaniel leaned back, staring at the graft through the half-light.

And wondering how much more this orchard would make him bleed.

CHAPTER EIGHTEEN

ROT AND BLOOM

T he smoke began low, like breath beneath earth.

Elizabeth stood at the edge of the north row, pruning knife clenched in one hand, torch in the other. Her boots were caked in mud from the morning's inspection. The hem of her outer petticoat, already dark with ash, stirred faintly in the wind that rolled down from the hilltop, carrying the scent of rot.

The aphids had bloomed: white and woolly across bark seams like mildew stitched by ghosts. Several trees had already begun to ooze from beneath their graft lines. One, nearest the path, had split outright, cracked at the base as if it had died trying to hold itself upright.

They could not be saved.

She thought of Phoebe's face that morning, standing barefoot on the stool in the stillroom to copy down rootstock names. The girl had traced each curve of the grafting chart with the reverence of a prayer. "Do they feel it when they split?" she'd asked, half-whisper. Elizabeth hadn't known how to answer. Only that sometimes they did.

And William had hovered nearby with his questions about tinder and smoke. She'd sent him up to the cottage with firm instructions: *You're brave, but not fireproof.*

"Clear the ground," she said now to the two older boys from the village. "Branches, undergrowth, anything that'll feed the blaze."

John Thatcher approached behind her, jaw clenched, his chalk-streaked hands balled into fists. "We could wait another day," he offered. "Try the lime wash again."

She didn't look at him. "That tree was my father's."

Silence. Then he stepped back.

Elizabeth struck the flint against the iron bracket three times before the pitch-soaked torch cloth caught. The resin hissed, then flared: a small, brutal light. She lifted it high. The fire painted her hand in gold and shadow.

"Miss?" one of the boys said, uncertain.

But she didn't answer, simply walked forward, one deliberate step after another, into the row that had once been her inheritance and was now her shame.

Halfway to the center, someone fell into step beside her. Nathaniel.

He didn't speak, but he matched her stride, his coat dusted with wood ash and the faint damp of afternoon mist. In one hand he carried a bucket of water, sloshing slightly. His other hand hovered near hers, but didn't touch.

She felt his presence like heat.

When they reached the first tree, she lowered the torch, let it kiss the base of the brush pile she'd arranged. The leaves crackled, hissed, and caught. Flames jumped like startled birds.

Another pile. Another tree. Another strike of fire.

"Why now?" Nathaniel said quietly. "You could have waited. Could've tried another field."

"Because they're all watching," she said. "And they want me to flinch."

She turned toward the next tree, the torch blazing brighter now. "If I burn my own rot, there's less left for them to take."

Wind rose, smoke curled, and a branch snapped somewhere in the flames with a noise like a closing jaw. The boys backed up. John crossed himself. Elizabeth didn't.

She moved to the last tree, the one closest to the stone wall. Its trunk bore a faint line of graft wax still visible: her father's work, she thought. It had always leaned slightly, like it wanted to grow somewhere else.

She pressed the torch to its roots. The flames answered.

When she turned to move back, the smoke stung her eyes and made her cough once, dry. Nathaniel caught her elbow before she stumbled.

"I'm fine," she said, not pulling away.

"I didn't ask," he said softly.

They stood together then, watching the orchard burn—not to ash, not yet, but to a blackened future. The air was sharp with the scent of wet bark, the sweetness of spoiled fruit, and something old and bitter beneath it all.

"Your boots are ruined," she said finally, staring down.

He gave a low, dry laugh. "First casualty of war."

She handed him the torch. "You want to help?"

He dipped it in the bucket, dousing the flame with a hiss. "Always."

Elizabeth nodded once. Then turned toward the rising smoke.

Some rows bloom, others rot. And still we plant again.

She said nothing more. But she thought of a small girl in the still-room, fingers ink-stained, copying graft charts with quiet devotion. Of a boy too young for pruning, too proud to stay out of danger's reach. And of a man who had once followed shortcuts, and now chose to follow her instead.

The first rumble was distant—a low shudder in the bones of the sky—but by the time Elizabeth reached the edge of the lower orchard, the heavens had split.

Rain fell in sheets. Not the gentle, cleansing kind, but a pounding deluge that flattened ash piles, muddied the footpaths, and sent the boys fleeing toward the village sheds with shouts lost to wind. She stayed until the last flame hissed out beneath the downpour, shoulders soaked and shawl clinging to her arms like wet bark.

"Nathaniel!" she called into the grey blur.

"I'm here." His voice came from behind, and then his hand—a firm grip on her elbow, guiding her gently but without question. "Come on."

She let him lead her across the rutted track to the cider barn, half-sliding in the churned mud. The doors groaned as he shoved them open. Inside, it smelled of pressed apples, old wood, and rain-damp stone. He latched the door behind them with one heavy bar.

"Phoebe and William?" she asked, pulling hair from her eyes.

"They made it inside...John took them up," he said. "Phoebe was trying to count thunderclaps. William was making slingshot threats at the clouds."

Elizabeth let out a half-breath of laughter. "Stubborn as lichen, both of them."

The storm struck full then, battering the roof like fists on a tavern table. Thunder cracked, close enough to rattle the shuttered window above the still. She stood dripping just inside the doorway, water running from her sleeves, braid plastered to her neck. She stripped off her sodden shawl and hung it over a hook near the barrel staves. Her shift clung to her calves.

Nathaniel moved quickly. He fetched a lantern from the nail peg, lit it with a brisk strike of flint, then crossed to the hearth pit. The soft orange glow illuminated the barn's beams, slick and blackened with storm mist.

"Give me a minute," he said, tugging off his coat. He laid it over the press table and returned with a coarse wool blanket from the loft cubby. It smelled faintly of herbs and woodsmoke. "Sit. You're shivering."

"I'm not—" she began, but her voice wavered. She sat anyway, curling her hands over the edge of the bench.

Nathaniel crouched low by the hearth. The firewood was reluctant, but he coaxed it with wadded paper, shavings from a pruning pile, a bit of beeswax. Soon a narrow tongue of flame licked upward, casting gold shadows along the cider barrels. The storm howled beyond the walls.

He came back with a linen-wrapped parcel. "Stolen from your kitchen," he said lightly.

She raised an eyebrow.

He unwrapped a heel of dark rye, a wedge of soft cheese, and a few shriveled pears. "Phoebe said you never remember to eat when you're angry."

Elizabeth accepted the bread without comment. "She watches everything."

"She does."

They ate in silence, fire snapping, rain pelting the roof in thick, erratic rhythms. The barn creaked around them, old wood shifting under the weight of a storm England had been waiting all summer to unleash.

Nathaniel handed her a pewter flask. "Here. For the bones."

"What is it?"

"Mostly apples. Some blackcurrant. I added a pinch of bark to make it 'more colonial.'"

She sipped and coughed. "God's blood."

He grinned. "Soothing, no?"

"Burns like heresy."

"Exactly."

She wiped her mouth with the corner of the blanket and leaned back, watching the rafters drip.

The silence that settled was different this time—less wary. More worn-in. Like a quilt pulled down in winter. They were two soaked souls under timber and fire, and neither of them moved toward the door.

"You didn't ask questions," she said after a long while. "When I lit the torch."

"It wasn't mine to speak over."

That silenced her more than any comfort might have.

The wind tore past the walls again. The barn shivered but held. Elizabeth stared at the fire until the orange flicker stung her eyes. "You should have stayed inside," she murmured.

"So should you."

She didn't argue.

Instead, she pulled the blanket closer around her shoulders, thought of Phoebe's fingers smudged with ink, and the muddy trail where William had run shouting toward the kitchen for biscuits before the storm. Her family—ragged as it was—had held.

And she hadn't done it alone. Not anymore. The thought startled her, and then she took a deep breath. Her shoulders relaxed.

The fire had settled into a steady glow, throwing wide ribbons of warmth across the barn's stone floor. Elizabeth set down the empty tin of pears and let herself sag slightly against the press frame behind her, legs stretched out before her in her stockinged feet. Her boots steamed by the hearth, one of them split at the seam.

Nathaniel sat beside her, close but not pressing, a quiet presence shaped by patience. His sleeves were rolled, forearms flecked with soot from coaxing the fire, and there was a new scrape across his knuckle, likely from the door latch or a stubborn barrel.

"You don't have to wait out the storm," she said at last, voice low. "It's not your orchard."

"No," he agreed. "But it is your orchard. And you're soaked through. And I don't make a habit of leaving women to sit alone in cider barns after setting fire to their family trees."

A slow breath escaped her. "Is that gallantry?"

"Stubbornness, mostly. And a fondness for graft wax and impossible women."

She gave a dry, tired laugh.

He shifted, reaching for something behind the nearest press—a folded bit of waxed cloth. From it, he unwrapped a small bundle of twine-bound papers and laid them beside her.

"What's that?"

"Your ledger from the stillroom. Phoebe asked me to bring it down earlier...said you'd be too proud to fetch it yourself once the storm hit."

Elizabeth blinked, then smirked. "She's getting bolder."

"She also left a note." He flipped the cover open, revealing a scrawled message in slanted ink: "*Mark the ones that matter most. You said the oldest trees forget their names. Don't let them.*"

For a moment, Elizabeth stared at it. The page blurred slightly, not from rain now, but from heat behind her eyes. "She's right," she said softly. "They do forget. Or we do, on their behalf."

Nathaniel nodded but didn't comment. Just watched her gently close the cover again and rest her hand on top.

"I've hated this barn," she murmured.

He waited.

"It's where he drank. Where he bragged. And where he lied...about the shipments, about the audits, about the gold he never sent to market." She didn't say her late husband's name. "I tried to scrub it all away. Made the boys whitewash the far wall. Swapped out the hooks. Moved the barrels. But still, when the wind comes from the east, it smells like the night he told me we were solvent."

Nathaniel looked at her, gaze steady. "And you stayed anyway."

"I had to."

"No. You chose to."

She closed her eyes. "I stayed for Phoebe. For my father's name. For trees that couldn't speak for themselves."

"And maybe," he said quietly, "for yourself too."

She opened her eyes.

"I've read your records," he said. "The entries are marked by hands that didn't always agree. Your father. Your grandfather. Thomas, maybe. But yours... yours are the ones in ink, not pencil. The ones with root measurements and bloom dates and frost resistance. The ones with the real names. And damned if I don't think that you run this orchard better than any of them ever could have."

Elizabeth stared at the fire. Then at him. "You know your way around a strong, bitter woman's heart," she sighed.

"I was raised by one," he replied.

That made her laugh, genuine and sharp, like bark cracking in the cold. He smiled too, and they sat like that for a moment, warmed by nothing but fire and truth.

"You're soaked through as well," she said after a beat.

"Didn't have time to notice."

"You will by morning."

He tilted his head. "If you're offering a blanket, I accept."

"I'm offering floorboards and a leaky roof."

He grinned. "Then I accept with thanks."

The wind worried the shutters, then eased, as if the fury of the rain had finally spent itself. The barn breathed. Elizabeth rose first, gathering the blanket to her shoulders, then glanced toward the door. "It's less vicious," she said. "Come, before the next squall remembers us."

They stepped out into a bruised light. Dusk clung along the hedges; the orchard lay wet and smoking, each ash heap a low ghost. The paths ran black as ink. They walked the central row without speaking, boots sucking softly at the ruts.

At the Widow tree Elizabeth paused, fingers brushing the linen wrap of yesterday's graft. The wax had held. A single drop of water swelled along the seam and fell.

Nathaniel stood a pace off, hat in his hand, as if the tree were a chapel. "She looks stubborn," he said, the smallest smile in his voice.

"She learned it from me," Elizabeth replied, but the humor drained quickly. She rested her palm on the scar where an old wound had knitted the wrong way and said, almost to the bark, "I keep thinking if I cut away enough rot, the rest will behave."

He didn't answer with comfort. "Some years the cut is the kindness," he said. "And some years the kindness is not cutting at all."

She let her hand fall. "I don't always know which is which."

"Neither did my mother," he said. "She kept a pear that never once gave a pretty fruit. She called it a truth tree and swore the ugly pears kept the rest honest."

Elizabeth huffed, then quieted. "If I keep the wrong ones, they pull the row crooked. If I cut the right ones, I'll never forgive myself."

They moved on, slow. A thrush scolded from the hedge, sounding older than birds ought to. Phoebe's upstairs candle showed faintly through the house's wavering glass. one small star.

"At first," Nathaniel said, "I wanted roots I could sell. Now—" He stopped, as if the words had weight. "Now I want them to belong to the people who've already bled for them."

"To her," Elizabeth said. Not a question.

"And to you," he answered. "I won't pretend it's noble. It's...clear." He looked down at his hands. "If the buyers push, they'll push against me. I've written as much."

"Paper won't shield bone," she said, but her voice softened.

"I know," he said. "I'm naming the wound I'll take."

A breeze lifted the damp from the grass and set the last leaves ticking together. They passed the Redstreaks, their trunks slick and dark, and came to the gap where a tree had stood that morning and now didn't. The ground there was raw, the circle of ash faintly warm beneath the rain.

Elizabeth stopped. "My father planted that one with a prayer he never told me," she said. "He died before it bore the way he swore it would. I think that's what I fear most, that I'll hand Phoebe a promise that never fruits."

Nathaniel didn't reach for her. He only stepped close enough that she could feel his steadiness. "Then let me keep watch with you," he said. "Not over land you own. Over the promise you made."

She looked at him. Dusk turned his features gentler than daytime did. He met her gaze without asking for anything to be returned.

"What would you keep?" she asked.

He answered without hurry. "Her right to walk these rows like they're hers." A beat. "Your right to decide what lives here, names, trees, futures, without a man's signature to sanctify it."

Silence laid itself between them like a soft cloth.

He lifted a hand, slow, and, with two fingers, brushed a wet curl back from her cheek. She caught his wrist, not to stop him, but to feel the pulse there. He bent then, near enough that the storm-smell of him braided with the cider-smell of her, and they both knew how easily the space could close.

It didn't.

Not yet.

She exhaled. "Not under their eyes," she whispered, glancing toward the house where a child's shadow crossed behind the curtain. "Not when every promise feels like a ledger."

He nodded, relief and hunger tempered into something steadier. "Then we wait," he said. His hand slipped to hers, palm to palm, nothing more. Their fingers pressed, learned the shape, let go.

They turned back together, walking the last stretch in companionable quiet. When they passed the graft again, Elizabeth touched the linen lightly. "Hold," she said to it, almost smiling. "We'll bind you again tomorrow."

"Tomorrow," he echoed, and neither of them made it sound like a threat.

They reached the barn door as the sky deepened from pewter to ink. Somewhere behind them, the thrush had fallen quiet. Ahead, the small light in the stillroom window burned on—Phoebe's small star.

The storm broke just before dawn, the clouds dragging east toward the estuary like sacked soldiers. Mist clung to the trees, and the orchard smoldered low, wet ash where fire had danced the day before. From the barn's open door, Elizabeth watched the pale grey light spill across the rows. Her arms ached. Her lungs felt heavy.

Behind her, Nathaniel stirred near the hearth. He'd slept on a folded canvas, coat bunched beneath his head, the blanket now pushed half-off his back. A single curl had fallen over his brow. He looked younger in sleep. Less burdened.

Elizabeth stepped outside. Mud sucked at her heel as she moved toward the old well, careful not to slip. She splashed water on her face, teeth gritting against the chill. Her shawl, still damp, clung to her shoulders.

By the time she returned, Nathaniel was awake and lighting the lantern again. He handed her the bread heel he'd tucked beneath a crate overnight, now firm but edible. "Still warm?" he asked, teasing.

"Still bread," she muttered, tearing it in half.

He took his piece and leaned against the press beam. "What now?"

"We rake the ash. Clean what can be saved. Document the rest."

"Does it go in the official ledger?" he asked, nodding toward the stillroom book on the bench.

"No," she said. "That one's for truth. Not for show."

A knock startled them both...three quick taps against the barn door.

William's voice came through the crack. "Miss Elizabeth? Thatcher says come quick. There's someone...someone near the wall."

She was moving before he finished.

Nathaniel caught up easily, long strides matching her quicker ones. They reached the edge of the scorched field just as John Thatcher emerged from the mist, a shovel in one hand, worry scrawled across his brow.

"He was sleeping beside the wall," Thatcher said, nodding toward the figure crouched beside a half-felled tree. "Said he knew you."

Elizabeth squinted.

"Miles Hardwick," the man said, standing now. His coat was travel-stained, hat tilted at a jaunty angle that didn't match the soot on his face. "Nathaniel and I go back. Quite far, depending who's asking."

"Miles." Nathaniel exhaled the name like a warning. "What in hell—?"

"Thought I'd pay a visit. Heard from a London broker you were sniffing after colonial rootstock again. Thought I'd offer my services. Just happened to find myself near Ledbury when the smoke started." His grin sharpened. "Wasn't going to interrupt a lady's bonfire."

"You've no business here," Elizabeth said coldly.

"That's where you're wrong." Miles reached into his coat and produced a small folded parchment, sealed with a crude wax stamp. "Document of intent. I represent a buyer interested in heirloom cultivars. The kind that survive both blight and stubborn orchard mistresses."

Nathaniel stepped forward. "I didn't summon you."

"No," Miles said. "But the kind of silence you've been keeping usually means you need someone like me."

William tugged at Elizabeth's sleeve. "Do you want me to run for the constable?"

"No," she said, voice steady. "Not yet."

"Miles," Nathaniel said, tone dropping, "this isn't one of your usual ports. These people, this place, it's not for trade tricks."

Miles didn't flinch. "Then maybe you shouldn't have borrowed from the sort of men who expect tricks in return."

A beat of silence passed. Elizabeth glanced sharply at Nathaniel, whose jaw tensed, but he said nothing.

"I'll leave," Miles said, raising his hands. "But I'll be back tomorrow. With terms. If you're clever, you'll read them."

He turned with a theatrical bow, stepping carefully around a pile of wet ash and whistling as he walked off down the track.

Elizabeth didn't speak for a long time. Then she said in a clipped voice, "I don't like him."

"You're not meant to," Nathaniel said. "I'll make sure he doesn't return."

William looked up at her. "He smells like rum and foxes."

Elizabeth's mouth twitched. "You're not wrong."

Thatcher cleared his throat. "What now?"

She stared at the path for a moment, then at the trees. "Now," she said, "we clean the rot. And we don't let foxes in the orchard."

The fire's last smoke drifted in ribbons across the orchard, a damp, bitter perfume of charred lichen and sap. Twilight settled in layers: ash grey, then ink. The boys had gone home; even Thatcher's lantern bob had disappeared down the lane.

Elizabeth remained by the north wall, rake leaning against her shoulder. The ground underfoot squelched with the evening's rain, every footprint a dark oval in the sodden earth. What remained of the burned trees were blackened crowns and the faint hiss of cooling embers.

Nathaniel came from the direction of the barn, coat collar turned high. He carried a lantern whose light flared against the wet stone and carved shadows into the smoke. He said nothing at first, only set the lantern on the low wall and passed her a tin cup that steamed faintly.

"Thatcher left a kettle on the hearth," he murmured. "Cider, with a splash of the blackcurrant you threatened to throw out."

She wrapped chilled fingers round the tin. The heat bit, then softened her knuckles. "You've a talent for stealing what's needed," she said.

"I call it borrowing." He stood beside her, close enough that the damp of his sleeve brushed her own.

They drank in silence. The night smelled of wet ash and fallen apples, not blossom but bruised fruit, the scent of a season almost spent. A single thrush gave a late scold and fell quiet.

Elizabeth tipped the cup and watched steam curl like ghost breath. "When my father burned the blighted pears, I thought it was the end of something sacred," she said. "He told me it was a kindness. Rot left standing will walk through a whole orchard before winter."

"And you believed him?" Nathaniel asked.

"Not then. I do now." She drew the rake slowly through the muck, pushing aside a wedge of blackened branch. "This is the season for cutting back, not for saving what will only poison next year's bloom."

Nathaniel rested his forearms on the wall. "Where I grew up, we called it the watch month—after harvest, before the hard frost. The ground still soft, the trees asleep but listening. We kept vigil the way some people keep holy days."

She glanced at him. "Vigil for what?"

"For what we wanted to see again come spring. For what we feared might not return." His voice was low, almost lost beneath the sigh of wind through bare limbs.

The lantern light caught the damp in her hair. He reached without thinking, brushed away a strand that clung to her cheek. She did not flinch.

"My father used to say the orchard remembers every cut," she whispered. "Even the merciful ones."

"Then tonight it knows you chose mercy," Nathaniel said.

The rake slipped from her grasp and landed softly in the mud. She looked at his hand where it still hovered near her face, the callused thumb dark against the glow.

"You stayed," she said.

"I wasn't about to leave you to keep watch alone."

For a long breath neither moved. The orchard steamed around them like a field of sleeping beasts. From the far slope came the dull crack of a limb settling, then silence again.

Elizabeth set her cup on the wall and eased her chilled fingers over his. "The watchers," she said softly, "need more than one set of eyes."

His palm turned upward beneath hers, a quiet acceptance.

They stood like that until the lantern began to gutter. When at last she drew her hand away, the imprint of his warmth lingered in her skin like an unspoken vow.

Nathaniel straightened and picked up the lantern. "We should check the southern rows before the frost sets. Ash drifts can hide embers."

She managed a small, rueful smile. "Ever the caretaker."

"Ever the stubborn mistress of the orchard," he returned.

They walked the perimeter together, lantern throwing brief islands of light across the wet grass. Each blackened stump looked almost sculpted in the shifting glow. Their boots left shallow prints that the night would fill before morning.

When they reached the last row, Elizabeth paused, gazing down the slope where the burned trees lay like a map of old wounds. "Tomorrow we rake again," she said. "Next week we cut the suckers. By first frost, the rows will be ready for their winter sleep."

"No blossoms till spring," Nathaniel said. "That's the right order of things."

She nodded. "And no false blooms to fool us."

The late-season moon, thin and cold, rose through a gap in the clouds. Its light silvered the soot and turned every branch to drawn steel. Elizabeth drew a breath, the cider's warmth still in her chest, and felt the weight of the day settle, not despair, but something steadier, a promise of work and of keeping watch.

Side by side they turned back toward the barn. Behind them the orchard lay dark and clean, its wounds cooling under the early-autumn sky.

Phoebe was already in the stillroom by the time Elizabeth returned, her small frame perched on the tall stool, sleeves rolled up, one stocking slightly askew beneath her hem. Her hair had been hurried into a braid but bits stuck out like wind-snagged twigs. The walking stick leaned against the bench at her side, its sling tucked neatly beneath a drying sieve. "William said the smoke was taller than the roof," she reported, dipping her pen carefully. "He said it looked like a ghost orchard."

Elizabeth stepped inside, brushing soot from her skirts. "It was just fire. It burned hot, but not all the way through."

Phoebe eyed her over the ink bottle. "But it smelled like medicine. Like when you clean wounds."

Elizabeth paused. "That's not wrong."

Phoebe nodded, then tapped her quill against the parchment. "I copied the rootstock list again. The tree that split yesterday wasn't on it."

Elizabeth moved to the bench and lifted the page. The girl's steady, deliberate handwriting bore tiny smudges but no errors. She'd even drawn a faint line to mark where the unnamed tree had stood. "You remembered where it was?"

"I watched from the wall," Phoebe admitted, "after William said I shouldn't."

Elizabeth raised an eyebrow.

"I brought the slingshot," Phoebe added. "In case that stranger came near."

Elizabeth sighed, not unkindly, and rested her hand lightly on the girl's shoulder. "Thank you."

Phoebe beamed, then returned to her writing.

Across the room, William swept the hearth, a bundle of kindling under one arm and ash streaked across his brow. He looked up as Elizabeth crossed the room. "Thatcher said he'll start hauling out what's left near the north slope. Wants me to help with the big rakes."

"You may help," she said, "but stay where he can see you. No wandering near the wall."

William nodded, then hesitated. "That man—Miles—he knew Mr. Carter?"

Elizabeth's mouth pressed into a line. "He claims to."

The boy fidgeted. "He asked me how many hands work here. And if we send cider downriver."

She stilled. "When?"

"While you were still out by the burn piles. He was leaning on the gatepost like it belonged to him."

Elizabeth crossed to the ledger and flipped back two pages. "And what did you say?"

William's ears flushed. "I said I was the only one who could outrun him, so he'd best not try anything."

Despite herself, Elizabeth smiled faintly. "Good."

He beamed, then bolted out the door with the kindling still under his arm, calling back something about oxen and puddles.

Phoebe looked up again. "Will he come back?"

"Yes," Elizabeth said. "I know men like that. He will." She moved to the cupboard and withdrew the smaller ledger—the one she hadn't shown to any official in three years. It bore her father's handwriting, and her husband's, and then her own. She flipped past the orchard maps, past the graft dates and cider tallies, until she reached the blank page she'd marked with a ribbon.

She dipped her quill. The ink clung dark to the nib.

Tree burned. Third row, northern slope. Split beneath old graft. No viable scion. Rootstock unrecoverable.

She paused.

Then added:

Witnessed: William, age twelve. Observed and recorded by Phoebe, age twelve.

She let the page dry, then shut the book.

Outside, the orchard steamed in the rising sun. Miles would return. So would the excise. And still, she had mouths to feed, trees to mend, and a harvest to coax from wet ground.

But this morning, at least, she had her ledger.

And her witnesses.

CHAPTER NINETEEN

THE ROOT OF IT ALL

The afternoon sky hung low and heavy, the kind of grey that made the orchard rows seem darker than they were. Nathaniel had been checking the bracing on the younger trees along the slope when he heard the crunch of boots on the track behind him.

Miles Hardwick stood there, collar turned up against the wind, grin sharp as ever, but his eyes flickered with something harder.

"So this is it?" Miles said, sweeping a hand toward the trees. "You're still playing orchard hand? Thought I'd find you ready to talk sense."

Nathaniel rested one gloved hand on the stake he'd just driven into the soil. "We've talked sense. You just don't like the answer."

Miles took a step closer. "The answer being you turn down coin you could've had in hand by now. You could be halfway to Virginia with Whitcombe's grafts locked in the hold. Instead, you're..." he glanced around in mild contempt "...mucking about in mud."

Nathaniel's jaw tightened. "I told you, Miles. I'm not pressing her before she's ready."

"You think she'll just hand them over out of the kindness of her heart? You've gone soft, Nate. Softer than orchard loam."

"Better soft than rotten," Nathaniel said evenly.

Miles barked a humorless laugh. "And when this 'honorable' plan of yours fails, what then? How will you make your fortune without me?"

"I have Haverford Green," Nathaniel replied. "Their scions ship next month. Honest work. Enough to start the way I should have from the beginning."

Miles' grin thinned into a sneer. "Honest work won't keep your pockets full. You'll regret this, mark me."

"Maybe," Nathaniel said. "But if I regret it, it'll be mine to regret."

For a moment, they just stood there, the wind rattling the bare branches overhead. His old friend's gaze hovered on him—calculating, maybe even disappointed—before he shook his head. "You're a fool," Miles said, voice low. "And fools learn the hard way."

"Goodbye, Miles."

Miles gave a mocking little bow and turned, boots crunching away down the track until the mist swallowed him.

Nathaniel stood alone in the quiet, the wind cutting sharper now. For years, Miles had been his constant...through storms, through bad deals, through ports where neither of them had friends. The loss felt like the slow closing of a door he'd thought would always be open.

But as he looked back over the orchard—its braced trees, its frost-silvered grass—he knew some doors had to close for better ones to open.

***

The house had finally quieted. Phoebe had fallen asleep curled beside her sketchbook, a pressed leaf tucked between the pages and Elizabeth's whispered promise of morning lessons still warm in her ear. Only then had Elizabeth slipped away to the stillroom, barefoot, unhurried, the hush of the hour wrapped around her like a second shawl.

Nathaniel had stayed behind under the pretense of checking the last barrel seal, but the truth sat quieter and closer to the bone.

She moved across the stillroom like a prayer made flesh: skirts hitched just above her ankles, arms bare from a long day's labor. Her braid was unraveling down her back, strands curling from steam and sweat. She bent slightly over the ledger, candlelight catching the slope of her cheek, the loose threads at her elbow, the ink-dark smudge at the edge of her wrist.

He watched her as a man might watch a tree heavy with its finest fruit, knowing that to reach for it too soon might spoil the sweetness, yet feeling the ache in his hand all the same.

The room was warm and breathing. Copper stills glinted in the corners like waiting saints, their hammered curves catching firelight in scattered crescents. Above the table, rosemary and meadowsweet hung drying, their green-sweet scent curling in the air like something sacred.

Nathaniel took a quiet breath. Then another.

"You're staying longer each evening," Elizabeth said without looking up.

"I'm learning," he replied.

She turned the page, dipped her quill again, and said nothing.

His voice came rougher the second time. "You know the orchard's not all I'm trying to protect."

That gave her pause. The pen halted mid-figure.

She glanced at him, unreadable. "Do you mean my trees? My land? Or the half-sealed ledger you think I don't know you've read?"

"I meant you."

She looked at him squarely then.

"You cannot mean me. You're a young merchant," she said, voicing what had been whispering unwanted in her head. "I'm an old widow."

"You're a beautiful, incredible woman, and I'm only a man," he answered, quiet but certain. "One who's stood in fields all his life and never seen anything take root like this."

Silence stretched between them, warm and taut. The candle cracked.

"You should be gone by now," she murmured. "If you were making the smartest business decision."

"I know what I'm doing."

She set her pen aside. "And yet you linger."

"Of course I do." His voice dropped to something near reverence. "Because you move like the orchard breathes through you. Because I keep thinking if I leave tonight, I'll never get back to the place I didn't know I was looking for until I found you here, wrist-deep in vinegar and stubborn hope."

She crossed to the still and ran her hand lightly along the rim of the copper bowl. Her back to him, she said, "You speak sweet for a tradesman."

"I've bitten my tongue all week."

"Then bite it again."

"I will," he said, taking a step closer, "if you truly want me gone. But you should know that I've sent Miles packing. He's no longer any friend or partner in any way."

A beat.

Then, softly, like linen pulled taut, Elizabeth whispered, "Bar the door."

Nathaniel just stared at his for a moment in disbelief. Then he crossed the room in three long strides and slid the iron bar into place. The sound rang out loudly, and his hands shook slightly as he let go.

The fire popped behind them.

He turned back to find her waiting.

Elizabeth stood in the halo of candlelight between the herbs and the stone wall. She reached behind her and untied her apron, folding it with the same care she used to bind a graft. She laid it across the table, methodical and slow.

Nathaniel stood very still.

"Are you afraid of me?" she asked quietly. It feels like you are."

"No," he said. "But I'm aware of the moment."

Elizabeth turned.

The firelight kissed her collarbone, her shoulder, the linen of her chemise already loosened from hours of heat and strain. Her shift had slipped slightly, leaving one sleeve to fall down her arm.

She came to him slowly. Her fingers found the edge of his coat and tugged once, lightly. "Then don't ruin it."

Nathaniel swallowed hard and obeyed.

His coat slid to the floor. She unlaced the front of his waistcoat with steady hands, like unwrapping a parcel she meant to learn by feel. He let her. Only when her fingers reached his shirt buttons did he lift a hand, just one, to her cheek. "You smell like rosemary and apples," he whispered.

"I smell like work."

"You smell like home."

She didn't reply. But her breath caught.

Elizabeth stepped closer, sliding her hands beneath his waistcoat. He kissed her then, heat meeting heat. Her mouth opened against his with a hunger that startled him in its certainty.

The world narrowed.

To the shape of her spine under his hand. To the sound of her breath. To the taste of something tart and unspoken.

She kissed like a woman who had waited too long, and who had too many people depending on her to waste even one second on something untrue.

Nathaniel's hands traced the slope of her back, careful not to rush. But she pulled him closer, her body all fire beneath work-worn linen. He felt her pulse at her throat, at her wrist, at the base of her spine where his palm settled like an anchor.

"You don't need to handle me like spun sugar," she murmured, lips grazing his ear.

"You are spun steel," he answered. "But I've never touched something that mattered this much."

She stilled.

And then, without a word, turned toward the pallet they kept beneath the press, blankets folded, tucked out of sight. She drew one up, laid it over the hard cider-wood floor, then knelt and held out her hand.

Nathaniel followed.

Above them, copper stills gleamed like watchful saints. Dried lavender crumbled slightly as she brushed past it, releasing another note of sharp sweetness into the air.

He reached for the laces of her stays. When he fumbled, she laughed once, quiet, almost breathless. "You undid a whole graft by candlelight. Surely you can manage three ribbons."

Nathaniel laughed, though his fingers trembled with desire. "That was less intimidating."

"You're doing fine."

When the last ribbon fell, he kissed the skin at her shoulder, and she leaned into him. He whispered a line his mother used to murmur about springtime: "Cider and honeysuckle, ripe on the same air, meant for soft hands and slow mouths."

Elizabeth inhaled like the words hit her lungs and stayed there.

"Nathaniel..." she said once.

He quieted her with his mouth.

They lay together, half-dressed and fully open, limbs tangled on the blanket, the scent of fire and apples wrapped around them like cloth. His hand stroked slow circles into her waist. Her lips found his again. And again.

When he moved toward more, she met him with a heated kiss, but slowed, bracing a hand against his chest.

"Not here," she whispered, not with fear, but with promise. "Phoebe sleeps light."

He stopped instantly. "I can wait."

They stayed like that, listening to the fire tick down. Listening to the stillroom hold them like it held everything else that mattered: sealed, warm, and waiting to be pressed into something lasting.

The fire burned to a dull orange, casting soft, uneven light across the room. Copper vessels gleamed faintly, halos of past use and warmth. The stillroom, for once, was quiet, not bustling with tinctures or tallies, not heavy with tasks. Just breath. Shared.

Elizabeth lay half-curled against him, cheek tucked to his bare shoulder, her legs drawn up beneath the old wool blanket he'd pulled around them both. She hadn't spoken for some time. Her fingers rested lightly at his sternum, rising and falling with each breath.

Nathaniel didn't move. He hadn't realized silence could feel so full.

Her braid had mostly unraveled. A strand of hair trailed against his ribs, impossibly soft. He let his hand drift lazily and fondly along her spine.

He'd spent years aboard decks and dockyards, where men like Miles could trade affection like silver and walk away without so much as a glance back. But this was not that. There was no bargain here, no convenient departure at dawn. Just her, real as earth. Holding more weight than any ledger he'd ever kept.

When he finally spoke, his voice was low, steady. It didn't feel rehearsed, but it had waited long enough. "I won't trade your name," he said. "I won't barter your orchard, or what you've built here. You are not part of the shipment. You're the root of it all," he added.

Elizabeth shifted, resting her chin against his chest, her eyes on his. She studied him a long moment. Then, without a word, she reached up and touched the edge of his jaw with her knuckles. "I believe what I can. I'll see the rest."

He swallowed. "I've made a vow," he said. "I don't need one back. Just the chance to keep mine."

She nodded.

Above them, the beams creaked faintly in the rising breeze. Somewhere beyond the stone wall, an owl called once—low and sure. The fire snapped, releasing a waft of spiced apple and pine smoke.

Elizabeth exhaled into his skin, and for the first time since stepping off the ship in Bristol, Nathaniel felt something deeper than desire or risk. He wasn't sure what it was quite yet, but he hoped it was trust.

***

The scent of cider pulp and burnt rosemary had dissipated, softened now by the hush that comes only after something tender has unfolded and held. Dawn stretched her fingers through the cracks in the shutters, casting long, honey-colored lines across the stone floor.

Nathaniel rose quietly, careful not to wake her. Elizabeth lay near the hearth, one arm flung across the folded edge of her shawl, a faint furrow still between her brows even in sleep. He resisted the urge to smooth it with his thumb. Some things could only be unknotted in their own time.

The stillroom looked different by morning. Gentler. The copper stills sat like sleeping giants, and above them, herb bundles stirred faintly in the draft that crept through the loft slats. Somewhere overhead, a faint shifting sound—Phoebe, perhaps, rolling beneath her quilt. Or young William stirring in the eaves where the boys sometimes slept when the beds were full and the harvest heavy.

Steam from the kettle drifted with rosemary and cider, bitter-sweet and dizzying. She undid his damp cravat with work-stained fingers; he laughed, low and disbelieving, until she swallowed the sound with her mouth. Buttons gave. Stays loosened. He learned her like a map made by touch: the hollow of her throat, the small startled gasp when his palm found the heat at her ribs. "Care," she breathed, a command and a mercy. He answered with care, and more than care, until the lamp burned to a quiet pearl and the room forgot their names.

He pulled on his shirt slowly, boots dangling from one hand, and padded toward the press bin at the far end.

And there it was.

Half-buried beneath a discarded mesh of pomace and crushed leaves, still bright in its bruised red way: a Foxwhelp blossom.

Nathaniel plucked it gently free from the ground, the edges slightly frayed. One petal torn. Not flawless. But vivid, and stubborn enough to outlast the frost. He glanced back once, toward her sleeping form. Then he moved to the table where her ledger lay, its corner ink-smudged, pages curled from long use. He turned gently to a place he'd seen her mark before. A single past entry:

Survived frost. Uncertain yield.

Carefully, reverently, he pressed the blossom between that page and the next, just above the line. A bright echo. A small offering. Then he closed the book.

"Let it grow," he murmured aloud.

Then, tucking a final glance toward her form beneath the hearth-light, and up, briefly, toward the loft where a girl dreamed in ink and grafts and legacy, he stepped barefoot into the morning.

The stone threshold was cold beneath his feet, but something inside him had already rooted.

CHAPTER TWENTY

THE AUDIT

T he sound of hooves reached her before the dust did…clipped, purposeful, and too well-timed to be a neighbor or a passing merchant. Elizabeth stood at the edge of the courtyard, shawl pinned fast, ledger pressed firm against her hip. When the riders came into view, her posture didn't change.

But her stomach did. It turned once, sharp as a plow edge.

From the window above the stillroom, a flutter of movement caught her eye: Phoebe's face, round and pale behind the glass, before a hand (likely Meg's) gently drew the curtain closed.

Good. She didn't want her seeing this part.

Three men dismounted. The one in front—tall, meticulous in a charcoal-gray coat with silver trim—stepped forward and removed his gloves finger by finger. His boots were polished enough to show her orchard sky in their shine.

"Elizabeth Whitcombe?" he asked, voice like oiled steel.

"I am." Her tone was dry, clipped. Neutral enough not to betray the knot behind her ribs.

"I'm Mr. Wainscott. Appointed by the Excise Office on behalf of His Majesty's Crown." He produced a folded document sealed in red wax. "This is a notice of provisional audit, in light of recent irregularities among cider-producing properties in Herefordshire."

Behind him, the two junior clerks were already scribbling in thin black books.

Elizabeth accepted the paper with practiced calm, even as her throat tightened. She didn't need to read the whole thing—not now. The red wax said it all.

"I was not made aware the date had changed," she said, not accusing, but not deferential either.

He smiled without warmth. "Efficiency. The Crown prefers its records kept in real time these days."

Wainscott unfolded the notice with two neat taps of his finger. "By this writ I am empowered to compare the Excise Register against your house ledgers, manifests, and seal receipts, and to request warehouse acknowledgments from Gloucester and Hereford. Where register and private books do not align, the Crown presumes intent to defraud until the discrepancy is corrected or stamped proof is produced."

Elizabeth kept her face still. Plain speech: if my numbers and theirs argue, they'll call it theft until I prove otherwise.

"Of course," she said, though it wasn't.

Her eyes flicked behind him. No constable, no magistrate. That, at least, was something. For now.

Wainscott let his gaze drift past her shoulder, over the yard—pausing at the stillroom doors, the stacked barrels, the shadowed cider barn. His expression didn't change, but the calculation in his eyes sharpened.

"No husband present?" he asked, too casually.

"No," Elizabeth replied evenly.

"Male heir?"

"No."

For half a breath, she thought of Phoebe...just twelve, lame-footed, with her mother's stubborn mouth. A girl, and not by law an heir. But everything that mattered.

Wainscott's gaze returned to her face. "Then I suppose the operation falls entirely to you."

"I was under the impression that was legal," she said, voice cool.

"It is," Wainscott said. "But unusual. And unusual things are often worth a closer look."

Before she could reply, the cider barn door creaked on its hinges, and Nathaniel Carter emerged into the morning light, sleeves rolled, shirt damp from the barrelhouse humidity. He paused only a moment at the sight of the visitors, then adjusted his gait and came forward at a worker's pace, wiping his hands on a linen cloth.

Wainscott's attention shifted. "Is this one of your workers? I was under the impression that most of them had been hired away."

"And how would you know that?" Elizabeth asked, fixing him with a contemptible look.

He ignored her. "And you are?"

Nathaniel inclined his head with just enough humility to make it believable. "Nathaniel Carter, sir. A grateful steward to Mistress Whitcombe's orchard. I manage what I'm told." He stepped back, palms open, and pitched his voice for the clerks to hear. "Mistress Whitcombe keeps the books. I fetch what she names and answer what she permits. If you've questions of account, you'll have them from her."

"Colonial," Wainscott noted.

"Virginia-born," Nathaniel answered easily. "But loyal to the trees, wherever they grow."

The inspector gave a tight, unreadable smile. "We'll begin with the ledgers."

Elizabeth stepped forward, producing them without ceremony. "This year's entries are here. Yield reports, barrel seals, and tax markings on the inside covers. I've cross-checked them against our culling log and spring frost losses."

Wainscott took the book and flipped it open without looking at her. The pages fluttered under his fingers like a priest rifling scripture for heresy.

"Very thorough," he said.

"I have to be," she replied. "I've no husband to answer for me." That earned a stern look from one of the junior clerks. Elizabeth didn't care.

Behind her, Nathaniel moved toward the barn without waiting to be asked. He carried himself with a kind of cultivated invisibility...steady, deferent, hands callused just enough to be believed. Not a merchant now. Not the man who'd ever kissed her by firelight.

Just a hired steward. Exactly as planned.

She let her breath slow.

From somewhere behind the shuttered window, a quiet thud...Phoebe's notebook dropping, maybe, or a stool leg shifting. The child would be listening, wide-eyed, tracing orchard names in ink while grown men tested the soil with knives.

Elizabeth tightened her grip on the ledger.

Let Wainscott circle. Let him sniff out softness. He'll find none here.

The barn smelled of damp oak and crushed apple skin; it was the comforting scent of routine. But nothing felt routine today.

Wainscott did not waste time. "Your winter manifest lists two Gloucester consignments; the Register lists three. A February lot appears in the register dated the twenty-fourth with two hundred and forty-one gallons and a receipt noted, yet your book records only a delayed sealing and no second stamp. If the 'held over' barrel exists, we will see its stamp number and carter's mark."

"It exists," Elizabeth said, level. "Blight delayed sealing. The carter marked by cross—he cannot write—and the duty was paid when the hoops cooled."

Wainscott's mouth thinned. "Then we will find a matching stamp or a warehouse acknowledgment. Otherwise, I record presumed surplus."

Elizabeth stood just inside the threshold, posture controlled, while Wainscott prowled the rows of barrels with the cold attentiveness of a man sniffing for fraud. His junior clerks trailed behind, recording barrel counts and scribbling notations without lifting their eyes.

Nathaniel was already there, sleeves rolled to the elbow, shirt slightly open at the collar. He moved with calm purpose, looping a leather strap through a pulley and guiding a cask into place with deliberate steadiness.

He did not look at her.

It made her chest ache.

From the corner of her eye, Elizabeth noticed a flash of calico behind the slats of the far wall. Meg's skirt, and beside it, still and silent, Phoebe's silhouette. Watching, hidden. No one had told her to, but she'd come anyway. She always came for moments that mattered.

Wainscott turned sharply. "Mr. Carter, is it? You were present for the last pressing?"

"Aye, sir," Nathaniel said, voice mild.

"What method was used?"

"Rack and cloth," he said without hesitation. "Redstreak and Foxwhelp blend. Yielded lighter than expected. We let the must sit twelve hours before second press."

"Good," Wainscott said, noncommittal. "Now the stamps. Bring me the slips for last Michaelmas through February, and the seal disk tied to any 'held over' barrel."

Elizabeth crossed to the press ledger box. "Slips are bundled by quarter." She set the packet down; Wainscott fanned through, pausing at a red-edged slip. "Gloucester, 24 February, 241 gallons." He tapped the margin. "Note: delayed sealing." His gaze lifted. "And the barrel mark?"

"Fourteen...KB," Elizabeth said. "Cross-signed by the carter. You'll see it echoed on the bung."

Wainscott's gaze flicked to Elizabeth. "No additives?"

"None," she answered. "Our orchard is old. It doesn't need fortifying."

Nathaniel didn't speak. He only returned to his work, tightening barrel rings, inspecting wax seals, moving as though his only loyalty lay in the press and the pulp. But Elizabeth saw it in the slope of his shoulders...he was listening to every word.

Wainscott turned predictably back to him. Men. For more than once, she was grateful for Nathaniel. He was a marvelous buffer, but still allowed her to take the lead when appropriate. If only her late husband had been that way. "And how long have you served under Mistress Whitcombe?"

"Since harvest began," Nathaniel said. "I serve where I'm permitted."

The clerk beside him raised an eyebrow. "That isn't long. How do you know the records are accurate?"

Nathaniel straightened slightly, not enough to challenge, but enough to be noticed by the smaller man. "I read what I'm given. I lift what's marked. If the numbers lie, I haven't seen them do it."

Wainscott stepped closer. "You speak like a man who's held authority."

Nathaniel smiled. "Not lately."

Wainscott studied him. "And how long do you plan to stay?"

There was a pause. Then Nathaniel answered, "As long as the orchard will have me, and the work is honest."

Elizabeth's throat tightened.

She didn't look toward the slats again, but she still felt Phoebe's attention. Later, she'd have questions. About truth, and performance, and who decided which was which.

The moment passed.

"Barrel fourteen," Wainscott called, gesturing to one near the corner. "Unseal it."

John, watching from the back wall, stepped forward, but Nathaniel beat him to it, moving smoothly with the pry and catching the lid before it clattered.

The cider inside was dark gold, clean-surfaced. Elizabeth swelled with pride, despite the tense moment.

Wainscott dipped a ladle, sniffed, then nodded. "This matches the account." He handed the ladle to the younger clerk and moved on.

Elizabeth let herself breathe again.

As they walked to the outer row, Nathaniel passed within inches of her. His eyes never met hers. But his hand brushed a stave near her hip, steadying a barrel she hadn't realized she'd leaned into.

It wasn't the touch that burned. It was the absence of recognition. The perfect performance. The lie that kept her orchard safe.

She hated how much she needed it.

Wainscott stopped again. "Mistress Whitcombe, I'll need to see last year's excise slips."

"Of course," she said evenly. "They're stored in the press ledger box."

She crossed the barn and opened the worn lock, fingers smooth on the iron. Inside, bundled by season, were the folded papers and stamped verifications of every taxed barrel in the previous fiscal cycle. No ghosts today. No missing slips. Not in this box.

She handed them over, and Wainscott flipped through them silently, then laid one slip against his register extract. "Your tally says seventy pressed last fall with one held. The Register shows seventy-one received. If the 'held' was the twenty-fourth of February lot, your **house book must show the second stamp tied to the same barrel mark."

He turned to his clerk. "Mark discrepancy pending under Section VI, presumed surplus unless stamped proof produced by return."

His gaze cut back to Elizabeth. "Three days. We return with the magistrate and a seal officer."

Elizabeth's spine stayed straight. But inside, she was starting to coil.

A flutter of movement from the loft above...a shadow, barely there. Phoebe, surely. Lurking in the hay by the rope pulley, where she sometimes sat to study leaf journals or listen to the ferment gurgle through staves. Elizabeth had told her not today. But the girl never missed a moment that felt like a verdict.

Wainscott moved toward the open ledger, still flipping. "Seventy-one recorded last fall. Seventy pressed. One held over."

Elizabeth passed him the current count sheet. "This year's total is sixty-eight, as shown. We culled a row due to aphid rot. And one barrel cracked during the June heat."

Wainscott's gaze flicked to the sheet. "And yet... these figures don't align."

Elizabeth's pulse skipped. "We accounted for that. I marked the spoiled barrel with asterisks. The cull is noted under the yield adjustment column."

He didn't read it. He leaned forward instead, close enough that she could smell the sharp lavender oil in his collar. "Do you expect me to take your pen marks in place of stamped record?"

"I expect the Crown to recognize a working orchard in a blight year," she said evenly.

He gave here a serene, wolfish smile. "And I expect a business-woman to account for all her stock. You are, after all, operating alone."

The words hung in the air. *Alone.*

Behind her, Nathaniel shifted...just enough for her to feel it like gravity. He didn't speak or move toward her. But she could sense his body beside the press, the warmth of him like a brace beneath her ribs. And above her, unseen but known, Phoebe still watched. Both thoughts gave her strength.

She'd tell her niece later: *You are never alone. Not in this house. Not while I stand.*

Wainscott turned back to his clerk. "Mark the file: discrepancy pending."

The younger man nodded and inked a red line across the parchment's margin.

Elizabeth's jaw clenched. The sound of the quill's scratch felt like a verdict.

Wainscott looked at her again, his expression one of cool civility. "You'll receive formal summons within three days. The magistrate will accompany me on my return, along with a seal officer. If the discrepancy cannot be resolved, your surplus may be seized."

"I have no surplus," Elizabeth said flatly.

"Then you'll have no difficulty proving that," he replied. He gathered his gloves and tipped his hat. "Good day, Mistress Whitcombe."

The clerks followed without comment, and the barn door creaked closed behind them, leaving a brittle silence.

Elizabeth gripped the edge of the table, knuckles white. The blood had drained from her fingers, but her face held.

John appeared from the far end of the barn, wiping his hands on a cloth that was already filthy. "I've seen softer dogs," he muttered. "That man could poison a beehive."

William, lingering near the threshold with a stick half-carved in his hand, looked up. "Next time he comes, I'll pitch a hornet barrel toward his boots."

"Don't tempt fate," John muttered, though one corner of his mouth twitched.

Elizabeth didn't laugh. She couldn't. But from above, in the hay loft, a faint rustle told her Phoebe was slipping down the rope ladder.

Even before she turned, Elizabeth knew the girl would have that same fierce look she wore when a graft failed: unshed tears and a straightened spine.

The kind of bravery no man expected to find in a child.

The pencil in Phoebe's hand hovered, then moved: one small X beside a sketched barrel and, beneath it, 14-KB in careful figures. *If they forget, I won't,* the drawing seemed to say.

***

The light was gold and thinning, the kind of dusk that softened edges but didn't dull the ache behind her eyes. The orchard wall, built of old stone and mossy at the base, held the last of the sun like a shallow breath.

Elizabeth leaned against it, arms crossed, as John and William arrived from the south slope. Nathaniel followed last, quiet as ever, his shirt sleeves rolled to the elbow, ink still on his thumb from marking cider tallies.

Phoebe wasn't far. She sat cross-legged near the press basin, her journal open and pencil poised, though unmoving. Her eyes watched the men with a kind of grim steadiness, absorbing everything though no one had asked her to.

Elizabeth didn't send her inside. She couldn't, not after today.

"We can shift the extras," John said first. "Barrels from the west barn...stack them in the press yard, label them for fall yield."

"They'll ask for dates," Elizabeth replied. Her voice came out hoarse, gravel-edged. "Wainscott wants proof, not appearance."

William kicked at a clump of dry moss near the wall. "Then give him both. Empty barrels, chalked and sealed. If he wants to open one, let him pick wrong."

"Some do," John muttered. "Especially if they've been told where to sniff."

Nathaniel stepped forward, voice even. "What if we don't fake anything, but shape what's already true? The barrels are real. The yield was damaged. The cooper's last delivery came late; we could say that's why we held one over."

Elizabeth turned to him. "You want me to lie without lying."

"I want you to survive," Nathaniel said quietly. "The orchard's truth is already written. We just... underline the parts that won't damn you."

A breeze stirred Phoebe's hair. She didn't look up, but her hand had begun to move, sketching lines in faint graphite. Barrel staves. Possibly faces. That was how she worked through fear...she drew it down until it couldn't bite.

Elizabeth exhaled. "No forged stamps. Not again."

Nathaniel gave a slight nod. "Then we do what's honest, and let them call it what they will."

John cracked his knuckles. "I can shift seven barrels by morning, maybe eight. Meg can wax the rims. William and I'll chalk the dates."

William's face lit, then sobered with exaggerated gravity. "Only if I can write Wainscott's name on one. In piss."

"Don't tempt hornets, boy," John said, but ruffled his hair all the same.

Elizabeth managed half a smile, brittle at the edges. "Make sure the marks look hand-stamped. Real, but rough."

Nathaniel nodded. "And I'll draft the cooper's letter. Say the iron hoops were delayed. That gives us grounds for one held barrel, maybe two."

Phoebe was still scribbling, but now her pencil danced more deliberately. Elizabeth caught the corner of the page, barrels lined in rows, one with a fox curled beside it, nose tucked in its tail. The girl hadn't missed a single word.

Elizabeth turned toward the trees. The rows stood quiet now, their outlines softened by dusk and fatigue. Her gaze slid past them to the ridge, where wind caught the upper branches. She squared her shoulders. "They've already marked me a liar," she said. "If I'm to be called one, let me do it clean."

John straightened. "I'll be in the barn. William...light that kettle. We've work." They disappeared into the growing dark, leaving only the rustle of the leaves and Phoebe's pencil scratching paper.

She rose slowly, brushed the dust from her skirt, and padded toward Elizabeth. She didn't speak, but she pressed a folded sketch into Elizabeth's palm.

A dozen barrels. Glyphs chalked above them in a system Elizabeth didn't recognize...Phoebe's own symbols. And beside the row, half in shadow, a little fox crouched low.

"I didn't forge," Phoebe whispered. "I just imagined." Then she walked on.

Elizabeth remained still, facing the orchard.

The warmth of Nathaniel's nearness stayed behind her, not quite touching, but felt all the same, like the strength of a wall, or the hush before frost.

"Three days," she said aloud.

Nathaniel's voice was quiet: "We'll make them count."

CHAPTER TWENTY-ONE

THE BLANK PAGE

The light slanted low across the cider barn, catching the dust in lazy gold spirals. Nathaniel sat at the long bench with a blank customs folio spread before him, his sleeves rolled back and a pot of thick brown ink uncorked beside his elbow. He hadn't dipped the quill yet.

The page—laid paper, coarse at the edge and watermarked faintly with the Crown's stamp—stared up at him, brittle and expectant.

He could already feel what it would cost.

He ran a finger along the grain, testing it like bark before a graft. His jaw worked soundlessly. This was the part he hated. Not the lying, not even the risk, but the moment before he decided to do it. When a man weighed the truth against what was worth preserving.

He'd already done this once...in Annapolis, with fewer scruples and a far worse outcome. The ink had run thin that time. The paper had warped in the damp. The lie had been clumsy. This one couldn't be.

Miles would've made quick work of it, no doubt...half-drunk, candle barely lit, stamping a forgery with the heel of his boot. And it might've worked, for a day. But Nathaniel needed this to hold longer. To protect more.

He shifted slightly on the bench, dislodging a small square of paper that fluttered to the ground. He bent to pick it up.

It was a child's drawing, ink smudged, uneven. A tree with two trunks joined in the middle, roots sprawling beneath. A single word beneath it, in blocky capitals:

GRAFT.

He smiled despite himself. Phoebe's doing, no doubt. She'd taken to trailing Elizabeth in the stillroom, mimicking her lettering in the margins of scrap folios. She must have slipped this one into the bundle when they'd gathered supplies that morning.

He set it aside gently, brushing a fingerprint off the corner, then turned back to the blank page. The empty line waited.

The fire had burned down to a deep amber glow. The stillroom was quiet but for the occasional hiss from the copper kettle cooling beside the hearth. They'd moved from the barn an hour ago, bringing the folios, ledgers, and sealing wax with them. Elizabeth had lit two tallow candles, one each for their ends of the table, but now they sat closer...ink smudged on her cuff, wax flecks on his sleeve, documents laid like cards in a gambler's spread.

Nathaniel reread the forged manifest aloud, carefully measured.

"Whitcombe Orchard. Shipment Date: April 16, 1763. Quantity: One barrel. Not for sale, exported for sample only. Authorized by steward of record under seasonal exemption."

He looked up. "Will they buy that?"

Elizabeth drew the page to her and tapped the margin where he'd left space. "Then say it plain enough to soothe a clerk: 'Covers barrel mark 14-KB; held as sample under seasonal exemption.'"

Nathaniel's quill hovered. "Name it on the face of it?"

"Put the bait where Wainscott expects to find it," she said. "If he thinks 14-KB was the sample and not a sale, he'll kick it to correspondence. That buys us three days while he waits on the warehouse reply."

She added, quieter, for the empty air between them: "Plain speech...we're telling him it wasn't taxable stock because it never entered trade. If he swallows that, he can't seize while the query's open."

Elizabeth rubbed her fingers together to warm them. "They won't buy anything. But they'll want the illusion they were right to ask."

She tapped the margin. "Add frost damage. Let them think we're the ones who paid the price."

He obeyed, scratching the words in his sharp hand. The ink smelled slightly of iron and vinegar, thicker than what Miles would've used. Miles preferred speed, shortcuts, contraband stamps slipped under coat-linings. Nathaniel, now, found himself careful, deliberate.

"Grain's too fresh," Elizabeth murmured, feeling the folio's edge. "A real April paper would've seen damp."

Nathaniel nodded, reached for the sand shaker, and dusted the ink just enough to pit it. He smudged a corner with the heel of his palm, then pressed the sheet beneath the warm copper still lid for a count of twenty. When he lifted it, the watermark had bloomed faintly, warped as if it had ridden in a steamy satchel.

"And a steward in a hurry would blot oddly," she added. He blotted—once sharp, once crooked—then nicked the lower margin with a penknife and ground a touch of pumice into the cut. "Let them see haste," he said. "Not guile."

On the sill behind her, Phoebe's primer lay shut but not forgotten. Its cover was singed at the edge from a candle left too close earlier that week. Elizabeth hadn't moved it. Phoebe had left it there during her late-night copying, trying to match Elizabeth's steady script in the margins of a practice ledger.

The girl had nodded off beside the hearth not long ago, bundled in a shawl with a handkerchief of dried lavender at her wrist. Elizabeth had carried her to bed before they crossed to the stillroom but the scent lingered, stubborn and soft beneath the sharper notes of sealing wax and cider lees.

Nathaniel shifted his foot and felt something under his boot…a snapped quill. One of Phoebe's, he guessed. She'd taken to hoarding the broken ones like relics, convinced they held stories too old to waste.

Outside, the wind pressed faintly at the shutters. Elizabeth reached for another parchment and drew it toward her, scanning quickly, lips pressed thin. Her hand shook, and she set down the paper. "I stayed up most of last year re-copying the ledgers after he died," she said. "All so they'd believe me capable. All to erase the errors he left behind."

Nathaniel didn't interrupt.

"I thought if I made it clean enough, with tight script, exact sums…they'd forget I was a widow." She glanced at him, the candle-light sharpening her cheekbones. "I didn't expect to outlast the ink."

"Wainscott said three days," Nathaniel reminded, soft but steady. "He'll come back with a magistrate and a seal officer. This gets us to that door without our barrels hauled off the yard."

"Three days we buy," Elizabeth said, "and three more we make him spend to prove he's right. That's six he won't have for my neighbors."

He studied her in silence for a moment longer, then said, "My mother used to say grafting was just hope made visible. A wound bound up in trust."

Elizabeth's voice turned dry. "Hope doesn't pay fines or stop the Crown from seizing your press."

"No," he said. "But I've found it makes for a better night's sleep than certainty ever did."

That earned a half-smile. A real one, barely there.

He reached for her hand across the table. "You aren't alone," he said. "Don't forget that."

Her fingers curled around his.

The stillroom smelled of steeped herbs, old ink, lavender, and the faint sharp scent of applewood smoke. Outside, the wind stirred the hedges.

But inside, the candlelight held. And so did they.

By the time the moon angled past the shutters, the table had become a small topography of ink-dark valleys and parchment hills. Ledgers lay open to carefully modified entries. Blank folios bore fresh stamps. Elizabeth now sat cross-legged in her chair, hair loosened, sleeves rolled, the edge of her boot tapping softly against the floor in rhythm with her thoughts.

Nathaniel had spread the pages into a mock-inspector's path. "He'll start here," he said, pointing to the inventory list. "Then he'll compare it to the spring shipping manifest. Which we'll leave in plain sight, with this." He held up a folded sheet: a mocked-up receipt, deliberately smudged, initialed, and sealed with an old die-cut stamp he'd salvaged from the bottom of Thomas Whitcombe's desk drawer.

Elizabeth raised a brow. "Won't that raise more questions?"

"Only if it's perfect," he said. "This one's credible. Messy. Like a steward in a hurry who barely understood the rules." A pause. "Which is almost true."

She reached for the sheet, scanned it, and nodded slowly. "You're good at playing someone else."

"Only when the stakes are worth it."

Nathaniel fanned their papers into a neat corridor. "He starts at inventory, checks your spring manifest, then jumps to slips. We'll leave this 'sample' receipt a shade too obvious. He'll copy the mark 14-KB and write to Gloucester for an acknowledgment. While the query travels, he can't seize on a presumption. It's his own rule."

Her gaze flicked up to his. "And they are?"

He didn't look away. "Yes."

Elizabeth stood and crossed the room to fetch the master ledger, the one no one else touched. She laid it beside the others, opened to the back flyleaf, and turned to the only unmarked page. She hesitated a breath, then wrote one line across the top:

Correction Ledger – 1763

She underlined the first entry and said, almost to herself, "This ledger answers for 14-KB until his letter comes back. It buys three days if he's quick, five if Gloucester is lazy, and more if God is kind."

Below it, she began to list the barrel numbers they'd just rewritten into existence. Each stroke was precise. Intentional.

Nathaniel glanced toward the shelf where Phoebe's pressed-flower samples stood in mismatched jars. Tiny labels fluttered beneath them—"Bittersweet," "Russet moss," "April twine"—each scrawled in a mix of Elizabeth's measured hand and Phoebe's crooked mimicry. One jar was labeled simply: Survived frost.

He smiled faintly. "You're risking a charge of falsification if he looks too close," he said.

"I'm correcting a record," she replied. "If the truth costs me the orchard, I'd rather survive on ink."

When she finished, she laid down the quill. Her fingers were ink-stained; a wax fleck clung to her sleeve. She looked older than she had an hour ago, and stronger.

Nathaniel rose, walked around the table, and placed his hand atop hers. "Three days," he said. "That's what we've bought."

"Bought for you," he added, low, "and for a girl who draws roots like hands. Not for buyers. Not anymore."

Elizabeth met his eyes. "Then let's make them cost him."

They stood like that a long moment, hand to hand, ink and bloom between them.

Outside, the wind quieted. And the orchard, though sleeping, was still hers.

"Say it back to me," Elizabeth said, hands braced on the table's edge, eyes on the forged sheet.

Nathaniel obliged, voice low and deliberate. "Barrel fourteen-KB marked as sample; steward's blot shows haste; frost damage explains the delay. Held over, no sale entered, awaiting warehouse acknowledgment."

"And if he asks why a widow kept a steward's note at all?"

"Because the carter couldn't write," Nathaniel answered, meeting her gaze, "and you've learned not to trust any man's memory."

Her mouth twitched, half a smile, half defiance. "And the effect?"

"This buys you three days," he said. He tapped the margin where the false exemption lay. "Three clean days before Wainscott can petition the magistrate, three days before the Crown can force the barrels open."

Elizabeth drew a slow breath, the tension easing from her shoulders by the smallest degree. "Three days," she echoed, as if testing the number against her pulse. "Enough to finish the cull and move the surplus."

"Enough to win the time you need," Nathaniel said quietly, "if we keep our story straight."

The candles guttered; the ink gleamed dark and wet. For a heartbeat the stillroom held only their joined silence—two conspirators, three borrowed days, and a single line of forged ink standing between them and the Crown.

CHAPTER TWENTY-TWO

THE PRICE OF TRUTH

E lizabeth's voice was raw with fever, but the sharpness of her gaze hadn't dulled. The quilt was pulled high at her collarbone, her hair falling in a dark tangle over the pillow. On the table, a cup of broth had cooled untouched.

Nathaniel knocked once before stepping inside, a folded scrap of paper in hand. "We need to talk."

"If it's about cider shipments..." she started, but he cut her off.

"It's about a debt. Mine."

Her eyes narrowed, though the effort cost her. "What debt?"

"The one I carried when I first came here," he said. "There were men in Portsmouth who wanted their coin. I thought if I could convince you to sell your scions early, I could pay it off in one stroke. I didn't tell you because... I didn't want you to think I was only here for that."

"How dare you." Her fever-bright gaze didn't waver. "You remember, I told you about my husband's debts before we ever discussed graftwood. I told you because trust is coin in my ledger. You chose to keep yours in a locked box?"

"I'm so sorry." He took the reproach without flinching. "You're right. I was wrong to keep it from you." He unfolded the paper and laid it on her quilt. "The last of it's paid. Went out with the Bristol packet last week."

Elizabeth stared at it as though it might scorch. "And what am I meant to do with this information? Forgive you?"

"No," he said quietly. "Give me your list instead."

"My...list?"

"The list you keep in your head, the running list of everything you're meaning to tackle with everything else you're juggling."

She blushed. "There's no need."

"There is," he argued. "You're sick, you need the help, and I'm willing and ready to attempt to gain back your trust."

Sighing, Elizabeth sank back into the pillow. "I hate that you're right."

"All of it. Every chore, every repair, every miserable task you've been putting off since the season started. I'll do them all. Until it's square between us."

Her lips pressed together. Slowly, she reached for the notebook on her nightstand. When she began writing, her pen scratched like a rasp. The list grew long enough that he almost laughed, until he realized she was still writing.

- *Muck out the west paddock*
- *Clear the east ditch before the next rain*
- *Repack the graft vault crates*
- *Weed the north slope rows*
- *Split and stack three cords of wood*
- *Scrub the press floor and stone yard*

• *Tighten the stillroom gutter before frost*

• *Mend the south fence line and replace the rotted post near the lane*

• *Carry cider barrels from the cooper's shed to the cellar without rolling them*

• *Sort the seedling nursery by graft type*

• *Pick the late pears without bruising*

• *Oil every latch on every outbuilding*

• *Repair the tool shed hinge and lock*

• *Paint the henhouse trim*

• *Haul the failed beams from the cider barn to the burn pile.*

And at the very bottom, in a sharp hand:

Find out why the barn failed.

She tore the page free and handed it to him. "Do them all, Mr. Carter. Then we'll see."

He did them. Every back-breaking, splinter-drawing, blister-making task. His boots were caked in ditch mud, shoulders burned from hauling wood, palms scored from fence wire. Each evening, the list grew shorter. But the final item—why the barn failed—stuck like a thorn.

Nathaniel spent hours in the ruin's shadow, studying the grain of the fallen beam. He searched old ledgers, questioned John Thatcher, and climbed into the loft where dust lay thick enough to hide secrets. There, in the back of an old tool ledger, he found it: a folded scrap in the late Mr. Whitcombe's hand.

Cost for full beam: 3£ 4s: cheaper supplier offers 2£ 1s. Reinforce after harvest.

The harvest in question was five years past.

Elizabeth was still pale when he brought the paper to her bedside. He stood at the foot of her bed, hat in hand, feeling every mile between them. "It wasn't the storm," he said. "Your husband bought a beam too narrow to bear the load. Planned to brace it later. Never did."

She stared at the paper for a long moment, then set it aside as if it weighed too much. "He saved his coin and spent the risk on us."

Nathaniel hesitated, then laid another page beside it—his own notes. "These other beams were cut in the same season. The still-room rafter. The drain near the apple vault. You'll want to have them checked before winter."

Her gaze lifted, measuring him in silence.

"You told me once," he said, "that trust is coin in your ledger. I'm paying in more than chores now."

Elizabeth's mouth twitched, with not quite a smile, not quite a surrender. Slowly, she reached for the list on her nightstand, drew a neat line through the last item, and set it back down. "You've made it up to me," she said softly. "In my ledger, Mr. Carter, you're well in the black."

He allowed himself a small smile. "Then I'd best not earn myself another list."

Nathaniel set the list on the table, then dipped a cloth in the basin and wrung it tight. "May I?"

She hesitated before nodding wearily.

He brushed the fever from her brow with maddening gentleness, the way a man steadies a graft with two fingers and a prayer. "Sleep now," he said. "I'll sit a while and count the lamplight like harvest."

"You count barrels," she murmured.

"Only until you're well."

Her lashes lowered. He stayed, quiet as breath, refolding the blanket when she turned, lifting the cup when she coughed, and when her hand slipped from the coverlet, threading his fingers through hers so the heat had somewhere kinder to go.

***

Elizabeth sliced the twine with her pruning knife.

The letter had been delivered by a boy with no name...just a red wool cap, a crooked gait, and mud crusted thick on his cuffs. Phoebe had reached the door first and opened it, her soft voice drifting ahead of Elizabeth's: "Are you the barrel runner?" The boy had shrugged and held out the folded page without speaking, then turned and vanished down the lane.

Now, in the stillroom, Elizabeth sat at the worktable while Phoebe perched on the low stool nearby, carefully copying cider-apple names into a small ledger. The child's tongue stuck out ever so slightly as she bent over the page, brow furrowed. Elizabeth couldn't bring herself to look at her just yet.

The wax seal bore the Crown, crude and iron-hard, the jagged edge of Parliament's reach pressed deep into the page.

She broke it cleanly and unfolded the letter.

To Mistress Elizabeth Whitcombe, Whitcombe Orchard, Hereford-shire

Be advised the Excise Office has reviewed your Petition for Relief under the Cider & Perry Duties (1763). Upon examination of your ledgers, stamped slips for the prior harvest, and your asserted losses from frost and aphid blight:

1. Relief Denied. No exemption is admissible under Clause IV; your operation does not meet the qualifying tests for charitable, clerical, or military supply.

2. Adjustment Denied. Declared yield variances remain unsupported by Crown-stamped warehouse acknowledgments.

3. Inspection Advanced. A provisional re-inspection is scheduled three (3) days from receipt of this notice. Inspector Wainscott to attend with the magistrate and a seal officer.

4. Sanction. If discrepancy persists, surplus and implements may be seized pro tempore pending assessment; fines to be levied at 2s per missing barrel equivalent, plus costs.

5. Appeal. You may lodge appeal at the next Quarter Sessions within 14 days, upon posting bond equal to the estimated duty; trusteeship or lawful marriage to a qualified freeholder may establish standing for certain petitions.

— *Office of Excise, Worcester District*

Elizabeth read it twice. The words didn't soften. "Three days," she said, the syllables flat as a date cut into stone.

As if she hadn't walked every inch of this orchard since she could stand. As if she hadn't bent her back packing frost-blankets, counted the barrels through fever and rain, and stitched every harvest line by hand. As if Whitcombe's ink still outweighed Trewyn's grafts and sweat.

She felt the letter tremble in her hands.

Phoebe glanced up. "A bad one?"

Elizabeth tried to lie and couldn't. Her throat closed. "A foolish one," she said instead. She attempted a smile, but it didn't hold. Phoebe returned to her writing, slower now, her small ink-smudged fingers gripping the pen tightly.

From above, the faint creak of boots on a floorboard. William again, likely dangling his string from the loft to try and catch the barn cats by the tail. She'd remind him later that even cleverness needed reins.

Elizabeth let the letter fall flat on the table. Her hand hovered above it. For one breath, she imagined tearing it clean in half and feeding it to the mash. Let the pulp soak it through. Let the next inspector come sniffing after vinegar.

But fury wasn't enough, not anymore. Not when she had five days. Not when a man named Wainscott would return with writs and wax and the Crown's contempt packed neat in a box.

She looked again at the signature:

E. Whitcombe...not even Elizabeth. Just a placeholder.

Phoebe stirred. Then reached carefully into her apron and withdrew a flattened flower, pressed too soon, the edges already browning. "I saved this," she said. "From the Foxwhelp graft. You said it might not bloom again."

Elizabeth took it gently. The petals crumbled slightly between her fingers.

"I thought it was lucky," Phoebe added, barely audible. "You don't have to keep it."

Elizabeth set the letter aside and placed the browned bloom atop it, like a final word on a grave. "Thank you," she said. "I'll keep it."

Her hand found the edge of the ledger. Her fingers clenched it, white-knuckled. Then she breathed, slow and deliberate, like pruning thornwood from a fruiting branch.

"Right," she murmured aloud. "So that's the price."

Behind her, the copper hissed. Outside, a crow gave a sharp call, like a hinge swinging open on winter's door. The paper crackled in her hand as she stood.

"Phoebe," she said gently, "can you mind the mash for ten minutes?"

The girl nodded without hesitation, already sliding off the stool, careful not to catch her twisted foot on the stool's edge.

Elizabeth didn't fold the letter again. The words had already branded themselves beneath her collarbone. She walked to the hearthroom without looking back.

In the hearthroom, the fire had burned down to soft orange coals. The longcase clock ticked solemnly, an old Dutch piece her grandfather had brought back through Harwich, its hands still accurate, its chime stilled long ago. The ash box sat squat beneath the grate, soot-slick and square, its iron lid slightly warped from years of damp heat.

Elizabeth knelt beside it, the hem of her apron brushing the hearthstone. The air smelled of ash, beeswax, and buried paper.

Inside the box were all the things she hadn't let herself look at for weeks: the solicitor's first letter, the list of untaxed barrels, the foolscap Thomas had written on with his beautiful, damning pen. Receipts he'd folded so carefully, sealing his debts with flattery and flourish. She had let them lie here, quiet and smoldering.

Phoebe's small feet padded into the doorway behind her. "I stirred the mash," she said. "And shut the vent."

Elizabeth didn't look up. "Good."

Phoebe hesitated on the threshold. "Was the letter very bad?"

Elizabeth reached for the iron lid and placed the newest wound atop the pile, folded, but not hidden. "It was... as expected." She closed the lid slowly. The thunk of iron on iron made her flinch.

Phoebe lingered a moment longer, fingers plucking at her sleeve. The child had her mother's stillness...that quiet watchfulness Ruth had once turned on Elizabeth like a mirror.

"Why don't you go up and rest?" Elizabeth said, not unkindly. "I'll finish the evening check."

A pause.

"I'll leave the lamp for you," Phoebe said, and padded back down the hall, her steps slower now. One foot lighter than the other.

The house creaked as she went. William's voice drifted faintly from upstairs, some boyish sing-song about barrels or cats. Elizabeth let it pass.

Elizabeth stared at the ash box another moment, then stood, brushing cinders from her knees. She spoke aloud, voice raw as a root: "I said I wouldn't forge. But truth has a price."

Her mind leapt, unbidden, to the slope by Phoebe's cairn...the Foxwhelp cross they'd set after midnight, Phoebe's little drawing tucked at its root. Fourteen-KB buys the hours, Nathaniel had said softly then. This buys the years.

She shut the iron lid. "We have to win both."

Behind her, the door creaked, and her heart leapt. She recognized the careful cadence of his boots, the pause he always gave her, as if measuring whether she'd throw him out again or let him stay.

Nathaniel waited at the threshold. "Was it the answer we feared?"

She nodded once, not looking up. "They've made it simple. A marriage or a sale. That's the shape of my freedom now."

He stepped in, but not close. His voice was calm, but it carried the weight of steel wrapped in linen. "Then marry me."

The air shifted. The coals clicked in the grate. Elizabeth rose slowly, ash still clinging to her palms. "You've a talent for blunt proposals," she said, not quite meeting his eyes. "You should marry a young American homemaker."

"It's not the romantic proposal I wanted to give you," he replied. "It's a line in the dirt. I'll stand behind you, by law, if I must."

She turned to face him, mouth tight. "Don't dress this up as selfless," she said.

"I'm not," he said. "It would protect you. It would protect the orchard. But it wouldn't be selfless."

Her voice dropped. "Because you'd gain what? A stake? A legacy? A piece of England to call your own?"

Nathaniel's jaw shifted. "Because I'd gain you. And I've already staked myself here," he said, voice low. "Not in your ledger. In your life."

That silenced her.

He didn't move, didn't reach for her, but just stood still, fists quiet at his sides, waiting.

"I don't want to marry for paperwork," she said. "Not again. Not to stamp a seal and watch another man gamble with what I love."

"I won't sign over you," he said. "I'll sign with you. If the magistrate needs a name, he can learn to read two. You won't be alone," he said, evenly. "Not while I have breath or ink in my hands."

Ash dusted his jaw; she almost brushed it away, almost pressed her mouth to the vow he'd made her. "Ink fades," she said, but too softly to convince either of them. He didn't reach for her. He let the wanting stand between them.

The fire gave a low pop.

"You don't know what it costs," she whispered.

"I do," he said. "And I'd pay it. Every damn day."

***

The sky had darkened by the time Elizabeth left the hearthroom.

She stepped out onto the orchard path, apron strings loose at her back, her boots finding the ridged earth by memory. The night held no wind. The trees loomed still and watchful, silent silhouettes in rows, their limbs knotted with the weight of too many seasons.

Somewhere up the hill, the press gear groaned as it settled. The house behind her glowed faintly in the windowpanes. A single lamp still burned in the stairwell; Phoebe had left it, just as promised.

A soft sound followed her onto the path. Not the tread of Nathaniel's boots...this was lighter, and barefoot.

"Phoebe?" Elizabeth asked, not turning.

The girl's voice came from behind, quiet as leaf-fall. "I couldn't sleep."

Elizabeth turned slightly. Phoebe stood in her nightdress, a wool shawl wrapped clumsily around her shoulders. Her hair, unbraided, clung in wisps to her temple. "I heard voices," she added. "I thought you were angry."

"Not angry. Just... deciding."

Phoebe didn't ask what. She only stepped closer and looked toward the slope where the orchard bent east. "You always walk here when you're thinking."

Elizabeth gave a dry half-smile. "Hard habit to break."

"I like it better when you walk," Phoebe said. "Not when you sit at the table with your fists tight."

"You notice that?"

"You breathe different too. Shallow, like you're bracing."

Elizabeth's throat went tight again.

"Will's the same before he drops a ladder," Phoebe added. "He doesn't think anyone sees."

A small silence fell between them, then Phoebe whispered, "Is the Crown taking us?"

"No," Elizabeth said firmly, before she could stop herself. "No one's taking anything. Not without a fight."

Phoebe nodded resolutely. "I can help."

"I know you can." Elizabeth's voice nearly broke. She reached out and tugged the shawl a little higher around the girl's shoulders. "Back to bed, love. Before your feet go to ice."

Phoebe hesitated, then obeyed, limping lightly up the slope toward the glow of the kitchen window. Elizabeth watched until she disappeared inside.

A moment later, Nathaniel joined her near the rise, where the Old Widow loomed above the younger saplings. Moonlight filtered through the bare branches, painting silver along the graft's linen wrappings.

"She's holding," he said quietly.

Elizabeth exhaled. "For now."

They stood side by side, the silence between them full of all they hadn't said, and all they had.

"I meant what I said," he added. "About marriage."

"I..." She folded her arms. "You'd take on my debts. My risk. My name."

"I'd take any of the weight that you allow," he said. "If you'd let me."

"And if I say no?"

"Then I stay anyway. If you'll have me."

Elizabeth huffed a breath that wasn't quite a laugh. "You've a gift for wearing me down."

"No," he said gently. "Only for listening long enough to hear the part you don't say."

She turned to face him, her hands no longer clenched. "You don't know what I'm like in a marriage," she said. "You think you've seen my temper. You haven't. You think you've seen how far I'll bend. You haven't. I'm not a wife who smiles and yields and lets the man sign the ledger."

"I wouldn't want her," he said. "I want the woman who nearly bit my hand off the first time I offered her a contract."

She snorted. "You're mad."

"Only about you."

The silence fluttered, then steadied, like wind testing a sail.

Elizabeth reached for the lowest branch and touched the scar where they'd joined scion to rootstock. The wax held. The wound was sealed, but still fresh. Still healing.

"You're not the only one who's planted something here," she murmured. "And I've no mind to see it trampled just because Parliament likes its titles neat."

"I wouldn't sign you over," Nathaniel said. "We'd sign beside each other."

She looked up at him. This time, her expression wasn't wary or guarded.

It was tired, brave, and something he could fall in love with all over again.

She stepped toward the barn's soft yellow glow. "I'm not saying yes," she said, gentler now.

"I know."

"And I'm not promising you anything."

"I wouldn't ask you to."

"But if I let you stay... if I let you keep standing beside me, even when the wind turns..."

"I will," he said.

They paused beneath the Old Widow. Moonlight silvered the new bandage on the Foxwhelp cross farther downslope.

"She's holding," he said.

"For now," she answered.

He didn't reach for her; he waited until she lifted her hand first. When her fingers found his, he closed around them like a brace at the seam of a wound. "If you let me stay," he murmured, "I'll guard what you name. The child. The line. Your right to sign your own page."

She nodded once, the movement small and sovereign. "Then stay. And don't forget who leads."

"Never," he said.

Their hands stayed linked all the way back to the lighted door.

CHAPTER TWENTY-THREE

A KIND OF GRAFT

The hearth in Nathaniel's room at the King's Arms had burned down to embers, though the chill of morning hadn't yet breached the stone flags underfoot. He stood at the foot of the bed...sleeves rolled, boots scuffed, and everything he owned in England laid out before him.

Not much, really.

His satchel—leather-soft and sweat-worn—lay open beside a modest stack of shirts, a rolled vellum map of transatlantic shipping routes, and the tin case holding his mother's pruning knife. He packed slowly. Not out of doubt. Just because he wanted to remember this room, the scent of last night's fire, the stubborn window latch, the ghost of apples still on his palms.

The knife went in first. Then the ledger he hadn't dared to send.

And finally, the Foxwhelp blossom.

It had dried, mostly. Curled in on itself like something sleeping, still edged with a faint smudge of red-gold. The same one he'd pressed between her ledger pages. The same one he'd found by the stillroom vat after she'd let him touch more than bark or paper.

He didn't throw it away. Instead, he wrapped it in a strip of linen and tucked it deep into the crease of his mother's cultivar book. A strange kind of prayer. A keepsake he hadn't earned.

Beside the book, half-covered by the folded map, lay something he'd nearly forgotten: a small wooden token shaped like an apple, carved clumsily from orchard scrap. He'd bought it in Ledbury weeks ago, thinking Phoebe might like it...she had a sharp eye for orchard shapes and a way of turning discarded things into meaning.

He picked it up, thumbed the notch at its stem.

Miles would've laughed at that. Sentimental nonsense, he'd say. Give the girl coin, not carvings.

But then again, Miles didn't have a niece with twine on her fingers and bark in her boots. He slipped it into his pocket.

Nathaniel sat at the narrow writing table, drew a fresh sheet from his satchel, and uncapped his pen. The letter to Philadelphia had written itself half a dozen times in his head over the past week, but now that the moment had come, the words landed heavy.

To R.H.,

Sapling shipment is suspended indefinitely. The Whitcombe orchard will not be divided, sold, or contracted without full ownership rights. The line remains hers.

I resign my claim.

—N. Carter

He let the ink dry naturally. No blotting sand. No hurry.

Then folded the sheet, sealed it with the old wax stamp that had once been his mother's, and placed it atop the mantel, where the post rider stopped twice weekly for Bristol-bound parcels.

He stared at the cooling hearth a while longer.

No sign of her, not that he'd expected one. He shrugged on his coat, slung the satchel over his shoulder, and paused in the threshold. "I asked for nothing," he said aloud, quiet as confession, "and she gave me more than I dared. And still... I wanted more."

He pulled a second sheet and wrote more slowly than was his habit.

To Mr. Bowman of Haverford Green

Withdraw my commission and any finder's fee attached. If you seek Whitcombe grafts, you will apply to Mistress Whitcombe directly and on her terms. Any credit extended in my name is rescinded; any profit owed to me by custom I assign to her in full.

This forfeiture is voluntary and final.

— N. Carter

He sanded, sealed, and, because he knew how rumors traveled, carried both letters down to the common room and read the Bowman notice aloud at the keeper's desk. Two factors at the fire looked up sharply; one smirk faltered. Nathaniel laid a half crown and his mother's apple-blossom ring as surety for the courier fee.

"Mad to cut yourself out, Carter," the elder factor muttered.

"Not mad," Nathaniel said. "Resolved."

He collected the ring only when the keeper nodded to the stamped receipts cooling in the wax.

He stepped out into the morning.

The day was clear, windless. The kind of pale-washed spring sky no one remembers unless something happens beneath it. Nathaniel didn't yet know this would be that kind of day.

***

The orchard was already humming by the time Nathaniel reached the gate, the scrape of pruning hooks, a wheeling of birds over the hedgerow, the rhythmic thunk of barrels being turned near the press barn.

And there she was.

Elizabeth Whitcombe. Hair unpinned, cheeks wind-flushed, her shawl clutched but slipping, boots muddied at the hem. She looked like she'd left in a hurry and hadn't stopped second-guessing herself since.

In her hands was a folded sheet of parchment, creased soft at the corners, gripped hard at the edges.

A long silence passed, the orchard rustling behind them with the sound of small lives at work...birds, branches, a spade hitting dirt.

"I heard," she said at last, "you told the innkeeper you'd be gone by sundown."

"I planned to be."

Her chin lifted slightly. "Unless something's changed?"

He didn't answer with words. Just watched her.

She stepped forward and held out the parchment—not like a demand, but like an offering.

"I drafted this last night. Didn't sleep." Her mouth tilted in a half-smile. "That's your fault."

He took the paper with care.

It was formal but spare: a deed of joint stewardship. One small parcel of orchard land, bounded in ink and witness, assigned equally to Nathaniel Carter and Elizabeth Whitcombe. For shared cultivation. Mutual responsibility. Neither party with power to sell or split without the other's consent.

Her name. His. "You're offering me land," he said slowly, "not marriage."

"No," she said. "Not ownership. Partnership. And perhaps, this would both enable you to not go destitute after your clean break with Miles. And...maybe we could court a bit more before we speak of marriage again."

"Elizabeth…" His throat felt tight. "This is more than I deserve."

"It's what you've earned. And what I choose." She lifted her chin stubbornly. "Don't argue."

He looked down again at the page. "You're sure?"

"Only fools are sure," she said. "But I'm not planting certainty. I'm planting a chance." She reached for his hand, steady and clear-eyed.

He took it.

They walked together in silence past the lower rows, where Phoebe's linen basket still waited like a small altar of scraps and use. The girl looked up but said nothing, only resumed her sorting…twine, cloth, threadbare bits. Her fingers moved quickly, but her eyes followed them as they passed.

They stopped beneath the Old Widow.

The tree stood as it had on the day of the graft, bark weathered but firm, linen wrap darkened by dew, the wax joint still sealed like a stitched wound.

Nathaniel touched the graft, thumb grazing the seam. "She took," he murmured.

Elizabeth stood beside him. She unfolded the parchment, smoothing the page with one palm, then reached into her apron for a small walnut-stained inkwell and a stub of quill trimmed short for control. "I'd rather not carry this back unmarked," she said. "If you're still willing."

He took the pen. His fingers didn't tremble, but the weight of the moment settled through his spine. The ink bore her stillroom scent of oak gall, vinegar, ash, now so familiar. He bent his knee, resting the parchment on his thigh, and signed his name beneath hers.

When he rose, Elizabeth reached to steady the page in the breeze, then pressed her hand lightly against the tree's bark, just above the join. "Some grafts don't take," she said.

Nathaniel glanced at her.

She didn't look back, but her voice carried certainty. "But if the rootstock's good..."

He finished quietly, "You get something new."

A sound of movement behind them.

Phoebe stood near the path, one hand on her cane, the other brushing the leaves of a nearby sapling.

"You came to check the graft?" Elizabeth asked.

Phoebe nodded. "You said it might need rebinding."

Nathaniel crouched to let her closer. "Well?" he asked. "What's the verdict?"

Phoebe peered at the join like a tradesman inspecting barrel hoops. "It's holding. But it needs watching."

He smiled. "Most worthwhile things do."

Phoebe pulled something from her apron: a twist of cloth. She unwrapped it carefully to reveal a Foxwhelp blossom, fresher than the one he'd carried, though slightly bruised at one edge.

"I pressed this one," she said, holding it out to Elizabeth. "For when it's time to write again."

Elizabeth accepted it gently. "Thank you."

Phoebe nodded and turned, her steps steady on the damp grass.

Nathaniel watched her go. "She'll outgrow us both."

Elizabeth's voice held pride. "That's the point."

***

By noon the taproom at the King's Arms was warm with stew and speculation. Elizabeth stepped onto the settle, knuckles white around the nail she'd brought from the cooper's bench.

She pinned the NOTICE beside the grain prices. A murmur rippled the room.

"That's the widow's hand," someone near the door said.

"Steward?" someone else sniffed. "Smells like marriage by halves."

"Looks like law by wholes," the keeper replied, reading the line about Quarter Sessions.

Nathaniel stood two paces back, hat in hand, silent as a brace. When the room's noise swelled toward her, he shifted just enough that the attention slanted his way.

"Questions to me," he said mildly, "complaints to the magistrate, and respect to the mistress of the orchard whose name is on every barrel you drink."

Elizabeth didn't look at him, but her shoulders eased the barest fraction. Outside, a child's laugh skittered along the lane; when they stepped into the daylight, Phoebe was there with William at her side, bright-eyed.

"You posted it," Phoebe breathed.

"We did," Elizabeth said.

"And you didn't faint," William added, impressed.

"Not even a little," Nathaniel said gravely, earning a snort from Elizabeth that made William grin.

They stood a moment longer beneath the Old Widow, the parchment signed, the graft holding. Not yet fruiting, but rooted now.

When the children ran off, Elizabeth and Nathaniel took the long path by the east wall, where the wind always found a way in and old stone held the day's heat.

"I should tell you something," he said. "The orchard in Virginia...my mother's...may yet be lost. A Threadneedle Street firm bought the debt. I've kept that truth like a thorn in my boot. It bleeds when I stand, and I stood here anyway."

She walked a few steps in silence. "Then I'll tell you something of equal weight," she said. "I've been afraid to let my name sit beside any man's again. Not because I doubt my strength, God knows I don't, but because the ink dries faster on a woman's mistakes."

He looked at her. "Then we won't hurry the ink."

She nodded. "But we won't let fear hold the pen either."

They stopped where the hedgerow broke just enough to see the river glint. She turned to him and, very simply, said, "We will take the next blow together. We will answer Wainscott together. We will lose, if we lose, together."

"We will win together," he answered, and the way he said we put a knot in her throat that felt like release.

He reached in his coat and pressed something small into her palm: the clumsy apple token he'd bought weeks ago and then forgotten. "For Phoebe," he said, a little sheepish. "Or for the graft book, if she turns up her nose."

Elizabeth turned the little apple over once with her thumb, the notch at the stem catching the light. "We'll have her name the Foxwhelp cross," she said. "We started it. She'll carry it."

"We will," he said.

They walked on, speaking mostly in practicals—barrel counts, seedling trenching, the timetable to Quarter Sessions—but the grammar had shifted. Every sentence found its way to we.

There were no footsteps but theirs now...soft against the moss-heavy earth. No birdsong but the high, circling cry of a kite wheeling far above the hedgerow.

Nathaniel slowed, then turned back toward the graft, the scion, the rows of trees he had once measured by ledger and route. Now he knew them differently. By wound and weather and the shape of her care.

He exhaled, steadying himself to leave, but she caught his sleeve. When he turned, her eyes were already on him, clear and windlit and full of some unspoken truth that asked no permission.

And then she kissed him. Not like the first time, when uncertainty clung like ash. Not like the second, where need had fought silence. This kiss claimed, answered, promised. It was everything they didn't know they needed,

Her fingers slipped into his hair. His hand found her waist, her back, the warmth he already knew like a map inside him. He held her as if the orchard might vanish. She kissed him like it never would.

When they parted, barely, her lips brushed the corner of his mouth. "You're still the gamble," she said softly.

He smiled into the space between them. "Always."

Her fingers traced his jaw, rough with travel, ink, and all he hadn't said. "But I'm willing," she murmured, "to plant."

Behind them, the newly posted NOTICE snapped once in the courtyard wind; in the inn's ledger, Bowman's clerk would find a seal that cut Nathaniel out of profit by his own hand.

The gate creaked faintly, but neither of them stepped through.

Not yet.

CHAPTER TWENTY-FOUR

FIRST FRUIT

The green had been swept, the press scrubbed, and every able hand in the village turned out in coats a touch finer than usual. Bunting strung from cider barrels to fence-posts fluttered in the wind, cut from scrap cloth and dyed with beetroot, onion skin, and apple bark. Children in scuffed shoes darted between stalls holding caramel apples on rush-wrapped sticks. Someone was playing a fiddle off-key.

Elizabeth stood at the edge, her shawl tucked close and a basket cradled in both hands. It was still warm, lined with a linen cloth and heavy with the scent of spice, cider vinegar, and just a hint of rosemary. Beside her, Phoebe leaned slightly against a painted post bearing the Whitcombe crest. "You sure they'll take it?" Phoebe asked, craning to peek under the cloth.

Elizabeth gave a faint shrug. "They'll take it. Whether they like it is another matter."

Inside the basket sat six small tarts: deep golden in their rosemary-laced crusts, the filling a thick reduction of Foxwhelp apples, cider syrup, and a touch of grated quince. Phoebe had helped with the lattice tops, her uneven hands forming crooked but cheerful Xs across each one.

They were entered under the name:

Spiced Foxwhelp Tarts – A Whitcombe Orchard Heritage Recipe.

Phoebe gave a sideways glance at the other entries: a treacle apple pudding, a honeyed dumpling in muslin, a jar of jelly so clear you could read through it. "Ours smells best."

Elizabeth didn't reply. She'd spotted Nathaniel at the far edge of the green, talking with the cider stewards and laughing at something John Thatcher had just muttered. The sight was strange still...familiar, but new. He belonged, and yet hadn't always. The orchard had a way of changing people, herself included.

From the central table, a call rang out:

"All entries for tasting, please! Judging begins on the hour!"

Elizabeth stepped forward to place her basket on the linen-covered table. She did not smile. But her hands were steady.

Phoebe followed, limping slightly, her notebook tucked under one arm. She had entered something too...drawings and grafting notes carefully labeled in her slanted hand, tied with a sprig of dried apple blossom and tucked in the "young naturalist" category.

Behind them, the village stirred: women comparing spice blends, a girl with ribbon-tied braids showing off her painted cider mug, an old man asleep under the barrel rack. Music drifted through the smoke of roasting pork and pressed cakes.

And the wind, sweet with blossom and yeast, carried the scent of Elizabeth's tarts toward the judges' tent.

The sun had crested, warming the green just enough to draw out the scents of sugar, peel, and yeast. Judges in well-brushed coats made their rounds like parsons at a christening, leaning, sniffing, murmuring to one another over folded papers.

Elizabeth stood back with the rest of the orcharders, arms crossed and basket empty. Phoebe hovered beside her, shifting her weight between feet, her expression caught somewhere between pride and dread.

One of the judges, Mrs. Templeton, who'd run the village bake-house since before Elizabeth had married, paused before the Foxwhelp tarts. She wore her apron like armor, her spectacles low on her nose, and her silver hair coiled into something not unlike a grafted knot.

She took a bite. Then another. She said nothing.

Another judge, the vicar's wife, leaned in and murmured something. Mrs. Templeton raised a hand, finished chewing, and only then said, "That crust *sings*."

Phoebe let out a breath loud enough that a boy nearby turned his head. Elizabeth's lips didn't twitch, but her fingers flexed slightly at her sides.

Next came the naturalists' table. There, laid out beside a child's pressed-flower page and someone's crude drawing of an orchard mouse, sat Phoebe's ledger, opened to a diagram of cleft grafting techniques, each step inked and captioned. A young steward examined it, tracing the sketches with one finger.

"She did those herself," Elizabeth said softly.

The steward looked up. "This is hers?"

Phoebe nodded, one heel dragging back half a pace. "I used a twig dipped in ink. Quills splatter too much."

The steward glanced at the ribbon on her ledger's corner—white for youth entries. Then he turned back to the page, brows lifted. "You've shown cambium detail."

Phoebe blinked. "I have?"

"Yes. This... this is not beginner's work."

She said nothing, but her grip on the ledger tightened, and her spine seemed to straighten with pride.

A bell rang. The tasting had ended. Judging began.

Elizabeth didn't watch it happen. She turned toward the far end of the field, where someone had tapped open a barrel and children were pressing small cups to the spout. The sun on the copper hoop glinted like a seal.

She remembered that feeling...waiting for a verdict. It had never favored her.

But this time, something was different.

"Miss Whitcombe," someone called. She turned.

Mrs. Templeton held out a ribbon. Red, stitched with white. "You've won."

Elizabeth took it with both hands. "Thank you."

"It's the rosemary," Mrs. Templeton added, as if unwilling to let the moment pass without explanation. "Everyone forgets apples have bitterness, too. Yours let that speak."

Elizabeth inclined her head. "It's a truth we know at the orchard."

Phoebe was next. Her name, called by the young steward who now looked slightly awestruck. "Miss Phoebe Trewyn," he said. "For contribution to botanical record and emerging expertise in English grafting methods." He offered her a ribbon, white with green edging.

Phoebe didn't reach for it immediately. She looked at her aunt first.

Elizabeth smiled.

Then Phoebe stepped forward and took the ribbon, then her ledger, clutching both to her chest like heirlooms.

From behind them, Nathaniel's voice rang out: "Does this mean we're taking home two prizes?"

Elizabeth turned. "Three," she corrected, eyes on Phoebe.

The girl was still standing tall, cheeks flushed, spine straight. She'd earned every thread of it.

Elizabeth felt Nathaniel's hand graze hers. "Walk with me," he murmured.

They slipped through the milling crowd to the orchard gate where the dusk gathered like blue smoke. The festival music thinned behind them until only the hush of leaves remained.

Nathaniel rested his shoulder against the old gatepost. "I've been thinking about what comes after prizes and ribbons."

Her pulse ticked once, hard. "And?"

"I'll stay through the winter grafts. The Old Widow needs watching. So do you."

She arched a brow, but her smile betrayed her. "Co-stewards, then. Through the winter at least."

"And longer if you'll have me." He caught her gaze. "We can draw up a plan. Foxwhelp lines, spring cuttings, side by side."

Elizabeth reached for his hand and laced her fingers through his. "We will," she said, the we landing with quiet certainty.

He glanced toward the green where Phoebe stood with her prize ribbon gleaming in the last of the light. "And the junior steward?"

"An apprenticeship," Elizabeth answered without hesitation. "By spring she'll know every graft in the orchard."

Nathaniel's eyes softened. "Then we're agreed...three stewards, three seasons to come."

Elizabeth's breath left her on a quiet laugh. "A family, of sorts."

He tilted his forehead to hers. "Of ours."

She let the words settle like a vow, then rose on her toes and kissed him, slow and certain, a promise of all the winters and harvests ahead.

He tasted of apple and smoke. His hand slid to the nape of her neck, gentle through her ribbon, and for a breath the music fell away to the thud of his heart under her palm.

The orchard slept again. The sky had gone lavender, and a hush had settled over the kitchen, flour dust drifting in the quiet, a single candle throwing light over the scuffed table.

Phoebe sat curled on the bench, her legs tucked under her skirt, a blanket around her shoulders and her prize ribbon still pinned at the corner. Her ledger was open across her knees, one twig-quill held loose in her fingers. She was trying to sketch a rosemary sprig with cross-hatching, her brows furrowed in deep concentration.

Across from her, Elizabeth sat with a different book, the orchard's household journal. It had never held recipes before, only barrel yields, weather notes, and grafting charts. But tonight, she turned to a blank page and wrote carefully across the top:

Foxwhelp and Rosemary Apple Tart

Her handwriting was slow and deliberate, the kind she used for grafting diagrams or ledgers destined for the Crown.

Pastry:

- 8 oz fine flour
- 6 oz cold butter
- 1 oz lard (if on hand)
- A pinch of salt
- Cold water to bind

Filling:

- 2 lbs tart apples (Foxwhelp preferred)
- 2–3 sprigs rosemary, chopped fine
- 3 oz dark sugar
- 1 oz cider vinegar
- A grating of lemon peel (if not dear)
- Pinch of salt and pinch of ground clove
- Optional: a spoon of thick cream stirred in before baking

"Should I draw it?" Phoebe asked suddenly.

Elizabeth glanced up. "Draw what?"

"The tart. So someone reading it knows it's not meant to be neat."

Elizabeth smiled. "Yes. Show the cracks."

Phoebe grinned, then turned to a fresh page in her own ledger.

Elizabeth finished the final line:

Bake in a hot oven until the scent alone could bring an orchard back from frost.

She paused.

Then, beneath it, in smaller script:

Best served warm. Even better shared.

Phoebe hummed softly, her quill dancing. "Do you think someone will find it, years from now?"

"I hope so."

"And make it?"

Elizabeth folded the book shut, her thumb pressed gently against the spine. "They'll have to. It's a winning recipe now."

Nathaniel appeared in the doorway, sleeves rolled, curls damp with mist. "Have either of you left that bench since dusk?"

"No," they said together.

He crossed to the hearth, then leaned against the lintel with a soft, crooked smile. "Good. I rather like you both there."

She reached to smudge the ash from his cheek; he caught her wrist and kissed the heel of her hand. The room felt smaller, safer...two people and a future the size of an orchard.

Phoebe held up her drawing: a lopsided tart, steam curling in the shape of apple leaves. "I'm illustrating the legend."

"Ah," he said. "Then you'd best put both your names on it."

Elizabeth looked at him over the candlelight, eyes steady.

"No," she said. "One name."

She nodded toward Phoebe. The girl blinked, then sat a little taller.

Elizabeth opened the journal once more and added beneath the recipe title:

From the kitchen of P.T., junior steward of Whitcombe Orchard.

Nathaniel moved behind her, the candlelight catching the copper in his hair. He set his palms lightly at her waist.

"You've given her the orchard's first fruit," he whispered, voice roughened by the long day.

Elizabeth turned. The warmth of his hands anchored her; the quiet pressed close around them. He brushed a stray curl from her cheek.

"Elizabeth..." His voice faltered, then steadied. "We're not only keeping trees alive. We're building something worth inheriting."

Her answer was a kiss that left no doubt, deep and unhurried, tasting of sugar and smoke and every risk they had chosen together. He drew her nearer until the world shrank to breath and heartbeat and the faint rustle of Phoebe's even breathing on the settle.

When they parted, she rested her brow against his. "We will tend it," she whispered. "The orchard. Her future. Us."

He smiled, the quiet surety of it a promise. "Together."

Outside, the orchard stood dark and waiting. Inside, the candle guttered and flared, sealing their vow in light and shadow.

Outside, the trees stood silhouetted against the darkening sky.

Inside, the kitchen glowed, warm with candlelight, sugar, rosemary, and the quiet promise of things that would last.

SPICED FOXWHELP TARTS

B ased on 18th-century English apple tart recipes, this includes:

   • Foxwhelp apples (or any tart heritage apple)
  • Boiled cider or cider syrup
  • Grated quince or lemon zest (for sharpness)
  • Nutmeg and clove (limited cinnamon, as it was expensive)
  • Rosemary-laced crust (a nod to savory-sweet pairings common in
the 1700s)

A Tart of Foxwhelps & Rosemary
As set down by P.T., junior steward of Whitcombe Orchard
Anno Domini 1764

To be served warm when the frost hath fled, and shared whilst the
hearth still glows.

<u>For the Crust:</u>

Take 8 ounces of fine flour and rub therein 6 ounces of butter cold, with 1 ounce lard if the kitchen allows. Add a pinch of salt, and bind all with cold water 'til it gather as paste. Roll not overmuch. Let it rest in a cool place while the filling is prepared.

For the Filling:

Pare and slice finely 2 pounds of Foxwhelp apples (or any sharp sort), and stew them gently with 3 ounces dark sugar and a single spoon cider vinegar 'til softened but not lost. Stir in 2 or 3 sprigs rosemary chopped most fine, a scant grating of lemon peel if not too dear, and a pinch each of salt and ground clove.

If cream is at hand, stir in one good spoon just before baking. Else, it may be left plain.

To Bake:

Lay the paste in a shallow tart pan, fill with the apple compote, and cover loosely with strips or a crumbled crust as suits the kitchen. Bake in a hot oven until the scent may rouse even a sleeping tree.

Let stand, then serve warm with strong tea or fresh cider.

Nota Bene:

This tart needs no fine form. Cracks are welcome. Sweetness and sharpness may be amended to taste.

AFTERWORD

AUTHOR'S NOTE

By 1766 the Cider Act was gone, repealed under pressure from both Parliament and the public. The protests had been fierce enough to turn cider from a quiet country drink into a political flashpoint. But the damage was done. Many small orchards never reopened, and some families left cider-making entirely, turning their land over to grazing or grain.

Herefordshire, though, kept its reputation for sharp, fragrant cider apples. The varieties in this book (Foxwhelp, Kingston Black, Dabinett) still crop up in orchards today, though many of the old varieties have nearly vanished. The early bracing, the stillrooms scented with rosemary and meadowsweet, the long fermenting in oak barrels: these were real enough, passed from hand to hand over generations.

Elizabeth Whitcombe, Nathaniel Carter, Miles, Phoebe, William, John: these were inventions. But the stakes they lived with, the narrow margins of survival, and the stubborn pride in a good apple crop all belong to the time and place. In 1763, Herefordshire's orchards stood at the edge of change. Some endured, some were lost. And maybe somewhere a woman still tends a tree planted in those years, and a man still walks beside her, knowing the roots will hold.

MANY THANKS

Chris, my husband, who supports me and my writing with every breath, every bookstore visit, every bubble bath of me time.

Katherine and Michael, my parents, who have supported my writing and believed in me since before they taught me to use a pencil.

My darling daughter Bailey, who inspires me with her own incredible reading and writing every day.

Maria, my editor from Juicy Details Editing, who gave me a manuscript critique for this book I shall treasure forever.

Nicola, my friend and artist who reads all my books and drew the logo for my own cider CANDY company years ago: Cider Sweets.

The most wonderful writing group in the world: Katherine, Arlyn, Gretchen, Carrie, and SarahAnn, who read my writing every single month.

My beta readers for this book, Tehniat and Lorraine, whose feedback that helped shape this story into the book it is today.

The Emerald City Romance Writers, a group I'm honored to be a part of, and whose excellent workshops and intentional events bring alive the experience of writing. Thank you for connecting me with so many others in this space.

ABOUT THE AUTHOR

Matilda Lockwood is a writer, artist, tea drinker, and passionate believer in the magic of humans.

A eager graduate of culinary school and a lifelong history enthusiast, she creates richly imagined stories that celebrate resilience, creativity, friendship, love, and the power of reclaiming one's voice.

When not writing historical romance with a touch of rebellion, she can be found sketching her characters, paper crafting, swimming in the Puget Sound, or browsing a good bookstore. She is a proud member of Emerald City Romance Writers and Moms Who Write, as well as being an avid researcher who believes that every story is rooted in something true.

She lives in the Pacific Northwest with her husband, daughter, chickens, dog, and far too many books.

Matilda Lockwood believes good stories, like good recipes, are meant to be shared. A proud culinary-school graduate, she fell hard for the delicious history of food, from medieval feasts to the cider presses of New England. That curiosity once whisked her into running a tiny cider-caramel company, where she stirred apple cider into ribbons of buttery sweetness until the mountain of permits and insurance forms proved stickier than the candy. (She still makes a batch when the craving wins.)

These days she practices a different kind of alchemy: turning history into love stories. From a small Pacific Northwest town she shares with her husband, their spirited daughter who has already surpassed her in books written, a flock of opinionated chickens, and a heroic stack of books, Matilda writes historical romances that celebrate resilience, creativity, and the delicious ways people find one another. She credits her lively writing, reading, and art groups for keeping her imagination well-fed, and her teacup never empty.

Also By

Matilda Lockwood

Secrets of Castle Rowley
Treasures of Castle Rowley
Timeless Flavor
When Witches Can't Cast

READER REQUEST

Dear Reader,

Thank you for spending time in the Whitcombe orchard with Elizabeth and Nathaniel. If the cider press, the autumn rows, or their slow-burn romance resonated with you, I'd be truly grateful if you'd leave a short review, on the store where you bought the book, on Goodreads, or Amazon.

One or two sentences about what you enjoyed (a favorite moment, a character you rooted for, the harvest setting) helps other readers find the story and helps me keep writing them! Your words matter more than you know.

Now, I'm off to write Phoebe's story...

With thanks for every page we shared,

Matilda Lockwood

♡ *Matilda Lockwood*

www.ingramcontent.com/pod-product-compliance
Lightning Source LLC
Chambersburg PA
CBHW030244120726
47903CB00005B/1615